Praise for *Untold*

"Astonishing . . . Tightly structured and lyrically told."
—Meredith Maran, *People*

"Ms. Ali builds tension as slickly as any thriller screenwriter."
—Michiko Kakutani, *The New York Times*

"An unapologetic hybrid of a novel, a literary examination of identity, and a page-turning thriller, complete with car chase."
—Sara Nelson, *O, The Oprah Magazine*

"A dazzling feat . . . All the pistons are firing."
—Marie Arana, *The Washington Post*

"Haunting and intensely readable, this is something between a thriller and a ghost story."
—Lady Antonia Fraser

"Ali, a gorgeous stylist, has a wicked good time describing Grabowski in all his rumpled, greasy glory. . . . Beautifully written and cleverly imagined."
—Andrea Simakis, *The Cleveland Plain Dealer*

"Thoughtful, compassionate . . . A suspenseful and gripping read."
—Suzi Feay, *Financial Times*

"Irresistible . . . Lydia's unsent letters . . . are delightful, containing the novel's emotional core."
—Curtis Sittenfeld, *The New York Times Book Review*

"Ali tells her story with unobtrusive, restrained prose. . . . Remarkable . . . Astounding."
—Martha McPhee, *San Francisco Chronicle*

"One wonders, why didn't someone write this novel sooner? . . . [Ali is] a true thriller writer."
—Susan Salter Reynolds, *Los Angeles Times*

"Norman Rockwell couldn't paint a more affectionate portrait of small-town America."

—Deirdre Donahue, *USA Today*

"Monica Ali puts a literary gloss on a beach-read subject."

—Lisa Schwarzbaum, *Entertainment Weekly*

"Brilliant . . . Riveting to the end."

—Karen Brady, *The Buffalo News*

"A great beach read . . . [Ali] is a gifted author."

—Jane Buckingham, *Good Morning America*

"Rich . . . heartfelt writing."

—Ellen Kanner, *The Miami Herald*

"Higher-caliber writing."

—Kristin Tillotson, *Minneapolis Star Tribune*

"A thriller . . . The denouement of *Untold Story* is satisfyingly unpredictable and perplexing."

—Judy Krueger, *New York Journal of Books*

"An intriguing story filled with twists and turns."

—Sharon Galligar, *Las Vegas Review-Journal*

"Builds to a thrilling and rewarding finish . . . Daring and engrossing."

—Kristine Huntley, *Booklist* (starred review)

"A revelation . . . A compassionate portrait of the flawed and magnificent woman."

—Donna Bailey Nurse, *The Globe and Mail* (Canada)

"Sensational . . . The psychologically suspenseful chapters show what Ali is capable of."

—Dusan Petricic, *Toronto Star* (Canada)

"A sympathetic . . . insightful portrait of a woman held captive by the demons from her past."

—Akin Ajayi, *The Jerusalem Post*

"A masterpiece of suspense . . . This is a startlingly intelligent, perceptive, and entertaining piece of fiction. It's quite brilliant."

—Henry Sutton, *Daily Mirror* (UK)

"*Untold Story* is a superior thriller."

—Philip Womack, *The Daily Telegraph* (UK)

"Ali's third-person princess is a very convincing and sympathetic figure. . . . Extremely skillfully done."

—Tibor Fischer, *The Observer* (UK)

"Absorbing . . . Ali has written a thoughtful book about a serious theme: the insanity of celebrity culture. . . . But the artistry of Ali's execution justifies her risky choice of material. . . . While reading this book, you genuinely feel she might still be out there somewhere."

—David Free, *The Weekend Australian*

"Ali builds the tension masterfully. . . . A compelling and intriguing look at celebrity and the media through a fascinating and complex character."

—Lucy Clark, *The Sunday Telegraph* (Australia)

"An exciting psychological thriller with several unpredictable twists . . . Ali takes the testosterone-loaded concept of the stakeout and adds a feminine touch."

—Michelle Griffin, *The Age* (Australia)

"Monica Ali has always been a brilliant and provocative writer, but *Untold Story* is not only a gripping read but a compassionate portrait of a woman in turmoil—her finest novel yet."

—Gary Shteyngart, author of *Super Sad True Love Story*

"A terrific, clever, multilayered, and subtle book (and let's not forget—hugely entertaining!)."

—Joanne Harris, author of *Chocolat* and *Blueeyedboy*

"It is always said that Princess Diana was hunted and haunted, that her story contained the seeds of a contemporary myth. It was obvious that only the imagination of a first-rate novelist could master that material and make it fully and unforgettably alive. We now have the book we have been waiting for in Monica Ali's *Untold Story*. It is a beautiful, gripping accomplishment, a treat for the heart and the head, and will be a joy to readers who believe in the possibility that a book can transform your basic sense of life."

—Andrew O'Hagan, Man Booker Prize–shortlisted author of *Our Fathers, Be Near Me*, and *The Life and Opinions of Maf the Dog, and of his friend Marilyn Monroe*

ALSO BY MONICA ALI

Brick Lane

Alentejo Blue

In the Kitchen

UNTOLD STORY

A NOVEL

MONICA ALI

SCRIBNER

New York   London   Toronto   Sydney   New Delhi

SCRIBNER

A Division of Simon & Schuster, Inc.
1230 Avenue of the Americas
New York, NY 10020

First Scribner trade paperback edition June 2012

SCRIBNER and design are registered trademarks of The Gale Group, Inc.,
used under license by Simon & Schuster, Inc., the publisher of this work.

For information about special discounts for bulk purchases,
please contact Simon & Schuster Special Sales at 1-866-506-1949
or business@simonandschuster.com.

The Simon & Schuster Speakers Bureau can bring authors to your live event.
For more information or to book an event contact the Simon & Schuster Speakers Bureau
at 1-866-248-3049 or visit our website at www.simonspeakers.com.

Manufactured in the United States of America

1   3   5   7   9   10   8   6   4   2

Library of Congress Control Number: 2011018104

ISBN 978-1-4516-3548-5
ISBN 978-1-4516-3550-8 (pbk)
ISBN 978-1-4516-3551-5 (ebook)

For M.M.S.

UNTOLD

STORY

Chapter One

Some stories are never meant to be told. Some can only be told as fairy tales.

Once upon a time three girlfriends threw a little party for a fourth who had yet to arrive by the time the first bottle of Pinot Grigio had been downed. Walk with me now across the backyard of the neat suburban house, in this street of widely spaced heartlands, past the kid's bike and baseball bat staged just so on the satin green lawn, up to the sweet glow of the kitchen window, and take a look inside. Three women, one dark, one blonde, the third a redhead—all in their prime, those tenuous years when middle age is held carefully at bay. There they are, sitting at the table, innocent of their unreality, oblivious to the story, naively breathing in and out.

"Where is Lydia?" says Amber, the blonde. She is a neat little package. Delicate features, Peter Pan collar dress, French tip manicure. "Where the heck can she be?"

"We holding off on the sandwiches, right?" says Suzie, the dark-haired friend. She didn't have time to get changed before she came out. There is a splash of Bolognese sauce on her T-shirt. She made it in a hurry and left it for the kids and babysitter to eat. "These reduced-calorie Ruffles? Forget it, not going there." She pushes the bowl of chips away.

"Should I call her again?" says Amber. "I left three messages already." She closed up her clothing store an hour early to be sure to get everything ready on time.

The redhead, Tevis, takes a small phallus-shaped crystal out of her pocket and sets it on the table. She says, "I had a premonition this morning."

"You see a doctor about that?" Suzie, in her favorite khaki pants and stained T-shirt, sits like a man, right ankle on left knee. She gives Amber a wink.

"You guys can mock all you want," says Tevis. She has come straight from work. In her pantsuit, with her hair in a tight bun, pursing her lips, she looks close to prim—the opposite of how she would want to be seen.

"We're not mocking," says Amber. "Was it about Lydia?"

"Not specifically," says Tevis in a very Tevis way. She cups her hands above the stone.

"You carry that around with you?" says Suzie. Her hair is aubergine dark, a hint of purple, and has that freshly colored shine. She plucks a carrot out of the refrigerator and peels it directly onto the table that has been laid with the pretty crockery, hand-painted red and pink roses, fine bone china cups and saucers with handles so small they make you crook your little finger, just like a real English high tea. "Don't worry, I'm clearing this up."

"You better," says Amber, but she reaches across and scoops up the peelings herself. If Lydia walks in that second everything has to look right. She feels guilty about packing Serena and Tyler off to friends' houses when they'd wanted to stay and say happy birthday to Lydia. Wouldn't Lydia have preferred to see the children rather than have everything arranged just so? Amber tucks her hair behind her ears and pulls a loose thread from her sleeve. "Please say it wasn't about her."

"Jeez Louise," says Suzie. "She'll be working late. You know how she loves those dogs."

"Why isn't she answering her phone?" says Amber.

"I didn't wrap her present. Think she'll mind?" Suzie snaps off the end of the carrot with her front teeth. The teeth are strong and white but irregular; they strike an attitude.

"I'm not trying to worry anyone," says Tevis. She puts the crystal back in the pocket of her tailored jacket. She is a Realtor and has to look smart. It's not who she is. It's what she does. As she herself has pointed out many times. But this is a town full of skeptics, people who buy into all that bricks-and-mortar-and-white-goods fandango instead of having their chakras cleansed.

"Seriously," says Suzie, "you're not." She loves Tevis. Tevis has no kids so you talked about other stuff. Suzie has four kids and once you'd talked about those and then talked about the other moms' kids, it was time to head home and pack sports gear for the following day. Tevis being childless meant you felt a bit sorry for her, and a bit jealous. Probably the same way she felt about you. She could be dreamy, or she could be intense, or some strange combination of the two. And she was fun to tease.

"Remember what happened last time?" says Tevis.

"Last time what? You had a premonition? Is it about Lydia or not?" Amber, she is pretty sure, knows Lydia better than the others do. She got friendly with her first, nearly three years ago now.

"I don't know," says Tevis. "It's just a bad feeling. I had it this morning, right after I got out of the shower."

"I had a bad feeling in the shower this morning," says Suzie. "I felt like I was going to eat a whole box of Pop-Tarts for breakfast."

"How late is she anyway? God, an hour and a half." Amber looks wistfully at the silver cake forks fanned out near the center of the table. They were nearly black when she found them in the antiques store over on Fairfax, but have cleaned up beautifully.

"And guess what," said Suzie. "I did. The whole freakin' box."

Tevis takes off her jacket. "The air always gets like this before a thunderstorm."

"What?" says Suzie. "It's a beautiful evening. You're not in Chicago anymore."

"I'm just saying," says Tevis. She fixes Suzie a stare.

"Come on, Tevis, don't try to creep us out." The cucumber sandwiches are beginning to curl at the edges. It is kind of dumb, Amber knows it, to have English high tea at seven in the evening. More like eight thirty now.

"Yeah, let's just hear it, girl, the last time you had a premonition . . ." Suzie begins at her usual rat-a-tat pace, but suddenly tails off.

"So you do remember," says Tevis. She turns to Amber. "Please try not to be alarmed. But last time I had a premonition was the day Jolinda's little boy ran out in the street and got hit by the school bus."

"And you saw that? You saw that ahead of time?"

Tevis hesitates a moment, then scrupulously shakes her head. "No. It was more like a general premonition."

"And that was—what?—two years ago? How many you had since then?" Amber, her anxiety rising, glances at the Dundee cake, enthroned on a glass stand as the table's centerpiece. It is mud brown and weighs a ton. Lydia mentioned it one time, a childhood favorite, and Amber found a recipe on the Internet.

"None," says Tevis, "until today."

"You never get a bad feeling in the mornings?" says Suzie. "Man, I get them, like, every day."

Amber gets up and starts washing the three dirty wineglasses. She has to do something and it's all she can think of except, of course, calling Lydia again. But when Lydia strides through the door, that swing in her hips, that giggle in her voice, Amber doesn't want to feel too foolish. "Damn it, I'm calling again," she says, drying her hands.

"There's no reason why it should be to do with Lydia," says Tevis, but the more she says it, the more certain she feels that it is. Only a couple of days ago, Lydia came over and asked for the tarot cards, something she had always refused before. Tevis laid the cards out on the mermaid mosaic table but then Rufus wagged his tail and knocked two cards to the floor. Lydia picked them up and said, "Let's not do this," and shuffled all the cards back into the deck. Tevis explained that it wouldn't matter, that to deal the cards again would not diminish their power. "I know," Lydia said, "but I've changed my mind. Rufus changed it for me. He's very wise, you know." She laughed, and though her laugh contained, as usual, a peal of silver bells, it also struck another note. Lydia was intuitive, she knew things, she sensed them, and she had backed away from the cards.

"Absolutely no reason," Tevis repeats, and Suzie says, "It's probably nothing at all," which sounds like words of comfort and makes the three of them uneasy that such comfort should be required.

4

Amber tosses her cell phone onto a plate. Lydia's phone has gone to voice mail again and what's the point in leaving yet another message? "Maybe she took Rufus on a long walk, lost track of time, forgot to take her phone." She knows how lame it sounds.

"She could've got the days mixed," says Suzie, without conviction.

"Suzie, it's her birthday. How could she get the days mixed? Anyway she called this morning and said see you at seven. There's no mix-up, she's just . . . late." Lydia had sounded distracted, it was true. But, thinks Amber, she has frequently seemed distracted lately.

"What the . . ." says Suzie.

"I told you," says Tevis. "Hail."

"What the . . ." says Suzie again, and the rest of her sentence is lost in the din.

"Come on," shouts Amber, racing for the front door. "If she arrives right now we'll never hear the bell."

They stand outside on the front deck and watch the hail drum off Mrs. Gillolt's roof, snare sideways off the hood of Amber's Highlander, rattle in and out of the aluminum bucket by the garage. The sky has turned an inglorious dirty purple, and the hail falls with utter abandon, bouncing, colliding, rolling, compelling in its unseemliness. It falls and it falls. The hail is not large, only dense, pouring down like white rice from the torn seam above. "Oh my God," screams Amber. "Look at it," Suzie screams back. Tevis walks down the steps and plants herself on the lawn, arms held wide, head tilted back to the sky. "Is she saying a prayer?" yells Suzie, and Amber, despite the tension, or because of it, starts to laugh.

She is laughing still when a car pulls off the road; the headlights seem to sweep the hail, lift it in a thick white cloud above the black asphalt driveway, and spray it toward the house. Tevis lets her arms drop and runs toward the car, her Realtor's cream silk blouse sticking to her skinny back. The others run down too. It must be Lydia, although the car is nothing but a dark shape behind the lights.

When Esther climbs out of the front seat, clutching a present to her chest, they embrace her in an awkward circle of compensation that does little to conceal their disappointment.

* * *

Back in the kitchen, Amber sets another place at the table. Esther brushes hail from her shoulders, unpins her bun, and shakes a few hailstones out of her long gray hair. "Forgot I was coming, didn't you?" she says, her tone somewhere between sage and mischievous.

"No!" says Amber. "Well, yes."

"That's what happens to women," says Esther. "We reach an age where we get forgotten about." She doesn't sound remotely aggrieved.

Amber, through her cloud of embarrassment and anxiety, experiences a pang for what lies ahead, fears, in fact, that it has already begun, at her age, a divorcée the rest of her life. She gathers herself to the moment. "The thing is, we've all been a bit worried about Lydia. Has she been working late? She's not answering her phone."

"Lydia took the day off," says Esther. "You mean she's not been here?"

Nobody answers, as Esther looks from one to the next.

"We should drive over to the house," says Suzie.

"Wait until the hail stops," says Tevis.

"We can't just sit here," says Amber.

They sit and look at each other, waiting for someone to take charge.

Chapter Two

For a town of only eight thousand inhabitants, Kensington pretty much had everything: a hardware store, two grocery stores, a florist, a bakery, a pharmacy with a wider-than-usual selection of books, an antiques store, a Realtor's, a funeral home. When there was a death in Abrams, Havering, Bloomfield, or Gains, or any of the other not-quite-towns that tumbled across the county, nobody would dream of calling a funeral home in the city. They would call J. C. Dryden and Sons, a business established in 1882, a mere four years after the founding of Kensington itself. If, as sometimes happened, demand was running so high that a funeral could not be accommodated in timely fashion, Mr. Dryden would call the bereaved to advise personally on alternatives. Kensington was thus sought after in death, and if it was not quite equally sought after in life, real estate prices were certainly on the high side. A couple of Kensington's stores were located on Fairfax but the majority lined Albert Street or turned the corner into Victoria Street. From Albert, the town fanned away on a gentle incline to the north, to the south reached down within five miles of the interstate, handy for those with a city commute, to the east was bounded by a thirsty-looking river, and to the west by the sprinkler-saturated greens of the golf course that eventually gave way to a forest of tamaracks, sweet gums, and pines.

Lydia drove past the golf course on her way into town. Wednesdays she worked a half day at the Kensington Canine Sanctuary, a sprawling block of kennels and yards just outside of town that picked up mutts or had them delivered from "the area of darkness"; that was how Esther described the county, which had no other dog shelters at all. Four days a week Lydia worked until six in the evening, ordering supplies, cleaning kennels, training and handling, humping thirty-pound bags of Nature's Variety dried dog food, eating Esther's chicken rice salad out of Tupperware. But Wednesdays Lydia nudged Rufus awake with the toe of her sneaker at noon. He'd be sleeping in the office with his ears flapped over his eyes, and he'd stretch his butt up in the air, shiver his front paws, and shake his head as if he knew not what the world was coming to, then race ahead of her to leap in the back of the dusty blue Sport Trac.

Usually Lydia scooped him out of the cargo box and set him on the front passenger seat but today she let him ride in the box with the wind streaming back his ears, so when she said, "Do you think I should stop seeing Carson?" there was no quizzical face looking up at her, urging her to continue. She shrugged at the empty passenger seat and switched the radio on.

She drove up Fairfax, past the sports field, playground, elementary school, and bed-and-breakfast and turned into Albert, parking by the bakery where she bought two toasted pastrami and Swiss paninis and walked up to Amber's store, Rufus padding so close to her ankles she had a job to avoid tripping over him.

The store didn't close for lunch and Wednesdays Amber's assistant went to hairdressing school in the city so Lydia always took sandwiches in.

"Hey," said Amber, looking up from a magazine. She came around from behind the counter adjusting her skirt and her hair, touching her finger to the bow of her lip to make sure no lipstick had strayed.

The first thing Lydia had learned, the first among many first things, when she had taken the job she had held, or that held her, for most of her adult life, was never to fiddle with any part of her wardrobe or makeup. Yes, they had taught her that explicitly, though there was much that they had not. It was a lesson she could hand on to Amber. Amber, who could not pass a mirror without checking it, who used a window if a mirror was not available, who was fearful of being looked at by everybody and terrified of being looked at by no one. But poise, Lydia had decided, was overrated. Only fools and knaves gave a fig about that.

"You look great," she said. "New skirt?"

Amber said that it was and probed Lydia for a detailed opinion, explaining that it was from a range she was considering for the store. Lydia wore jeans and a T-shirt nearly every day but Amber seemed to think she knew a great deal about clothes and fashion, which was not an impression Lydia was ever aiming to give.

They sat on the repro fainting couch by the window. Amber had bought it, she said, for the husbands who became a little dizzy when they saw the price tags. "Though there's nothing in here over four hundred bucks," she had added, a little wistfully.

"I've got to show you these photos," Amber said now. She retrieved the gossip magazine from the counter. "This one was taken last week. And then here she is in the nineties. Doesn't she look so different?"

"Don't we all?" said Lydia, barely giving the page a glance.

"Her nostrils are uneven," said Amber. "That's always a telltale sign."

Lydia took another bite of her panini so she didn't have to say anything.

Amber started reading aloud. "'She may have had a lower eye lift and, judging by her appearance, her surgeon may have employed a new technique by going in underneath the actual eyeball—this reduces the risk of scarring and can have excellent results.'"

Lydia pulled a face. "Why do you read this stuff?" She waved the sandwich at the stack of magazines on the coffee table.

"I know, I know," said Amber. "It's ridiculous. She's definitely had Botox as well."

"Who cares?" said Lydia. "Her and every other actress her age."

Amber tucked her hair behind her ears. Last year she had cut bangs and this year she was growing them out and her hair kept falling over her eyes so the tucking was a repeated necessity, but it had also become part of her repertoire of self-adjustments and taken on an apologetic quality. She laughed. "I don't know why I read this stuff.

But everybody does. There's even a college professor comes in here and she spends more time flicking through the magazines than flicking through the racks. Guess she doesn't like buying them herself, but what do you think she reads at the hairdresser's? Not one of her professor books, for sure."

Lydia held a sliver of pastrami out to Rufus. "Well, we think it's silly, don't we, boy?"

Rufus licked her fingers in assent.

"Oh my God," said Amber.

Lydia loved the way Amber said *oh my God*. It was so American. It reminded her of how English she felt after nearly ten years in the States, and that when everything else about her felt not so much hidden as worn away, her Englishness, at least, remained.

Almost ten years. It was 1997 when she arrived—not only a decade but a millennium ago.

"Oh my God, I'd forgotten—I've got these gowns in back I really want you to try. They are going to look so fabulous. I can't wait to see." Amber ran into the stockroom, and Lydia watched through the open door as she shucked plastic-sheathed dresses off the revolving rail and laid them over her arm.

When she'd arrived in Kensington, it was Tevis who had sold Lydia the house, but Amber with whom she'd first made friends. They had shared a table in the bakery, there were only four tables so you normally had to share. Over a cappuccino for Amber and an Earl Grey for Lydia they recognized in each other an instant acceptance, and Lydia, who for seven years had made only acquaintances, was relieved to give herself up to this inevitability. She was careful, of course, but after a few conversations, filling each other in on their backgrounds, there wasn't much need for caution, and Lydia found herself wondering why, for so long, she had held back from everyone.

That first afternoon Amber told Lydia about her marriage, to her childhood sweetheart, how he'd cheated on her with her best friend, how she'd forgiven them both because "it just kind of happened," they were attorneys in the same law firm and she was a stay-at-home mom and looked kind of schlubby most days, and how when she looked in the mirror she felt sort of guilty about the whole thing. She'd given herself a makeover, of course, and they did "date nights" and talked and got a whole lot of issues out on the table, like how he hated her meat loaf and had never been able to say. And it had been sweet and dandy for a while, before she found out about another affair, with a waitress at their favorite "date night" restaurant, but he said it was "only physical" and she had forgiven him again. She'd cried about it anyway, as anyone would, and it was Donna who comforted her. Donna, her best friend. Who was still sleeping with her husband as probably everyone knew except Amber, who, when she walked in on them, in the moments before they noticed her, fought the urge to tiptoe away and pretend to have seen nothing. At the age of thirty-nine with two children and no career, it seemed more sensible to treat it as a hallucination than to face the howling truth.

"You had to move out all this way from Maine," said Lydia. "I think I know why."

"I don't know. Getting away from him?"

"You were afraid you'd forgive him again." Lydia touched Amber's hand.

"Oh my God, you are so right. He was such a bastard. But"—she shrugged a little apology—"he would have talked me around. Not the talk, more the way he walked, the way his jeans fit. I'm so stupid. Why did I stay so long? Really? Because I liked the way he moved, and I liked the way he smelled."

Amber emerged from the stockroom and Lydia made way so that she could set the dresses down on the couch, which Amber did with such tenderness that no mortician at J. C. Dryden ever took more care in laying out the deceased.

"Ten gowns, three sizes, six-fifty wholesale. Tell me I'm not crazy."

Lydia wiped her fingers on the seat of her jeans before unshrouding the first offering. Closet, the store, turned over nicely on the staples of wraparound dresses, A-line skirts, and little beaded cardigans favored perennially by Kensington women, supplemented by the prom season business, flirty numbers in fuchsia and gold and white that retailed around $300, and formal floor-length durables that offered good bosom support and value to the Kensington matrons who invested for a silver wedding and expected, God willing, to be seen through to the diamond anniversary. The good women of Kensington were not short of a dime but wise enough to know that dimes didn't grow on sweet gums and, besides, there was little occasion for occasion wear.

"Wow," said Lydia, "gorgeous." Should she ask if the dresses were sale or return? She didn't want to dishearten her friend. Inspecting the needlework would give her time to think, and she traced a finger around the embroidered neckline.

Back when they had first met, Amber had poured out her story and it had seemed as natural and expected to Lydia as tea being poured from the pot. She hadn't been able to reciprocate exactly, but had talked about moving to the States in her thirties with her husband, how exhilarating it had been to get away from stuffy England, how everything here had been both strange and familiar, and how the marriage had not worked out. She was expert at telling the story and when she was talking it didn't feel like telling lies. No names and dates and places, best to leave that vague, just the weaving of little details—the novelty, for an English person, of having a flag fly over one's own home, the thrill of finding Marmite in a grocery store, the way she'd picked up words and phrases she had never dreamed she would use, *ass, hang it, darn.*

Over the weeks and months that followed there were questions, because when Amber wasn't with Lydia the story reduced to a bundle of threads that Amber would gather and later hold out for repair. Lydia told her some things that were not true—that she didn't have children, that was the worst, denying them got harder, not easier, over time, as if each telling made it more of a reality. Some things she said were true enough, for example, that her husband had been cruel. Amber never pushed too hard. And Lydia had done this professionally for a large part of her adult life—given moments to strangers that they treasured as candid and intimate, not knowing her at all. For this there had been no training, but it turned out that she had the gift. Amber and Tevis and Suzie were no longer strangers and they knew as much as she could let them, but in the early days what Lydia had supplied was a sense of taking them into her confidence, and they had supplied much of the material: assuming her husband had been violent, that he was a man of some influence, that she did not want to be found.

Amber held the fitting room door. "Please," she said. "Try it on. I want to see."

"Why don't you put it on?" said Lydia. "This green is definitely your color. You should take one for yourself."

"Oh, I tried them all already. I'm such a short ass, they don't look right on me."

"Nonsense," said Lydia. "Stop putting yourself down like that."

"Quit stalling, and get your butt in here." Amber shooed her in.

The dress was a pale green column with silver embroidery and soft ruffle flowers sweeping up diagonally that made Lydia think of Valentino, though of course the work was not as fine.

"Come out here," called Amber.

There was no mirror in the fitting room, because Amber said Kensington women were too quick and ready to make wrongheaded assessments without giving the outfits a chance: a few pins in the hemline, a switch of blouse, a scarf at the throat, could make all the difference.

Lydia strutted out like a catwalk model, hand to hip, face set, head turning left and right. Amber applauded and whistled and then took Lydia by the shoulders and turned her to face the mirror.

"Beautiful," Amber murmured, "just beautiful."

Lydia took a breath. Ten years since she'd worn a floor-length gown. There was a hot little hole in her stomach that she would not on any account pay attention to, focusing instead on equalizing the length of her inhale and exhale.

"Fits like a glove," said Amber. "How about that?"

"Not quite," said Lydia. "I'd take it in just a fraction on the hip."

"Know what?" said Amber. "You've got to have it. It's a present. I knew these gowns were going to look great on you, you have the figure, but I didn't know *how* great. And I didn't even know if I'd coax you into one. Thought I might have to get those jeans surgically removed."

"And when, exactly, would I wear it?" said Lydia, examining herself in profile. "Not very practical for cleaning out kennels. Can you imagine if I wore it to one of Suzie's cookouts?" As soon as she had spoken she regretted it. She had just pointed out why Amber had been wrong to invest so heavily.

Her friend gazed at her without speaking, her face frozen for a moment in its previous rapture, as if it had not yet received the bad news from her brain. "Oh," she said finally, "get Carson to take you somewhere nice."

"I will," said Lydia, rallying. "I'll do that. Can I try the others on too?"

"Of course," said Amber, sounding deflated. "Then pick out the best one. It's on me."

They passed the afternoon with Lydia trying on one after another and when a customer came in the gowns were much discussed, two women even donning the dark blue taffeta and promising to come back the next day. Amber's spirits were thus restored. By five o'clock they had cleared up and sat down with lattes.

"How's Serena?" said Lydia. "And how's Tyler getting on with the violin?"

"Oh, I keep nagging him about practicing but it's a waste of breath. Serena's up for a part in the school play—Dorothy in *The Wizard of Oz*."

"Fingers crossed," said Lydia.

"If she doesn't get it . . ."

"I bet she does."

"Tap lessons, singing lessons, ballet class—but they all do, you know, it's just so competitive out there."

"Wait until you hear. Don't start worrying about it now." Lydia gestured at the rack where they'd hung the new stock. "Will you keep one for yourself?"

Amber tucked her hair. "Oh, I don't know. I might end up with a few more than that."

They looked at each other and started to giggle.

"I mean," said Amber, between fits, "unless evening gowns become popular on the school run."

"You never know," said Lydia. "Stranger things have happened." She sipped her coffee and choked.

"Not around here." Amber patted Lydia on the back. "When I was in high school," she said, her hand still resting between Lydia's shoulders, "I was such a dreamer. I walked around in a dream. I was pretty but not spectacular, my grades were nothing to write home about, I had friends but I wasn't Miss Popular, I wasn't on any A-teams." She paused for a long moment, as if she had fallen back into the old dream. "But it was like I was carrying this big secret around inside of me, that I'd never tell anyone, only one day they would see it because inside I was just so special that the world, when I got out and lived in it, was bound to make me a star. I didn't think I'd even have to try. It would just *happen,* it was bound to, I was sure. So I was never really paying attention to anything around me, I was waiting for my life to begin. When it did, I'd be wearing these fabulous dresses and people would be a little surprised at first and then they'd say, of course, Amber, we should have guessed. It would all be perfect. The dresses, the houses, the cars, the charming prince who would propose." She laughed and rubbed Lydia's back, though she hadn't coughed again. "What a doofus. Maybe I still am."

Lydia pulled Amber's hand away from her back and held it between her own. "Listen, you're not a doofus. All girls feel like that."

Amber smiled. When she smiled there was something touching about it. The way she showed her top gum made her look open to attack. "I bet you were more sensible."

"Oh, I was hopeless at school," said Lydia. "Thick as a plank, that's me."

Amber ran up the road to get to the drugstore before it closed and Lydia waited a couple of beats after the door had shut before reaching for the pile of magazines. She pulled out the three that were from this week and rested them on her knee. First she centered her thoughts: she would not get upset either way. If she found what she was searching for she would tear out the page and put it in her purse to examine at home. If she found nothing, she would not take it as a blow but simply try again next week. She turned the pages and quickly discarded the first magazine. Then the second, then the third. Nothing. It was a blow. How could it not be?

Her cell phone bleeped and she read the text message from Carson. *Pick you up at 7. Ok?* She texted back *yes,* and then Amber returned and said she'd bumped into her new neighbor and he'd asked her out to lunch next week.

"Is it a date?" said Lydia.

Amber pulled at her blond bob and straightened her skirt seams. "I guess. No. I'm not sure. Maybe he's just being friendly."

"Will you go?"

"Lunch is probably not a date. And he's a neighbor. So I should go."

"What if it is a date?"

Amber pursed her lips. "If it's a date he's outta luck, he's too short for me."

"You're all of five feet three."

"I don't need someone tall, but tall enough, you know? So the gap is safe. Like if I wear heels it's not a worry, and so if you kiss you know the angle's going to be right."

"Ah," said Lydia. "Well, Carson is only a couple of inches taller than me. Think I should get rid of him?"

"No!" said Amber. "Don't listen to me. I already told you how silly I am."

Lydia stood up, tipping Rufus to the floor and gathering her purse and cell. She gave Amber a hug and promised to call her tomorrow to analyze the lunch proposition further, by which time Amber might have gleaned more intelligence. She took the green dress, the first one she had tried, deciding she would drop off cash with Amber's assistant to save them both the embarrassment of fighting over it now.

It was a quarter of six by the time she got home and the air was a little chill but Lydia desperately needed to swim. The pool was unheated and she completed the first length underwater, turning her mind to ice. She swam steady lengths of crawl after that for thirty minutes, feeling nothing but the extension of her arms, the stretch in her back, the flex in her thighs, and the gratitude that always came over her for this release. When she had finished she stood for a moment in the shallow end facing the house. It was the first place she had bought in the States. The first she had bought anywhere. She had owned a flat in London before her marriage, but that had been bought for her. The house was a one-and-a-half-story bungalow, with a low-pitched roof and deep eaves. It had square columns at the front and back that made it seem solidly rooted, and wood sidings that she had painted a soft dove gray. She had completed the job herself, politely declining all offers of help. A neat, modest home in a good neighborhood at the north end of town, set in nearly a sheltering acre lined with maples and basswoods that made it invisible from the road and other properties, and Lydia had said, I'll take it, before Tevis had got her upstairs.

She climbed out of the pool, wrapped her towel around her, and went inside. In the kitchen she paused before her open laptop, knowing she could search the Internet and find what she had been looking for in the magazines. But if she started she would never stop. She had to keep the bargains she had made with herself.

Lydia went up to the bedroom and turned on the lights. She peeled off her swimsuit and showered, and when she had dried her hair and pulled fresh jeans out of the closet she noticed the gown slung across the bed.

She slipped it on and sat next to Rufus, who had made a nest for himself at the bottom of the comforter. She used a compact mirror to do her makeup, then swept her hair off her shoulders and fixed it in a loose chignon.

As she stood before the full-length mirror, Lydia shivered. Despite the dark hair, despite the surgeon's knife, despite the wrinkles wrought by the years and a permanent tan, she saw a ghost looking back at her that had long been consigned to the past. Slowly she turned and gazed over her shoulder. The dress scooped low to the waist. The flesh sagged, not much, just a little, beneath the shoulder blades. How horrible that would look in a photograph, where no blemish was ever forgiven, where you were only as strong as your weakest point.

When the dress was hung away in the closet and she had got dressed properly in jeans and a crisp white shirt, Lydia opened a can of food for Rufus and held his bowl in the air.

"I have a question for you," she said as he stood with his front paws on her leg. "Do I have to stop seeing Carson? He's asking so many questions. It's getting to be a pain."

Rufus panted eagerly, and tugged at her jeans with one paw.

"You're getting your dinner. But answer me first. Bark once for yes and twice for no."

Rufus barked three times.

"Oh, useless," she said, setting his dinner on the floor. She gave him a pat. "You are a silly spaniel. And I'm talking to a dog."

Chapter Three

Grabowski had stopped for a Coke and a hot dog at a diner just off the highway when his cell phone rang again. This time he took the call.

"Listen," he said, "how am I supposed to get any work done when you're on my back the whole day?"

"Hello, mate," said Gareth. "I love you too."

"What do you want?"

"I've left you like a million messages. And you never ring me. Just want to know how the book is coming. Getting all the peace and quiet you need in—where is it—Pig Poke, Illinois?"

"Arse Wipe, Arizona. I left a week ago."

"Not peaceful enough in Arse Wipe? Where are you now?"

"On the road."

"Go back to Pig Poke or Arse Wipe or wherever, lock yourself in your room, and don't do anything else, don't even breathe, until it's finished. Please."

Grabowski drained the Coke can and belched. "Can't," he said. "That place gives me the shits. Got to find somewhere else."

"Don't drink the water, then," said Gareth. "Drink bottled water. Don't fuck around sightseeing, don't turn it into a road trip."

"I'm not going back there. It gave me the creeps."

Gareth sighed. "Look," he said, "as your agent I have to advise you to get yourself back to London and get a bloody shove on with this book. Forget the big skies and desert and contemplation and all that artistic stuff. Just get it done."

"Yeah," he said, "easy. Just like that." He signaled the waitress for another can of Coke. Arizona had worked like an enema on his brain,

cleaned it out completely. Since then he'd been driving around, looking for the perfect place, stopping to take photos sometimes, writing
so easily in his head, losing the words again when he sat in front of a
keyboard instead of a steering wheel. No, he didn't want big skies and
deserts, he wanted an ordinary little town, somewhere without dis-
tractions. But there were so many to choose from that he just kept on
driving through.

"No one's saying it's easy, mate," said Gareth, wheedling. "But
think about it. We need this book to come out for the tenth anniversary. Eleventh anniversary doesn't cut it, eleven's got no marketing
pull."

At the next booth a mother looked out the window while her tod-
dler chewed through a packet of NutraSweet.

Gareth went on. "Don't get hung up on the writing—you know
what they want. Few anecdotes, the first time you clapped eyes on
her, tricks of the trade, all the old war stories you pull out in the pub.
To be honest, no one's going to give a toss about the text, as such. It's
the pictures everyone wants—'never-before-seen images of the Princess of Wales, taken by the man who knew her best.'"

Grabowski snorted. He shook a toothpick out of the dispenser and
broke it in two.

"All right," said Gareth, "not that line exactly. The publicist will
cook it up. 'Never-before-seen images of the Princess of Wales, from
the private archive of the photographer who snapped the very first
pre-engagement picture and documented her life and work.' That's
a bit long."

A pair of teenagers, girl and boy, spun through the door and slid
together onto a red vinyl bench, tight as a slipknot. At the counter a
trucker flicked out six dollar bills and tried to tuck them in the waitress's blouse.

"I've got to go."

"Do you have something to send me?" said Gareth. "Send me
whatever you've got."

"I'll send you a postcard."

"Deadline's in a month. Don't let me down. Don't let yourself down. You need the delivery money, remember. Divorces don't come cheap."

"Thanks for reminding me."

"Where are you going? Are you coming home? You needed a rest, it's good, you had a holiday, now come on back to work."

"What?" said Grabowski. "I can't hear you . . . Gareth, you're breaking up."

The trucks that thundered down the highway made the hood of the Pontiac tremble as Grabowski unfolded and laid out the road map. He studied it, running his finger along the lines between the towns as if a picture might be revealed, like one of those dot-to-dot drawings. A low-slung customized Harley pulled into the lot, the biker a hard case in sleeveless denim, inked from shoulder to wrist. Grabowski reached into the passenger seat for his camera and fired off some shots. The biker ruined it by starting to pose.

Grabowski turned his attention to the map again. Abrams then Havering, Gains, Bloomfield . . . there was no way to choose. Kensington, Littlefield . . . He ran his finger back. Kensington. He smiled. He folded his map, stowed his camera, and got into the car.

Chapter Four

1 January 1998

One pays a premium for a sea view but on days like today I wonder why. Those tight-lipped waves rubbing at the pebbles, that mean gray emptiness beyond. A crashing surf, a raging sea, can lift the spirits. This blank indifference is always the worst.

2 January 1998

Patricia came down for New Year's Eve. I tried to persuade her to stay in London with John and the kids but she wouldn't be put off. I opened a bottle of champagne and we sat on the balcony wrapped in blankets staring into the dark. She said, "Brighton's lovely, isn't it? Sea air's probably doing you good." I said, "For God's sake, Pat." Then she cried. I apologized, of course.

She wants me to move back up to London and live with her. John's in favor, apparently, as are my niece and nephew. I blamed the work, said that we historians, we writers, need our splendid isolation, need to be alone with our thoughts. That seemed to cheer her up.

I'm not getting much done.

4 January 1998

Yesterday I worked all day and had little enough to show for it. Two hundred words on the Clayton-Bulwer Treaty and some light revision of the Belgian Indemnities Controversy paragraphs. My mind is elsewhere.

5 January 1998

Illusions of Conflict: A History of Anglo-American Diplomacy, by Dr. Lawrence Arthur Seymour Standing. How does that sound? Stuffy enough?

My magnum opus. My legacy. My only begotten child.

Nine years in the gestation, and doubtless it will be a stillbirth. If birth there is to be. Tom came down in December and took me out to lunch. I told him the manuscript is running at seven hundred pages and counting. He didn't blink. "It'll be great," he said. "We'll throw a party at the Carlton, no, at the Reform. Maybe the Garrick, whatever you want." The bastard. He's hoping I'll die before it's finished and that he won't have to honor the contract.

6 January 1998

Have been working on my "bio," as Tom insists on calling it.

Lawrence Standing was born in Norfolk in 1944 and educated at Marlborough College and Trinity College, Oxford, where he received a First Class Honours in History. After graduating he joined the Foreign Office and served in numerous foreign postings, including Turkey, Brazil, Germany, and Japan. (Should I spice it up a bit by talking about my brief innings as a spy?) In 1980 he left the Foreign Office to take up the role of Private Secretary to the Princess of Wales, a position he held until 1986. He continued to act as her informal adviser until the princess's untimely death in 1997. In 1987 Lawrence returned to academia, completing a PhD in Anglo-American History and becoming a Senior Lecturer at University College, London. Lawrence was a keen sportsman, taking a blue in cricket at Oxford and running nearly every day of his life, until he was diagnosed with an inoperable brain tumor in March 1997. He died in 1998. He died in 1999. (Delete as appropriate.)

8 January 1998

Another wasted day. Fiddled with the "bio." Like writing my own obituary.

12 January 1998

Kept my appointment with Dr. Patel though I couldn't really see the point. She said, "Apathy is a common symptom with frontal lobe tumors. Are you experiencing any aggression, irritation, loss of inhibitions?" I said, "Mind your own fucking business, bitch."

I didn't, of course. I'm not sure Dr. Patel can take a joke.

I gave her a full report on the headaches, sickness, a touch of blurriness in the left eye. I told her I can't smell anything anymore. She made a note.

13 January 1998

All I want to write about is

What else matters?

What have I done in my life that matters, except that?

14 January 1998

What is it that prevents me? If I get it down (get it down then get rid of it straightaway) maybe I shall be able to concentrate again. Go on, Lawrence, you fool.

16 January 1998

I'm going to see her one last time, in March, before I'm too weak to travel. It's all arranged. I fly to Washington to "continue my researches" and drive from there, or hire a driver if that's what it takes. I said, "I promise you that if I don't arrive on that day, it can mean only one thing." She said, "Oh, Lawrence." She held my hand. She's had a lot of practice in that area. Holding hands with the dying—it never made her a saint, but it made her an angel in this world.

Is it the tumor making me apathetic? I don't know. I know I felt alive when I wrote that paragraph just now.

Go on, Lawrence, go on. There's no betrayal here.

17 January 1998

Cynthia comes in to clean. She would never touch my papers. She's been trained. Friends I see only at restaurant lunches or, very infrequently these days, dinner at someone else's house. They ask about the book, with such bloody tact, such solicitous low-voiced delicacy, as if the book were what is killing me. Gail has been to see me once. Hard to believe we were almost engaged at one time. Who else comes? Only Patricia who, it has to be said, might be tempted to read my diary, were she to find one lying around. Discover if it's true what they say, what some say, that I never "came out." She probably heard, too, the other rumor that was once in vogue, that when I was working at Kensington Palace, there was a period when I was sleeping with the boss. Not that Patricia would ever mention either possibility, not even in jest.

She might sneak a look at a diary, but will she ever read seven hundred pages of manuscript while I am in the bath, or on the loo, and so stumble inadvertently upon this insert? Not a hope.

Have you convinced yourself now? Given yourself permission? What are you waiting for?

18 January 1998

Six months to a year, Dr. Patel tells me, is my allotted span. Although, as she always says, it is impossible to make accurate predictions and, as I always say, I quite understand. That's on top of the ten months I've had already so quite a good innings in the brain-tumor world. Only thirty percent of us get over a year. Fourteen percent of us get a full five. Some lucky bastards, the ten percent club, get ten whole big ones. My tumor is higher grade than that. I said to Dr. Patel, "Higher grade, that means a better quality of tumor, right?" She didn't laugh.

What will happen to this manuscript, in any case, after my death? Even if these pages were to remain here by some calamitous turn of events, it is vanity on my part to fear their being read. Tom, good old Tom, the clubbable viper, already has his regrets composed, and will be deeply sorry to be unable to publish what, very sadly, is only a *partial* manuscript.

Patricia will pack it up in a box and put it in the attic. Perhaps she'll take it into Tom's office, slam it on his desk. Maybe she'll throw it away. No, she won't.

But these pages won't exist by then. I will make sure of that.

19 January 1998

I used to encourage her to write. Writing can be a form of therapy, but it was one of the few that she wasn't willing to try. She had her own way of getting her story into print, more dramatic than the one I was advocating. She's a high-stakes kind of girl. I remember, someone once asked her if she ever gambled. She said, "Not with cards."

She wrote a lot of thank you letters. As soon as she got home from an evening out she'd sit down at her desk in Kensington Palace with a card propped up in front of her with all the words she found difficult to spell and write one of her gracious thank you notes. People were always surprised at how she found the time. "Lawrence," she said, "what do they imagine I'm going to do all alone in these empty rooms?"

20 January 1998

The last time I saw her was in November. When I left her in September she had been manic, hysterical with grief and fear, and one of the few things that calmed her was when I begged her forgiveness for what I had done, for what I had helped her to do. She sat without speaking until the tears dried on her face. "No," she said, quietly and clearly, "I couldn't go on. We both know that." And indeed I had feared for her sanity the previous few months, when she had lost "the love of her life," when her behavior had become so erratic it caused a tabloid furore, when she seemed to drift through too many of our conversations as if in a semifugue. Time after time, over the years, she had come out of the darkness (of her husband's betrayal, of her bulimia, of numerous scandals) and dazzled the world. The deeper the darkness, the brighter she shone. Impossible to sustain indefinitely, and I had seen her teetering, finally, at the edge of the abyss.

I said, and what about now? Now can you go on? And although moments before she had sobbed until she retched, choking on the impossibility of it all, she smiled that smile that she has, pure sex, and completely chaste, and said, "Oh, do give me a little credit, please."

But when I returned her mood was black. Two months of living in an unremarkable Brazilian suburb, working on her tan and roughing up her accent had perhaps already given her too much of the "normality" she thought she craved.

That's not a fair thing to say.

She is not the first person on this planet to walk out of her life and "start over" as they say in her adopted homeland. She is not the first mother to leave her children behind. These things do happen, though they shock us when we hear of them.

But her circumstances are extreme. What a dry formulation that is. Would that I could write of it, of her, with poetry and passion instead of my journeyman lettering. Were I able I would write not prose but an aria.

So, yes, the circumstances are extreme and her depression, her bleakness, is natural and inevitable. We talked of it before as a stage that she would go through. Though, given the delicate state of her mind, she perhaps didn't fully comprehend the finality of her actions, hadn't accepted the loss of her boys as permanent. No, she couldn't go on. But I didn't doubt, I still don't, that she will survive her losses. She is a survivor. She's the toughest woman I ever met.

"Real life," though, must have come as something of a shock. She always wanted it, or so she imagined. She fantasized about riding on a double-decker bus the way others dream about riding in a horse-drawn coach. When we were making our little plan (that's how she referred to it; she is often droll though princesses are seldom credited with a funny bone) she would remind me how many times she had walked down a London street "and got away with it." There weren't so many times, we could count them, because usually a photographer, or several, blew her cover. The cover being that it couldn't be the Princess of Wales in jeans and a sweatshirt browsing at the magazine stand. Other times she'd go out in disguise, a wig, dark glasses, once a policewoman's uniform, something she'd done once or twice in the early days, high jinks with her sister-in-law, and later, in desperation, to make pay phone calls to some undeserving object of her love. Disguise, she already knew, could work.

But the unrelenting day-in-day-out of shopping and cooking and cleaning and washing, despite her retention through the years of a touch of the Cinderella complex, has definitely been a bore. She hadn't hired a cleaner when I saw her. By the end of November she'd had over two months fending for herself. It's a point of pride on which she will eventually give way.

She's wearing a wig and dyeing her hair as well; never one to do things by halves. Her tan is deeper than I've ever seen it. Her eyes are dark brown and she complains that the lenses are a pain to take in and out.

Back in September, when we went to have the "filler" put in her lips, a local clinic in Belo Horizonte (the town where she was holed away), she could hardly breathe all the way there in the car. She had spent the previous two weeks hiding in the house, curtains drawn, rationing out the food that I'd bought. "Oh my God," she kept saying on the drive. "Oh my God."

I said, Might I venture a couple of observations, ma'am? First that we will be in and out of the clinic within forty minutes and that you can keep your sunglasses on if that would make you more comfortable. Secondly that truly nobody is looking for you. You are being hunted no longer, that is over, it's gone.

She pulled herself together then and commandeered the rearview mirror to reassure herself that she was a dark-haired, dark-eyed beauty now. She said, "Will you please stop calling me ma'am?"

Her lips are fuller and I think she was pleased with the result, when the swelling went down and it was apparent she wasn't going to be left with a permanent pout. "They're quite sexy, aren't they, Lawrence?" Even in the midst of anguish she can flirt.

In November she went through with the nose job in Rio, although I didn't think she needed it. But when you have been the world's most photographed woman it is difficult to believe that you are safe from discovery. And by the time I left her in North Carolina three weeks later (I had the house all arranged in advance of course) I could see that it had been done with artistry. Also that she was absolutely right to have had it done. Adding a new nose to the new mouth, the difference seemed not incremental but exponential, as it appeared to alter, as perhaps indeed it did, the very proportions of her face.

21 January 1998

God knows what she is doing with herself now. I try to imagine it and I can't. She imagined it so many times, a "normal" life, but always with a man, the one who would take her away from it all. That was never going to happen and even she could see that in the end.

I gave her some books, *Vanity Fair, Pride and Prejudice, Madame Bovary, Crime and Punishment.* She said, "It's terribly sweet of you, Lawrence, pretending I'm clever enough for this stuff."

What will she be doing now? What does her morning look like? Perhaps she's taken up gardening. Maybe she has a library card.

It is too difficult to imagine her living life on a human scale, and I don't know whether to put that down to exalting her too highly or patronizing her too much. When she wasn't out in public, she was frequently alone in a room with a sofa, an embroidered cushion, a television set.

She did love watching the soap operas, but there never was a drama to match the drama of her life. However difficult that was (again, the dryness) she must miss it, and when I was with her last she seemed almost to resent the fact that she could go about her business with ease. When, for instance, I took her to the hospital for the rhinoplasty, she did not gasp all the way there as she had on the previous trip to the clinic, although she would, according to the brochure, be under "close observation" during the stay. This time she was sullen, almost silent, and when I asked her if she was worried she said, "Why should I be? I'm just one amongst dozens."

That was true enough. Rio is probably the plastic surgery capital of the world. Buying a new nose was as simple as buying a new dress from a catalog; you can pick the style you prefer from a batch of photographs.

I blanched, though, when we went into the reception room and saw her picture gracing the cover of many of the magazines they had there. She, however, was a step ahead of me. She picked one up and told me to hold on to it. At the "consultation" with the surgeon, a pre-theater chat when she was already in a hospital gown, sitting up on a gurney, I had the magazine facedown on my lap and I felt it burning my knees. She was makeup-free with just a few strands of dark hair escaping from the plastic cap. After the preliminaries, the surgeon, a suave fellow, a lounge lizard in scrubs, began to scrutinize her profile. Two months since she was assumed to have drowned. Her portrait still plastered the press. As unremarkable as she looked in her gown and cap, was there any possibility of him recognizing her? I held my breath.

"Darling," she said, "pass me the magazine. Wasn't she beautiful? I'd like you to make me look more like her. Can it be done?"

The surgeon barely looked at the magazine. He said, "Such a tragedy. Such a beautiful woman. Now what I'd suggest for you, if I may, is that we streamline a little here, and here, and take the nostrils to there. I think you're going to love the result."

She acquiesced by little more than a murmur and he began marking her face with his pen. I sat by her side, in the role of husband, I suppose. The surgeon must see them every week. A husband taking his wife on a nip-and-tuck holiday in Brazil, a couple of weeks on the beach thrown in to recover, before returning home remarkably "refreshed."

Still, I was nervous, I must admit, in a way that I had not been since she was officially deceased. When I returned to visit her in the morning I stood for a full five minutes on the hospital steps holding myself up on a railing while my legs did their best to let me down. I am ashamed to recall that my fear was as much for myself as for her, and that as I trembled at the prospect of discovery I had in mind my own inevitable disgrace perhaps more than anything else.

I pulled myself together. For an instant I wished I could be felled right there and then, a sudden blood clot in the brain to trump the tumor, no more tightening and loosening of the hangman's noose, no more service to him, to her, to anything, anyone. And then I pulled myself together, called upon my birthright as an Englishman, a stiffening of the upper lip drafted in like the Household Guards to quell an uprising of the emotions.

I nearly laughed when I saw her, sitting on the bed, painting her toenails. With two black eyes, a bandaged nose, and swollen face I could barely recognize her myself. "I'm a mess," she said. "And the nurses think I'm just some rich spoiled wife who has nothing better to do than chop a perfectly good nose around." She sounded petulant.

I took her home two days later. The drive was long and, again, silent. I made some dinner, or rather, heated two plastic trays in the microwave, while she lay on the sofa beneath a blanket, only the crown of her head and two punched-up eyes revealed. For the next few days her mood was as somber as I have ever witnessed. Not distraught, not hysterical, and not punctuated by those rays of light with which she pierced even the blackest of her moods. She was absorbing, I think, the realization that she will not be recognized, not by the neighbors, the shopkeepers, the nurses, or anyone else. When she goes out now she may take all the precautions she pleases, in the way she dresses, the way she speaks, what she says, but the drama will be limited to the scenarios playing out in her mind. Her outings will not be adrenaline-filled. The curtain has fallen. The soap opera has been axed. And so here starts the rest of her life.

Chapter Five

Although she wasn't supposed to work the weekends Lydia liked to drop in on Saturday mornings because Saturdays were when families came to look for a new pet, meaning there were fewer staff available to exercise and care for the dogs. She pulled up in front of the pre-fabricated office and opened the passenger door to let Rufus bounce down ahead of her.

Esther was in the clinic with the Kerry blue terrier puppy they'd taken in a few days earlier. "This one," she said, "will not take his worming pills. Eric's been mixing them in his food but he finds them and spits them out."

"He's a smart cookie," said Lydia.

"With a sore backside to prove it."

Lydia stroked the puppy's wavy black coat. It wouldn't turn that lovely slate blue for another few months yet. She ran her hand over his little beard. "I'll crush a tablet," she said, "mix it with some peanut butter. That usually does the trick."

"I'll leave him to you," said Esther. "Got a family coming by in a minute and if I can get them to take one of the older dogs while this smart cookie is out of sight, all the better and amen."

Lydia took Tyson, Zeus, and Topper for a walk in the woods, along with Rufus, who proudly led the way. They were old dogs who had been at the shelter for years and would probably never be rehomed. Tyson dragged a back leg and Zeus and Topper grizzled at each other like the old bad-tempered men they were. She took them because the others would have more chances, were cute enough to find families who would throw sticks and rubber balls while Zeus and Topper chewed on their kennel's wire netting and Tyson curled up and chewed on his leg.

Last night Carson had come over and she had made chicken parmigiana and when the dishes were cleared he said, "Living by yourself is great. No one else to please."

She'd waited.

"But isn't it a little bit lonely? Sometimes?"

Lydia knew about lonely.

"Nothing's ever perfect," she said.

"Don't get me wrong. I'm not complaining. Just wondering if there might be another way. It crosses my mind."

"Don't turn all romantic on me," said Lydia.

Was there anything she didn't know about loneliness? She had tasted it so many ways.

"Now you know there's no danger of that." He rubbed the back of his neck.

"Phew," said Lydia. "I'm relieved."

"Being with other people doesn't stop you being lonely," said Carson. "Not necessarily. And living alone doesn't make you lonely. But if you're not spending enough time with the people you want to spend time with, that's when maybe it starts to get hard."

"Carson," said Lydia, "we've only been dating four months."

There was a time when Lydia had thought—oh, the arrogance, the almighty arrogance—that nobody had known loneliness like hers. Her life was so . . . singular, so *removed* from the common experience. What a fool she was. There were so many lonely people, and she was just one of them. Hadn't Lawrence been lonely too? She'd been blind to it at the time, but wasn't that something that had bound them together?

"I bought tickets to the ballet," Carson said.

"I love the ballet," said Lydia.

"I know. You told me. One of the few things I'm allowed to know."

Lydia laughed. "What are we seeing?"

"*Swan Lake* at Lincoln Center."

"You're taking me to New York?"

"Don't you have a birthday coming up? Thought we'd have a weekend away. Walk in Central Park. Nice dinner. The ballet."

She was quiet as she looked at him. She didn't know if she wanted to go to any of the places she used to go. A few years ago she definitely would have refused. Now she just wasn't sure.

"That's so sweet of you," she said.

"Then you'll come? I already bought tickets—the weekend after your birthday. Was going to keep it a surprise, but then I thought maybe you wouldn't appreciate being kidnapped."

She really should stop this thing right now before it turned into a mess. Already she was breaking her own rules, having him stay some nights at the house.

She said, "I'll have to find something to wear."

After Lydia had put the dogs away she watched Esther training Delilah in the yard.

"I'm not getting too ambitious here," said Esther. "A five-second sit-stay is where it's at for today. Good girl!" She gave Delilah her treat and the Lab jumped up, a great lolloping yellow ball of glee. "Don't spoil a good thing, now, Delilah. Down."

Lydia was still learning about obedience training. She'd read a couple of books. She'd worked with a number of dogs, including her own. But watching Esther was still the best.

"So does she do a little longer each day?"

"That's the idea," said Esther. "We add the three Ds—duration, distance, and distraction. We don't try to do too much at once."

They took a break in the staff room with mugs of herbal tea. It was a horrible room, with a leak-stained ceiling and a sink that dripped constantly. Aside from the table and plastic chairs there were two easy chairs that smelled of mildew. Esther kept saying she was going to throw them out. She kept saying too, that she was going to do something about the general nastiness of the room, but whenever they got any money Esther said the dogs had to come first—that's what people gave the money for.

"Kid came in with his mom this morning, gave thirty-two dollars he'd saved himself."

"What a darling," said Lydia.

"Darling is right. I told him so. Eight years old."

"Anything else come in?"

"Janice Lindstrom came by with the collecting cans. We counted up eighty-nine bucks and ten cents."

"Oh," said Lydia.

"Right again." Esther ran her hands up and down her bare arms. She always wore a sleeveless T-shirt and camouflage pants that she bought from an army surplus store in the city. It was a look she pulled off with panache. She had long steely gray hair that she wore tied back in a ponytail, up in a bun, or corralled in two thick braids.

Esther examined a bruise on her bicep. She was careless about letting the kennel doors swing against her arm, standing half-in, half-out of the doorway while she let one dog out and held another back. "Oh, and four new adoptions over the website, that makes another hundred and twenty dollars per month. We should say hallelujah for that."

"Every bit helps," said Lydia.

"I'm packing it all in," said Esther. "I'm packing it in and moving to Maui to sip margaritas by the sea."

"Can I come?"

"Sure. Let's go pack our bags." Esther laughed. "How did we end up in this town anyway?"

After all those years of moving and renting Lydia had been looking for a place to buy in Gains, ten miles down the highway. When the Realtor in Gains ran out of options she put Lydia in touch with Tevis and the idea of living in Kensington immediately appealed. If you kept a sense of humor you had not lost everything.

"It's not so bad," said Lydia.

"If you'd told me when I was twenty," said Esther, "that this is where I'd end up . . ." She shook her head, but she was smiling. "If you'd told me that I'd ever be *old*. Sixty-six! An old woman. Me. No way."

"When I was twenty," said Lydia. She stopped.

Esther had told Lydia about how she'd spent her teenage years and early twenties. (Have you heard of *The Electric Kool-Aid Acid Test*? I was there, baby. I was on that bus.) She'd stayed a hippie long after that, living in Haight-Ashbury, baking hash brownies with rare groove Lebanese black, sleeping with whoever wasn't too stoned to get it up. A friend of hers was arrested at a gay rights demo for kissing a police officer, who beat him and then booked him for assault. He got eighteen months in the state penitentiary and Esther bought herself some law books because the lawyers were all too dumb-ass for words. By the time she had a single clue about law, her friend was on parole but Esther went back to school. She straightened out. She wanted to specialize in international human rights, get a job at the UN in New York. Where she ended up was Boise, Idaho, in a corporate law firm where she made partner within eight years. Her BMW was top-of-the-line. Her lawns were mown by Mexicans. Her high heels hurt her feet. The day she handed in her notice was the happiest of her life.

"When I was twenty," said Lydia, "I had just got married. My husband belonged to a very stuffy family. It was all so suffocating. I scarcely breathed for years."

She had come to realize, slowly, slowly, now that she had a few friends, that it wasn't as difficult as she had assumed to mention certain things from her past. Nobody was out to get her; they weren't waiting to catch her out, trip her up. And they didn't find it so very peculiar that she had chosen to leave so much behind. In the States people moved around, lived far from families. Self-reinvention was American as applesauce.

"You poor kid," said Esther. "What did we know at twenty? I thought I knew everything. Think you'll ever get married again?"

"Not in a million years." She liked Carson. She liked him a lot but she wasn't going to allow herself to fall in love. Even when she was in her thirties she fell so hard it was always terrifying, out of control. Another form of addiction, of course.

Esther seemed to be studying her. She said, "Carson's a decent guy."

"I know," said Lydia.

They'd met about a year ago when he showed up at Kensington Canine, hitching his jeans with his thumbs. He filled in an application form, looked at some of the dogs, and arranged a date for a home inspection. When he returned he picked out an Irish red setter called Madeleine. Lydia had been certain he'd go for a bulldog, a boxer, or a German shepherd. She liked that she'd been wrong.

"Listen," said Esther. "Get out of here. Don't get married. Not to this place either. Not to the dogs. You're still too young for that. And I know you like to be needed, but I really do not need you today. I got more volunteers coming in. So go on out there and get yourself in some trouble while you still can."

Driving into town to pick up some groceries, Lydia said to Rufus, "Doesn't hurt to open up a little, does it?"

Rufus kept his counsel.

At the traffic light she leaned over and kissed the top of his head. He smelled of pet shampoo, forest floor, and dog. He pushed his nose under her chin.

"Of course it doesn't," she said.

She allowed herself a few moments to reflect on a memory. Her boys, flanking her on the sofa, watching a movie, flicking popcorn at each other, laughing when a piece got caught in her hair. Not too long. She pulled herself back. The past was an ocean, and although she swam toward the shoreline, she knew it could suck her down. The trick was to swim at an angle, not fight the currents directly yet not give in to them.

After she had finished the grocery shopping she remembered she had promised to lend Mrs. Jackson a book that had been sitting in the glove compartment for several weeks because she kept forgetting to drop it off. Mrs. Jackson was a pillar of Kensington society, and Esther kept muttering about trying to rope her into fund-raising. It was worth a little detour now. Lydia walked up to the bed-and-breakfast, a three-story colonial revival brick house on Fairfax, which the Jacksons owned.

Mrs. Jackson was on her way out with Otis who, only a few steps in front of the bed-and-breakfast, was already tangled up in his leash.

"Oh, goodness," said Mrs. Jackson. "This naughty dog."

Lydia pulled the book from her purse. "We've found this really useful up at the shelter," she said.

"*When Pigs Fly!*" read Mrs. Jackson. "*Training Success with Impossible Dogs*. Did you hear that now, Otis? Did you?"

Lydia knelt down, picked up the dachshund, and unwound the leash from his legs.

"Last night he pulled all the cushions off the couches and when I came in there were feathers all over the room."

"Oh dear," said Lydia. She made a fuss over Otis, who wriggled on his side while Lydia rubbed his belly and his back. She looked up at Mrs. Jackson. On the steps of the bed-and-breakfast, over Mrs. Jackson's shoulder, she saw the back of a man's head, square and gray, going inside.

"And there he was, lying on the floor, looking like butter wouldn't melt, with a feather behind his ear."

Lydia laughed. She set Otis down and stood up. She chatted a while longer with Mrs. Jackson and when she glanced up at the bay window, the curtain stirred as if moved by the breeze.

Chapter Six

Grabowski lay on the four-poster at the bed-and-breakfast. When he'd kicked off his shoes and loosened his belt he'd been thinking about knocking one out then a quick nap before lunch. But the prissy white lace curtains and the overstuffed room (colonial style furniture—mincing fiddleback chairs, haughty side tables with animal paw feet) was definitely a turnoff. His gut wasn't helping either, when he looked down at it now. He sucked it in. Then he closed his eyes and tried again.

Riffling through his stock of mental images, he failed to land on anything that caused a stir. He wondered if he'd bolted the door. Wouldn't put it past Mrs. Jackson to come busting in unannounced. She was desperate for someone to talk to and she'd already bored her husband to sleep in his armchair. That woman she was with earlier was pretty. Long dark hair, long legs, amazing blue eyes, which she'd turned up toward Mrs. Jackson just as he'd walked by and up the front steps. He'd gone into the sitting room and checked her out from the window, thought about going down and trying to strike up a conversation. Bottled it, of course. All mouth and no trousers. Funny, before Cathy kicked him out he'd found it easy to chat up women. It seemed so much harder now.

He gave up and zipped his trousers, stumbled over to the desk, and switched his laptop on. All the photos, even from the early days, were on the hard drive. He'd had all the film turned into digital files. He opened one at random, Necker Island. That was a "private" holiday, but she'd arranged a photo call, inevitably. She looked stunning in that red bikini, coming out of the surf. He zoomed in. She was smiling, apparently carefree and enjoying a little time to herself. Just her and a phalanx of photographers, out of view.

He spun through more shots. Why couldn't he get himself going? He hadn't even made a final selection of pictures, never mind got off the starting block with the writing. This book was supposed to be his retirement fund. Although Cathy might put a stop to that with her incessant financial demands. It didn't excite him. He was a photojournalist, not a bloody archivist. He liked the thrill of the chase. Crawling through the gorse at Balmoral, staking out her favorite restaurant haunts, getting tip-offs from his network of informers, intercepting the police radio with his handheld scanner while eating sandwiches in his car in Kensington. He'd broken the code almost straightaway—*52 rolling*—that meant she had passed the internal security checkpoint in her dark blue Audi and in another minute would be nosing out into the West London traffic. One minute and he'd be on the move.

Grabowski sighed. He pulled his rosary beads out of his pocket and rubbed them one by one through his fingers. Well, he wasn't going back to London to take more pictures of all the second-rate celebs. He'd had enough of them. When you start at the top, it's very hard to come down. Pop singers, soap opera divas, reality television goons. The occasional genuine Hollywood star. But even then . . .

No point being stuck in the past.

He picked his cell phone off the desk and jabbed in a number.

"It's John Grabowski," he said.

"Grabber," said Tinny, "what gives?"

"I'm coming out."

"Finally he comes to his senses. Why'd you want to be anywhere but LA? I'm sitting by the pool, drinking a Bud Light, I've got five guys on Britney, boy, is she going to blow, I've got three on Cameron, she's up to something, I've got . . ."

"Tinny, you don't need to persuade me."

"I been trying to persuade you for years. Get the fuck out of London. Hey, I'm sorry about you and Cathy, heard it from—I don't know who I heard it from, it gets around, and listen, there's a job for you here, the agency is booming, it's booming big-time, but some of these wetbacks I got working, they drive me nuts."

"You got Mexicans working for you?"

"Nah, I got French, I got Spanish, I got Italians, I got English. My European wetbacks. They can shove a lens up someone's nose, but they got no finesse, you know what I mean?"

Grabowski knew. The art was going out of the business. "I left London. I'm in the States. I'm on my way."

"Fucking-A," said Tinny. "The beers are on ice, the chicks are on fire. What the fuck's been keeping you?"

"I'm supposed to be putting a book together. Not just pictures— the definitive book, you know. It's taking some time."

"What? Ten years? You'll do it here. I'll put you on two, three days a week. Grabber, I gotta take a call. You know where to find me, right?"

Yeah, he knew where to find Tinny. They'd met on that Necker Island trip when Tinny had been working for one of the American news agencies. He'd set up his own shop shortly afterward and got himself some scoops straightaway. They'd stayed in touch. Tinny had offered him a job—payroll, decent split on the sales—and Grabowski and Cathy had gone out there for a week to get the lay of the land. Cathy said she couldn't stand it. It's all so false, she said. Said they'd be getting a divorce if that's what he wanted. Then she wanted a divorce anyway.

It was a good thing his mother was dead. Divorce, in her view, was a sin. Something a Protestant like Cathy would never understand. At the wedding his mother wept into her handkerchief, and they weren't tears of happiness.

He opened up another file on his laptop. A ski trip. No use for the cover shot, that's the one he wanted to find today. If he did that at least he would have achieved something. Another file from a polo match that she was watching from beneath some trees. She was wearing a horrible hat. It wouldn't do.

This was more promising, a charity gala at the Ritz. She wore her favorite pearl choker and a killer little black dress. He cropped in to head and shoulders. Then he zoomed in again to head and neck. He got in closer on her face. The picture was still clear and sharp. He stared into her eyes, looking directly back at him.

"Knock, knock," said Mrs. Jackson, opening the door without actually knocking on it.

"If you were hoping to catch me naked, Mrs. Jackson, I'm afraid you're just a few minutes too late."

She appeared not to catch his drift. "All decent?" she said. "Great. I've had a telephone call about vacancies. Now, will you be wanting the room tomorrow? You said you weren't sure when you registered."

"I'll be . . ." He turned to close down the image. It was about time to have some lunch. "I'll be going in the . . ." He stared once more at those eyes. How many hours had he spent, over seventeen years, looking at them, either through a lens, or in person, or in a photograph? Thousands and thousands, he reckoned. A great deal more time than any lover she ever had.

"In the morning?" said Mrs. Jackson. "Oh, Otis, you bad dog. You know you're not allowed in here. Scram!"

Over the years, thought Grabowski, she had changed so much. She grew into her beauty when she cast off the frumpy Sloane of the early years. She started off big and awkward, then became frighteningly thin, before filling out again. Her hairstyle changed and when it did it was cause enough for another front page. Her clothes and the confidence with which she wore them developed every year. But her eyes remained the same. They were mesmerizingly beautiful, and he'd never seen another pair that was half as striking. Until today.

"In a few days," said Grabowski. "I'll be leaving in a few days."

Mrs. Jackson had Otis, who had not scrammed, tucked beneath her arm. The dog looked frantic to escape and Grabowski decided he could not blame the little fellow. It was not a clinch in which he would like to find himself.

"We'll be happy to have you," said Mrs. Jackson. "Excuse us, I think someone is desperate to go potty."

"I won't keep you then," said Grabowski. "But just one question." He should at least try to meet that woman. So what if she knocked him back? You never knew unless you tried and maybe, just maybe, he would get lucky. He'd put on a little weight recently, all the stress, but he was a decent-enough-looking guy. "One question—who was that you were talking to outside this morning? She had a little spaniel with her."

Mrs. Jackson forgot about potty for Otis. She told him what she knew about Lydia Snaresbrook—little enough, but she plumped down on the end of the bed and spun it out for as long as she could.

Chapter Seven

23 January 1998

Had to stay in bed yesterday. Nothing too alarming—copious vomiting into a bucket, an almighty weariness. It's good that I can't smell a thing. The bucket sat by the bed until this morning and didn't bother me at all. While I'm in the mood for counting my blessings I shall offer up thanks that the tumor is not on the left side of my brain, my "dominant hemisphere," the one that controls language and writing. And I am, in truth, pathetically grateful for that.

I have been feeling so much better in recent days that yesterday really knocked me down. Hope is a sly old dog; it creeps up with a shy little wag of the tail and lodges its muzzle in your crotch, trying to worm its way back into your affections. I should know better. I do know better. If the tumor didn't respond to chemo and radiotherapy it is not going to respond to "positive thinking," as it is termed by the self-help brigade. All that "brave fight" nonsense. What is it that I should be fighting? Fight cancer with a smile?

The Macmillan nurse looked in, and she'll be back again later today. She's rather wonderful, Gloria. She has big square hands, a shapeless dress, and gray hair that looks as if it could be used for polishing pans. She's warm and thorough and competent, and she can tell a filthy joke. At no point has she suggested that I battle the tumor with willpower and a winning personality. Instead she checks and counts my medications, takes a blood sample, inquires about pain control.

Yesterday she did ask about my book and I confessed to her that I have become a little too absorbed in the byway of a *New York Times* article from the 1898 archive, discussing Chamberlain's speech in Birmingham from the perspective of German diplomats and journalists.

It was something of a false confession. Compared to the time I've spent dwelling on Belo Horizonte, my doodlings in the margin of fin de siècle history have been of microscopic proportions. The irony of the situation has not escaped my notice. An historian who is at pains to conceal a moment of history. That appears to be my fate.

24 January 1998

When I prepared the house in Belo Horizonte, or Beaga, as it is familiarly known, I fussed and fretted about how sterile it seemed. Naturally it was no palace but that wasn't my concern. Her informal drawing room and bedroom at KP were not grand, they were homely, filled with cushions and keepsakes, the children's artworks and photographs. I did my best. It was, perhaps, what is termed in pop psychology "displacement activity." I went shopping for soft furnishings, vases, and—my pièce de résistance—a menagerie of stuffed toy animals. I lined them up at the bottom of the bed, as she did in KP, and how baleful they looked, especially the elephant—I had to turn him around so I couldn't see those sad little eyes, that furrowed brow.

I chose a "safe" suburb, of course, and within that a gated and security-patrolled enclave. I am, though I say it myself, a diligent researcher and meticulous planner. It was better not to have too grand a residence (there were budgetary considerations as well), and I wanted someplace with a fluid demographic of internationals as well as locals, where a newcomer would attract little attention. Belo Horizonte has a significant business population among the nearly five million inhabitants of the metropolitan area, so it wasn't too difficult.

I'd bought clothes for her, and the other essentials of life, toiletries and so on. At first when we were devising our "little plan" she would say, "Oh, Lawrence, you will bring at least one photo album, won't you?" Or, "The two things I absolutely must have you take are the little wood carving from the drawing room and the painting in the blue frame on the mantelpiece. Masterpieces, both!" I had to work quite hard to persuade her that it was not wise to have anything go missing (even the children's artistic "masterpieces") at the time of her disappearance. I'm not so sure about that now. The whereabouts of numerous of her personal effects is presently quite unknown within the royal household, or at least known only to individual members of staff who may have spirited them away for "safekeeping."

Could I have worked more strenuously to persuade her that her schemes for seeing the children again were neither feasible nor advisable? I did try. But I couldn't bear to press the point too hard.

I did take one thing that she had asked for, an audiotape made by her former voice coach (how she used to dread giving speeches), one among many, which had never been cataloged or noted in any way. He filmed her during their sessions. I was present once or twice. I remember her sitting on the couch, she was wearing black capri trousers and a black polo neck above which her blond crop looked beautifully boyish, and she had her legs tucked up, and her feet in a pair of those flat ballet-style pumps that she favors, and he was pretending to interview her like a television presenter. He said, "You are well known for your charity work. What is it that draws you to do so much work for charity?" And she gave what may only be described as an impish grin and said, "It's because I've got nothing else to do." She fell about. She can giggle with great abandon.

How long will it be, I wonder, before one of those videotapes turns up on television, sold to the highest bidder? She can be remarkably, naively, trusting, as she was with that man, allowing him to keep the films of her talking so candidly. And she can take suspicion to the level of paranoid derangement. Just one of her many contradictions.

25 January 1998

It wasn't true, of course, what she said about having nothing else to do. Perhaps there was an element of that—not wanting to be simply a clotheshorse. But she is fantastic, sometimes, at putting herself down. One of her favorite lines to repeat is, "Oh, I wouldn't know about that, I never learned terribly much at school—the only prize I ever won was for Best-Kept Guinea Pig." But she was brilliant at the work that she did, and I think the key was that she was never merely fulfilling her public function, her allotted official role; she truly gave of herself and people sensed it, and that gave her something in return. Her husband resented that—the fact she got real pleasure from what he regarded as the dreary rounds of duty and destiny.

The voice coach had prepared an audiotape that he advised would help her "connect" more with the public by taking the edge off her cut-glass accent. She gave that short shrift. Public speaking was never her strong suit, but she is perceptive enough to know that it wasn't a question of the class divide, and that it is better to be posh than phony. Despite its aristocratic pedigree, and despite the work she put in with her coach, her voice remained really rather undistinguished and relatively unknown. That is an advantage now, but she won't believe it and is, or at least was when I saw her, wearing out that tape, determinedly chiseling away at the upper-crust diphthongs and pure vowels. I thought to tell her that nature would take its course and that they would fade over time but I refrained, because now she really does not have anything else to do.

I had some misgivings, as I say, about the sterility of the house when I leased it, but I did do my best, although home decoration is not my natural preserve. When I look around me now I can see that the coffee table might benefit from a strategically placed bowl, that a throw might soften the chesterfield, that the regimental order of this capacious desk could be relieved by a knickknack or two. But most of the time I remain in a state of grace, accepting my intimate surroundings as if they had been ordained from on high.

By the time of my third, no, my fourth, visit, she had wrought some feminine transformation, and—I was glad to see—kept the menagerie as well. I did have four stays at that house. The first was when I set up the rental, the second when I took her there, the third when I returned after the funeral, and the fourth when I went back in November and, after her recuperation from the surgery, took her to the Promised Land. The third time was the most fraught, though each visit was not without its challenges.

I had done what I could to protect her by removing the television set from the house. Although it is a favorite trope of the thriller writer, watching one's own funeral cannot be psychologically healthy; watching one's children in attendance would be enough to drive anyone over the edge. Had she imagined that scene while we were planning her escape? I think, most certainly, she had not. Toward the end she was so hunted and haunted and desperate, and there was a part of her mind—wherein the boys were safely stowed and sacrosanct—that was simply unreachable.

After the funeral I called her on the prepaid mobile I had purchased for her. She begged me to bring as many press cuttings from London as possible. I counseled against it. She called me back later, although we had agreed to keep calls strictly to the necessary minimum, and this time commanded me to do as I was told. For someone who has "the common touch" she can be quite startlingly imperious on occasion. "Lawrence," she said, "I am not your prisoner. You can't keep me in the dark." I said she most certainly was not my prisoner, that she was free to do as she pleased. She said, "I shall do as I please, Lawrence, and it pleases me to tell you to bring those cuttings with you, as many as you can manage in your suitcase."

She has always been a press junkie, particularly a tabloid addict, right from the early days, and that was both a strength and a weakness. I would have denied her access to her swan song had she not countermanded, but would that have been right? In any case, the coverage probably penetrated even to the darkest jungles of Borneo, and my shielding would have been partial at best. I took as much as I could reasonably carry along with my clothes.

Her initial response, on riffling through the newspapers and magazines, was as I had expected. I may have "saved" her from watching it on television but the pictures were there in full-color spreads. The boys walking with whey-faced bravery behind the hearse; the coffin, which was said (though no palace official confirmed it) to contain one of her outfits, chosen by them; and on top of the casket, a single word, spelled out in white flowers—*Mummy*.

Is it possible to die of grief? Apparently not. Were it possible, she would have achieved it that day.

26 January 1998

Her overwhelming grief. I record it for the sake of this process. And this process now does seem entirely necessary to me, this fleeting document more essential and sustaining than the array of pills in my bedside cabinet. I record it but I shall not dwell on it, just as, when she was able to hear me again, I pressed on her repeatedly the importance of not dwelling on their pain. The young do heal and mend. I said, You mustn't track their progress incessantly, you mustn't stalk them from afar. If you do, I told her, don't feel resentful when you see them happy, smiling and thriving in the fullness of their lives. She bristled at that, as I knew she would, the idea she could be so selfish; but I could see also that it hit home: they would be fine without her.

It didn't end there, of course. It went on, cyclically. I could have recounted, in my mandarin manner, the reasons that led to her cataclysmic decision and led me to aid and abet the same. But it wasn't the time. Why try to staunch an unstaunchable wound? I let it flow, and when I felt that it was ebbing, I made whatever poor and inadequate interventions I could.

I apologized. That helped a little. More than I could have predicted. I talked briskly of the boys' futures. That pulled her up a bit. More than anything, I tried to hold my nerve and remember the times when she was so seemingly out of control that I feared nothing would bring her back to terra firma again—the screaming, the hurling of heirlooms, the bingeing and vomiting, the cutting of her arms and her legs. There are very few aspects of life that remain private from a private secretary.

She did survive those times. That which does not kill us makes us stronger, as they say. That's a little glib for my tastes. Yes, she is tough, the toughest. But certain materials, as they harden, are always in danger of shattering. She knew it, and I knew it: she had had enough, more than anyone should be expected to endure, and it was my duty, my privilege, to help her escape—if I may resort to a cliché—the gilded cage.

Amid the heartbreak, her life strewn out in column inches across the floor, it has to be said, there was some comfort and strength to be drawn. I was supposed to be in Washington, continuing the research for my book. I spent two weeks with her and day after day she sat, or sometimes lay, reading the cuttings and weeping. And eventually she began to take a little solace: she was loved.

Whosoever had loved her previously had not loved her enough. There were many. I count myself among them. Although I escaped even temporary banishment from her circle (one of the few to be thus distinguished) I can recall some sticky moments when the fierceness of my attachment, my devotion, my unwavering loyalty, my willingness to talk on the telephone at three a.m., was called into question, subjected to her obsessive scrutiny. Many employees were sent to the guillotine (not, perhaps, as many as the press implied), severed not so much for any misdemeanor as for failing to take her fully inside their hearts. Friends fell by the wayside, cut off by the simple expedient of changing whichever of her private numbers she had given them. The causes, ostensibly, were wide and varied—a hint of betrayal, a perceived slight, a boredom setting in—but the underlying cause was always the same. A lack, as she saw it, of their true and undying love.

As for the lovers. Well. As for them. They did not always come up to the highest standards. I think I may safely say that without jealousy clouding my judgment. I seek neither to excuse nor condemn them, but merely to observe the extraordinary difficulty of their task. Her need for love is as wide as that sky out there and as impossible for an unwinged mortal to fulfill.

Does the love of an entire nation suffice instead? "Lawrence," she said, "all these people. All these people . . ." and could go no further. I could scarcely believe it myself, although I had borne witness to that scene. The sea of flowers, the poems and letters, the candlelit vigil at KP. I saw them, children and adults, of every class, every color, every creed. I saw a policeman wipe a tear away. I saw an elderly man in a wheelchair whisper a prayer. I saw a woman in a sari lay a wreath. I saw a man in a Burberry coat lean against a complete stranger and sob.

I cannot say what I felt that evening, after the official declaration of her death, when I had flown back to London. That night I stayed up with the mourners, I walked amongst them, shared their flasks and their sorrow and listened, now and then, to the stories they had to tell—of her visits to the hospital, the hospice, the homeless shelter, the anorexia clinic. I could think only of one thing: how I had taken her from them all. And I found myself appealing, to a god in whom I do not believe, that I not be judged too harshly for my sin.

27 January 1998

Of course my critical faculties were somewhat impaired. I was drained from the previous days' exertions, and overwrought with emotion and nerves. At some distance now, I perceive it differently. In a way she was not taken from the people but delivered to them. For she became that night a pure emblem, of goodness and suffering. A people can own an emblem, far better than a flesh-and-blood human being.

Her "death" changed the nation, so the leader-writers and columnists averred. It consigned the stiff upper lip to the annals of history. The Prime Minister spoke of her with a catch in his throat. The Queen broke protocol and bowed to the coffin.

The Queen broke protocol. How amazing it is to me to write those words.

There was a witch hunt, of course. The press and the public identified the culprits. She was hounded by the photographers, the paparazzi, and they were the ones to blame. They drove her to her erratic and risk-taking behavior, which culminated inevitably in her death.

She wasn't slow to see the irony there. "Are the press blaming themselves?" she said.

But she took strength from the outpouring, which reached far beyond the bounds of our shores. Two billion people, so it is estimated, watched the funeral.

28 January 1998

Did I act for the best? I have teased apart that moral knot so many times and still it tangles up. All I can say in the end is, I hope so. I hope I did not do wrong. Ultimately the answer lies with her. If she makes a life for herself then I was right to facilitate it. But I will not be around to see. On the other hand, were I not under sentence of death, I could not have done what I did. To carry the burden of secrecy and responsibility over decades would have made it unfeasible for me, and too risky for her.

So it goes around. One would hope that closeness to death brings some heightened sagacity. Perhaps when I start to feel very wise I will know that the end is near.

There are times when I wake in the night, as if from a nightmare. I can't recall a single dream anymore. If I do dream of anything it is surely her. I find myself falling into daytime reveries. I find myself yearning to call. We agreed that we would not, except in some extreme situation, pick up the telephone. "Even if I have an emergency, Lawrence," she said, "I know I've got to find a way to cope for myself, after all . . ." She did not finish the thought but we both knew what she meant. It wasn't that she was embarrassed by the prospect of my—of any—demise. Death has been deemed a kind of perversion and has been suitably sequestered from polite society. But not by her. "You've been the most terrific help already, you know." She kissed me on my bald pink head and giggled helplessly. "Oh God, Lawrence, what can I say? Anything I say to thank you sounds so ridiculous." It had, in fact, sounded as if I'd been awfully helpful getting the picnic packed, bringing the car around.

She hadn't her brown lenses in. We were sitting on the couch together in the little white wooden house in North Carolina, and I was wrapped up entirely in the ultramarine of her irises. Her eyes are worthy of a sonnet. They are the most beautiful eyes I have ever seen.

"Are you afraid?" she asked me.

I shrugged. I've been too distracted to think about it, I said.

"I would be afraid," she said. "Whenever I've thought about killing myself, I knew I'd never go through with it because I'd be too scared."

She can be as frank as a child.

"But you must be afraid," she said.

I conceded her point. Yes, when I allow myself to dwell.

She talked to me then of the old times, with such fondness that it felt like good-bye. We traded stories of our first meeting, of how when I had bowed to her, she had curtsied in return, that glorious spark in her eye.

After a while she grew serious again. "I'd be too afraid to die, Lawrence. Now I don't want to be too afraid to live."

29 January 1998

The night that she swam out to her new life she was raw, wild, magnificent. I had sat in the boat for nearly an hour before I spotted her, wondering if it could be possible that she had changed her mind, wondering after that if the whole "little plan" had existed only as a kind of delusional seizure of my malfunctioning brain. Then the still dark waters broke and her arm lifted up and she waved. She swam steadily toward the boat while I looked nervously around, checking for the millionth time on the possibility of being seen. The *Ramesses* was the only yacht this far from the harbor, keeping that royal distance to preserve her privacy.

I reached out my hand so that she could climb into the rowing boat. She nearly pulled me out; she had the strength of a tigress, if she had roared then it would have seemed natural to me.

I asked her if she was sure. "Row," she said.

But she was too impatient with my method, the near-silent slicing of the waters, the technique that I had honed, and when she had struggled into the jeans and sweater I had brought for her, she elbowed me aside.

I asked her if there was a possibility that anyone had noticed her get up (I meant, of course, her beau, although we had discussed how they would frequently take adjacent cabins because of his propensity to snore). She said that there was not. I asked her if there were any chance that one of the security team on night watch had spotted anything. "That poor oaf," she said. "Asleep. I checked." Even in the moonlight I could see the high color in her cheeks.

She had given up her royal protection long before, fearing—at best—that the officers were used to spy on her. Her beau's family had elaborate security arrangements, high cost, high tech, and hopelessly executed. It was a boon. The security cameras on the *Ramesses* were never turned on, her beau had ordered it, in case it should take his fancy to lock the door of, say, the dining quarters and tickle his princess (or one of her predecessors) on the table or the floor.

She stood up suddenly and the boat rocked. "I've done it," she said, so loudly that I automatically said hush. She laughed at that. It must have been many years since someone other than her husband had ordered her to pipe down. "Do you believe it?" she said. "I've done it. I really have."

30 January 1998

I had flown down to Brazil a few weeks earlier to conduct the "recce." The difficulty was knowing which one of the Pernambuco beaches would be closest to the *Ramesses*. After a few days with friends in Buenos Aires, they had flown to Montevideo to board the yacht and begin the sail up the coast of Uruguay. The superrich do not plan their vacations like mere mortals, like a page from a catalog. It was impossible to be sure of their exact schedule. So I scouted a few of the beaches, hired boats for a day in three using false identification, one can never be too cautious. I called her on her mobile when I was back in Washington and told her my preferred location, not the main beach, certainly. I told her—or tried to tell her—my reasoning, both strategic and tactical, in planning the retreat, first from yacht to boat, then from boat to land, and from the point of disembarkation to the interior. She swatted it all aside.

"What shall I do if he proposes?" she asked. I said I didn't know, but that she might have to accept. "Oh Lord," she said. I said that naturally she must speak as her heart dictated but if she turned him down and thus curtailed the holiday it would also bring about the end of the plan. "Well," she said, "it wouldn't be fair to string him along." It didn't seem to occur to her that she had already been doing that.

"Don't worry," she said, "I'll make sure he doesn't ask me." I enquired how she meant to achieve this aim. "By using my feminine wiles, of course. You know, hints about the best way, the best place, to propose, keep it just out of reach for now." All those cheap novels of hers may have come in useful after all.

She was certain she could make the mooring at the exact location that I thought best. "I'll work it in . . . what's the word . . . subliminally. I won't make it a big deal." I hazarded that her wish was her beau's command, or words to that effect. She said, "Lawrence, you know my trouble with men is . . ."

She dropped it. It's too big a subject.

We were away not long after three and she reckoned though she was normally an early riser they wouldn't think to check her cabin until about eight o'clock, thinking that she had decided to sleep in for once. That gave us five hours, and three hundred kilometers' distance. After that, the search would be concentrated on the water, the beaches, the reefs. In the car she put her feet up on the glove compartment and wound back her seat. I thought she was going to sleep but she didn't. She talked. I hardly knew what she said, and perhaps she hardly knew either. She scarcely drew a breath. I was fitter then than I am now and the rowing had not been a physical strain, easily manageable even if she had not insisted on taking over. But the drive was a demanding one, on strange dark roads, with my strange load, gripping the steering wheel so hard it hurt my hands. After a few hours she insisted that we switch. She drove and talked, small news and gossip about the friends she had seen in Buenos Aires, also a girlfriend who had terrible morning sickness, a film she had read about. In the first light of morning she wanted to stop and have breakfast and even browse some roadside stalls. "What about those beads?" she said, slowing the car. "That stall there. Are they made of some kind of seed?"

Perhaps the enormity of the situation was too much for her to comprehend. It may have been the only way she could cope. I do not know how to account for it, her preternatural calm. I took the wheel again for the short distance to the motel where I had planned to take a break. It was perfect. The Brazilian "motel" is rather different from its North American namesake. It is more akin to the Japanese "love hotel." It is a place you can rent for a couple of hours or more, and where secrecy and discretion rule the day. In this establishment, which I had previously scouted, one drives up to a kind of sentry box, where the check-in, such as it is, takes place. Money, naturally, must be proffered but no ID is required. One then drives into the motel grounds, set within a high-walled compound, and looks for the apartment number outside the row of garages, each of which is hung with a thick, opaque vinyl curtain from ceiling to floor.

She clapped her hands and hooted as she took cognizance of the setup. "My goodness," she said. "Lawrence, look at this, a proper tryst!"

I drove into our garage, lowered the window, and reached for the rope and pulley that closed the curtain behind the car. I explained to her that this type of motel is to be found all over Brazil, a country in which it is not uncommon for people to live at home until they marry, and that extramarital liaisons are frequently conducted in such an environment. More wittering from me, I fear, at that point, an attempt to cover my too-evident embarrassment.

"How fantastic," she said, as I located the door at the back of the garage that led to the apartment. "They've really thought this through. Nobody sees you get out of the car, nobody can see the car—how absolutely ingenious."

Before we went through the antechamber to the bedroom I hesitated, because I wished to explain more, and excuse. Words, however, failed me and all I could do was press on.

The large round bed was, naturally, the centerpiece of the room. By the window there stood a recliner with adjustable foot stirrups, set up as if for a gynecological examination. Two television screens played "adult" channels, which I rushed to turn off at once. I apologized profusely, of course.

"Why, Lawrence," she said, stalking the perimeter, "I've never seen you quite so pink."

She examined the minibar, the wall-mounted tissue dispenser, the lubricant sachets, and wore a puzzled expression as she inspected what looked a bit like a diving board, which was positioned to jut over the foot of the bed. "At least I understand this," she said, pulling back the sheet to reveal the mattress's plastic sheath.

I said to her that I would rent another apartment for myself if she preferred and that I had prevaricated about whether that would be better for her. "Of course it wouldn't be better," she said. "You're not going to leave me on my own."

Mother never got over her disappointment that the knighthood she believed was due me failed to materialize. She couldn't understand that I was simply in the wrong royal camp. That day, however, was all the reward I needed. I slept, or tried to, on the recliner and despite the farcical aspect of the arrangements, I was sorely honored that I was the one to be there.

Chapter Eight

On Sunday morning Lydia awoke to the smell of coffee and the sound of a chain saw. When she looked out of the window she saw Carson cutting down the dead oak. He stepped well back and raised his visor. The tree held its breath for a moment or two and then fell in a slow swoon across the lawn.

Lydia opened the window and poked her head out. "You forgot to say 'timber,'" she called.

"Did I wake you?" said Carson. "Good. It's breakfast time."

He had the pancake mixture ready and they ate them with blueberries and syrup at the kitchen counter.

"Who taught you to cook?" said Lydia.

"The television," said Carson. "What? I'm serious. Who taught you? Your mom?"

"No, she wasn't . . . I went on a Cordon Bleu cookery course when I was young, and then I didn't cook for years and years. I don't know. I taught myself."

"Okay, that goes in the dossier. Cordon Bleu course."

"What dossier?"

"The one I'm compiling. You hardly tell me anything, so it's a very slim document."

"What do you want to know?"

He folded his arms. "How about you start at the beginning and don't leave anything out?"

"You'd be bored to death," said Lydia. "Are you going to chop up that tree?"

"I'll chop it and stack it and when it's dried you can use it on the fire. You use the fireplace in winter, right?"

"You do come in handy."

"Thanks. Now, nice try with the distraction technique, but it didn't work."

Lydia started to clear the plates. He put a hand on her arm. She said, "I don't think I can do this."

"Once you stop holding back, it'll just get easier. It won't be so bad, you'll see. I'm a darn good listener."

"No, I mean, this whole thing. Us."

"Hey," he said, "come on."

"Really," said Lydia, surprised at how fast the tears had formed. "I don't."

He took his hand away and sat there with a dazed expression. "Okay."

She wanted him to argue with her but he didn't. She wanted him to tell her to stop being so ridiculous.

"Well," he said, finally. "Is it something I did? Something I said?"

"No, it's not you . . ."

He laughed. "'It's not you, it's me.' Don't I deserve better than that? Guess not."

She held on to her tears. He was getting up, and in another few moments he'd be gone and that would be for the best. It wasn't fair to him to let it drag on. And she wasn't going to get into a situation where she would be vulnerable. She liked her life the way it was.

"I'll chop the wood," he said, "and stack it, and then I'll be out of your way."

"You don't have to do that."

He shook his head. "I don't like to leave a job half done."

She could see him through the back door, which stood open. Rufus ran in circles around Madeleine, who had taken up a position close to her master and was getting her long red coat covered in sawdust. It would be a job to brush it out.

Carson stopped the saw for a moment and wiped his forearm along his brow. She felt her stomach contract with longing. At least she should go out there and talk to him, not let him leave without saying a proper good-bye.

When he'd walked into the shelter the first time, he'd been dressed in those same jeans and boots and checked shirt. She'd assumed he worked at something outdoors or manual. He looked like a carpenter. He told her he worked as a claims adjuster for an insurance company in the city. So will your wife be walking the dog? she asked, although he didn't wear a wedding ring. He told her, no, he didn't have a wife. If you're at the office all day, she explained, you wouldn't be a good candidate for a dog. They're social creatures, they get anxious if they're left alone too long. He surprised her again by saying he worked from home. That's the miracle of e-mail, he said. And when he went out to investigate a claim, he reckoned most times the dog could come along for the ride.

She took him a glass of water. "You looked thirsty," she said when the saw had juddered to a halt.

"You're not coming out here to give me the 'we can still be friends' speech?"

"No."

"I was going to tell you something," he said.

He drank the water and she waited while he finished.

"Is that allowed?" he said. "Okay. When I was twenty-two, just out of college, I went traveling in Asia. I met a girl." He looked away to the side, to the line of sugar maples at the edge of the yard. "She was Australian, backpacking her way around the world."

"You don't have to tell me," said Lydia. "Whatever happened, it was a long time ago."

"We fell in love," said Carson. She knew she would miss the sound of his voice, the way it seemed to come from within his chest and resonate in her own. "I took her back to Oakland, my hometown, and within six months she was pregnant so we got married. I quit graduate school and got a job. We had a beautiful little daughter named Ava, and she was just perfect, you know, the way babies are."

"I'll bet she was," said Lydia softly.

"By the time she was a few months old, her mother and I were fighting. It went on like that for two years. It shouldn't have come as any surprise but one day when I got back from work she said that she was leaving and taking Ava. I said, No, you stay, I'll go. She said, I'm taking Ava home. What do you mean, home? I said. I still hadn't understood. Her parents had sent the plane tickets. They were going back to Sydney, and that was that."

"Carson," said Lydia. He was looking at the empty glass in his hand.

"I kept in touch," he said. "I called, I sent letters and cards and presents. Sarah sent me a couple of photos of Ava, and she put paint all over her little hand and pressed it on a piece of paper and mailed it to me. Then about eighteen months later, when I'd saved up finally for a ticket, Sarah called. Said she'd met someone and wanted to marry him. Our divorce was nearly final. I said, congratulations, maybe I'll make it over in time for the wedding. I didn't mind. I'd stopped feeling that way about her. She was silent for the longest time.

"Then she just came out and said it. She thought it would be confusing for Ava to have two dads. She wanted me to stop all contact. And Gary wanted to adopt Ava, he really loved her already, treated her like his own."

"You gave her up," said Lydia. She'd given up her boys. If there was one person who would ever be able to understand that . . . but even Lawrence had never really understood.

"I thought about it. I called Sarah back the next week. I said, put Ava on the phone. I talked to her for a little while, she wasn't even four, and she babbled at me sometimes and sometimes she was talking to her doll. I made silly noises to make her laugh. Then I told her that I loved her and to go and get her mom. I told Sarah I was going to do what was best for Ava. I'd give up my legal rights."

She reached out her hand but he didn't take it. He stooped to put down the glass. Before he straightened up he rested for a moment with his hands on his knees, as if he had just been winded. "Today is Ava's birthday," he said. "She'll be twenty-five."

She wanted to tell him that she knew what he was going through. All she could offer was a platitude. "I'm sorry. I'm really sorry."

"It's all right," said Carson. "I wanted to tell you, that's all. I'm just going to finish this up." He started the saw and lowered his visor, and there was nothing she could say to him over the noise.

Lydia made a potato salad and took it over to Suzie's house. The kitchen had the air of a yard sale in preparation, the children's toys, books, and clothes stacked everywhere. Tevis had already arrived and was showing off the marks she had down her back.

"It's called cupping," she said. "It's a really ancient practice."

"So's leeching," said Suzie. "And it probably does you about as much good."

"Suzie, you are the most closed-minded person I have ever met," said Tevis.

"I have an open mind," said Suzie. "I just don't fill it with junk."

"No," said Tevis, "that's what you fill your stomach with."

"Oooh," said Suzie, "you are bitchy today. Weren't those cups supposed to suck all the negative energy out of you?"

"What am I missing?" said Amber, letting herself in through the back door. "I brought an apple tart. The kids are out in the yard with yours. They've brought a frog."

Suzie gave Amber a hug. "We're discussing cupping."

"Oh, like coffee tasting?" said Amber.

"No, like voodoo rituals. Tevis, show her your back."

Tevis pulled up her top.

"Oh my God," squealed Amber. "What happened to you?"

Tevis explained it all over again, how the air in the glass cups was heated with a flame to create suction against the skin when the cup was placed firmly against the flesh. The marks would be gone in a few days, and the benefits, in terms of relaxation and invigoration, would last for weeks.

"Well, you look relaxed," said Amber. It was true. Tevis was sitting on the grungy old kitchen sofa with her feet up, in cutoff jeans and a T-shirt, her auburn hair tumbled about her shoulders.

"That's because she's not doing any of the work around here," said Suzie. "Lydia and I have been slaving away."

"Let me help," said Amber. "What can I do?"

"You can fix us a drink for a start, and then you can tell us all about your date."

"I don't know if it was a date," said Amber. "It was lunch."

"Lunch can be a date," said Suzie.

"Of course it can," said Tevis.

Suzie said, "Hey, break out the champagne, someone. Me and Tevis just agreed on something."

"I see Pinot Grigio," said Amber. "I don't see champagne." She pulled a bottle out of the fridge.

"Let's sit down and concentrate," said Suzie, abandoning her knife. "Lydia, you can leave that to simmer, come on, sit down."

They all sat around the table. "Now," said Suzie, "spill."

"We went to Tiggi's," said Amber. She tucked her hair behind her ears, although it was already tucked. "I had the pea soup to start and he had the tomato and mozzarella salad."

"Don't give us the menu, Amber," said Suzie. "Give us the dirt. What's he like?"

"He's kinda nice," said Amber.

"So you had sex with him?" You could always rely on Suzie to get straight down to business.

And on Amber to get embarrassed. "No! Suzie, please!"

"Did you kiss?" said Tevis.

"No, I told you, I don't even know if it was a date. He's a neighbor, maybe he's just being neighborly."

"We sat down for this?" said Suzie. "Aren't you going to tell us anything juicy?"

Tevis said, "You know what I read the other day? If a man's ring finger is longer than his index finger that means he's got high testosterone. That is actually a scientifically proven fact."

"Really? A long ring finger means he's highly sexed? Amber, has what's-his-name got a rinky-dinky ring finger, or is he well endowed?"

"Suzie, you are so smutty," said Amber. She was smiling her slightly gummy, slightly daffy smile. "And his name is Phil, by the way."

"I've been married fifteen years," said Suzie, "to the man I dated in high school. I get my kicks vicariously."

"Well, I'll take my ruler along and measure all his limbs and digits next time," said Amber.

"Ah, so there's going to be a next time."

Amber sighed. She wore a wraparound blue cotton dress printed with white flower sprigs. Suzie wore khakis and Tevis was in cutoffs, and Lydia had on jeans as usual. But Amber always said she had to do her best to advertise Closet by making an effort with her wardrobe. "Yes, I think so. At least he said we should do it again."

"You don't sound too thrilled."

"I'd definitely go," said Amber. "But you know it's been so long since I've had—" She lowered her voice. "*Sex.* All my parts have probably dried up."

"Listen," said Suzie. "You are a very attractive woman. He'd be lucky to have you, this what's-his-name."

"I was out running the other day," said Amber. "You know, I go when I've dropped the kids off at school and before I open up the store. And I'm running along and I pass this woman going in the opposite direction, then another, we sort of half say hi, the way you do when someone's doing the same thing as you. I'm thinking something in the back of my head, some thought is forming, but I don't know what it is. And then I pass a third woman and bam! it hits me. These women's breasts don't move. I'm talking about women with good-sized breasts and they just don't move, and I'm wearing two goddamn bras and I'm, like, flop, bounce, flop."

"They've been done," said Tevis.

"Here in Kensington," said Amber, "women are having their breasts done. What's Phil going to think when, if—I mean if—he sees mine? They don't point up at the ceiling. They roll under my arms!"

They got back to the cooking. There'd be ten, including the children, for lunch. Mike was out on patrol and called to say he'd be home by four and to save some of the chicken fritters for him. Lydia chopped lettuce and cucumber and tomatoes, Amber shelled peas, and Suzie mixed eggs, half-and-half, and grated cheese for the quiche. Tevis sat in lotus position on the couch.

"I was in the bath the other day," said Suzie, "when Oscar walks in." Oscar was Suzie's five-year-old. "He takes a pee, and he's babbling away. He says, Mom, you know God? I say, yes, baby, I do. He says, how big is he? Is he, like, really, really huge? I start giving him this long answer, but he's not even listening, he's looking at my boobs. He says, Mom, you know your boobies? I say, yes, baby, I know those too. He says, well, like, why are they down on your belly?"

"Did you tell him, this is how a real woman looks?" said Amber.

"What I didn't say," said Suzie, "what I wanted to say but didn't, was because I breast-fed you and your brother and sisters, and this is what you did to them."

"Ha! But you stopped yourself."

Lydia thought about Carson sawing the wood, the flex of muscle where his shirt was open as his arm moved back and forth. Lawrence would like him. Of all the men she'd ever dated, he'd definitely like Carson. "But, ma'am," he would say, "as always I would counsel that it is preferable, in such situations, to err on the side of caution." She never listened. Or she'd listen, and then hurtle right ahead.

"Breast-feeding doesn't cause your boobs to sag," said Tevis. "There's no evidence for that."

"I don't know what makes you an expert," said Suzie. "I got all the evidence I need. I'm having a cookie. Anyone else want one?"

They all shook their heads.

"Man, you are self-controlled," said Suzie. "I'm starting a diet tomorrow. New week, new leaf, new me."

She was always starting diets, always wanting to lose a few pounds, just a few. Lydia looked up from her chopping board and appraised her friend. She was stocky, a little round across the middle but it sat naturally on her. In her khaki pants and white shirt, with her black hair cut into a crop, she looked attractive, full of mischief and energy.

"What's it this time," said Tevis, "cabbage soup?"

"You are so stuck in the nineties," said Suzie. "I know it seems like I'm on a different one every week, but you gotta try new things. What about you, Lydia? I bet you never dieted in your life. You're so lucky with your body shape."

Body shape didn't come into it, that much Lydia knew. She thought about the bowls of custard that the chef, on her instructions, would leave in the fridge before he went home at night. "I don't diet anymore. Suzie, you look just right as you are." She'd spend an hour or so bingeing. Eating the custard made it easier for it all to come up. Ice cream, too, was good for that. Much easier to purge your stomach than to purge your entire life.

"You okay?" said Suzie. "You're a bit quiet today."

"I'm fine, really, I am."

Suzie looked at her skeptically. "Everything all right with Carson?"

"Yes," she said, "he stayed last night, chopped down a dead tree for me this morning." She didn't want to talk about it yet, didn't want to have red eyes when the kids came in from the yard.

"Hey," said Suzie, "his ring finger must be long. What about Steve?" she said to Tevis. "How does he measure up?"

"He is perfectly balanced," said Tevis. "He has a feminine side. Personally, I have no desire for a caveman."

Amber started setting the table. "Do you want place mats, Suzie? Tevis, when are you and Steve going to take the next step? How long has it been, four years?"

Tevis unfolded her legs out of lotus and turned circles with her feet to give her ankles a stretch. "We've been dating four years, and I like going out on dates with him. I'm not moving in and he's not moving in with me. I don't need a man as the center of my life to make me whole."

"I do," blurted Amber. She giggled. "No, I don't. Well, maybe. It would be nice."

Four years of dating, thought Lydia. No need to change anything. Sounded perfect. If only Carson were around to hear that.

"I've got some news," said Tevis. She reached into her purse and pulled out a printed brochure. "I've been looking to buy a little retreat place for ages, and I've found somewhere up by the lake."

"Oh, it's so sweet," said Amber. "Did you get it? Is it yours? A log cabin, how romantic, and look how wild it is, there's deer up there, I think."

"Careful the bears don't getcha," said Suzie, taking a look. "Wow, it's really neat. When are we all going?"

"I thought we could go for Lydia's birthday, the weekend right after it. Amber, think you can get a sitter for the kids?"

Amber thought she could. That's the weekend of the ballet, Lydia thought. Maybe she ought to pay Carson back for the tickets. Or they could go as friends. No, he wouldn't want that.

Rufus ran in off the deck and fussed until she picked him up. She babied him. She stroked his silky ears. He sneezed right in her face, and then looked at her as if to say, aren't I just so adorable? She'd started letting him sleep on the bed. All the books said you shouldn't, and he used to sleep in his own bed in the kitchen, but somehow he'd wormed his way upstairs. When he started doing that she'd been stern with him, but then he would lie down so very close to the end of the bed that he was nearly falling off, as if she were being entirely unreasonable when there was so much room for a little chap who would be no bother at all.

A dog didn't ask for much. They were so much simpler than people. When she was telling Lydia how she came to set up the shelter, Esther had said, "It's not so altruistic as it seems. Sometimes I don't know if I'm sheltering the dogs, or the dogs are sheltering me. You see these celebrities who can't stand it anymore—what do they do? They go off and work with animals. It's better than therapy. I think that's what I'm doing." She laughed. "Me and Brigitte Bardot."

Lydia understood what she was saying and she loved her work at Kensington Canine, but Esther needed and preserved her solitude and Lydia still wanted people around. She enjoyed the warmth and clutter of Suzie's house, was grateful for these women, for their laughter, and for never making her feel like the interloper that she was.

Suzie called out to the kids that lunch was ready. They were making a racket upstairs so they must have gone around from the yard earlier and in through the front door. Oscar sat on Lydia's knee and talked with his mouth full. Amber's son, Tyler, sat opposite, fiddling surreptitiously with the cell phone on his lap. Maya, Suzie's eldest, said she wasn't hungry, and Serena (Amber's youngest and a year below Maya in school) said so too, although she had loaded her plate with a serving of everything.

"You girls gotta eat," said Suzie. "You'll waste away."

"Serena got the plum role in the school play," said Amber. "You're looking at the new Dorothy!"

"Terrific," said Lydia. "Book me a front row seat."

"My ass is getting big," said Maya. "I'll have salad."

"My ass you will!" said Suzie. "Eat. You too, Serena. And congratulations, honey, I'll be in that front row as well."

"Would it be bad to open another bottle?" said Tevis.

"This potato salad is delicious," said Amber. "Are these ramps in there, instead of scallions?"

"You know I throw half my lunch box away every day?" said Maya. "You put way too much fatty food in there."

"I'm not rising to it, Maya," said Suzie. "Did everyone wash their hands?"

The kids all mumbled unconvincingly.

"D'you miss Miami?" Tevis said to Suzie.

Lydia had heard the story of why Suzie and Mike had to leave. They'd been there ten years. "Half of Miami PD is on the take," Suzie had said, "and Mike's the one who gets investigated." Mike was straight, she said, a good guy. He bent the rules now and then but only in the interest of justice, so some piece of scum didn't get off on a technicality. She felt they'd been run out of town. "We like it here," she'd said. "But Mike does get a bit bored—it's all parking tickets and thirty-dollar litter fines."

"Not really, I don't," she said now, answering Tevis. "Kensington feels like home. I miss San Francisco sometimes, you can't get that kind of fog anywhere else. I'm going back for a high school reunion in September. Twenty-five years since graduation. I am so psyched for that."

"You keep in touch with anybody?" said Tevis.

"Of course. There's a bunch of us. We call, we e-mail, we do weddings, funerals, bat mitzvahs, and divorce. We gather for those."

"That's how it goes," said Tevis. "I'd be so up for a trip to San Fran. There are some healing shops I really love there."

"Come," said Suzie. "We'll go to all your nut job shops. I'd love it if you would come."

"September, my brother and his family are visiting," said Tevis. "If it doesn't clash with them . . ."

It had taken Lydia a while to realize it but she'd been wrong about this country. People moved around, lived far from families, invented new lives, but they didn't forget their pasts. This was a transient society. But there was an invisible glue that held it together in ways she hadn't seen at first, when she herself had been drifting from town to town. Suzie had her high school reunion. Lydia knew she would move mountains to get there. It gave her a warm, sad feeling in her chest. She crossed her eyes at Oscar, still sitting on her knee, and he stuck out his tongue, which was coated with quiche.

"Oh now, listen," said Amber. "What happened to that frog you were playing with?"

"Oops," said Oscar.

The other kids took a sharp intake of breath and looked at each other.

"Maya?" said Suzie.

"Serena?" said Amber.

Oscar slid off Lydia's lap and ran for the stairs. "Don't none of you guys remember?" he called back. "We left it in Mom's bedroom."

Back at home Lydia looked in the mirror in the bedroom. She tipped her head forward to examine the roots of her hair. They were brown but not as dark as the rest. If she let it all grow out she would end up mousy, not blond. She'd always had it colored and highlighted before. She examined her nose. Were the nostrils uneven? Amber had said it was a "telltale sign" of cosmetic surgery. Surely nature was asymmetrical sometimes. There were wrinkles around her eyes, not crow's-feet, maybe more like sparrow's or wren's. Her upper eyelids, which were puffy in the mornings, looked fine by the afternoon. It was great to have her old eyes back. When she'd moved to Kensington she'd decided not to wear the brown lenses anymore. Ridiculous how long she'd persisted with those. Maybe it was time to go blond again.

But she shouldn't get too careless. The ten-year anniversary was coming up. She hadn't seen anything yet in the magazines but she'd hardly looked. Only that one time at Amber's store. There would be some commemoration, surely, and it would involve her boys. She had tried her best to do as Lawrence said and not follow them obsessively. (Dear, sweet Lawrence, your advice lives on, through the long decade!) She had checked on their progress, knew all their milestones, pictures from the sports field, the last day of school, the first day of university, graduation, how handsome they looked in their military uniforms. Year by year she had seen how they had thrived, those motherless boys.

She had a fantasy. She lived it over and over again. They would be here in this house and she would pick their clothes off the floor, intervene in their squabbles, tell them off for drinking out of the milk carton. No butler. No maid. No boarding school. No Balmoral to keep them from her in the holidays. They'd come in late and raid the refrigerator and put their arms around her and lift her clean off the floor. She'd roll her eyes and say, now one of you turn on the dishwasher when you're done, I'm going up to bed. It was only a fantasy. When she left, and in the early days, she had thought she would be able to make it come true eventually. Now she knew she couldn't, although sometimes she pretended not to know. It was more bearable that way.

Lydia went out of the bedroom and down to the kitchen and stared at the computer, which wasn't turned on. She'd find what she wanted on there. She would never stop. The deal she had made with herself was that she would receive the bulletins when they came her way, like a distant aunt receiving a round-robin letter twice a year. To stalk them over the Internet would be unhealthy, and of no benefit to them. Maybe it was a stupid rule still to be following, as pointless as the brown lenses that she'd worn for years longer than she'd needed to.

When she was feeling this way she knew that what she should do was go for a swim. She checked the time. Five o'clock. Half an hour until the drugstore closed. She could make it in time to buy up an armful of magazines. There was bound to be a photograph or two.

She picked up her car keys, and Rufus, at the sound of them, headed for the front door.

"Clever boy," she said.

A sense of dread came over her like a clammy hand pressed over her nose and mouth. She had to sit down on a stool. How could she have left them? She was inhuman, despicable.

Judgment Day. Again.

Rufus trotted back and gave her a look, as if to say, that wasn't funny.

Mothers didn't leave their children. It was some kind of deformity she had. An abnormality of the soul. Maybe it just ran in the family. Hadn't her own mother left? She hadn't been able to take the children, which wasn't her fault. But Mummy was a bolter, anyway.

Stop it, she told herself, stop it. "Rufus," she said, "we're going right now."

Why had she bought this car? It was too big. She'd thought it would be useful for picking up supplies for the shelter, but most everything got delivered and it was just another bad judgment she'd made. If she couldn't get the small things right, how could she judge the big things in life?

Rufus draped himself over the hand brake and pushed his head onto her knee.

She walked up Albert Street toward the drugstore, counting her blessings, even though she knew that never worked. It never worked in the old days either, when she'd had everything, the world at her feet, supposedly. She browsed through the books above the magazine shelves to see if there was anything new. Most of it was rubbish—thrillers, horror, true crime, and swaths of cheap romance. She was going to buy one anyway, and chose a paperback with a picture of a young woman with a flower behind her ear. It had gold embossing on the cover which, she had discovered, was always a terrible sign. But it was like having a sweet tooth. Fine to give in to the cravings now and then. It would see her through this evening, no worse than sitting down with a big bar of chocolate.

There were twelve magazines she could buy and she stacked them all up. The cashier said, "Treating yourself today?"

"I suppose I am, Mrs. Deaver," said Lydia.

Mrs. Deaver wore horn-rimmed glasses and a knitted skirt and jacket. She looked more like a retired schoolmistress than a store clerk. "Is it the time of the month? Lot of girls come in here and buy a stack, along with a box of Tampax."

"Just going to curl up for the evening," said Lydia.

"You do that, my dear. That'll be seventy dollars and twenty-five cents. Are you sure you want them all? You'll find it's the same stories over again."

Lydia paid and went out. Carson was walking along on the other side of the road. If he saw her, would he stop? Would he see her? Her heart was racing. How pathetic. She was going to walk straight to the car and drive home.

Rufus darted out across the road before she could stop him.

Carson picked him up and got a big lick on the nose.

"I have something that belongs to you," he said, when he'd come over to her side of the street.

"Thank you," said Lydia. "He's pretty keen on you."

"I know. I thought maybe you were as well."

"Maybe I am," she said.

"Has anyone ever told you how astoundingly beautiful your eyes are?" He put Rufus down. "That's one question I already know the answer to." He rubbed the back of his neck. Lydia wanted him to rub hers too. He said, "I think I overreacted this morning. I'm sorry."

She had been horrible to him this morning, and now he was apologizing to her.

"It was my fault," she said. "As soon as I said it I wanted to take it back."

"We could have discussed it, if I hadn't gone off into my Iron John act. . . . That's a lot of magazines you've got there. Thought you didn't like those things."

Lydia looked down at the stack in the crook of her arm. "I was thinking about a different hairstyle. I might get some ideas."

Carson reached out and stroked her hair. "Really? I think it suits you as it is." He pulled her gently toward him and she rested her head on his shoulder. It wasn't a problem that he asked her questions. The problem was that she wanted to answer them.

Chapter Nine

31 January 1998

Here is a conundrum. My days are numbered. I am wishing these days away. They do drag on. I know that is because I am waiting to see her again. I have thought many times of bringing the trip forward but I believe that would not be right, dictated by my needs and desires and not hers.

What I ought to do is work. But I have scant appetite for it and what will the world be missing without my belabored pontifications on the dodge and feint of diplomacy across the pond? I remember when I first started lecturing, an undergraduate put up his hand toward the end of the seminar. "What would you say is the point of history? I mean, what is your personal view? Do we, like, learn from it so the same mistakes aren't made over again?" I smiled at that. I doubtless gave some fatuous reply about the telling of truth and the historian's role as mere impartial observer. The naive question is often the most telling, which is why we brush it aside. The point of my book? No one, thank goodness, will ask me that.

I had thought, when I began it, that this diary would allow me to clear my head, so that I could get back to work on the magnum opus. I write these pages and then reflect, and reflect again. March does seem a long way off. But only to me. I must remind myself that she is not sitting there in North Carolina waiting anxiously for me to arrive.

1 February 1998

We remained ten hours or so in the motel. The entire place was designed so that the clients and staff never set eyes on each other.

We ordered a meal, chicken and salad, that was left behind a service hatch in the anteroom. After that we again drove on in the dark. I half expected roadblocks, and to see billboard signs, reading *Princess of Wales kidnapped.* Of course there was no such thing. I tuned in to the radio, my Portuguese is passable, and it was the headline news. "They're talking about me," she said, "aren't they?" I said I would switch it off just as soon as I knew the situation. She turned her head to the window.

I had caught her expression, though, and it wasn't tears in her eyes, it was defiance.

The most difficult judgment of my life has been whether this "little plan" of ours should be implemented. Would it be the most extreme expression of her recklessness, one from which there would be no possible recovery? At what exact point would the line be crossed? Even as we were driving it occurred to me that we could turn around and go back. Say she had kept a rendezvous with me, wanting to explore a little of the country away from the media glare. There would be an uproar of course, more questions about her mental health, a storm of comment and fury about the conduct of the mother of the future monarch and those with whom she chose to consort. But it wasn't too late. I said as much.

She shook her head. "This wasn't a game."

She is simply the most extraordinary woman. The strictures of royalty, of motherhood, of overbearing fame—those things that should have kept her behavior in check—made her progressively more reckless. I remember a few years ago when she was on an Austrian ski trip (Lech, I think it was), getting a call from her bodyguard. He pleaded with me to make her see reason. How could he do his job? The princess had disappeared from the hotel by jumping from a first-floor balcony into the snow, a drop of at least twenty feet. She had stayed out all night, one presumes with her paramour. I think she herself feared how far she would go, how extreme she would become, if she didn't extricate herself from that life.

2 February 1998

I was compelled to leave her in Belo Horizonte after two days—despite the fact that she had begun to unravel somewhat. I had to travel back to Pernambuco and return the boat that I had hired, as just another tourist, for a week. It doesn't do to leave loose ends. From there I went back to Washington, where I was supposed to be buried in the Library of Congress, hard at work. I picked up, as I knew I would, a dozen or more messages.

My headache was intense. I spent the day lying down in the dark. The change in air pressure on the flight was only partly responsible. The first time I flew after the diagnosis—it was a short hop to Rome—I thought perhaps I would die on the plane. After all, my physician had said she could not advise it. Though neither had she advised against. Will it make the tumor worse? I asked. "There is no evidence," she said, "that air travel will predispose such tumors to grow or bleed. The risk is one of medical isolation. I'd be inclined to stay on the ground." Always hedging her bets. She possesses an encyclopedic knowledge of the brain and its malignant growths, does Dr. Patel. When she is able to speak in the abstract, as sometimes I encourage her to do, she can grow quite animated—the joy of speaking to a fellow PhD holder, though our fields are worlds apart. But ask her anything practical as it relates to my own condition and she grows rather sullen, as if I am trying to catch her out.

I thought it would be politic not to mention my anaplastic oligodendroglioma (what anagrammatic charms!) to the airlines when booking the flights. Naturally I would be mortified if I caused any inconvenience by keeling over in midair, but needs must, as the saying goes. I'd read up on civil litigations about passengers who had made similar disclosures and were subsequently denied the right to board.

So I lay in a darkened room in Washington, after the deed was done, wondering if my head would explode. It did not. I didn't return the calls for another day and by that time, everyone seemed to have forgotten that they had called me in the first place. Apart from dear old Patricia, who assumed I had been too distressed to speak. There had been no official declaration yet. "But they're not talking about search and rescue anymore, they're talking about recovering a body, if anything." There was that trace element of excitement in her voice that goes hand in hand with relating only distantly connected calamities.

I told her I'd be on the next available flight.

She took a deep breath, my little sister. "Is it wise?" she said. Although she is admirably restrained in keeping her opinions to herself, I know she fears I am shortening my life each time I step on a plane. She may be right. Who knows? Certainly not Dr. Patel.

"Everyone's so . . . stunned," she said. "I keep thinking about that time you brought her round for tea, how lovely she was, how natural, asking about the kids, admiring the garden. And then she did the washing up! I tell everybody that. And to think of her . . . Do you think . . . do you think it really was . . ."

She was overcome, either by emotion or the delicacy of the situation. Although the endless media speculation was of sharks, Patricia found the word unutterable.

3 February 1998

It was as I had planned. Had I selected the main beach of Boa Viagem, where there are notices warning that "bathers in this area at a greater risk of shark attack," it would have created a media storm when she insisted on taking her daily swim. Surfers are eaten with some regularity, but a princess is a different matter entirely. The beach I had selected was quite some distance from the Recife/Boa Viagem area and it was generally considered safe and the waters calm. What I had weighed in my calculations, however, was that five or six years ago, shark attacks in Boa Viagem were more or less unheard of. Easy for the press, then, to speculate that some new shift in the underwater eco-system had driven the bull sharks farther along the coast once again.

I had done my research so thoroughly that in one of our planning sessions I was perhaps a little too eager to share the information. "Oh, please would you stop?" she said. "I don't need to hear the gory stuff. I'll have to get in the water, you know."

The basic idea had been hers. She'd talked of it for a year or so.

"Isn't there some way, Lawrence, to make me disappear? People stage their own deaths, don't they, walk into the sea and vanish? Make me vanish, Lawrence. Make me go up in a cloud of smoke. I bet you did that at the Foreign Office, didn't you? Spies, and all that. You know how. You could do it. You're the cleverest person I know. You're the only person I'd trust."

There were variations on this theme—some joking, some semi-casual, and some delivered with heartbreaking earnestness. I must admit I was flattered more than alarmed. At least at first. She became increasingly desperate.

When I finally began to realize how serious she was, I told her it could—at some risk—be done. She sat quietly. We were in her private drawing room. A large vase of her favorite white roses stood on the table to my side, but either they were scentless or all my senses were tuned only toward her. I remember the drift of her perfume, 24, Faubourg, I believe. "Yes," she said, "please help me." And, with those simplest of words, I was entirely at her disposal.

4 February 1998

Spies, and all that. It was a line she delivered with her special mixture of knowing coquettishness and disarming naivety. There was a grain of truth. I know how to get things done. What I had to research from scratch was location, and the credibility of no body (or body parts) being found. In terms of absolute numbers, Florida and Australia have more shark attacks, but those in Pernambuco have a far higher ratio of fatalities. I favored Brazil too as a non-Anglophone nation, making it easier for her to disappear in those first critical weeks. That settled the location. Then I searched for cases in which people have gone missing at sea.

Sure enough, the media has obliged with a regurgitation of those very stories that I felt provided a strong enough precedent. On 17 December 1967, Australian Prime Minister Harold Holt went swimming off Cheviot Beach near Melbourne, and disappeared. After a massive search-and-rescue operation, which failed to recover a body, it was presumed he'd been eaten by sharks, and a funeral was held.

They dwelled too on Alcatraz escape attempts, such as those by Frank Morris and Clarence and John Anglin. It gave them a meaty narrative, and a chance for macabre speculation. All those who swam from the rock over the years were officially declared to have drowned, although no bodies ever surfaced, most likely providing meals for scavenging leopard sharks. There was a multitude of other stories too, famed or fabled, and the collated reports of workaday disappearances in Florida, Hawaii, Australia, Brazil, and so on. The list was long. It added a great deal of ballast to the story as I wished it to be told.

5 February 1998

The conspiracy theorists are out to play, which was only to be expected. Harold Holt was considered by the fantasists to have been abducted by a Russian (or sometimes Chinese) submarine. Morris and the Anglins were "sighted" by eagle-eyed citizens after they drowned. Probably the same keen individuals who went on to spot Elvis after his death. I keep an eye on the current conspiracies. She's been bumped off—that one leads the way. Various angles considered, including, most preposterously, that the murder was ordered by her father-in-law, the Duke of Edinburgh, and carried out by the security services. Pressure is mounting for a public inquiry, not as yet forthcoming. Suicide has been posited, with a nice twist that she had been pregnant and unwilling to bear a mixed-race child. There are a few theories, too, that she has absconded, and even "sightings" of her in Geneva and in a burka in a sprinkling of Muslim lands. Thankfully they are restricted to the Internet's lunatic fringe.

Chapter Ten

Last night he actually said his prayers in bed while turning the rosary beads through his fingers. Usually he just counted them off or clacked them together because he found the noise soothing. Looked like he was getting his reward—Lydia was right there in front of him, striding down Albert Street, the spaniel trotting so close it looked like the dog was glued to her ankle. He needed a moment to gather himself, think of an open-ended line with which to begin. He stepped off the street beside the coffee shop, where he could make a few sartorial adjustments out of view. He quickly tucked in his shirt. He ran a hand through his hair. Maybe he should use the camera. Say, I wonder if you'd mind if I took a few shots. You're very striking. Chicks liked that. No, only the younger girls liked that. A woman her age would think it was weird.

She'd be passing in a few moments. He couldn't make up his mind.

Now she was walking by and if she turned her head he would look like some kind of pervert, lurking in the shadow.

Grabowski, he told himself, you are an idiot. He automatically lifted the Canon and framed a shot. He didn't take it. Why take a shot of the back of her head?

He followed her at a distance down the street. He still didn't have a plan.

She had a good backside. It looked pretty fine in those low-rise jeans.

When she turned into the drugstore, he hesitated, wondering if he should follow her in. What are you going to do, Grabowski, ask her advice about which toothpaste to buy?

He looked around and then crossed the road. There was a big truck parked a short way to the left. If he stood behind it he could keep an eye on the store and in the meantime decide on his approach.

Mrs. Jackson had told him that Lydia was English and had lived in Kensington three years. "She works with the dogs, you know that place over west by the woods."

"I'm from out of town, Mrs. Jackson," said Grabowski, although he already knew that sarcasm was wasted on her.

The landlady blew her nose on a Kleenex. "Allergies," she explained. "I'm a martyr to that dog. I got him from the shelter, the place I was just telling you about. Here on business, are you? Is it the funeral home? Mr. Dryden will never sell. We've had a few trying to persuade him over the years, coming down from the city. But, of course, your accent, you're from overseas. Not that that means anything. We're quite cosmopolitan in these parts."

Grabber regarded Mrs. Jackson's beads and belt and patent leather shoes, the determined optimism of her manicured and heavily veined hands. "I'll bet you are," he said. "There's Lydia, she's foreign, isn't she?"

"Oh, Lydia," said Mrs. Jackson, "she's not foreign to us. She's one of the girls. Bought that house off the Merrywicks when they moved to Florida, lovely little house it is, Cedar Road, she's had me over, well, I drop by when I'm passing. Never too busy for a friend, that's the way around here. What line of business did you say that you were in?"

"I'm . . . an author," said Grabowski. "I'm writing a book. Thought this would be a nice place to hole up for a few days and work."

He wasn't about to tell her his curriculum vitae. People could be funny about it, especially now that it was coming up to the tenth anniversary and that whole debate was being brought up again, about hounding and press intrusion and irresponsibility. The hypocrisy made him sick. Those people bought the newspapers and magazines that bought the photographs. No demand, no money, no pictures. Simple as that.

"Ooh," said Mrs. Jackson. "A writer. What's it about, or shouldn't I ask? Writers don't like to be asked, do they? Well, you're welcome to stay just as long as you wish. Would you like a meal brought up? I don't do meals, only breakfast, but I could make an exception. I read about a writers' retreat once, they had all their meals brought to them so they wouldn't have anything to think about except their work."

Grabowski said that was very kind but he liked to get out now and then to get his juices flowing, creatively speaking. He was thinking about venturing out to find a sandwich now.

Mrs. Jackson fluttered her hands as she gave him directions to the bakery. He could have sworn she fluttered her eyelids as well. The writer angle was going down a treat. Before he knew it she'd be saying, I expect you'll be putting me in your next book.

When he went downstairs she was sitting behind the registration desk in the hallway (which she referred to as the "vestibule") and had added a smear of lipstick to her mouth. "Mr. Grabowski," she said, "this may only be a small town but we're not without culture. Just last year, Mr. Deaver held an art show in the school hall. My husband was indisposed on the opening evening but I, of course, was there. Mr. Deaver's watercolors are very much acclaimed. Yes, you'll find a great regard for artists generally. And if there's anything I can do for you, to get those juices flowing, please feel free to ask. See this little bell here on the desk?" She picked it up and gave it a shake. "Tinkle, tinkle, tinkle, and voilà, that's me at your disposal right away."

There was something Mrs. Jackson could do for him, thought Grabowski, as he peered through the truck windows and across the road. She could introduce him to Lydia.

Tinkle, tinkle, tinkle, Lydia served up on a plate.

He doubted it. It was no use asking, unless he could make it seem like her own idea. Mrs. Jackson wouldn't take kindly to playing second fiddle in her own orchestra.

When Lydia came out he would walk over the road and . . . say . . . Hi, you look really nice, and it's been a while since I got laid, so how about it, darling? Your place or mine?

Fuck it, he was going to LA. He'd go in the morning. But he'd never get laid in LA. It was a nightmare. Worst place on earth. He'd been on a date there once. It wasn't like a date, it was like a job interview. And he didn't get hired.

She was taking her time in the store. What was she doing in there?

Grabowski adjusted his camera strap. He lifted the camera and clicked off a few shots of the street. It was a cute street, it had character, proper stores, not those strip malls he saw nearly every other place. A kid rode by on a bike and Grabber reeled off a few frames. They'd be nice, kind of arty, the spokes would blur and the light was good with the sun low over the town hall. But art was not what sold, no matter what Mrs. Jackson said.

It was obvious what he should do. He'd go over and pet the dog.

She was coming out of the store now. Grabowski sucked his stomach in. He took a step forward. There was a man walking down the road toward him and next thing he knew the spaniel was across the street and yapping at the other guy's feet.

The guy bent and picked up the dog. That's my prop, you bastard, thought Grabowski. Put that dog down right now.

But he didn't. He loped over to Lydia.

They knew each other, clearly. Maybe they'd exchange a few words and head off in different directions.

Or maybe they'd arranged to meet.

At this distance, it was difficult to see the expression on her face. Grabowski pulled a long lens out of his bag. Never leave home without your camera bag. Even if you reckon you're just out to take a few photos of small-town life, because the camera is the only way of seeing what's in front of you, and you never know what you're going to need.

He zoomed in on her. He had a clear view just to the side of the dog thief's shoulder. It was pure reflex for him to take the pictures. He could see the way she was looking at that guy.

Thank you, Mrs. Jackson, thought Grabowski. One thing you forgot to tell me about Lydia, one detail that would have been useful.

Grabber went back to the bed-and-breakfast. He slung his camera and bag on the bed. Then he slung himself down.

He thought about going down to the "vestibule" and ringing that stupid brass bell. When Mrs. Jackson came running, asking what she could get for him, he would say, a bottle of Jack Daniel's, a gram of coke, and a couple of teenage whores. Help me stimulate some writerly juice, if you are a true friend of Art.

He picked up his camera and scrolled through what he'd shot, still lying on his back. They were average. None of the painterly qualities he'd been hoping for. He came to the shots of Lydia. The first was out of focus, on the second the frame was off, in the third one she was blinking, and the fourth was beautiful.

He scrolled back and deleted the first three, with a sigh he was about to delete the fourth. Then he took another look. He zoomed in even closer. Her lips were slightly parted, she was about to speak or laugh. Those eyes were amazing—ultramarine. You couldn't blame a man for trying.

That's exactly what he hadn't done. He'd only lurked.

Grabowski pushed in closer on the eyes. He stared at them. He sat up.

He got up and found the cable that connected the camera to the laptop, and loaded the photo onto the hard drive. He brought it up on the screen.

It was uncanny. He could have sworn it. It even had him a little spooked.

He brought up the picture he was planning to use for the cover shot. He arranged the two photographs side by side. It wasn't her, but the eyes were exactly the same. Exactly.

He needed a drink.

What if it was her? What if he had a story right here? The biggest story of his life.

Hadn't she been sighted in Abu Dhabi and Switzerland? What if all the cranks who said she had faked her own death weren't cranks after all? It was possible. There was no body. People have been known to fake their own deaths. And those were only the ones who got caught. What about Lord Lucan? What happened to him? Eventually declared dead, but he only went missing, right after someone, probably the merry lord himself, murdered the kids' nanny. Perhaps he was still living it up in Rio or wherever he fled. He'd be old by now, but still lucky. Lucky Lucan, that was his nickname.

His cell phone rang and he jumped as though someone had just shot at him.

"Tinny," he said, "can I call you back? In the middle of something here."

"Grabber, I got a hot one coming up, big bang, big bucks. I'm not telling you on the phone."

"Good, that's great. Don't tell me. I'll be with you as soon as I can."

"I'm not telling you on the phone, Grabber. You're not getting it outta me."

"I'm in, I'm in," said Grabowski. "I'm sold. I'm coming down."

He hung up and stared at the pictures on his screen.

Very possibly he was going mad. What had he been doing for the last few weeks other than driving around pissant towns and staring at boardinghouse ceilings? Working. That was a joke. He hadn't settled to anything. He'd brooded. He'd worked himself up. He'd calmed himself down with too many drinks. He'd hardly spoken to anyone.

Obviously it wasn't her. She was dead. She didn't fake it. She wasn't assassinated by the secret service. She wasn't kidnapped by aliens.

You could alter a lot with plastic surgery. Criminals on the run did it.

She wasn't a criminal.

Drowned, eaten, whatever. All the true icons die young. James Dean, Marilyn Monroe, Grace Kelly, whoever. The way it went.

He looked again at the screen. It was bizarre. The eyes, apart from a light smattering of wrinkles around them, were identical, down to the tiny, barely visible ring of green inset around the right pupil. He checked the left eye—pure, bright blue. And the right again. You had to look very closely to see. Grabowski saw it clearly, as he had a thousand times before.

Chapter Eleven

6 February 1998

Went for a long walk yesterday along the front. My left leg behaved, more or less, not as shaky as last week. I availed myself of a bench from time to time. Alan came down for lunch, which was good of him, pie and mash in the Crown and Anchor. I have to force myself really, interesting how food loses its appeal when one can no longer smell anything.

He gave me all the departmental gossip, although I don't know all the players these days, turnover has been high in the past couple of years. Spats about office space, rumored romances, minor scandals involving the spending of discretionary grants. Inevitable questions about the book, inevitable nervous questions about state of health, inevitable uncomfortable shifting in his seat. Was suddenly seized by the temptation to say that Dr. Patel had revised her opinion and decided to operate, and that I've made a miraculous full recovery. The urge was very strong. Do I take that as a sign of the "personality change" of which I've been warned? Or is the fact that I resisted a sign that I have not changed at all?

Useless to ponder on imponderables, although that does not usually prevent me from doing so.

It was good to see Alan. I wonder if he could be prevailed upon for the eulogy. What is the form? Should one organize such things oneself? A word with Patricia might suffice, although she does flinch rather when I attempt that type of forward planning.

7 February 1998

How many times did I go over "our little plan" while sipping Earl Grey, Darjeeling, or Lapsang souchong? I wanted every detail to be clear, every obstacle outlined, every tactic for overcoming them understood. I repeated myself ad nauseam, although in the end I knew I had passed the point of delivering any useful instruction and was merely becoming a bore. Let's think it through, I would say, you establish a pattern early on in the holiday of taking a morning swim. At first you will be photographed doing so. You will comment privately that you find this to be a nuisance and that you intend to beat the paparazzi by swimming earlier. You bring forward your swim times and alert the crew to be on watch for you. You swim farther and farther from the yacht, to the point where they begin to be discomfited. What will you do if they attempt to put a stop to it?

She rolled her eyes. "I'll seduce them."

I always like to imagine that when she teases like that I take it well in my stride.

She laughed. "Do you really think I would? What a low opinion you must have."

It had already been worked out, in any case. The plan was that she would continue with her early swims and, in the final days, take her swim before anyone else was awake but be sure to let them know, as soon as they got up, that she had already been out. Her beau would remonstrate but she knew where the power in that relationship lay. He wouldn't dare to risk thwarting her. As extra insurance, on the penultimate day she hopped on a launch with a bodyguard and headed to the motorboat carrying reporters from the *Mirror,* the *Sun,* and the *Daily Mail.* For ten minutes or so she chatted about life on board the *Ramesses* and then dropped into the conversation that she intended to do some Jet Skiing just before lunch the next day. With that promise of an ideal photo opportunity (the story would get around to the other press boats) we could be sure that the reporters and photographers wouldn't bother to leave their hotels and start buzzing around the *Ramesses* at the crack of dawn, only to get boring pictures of her doing a steady breaststroke.

All of this, as intended, surfaced in the media. At first her beau was at pains to suppress the information about her taking early and unsupervised swims. The crew and the bodyguards were instructed not to talk, but that broke down as soon as Scotland Yard arrived at the scene. Even prior to that, someone had leaked to the press. It was all to the good. It provided a smooth arc to the narrative.

8 February 1998

The context, in terms of her behavior, was far wider, and it reached back a considerable way in her history. But last summer it did seem that she really had lost control. "Lawrence," she had said to me (we were at KP, it was immediately after she'd had the place swept for bugs for a second time), "I know how I've got to behave in these last months. I've got to be very calm and collected. No antics, no outbursts. Nothing that might lead people to suspect that I've had a breakdown and run away."

I said I thought that to be a reasonable calculation and moved on to reviewing once again the mechanics of the finances. It was a subject that bored her despite its being vital to the whole enterprise. The amount was all that interested her and although I tried to explain why just under one million was the maximum I could spirit away without leaving traces, she merely sighed and said, "Do try again, if you can bear it. I won't have a single stitch to my name. Will I even have a name?" I reassured her once again about the construction of an identity, how the passport and documentation would be sound. These things can be done, with a little insider information. False passports can, of course, be purchased (and are, by the hapless souls who are desperate to enter our country) but I had no intention of going down that route.

Her understanding, in any case, was that she should be on her best behavior in the run-up to her disappearance. I can't say she managed that.

The pressures under which she was operating were almost unspeakable. A trusted confidant (a quack therapist-cum-mystic, how did she fall for these things?) turned out to be in the pay of the tabloids. Her own mother had given a paid interview in a gossip magazine. One could blame the booze, which had got the better of mother dearest, but if one's daughter is a princess, no excuse is good enough. Communications severed. The "love of her life" (there have been a few) had made it clear earlier in the year that he would not marry her, and dashed all her hopes once again. Her ex-husband began, as she saw it, "flaunting" his long-term mistress in public, and there was no doubt that the palace PR machine had begun to market her, with flagrant disingenuity, as "the woman who waited." Such cheek.

On top of all that there was her charity work and her campaign about land mines. Undoubtedly it fired her up (she felt her power then, and as a force for good) but the cognitive dissonance of spending one day talking to amputees in Sarajevo and the next being pursued by paparazzi while wearing a tiger-print bathing suit is hardly a recipe for emotional stability.

9 February 1998

She called me when she was away over those summer months, but no more than usual. I had impressed upon her that after her "death" her phone records would be checked and any strange pattern investigated. Having been through the "phone pest" scandal a little while ago, it was a lesson she easily took to heart. That particular front-page story had distressed her greatly. It was true that she'd been calling her lover's home late at night from public phone boxes, hanging up when his wife answered. But it was loneliness, not malice, that drove her to it. And it cut her to the quick that he did nothing to defend her.

Even without her phone calls to me, thanks to the daily deluge of photographs and reporting in the media and on the Internet, I could follow her every move. That came in useful for the Pernambuco assignation—I couldn't be sure in advance of the exact date of her arrival, but I could be sure to track her progress via the media.

In July she flitted between the Mediterranean and London and various charity commitments. At least she had her boys for most of that time. They were introduced to her beau's family and the press reaction was excoriating—should the heir to the throne be mixing with such folk? (Fascinating how the nouveau riche are looked down upon not merely by the Establishment, but also by the readers of the tabloids.) Her behavior could at best be described as volatile. One minute she would be posing for the photographers, the next she would be trying to hide. She initiated impromptu press conferences and then denied they had taken place. She gave tip-offs to photographers and was apparently furious when they turned up. I read every bit of coverage I could find. A photojournalist who had covered her for seventeen years wrote that he had "never seen her act more bizarrely." Apparently she had crawled along the balcony of the villa, a towel over her head, and then followed up by posing on the front stairs.

If I feared for her sanity, I could see too why a desperate remedy might be required.

10 February 1998

In early August, the antics that she had said she would avoid intensified. With the boys at Balmoral (always a low point for her) she could not be still—except in the embrace of her lover with a long lens trained on them. Then there was the Paris fiasco. Rumors of an engagement, ceaseless comings and goings within the two-day trip, an aborted dinner at the Ritz, a near-riot of paparazzi every time they moved. And move they did. No sooner, it seemed, than they reached a cocoon of luxurious privacy, they were in the car again. Why did she do it? I have not discussed it with her. I would have talked to her about it as it pertained to a forward strategy, but during our brief and infrequent phone conversations I always sensed another presence in the room with her. Afterward, the analysis bore no relevance and it would have been an impertinence on my part. A courtier to the last.

I did, however, give the matter a great deal of private thought. As it related to our project, I came to the conclusion that contrary to our previous supposition, it did no harm. After she had behaved in a somewhat extreme and unpredictable manner, the closing chapter of her life, though shocking, would take on an air of inevitability.

The apogee came with the "Near-Fatal Car Crash" as it was hysterically billed. The fact that the driver, who had not been wearing his seat belt, was the only one hurt, and not even seriously, did nothing to discourage the headline writers. The "near-fatality" angle was cooked up by saying that had the swerve to avoid the photographer on his motorbike come earlier, say in the Alma tunnel when the car had been clocked at around ninety miles per hour, death would have been instantaneous. There was, I suppose, a grim—if twisted—kind of logic to the headlines. What the press wanted to focus on was how she could have died trying to escape the paparazzi (the pursuit had certainly been reckless, if not downright crazy), a story of which they were robbed, albeit temporarily. It ran as a kind of rehearsal to the main event—when the mainstream consensus was that she died because she had tried to elude the press.

I do not believe, though, that she manipulated the circumstances. She can certainly, though it pains me to admit it, be manipulative. I think that she was sinking. Her manic need to be seen was a form of self-harm. Worse still, it harmed her children. She knew it. It was her worst addiction, one for which there is no recognized treatment or cure.

From London and then Washington I watched her closely, and by the time they flew into Montevideo in mid-August I was hugely relieved that we were moving into the final phase.

Chapter Twelve

Carson's first job had been as an insurance clerk and he had hated it. When Sarah left and took Ava with her all the way to the other side of the world he had stuck with it because he wanted to save up enough money to visit his daughter. That didn't pan out so he quit and drifted for a while. He worked dead-end jobs, busing tables, dealing cards in a casino, valeting cars, anything mindless and busy. One evening he went for a drink with his old boss, who started giving him a hard time. Know what your trouble is? The man looked like a wilted houseplant, not enough nutrients, but Carson liked him. He'd doubled his workload when Sarah took off and Carson understood that as a silent kindness. Know what your trouble is? You're a snob.

Carson knew he was anything but. He was hosing down cars for a living and got along with his colleagues just fine. He was nearly fluent in Spanish by then. Couldn't care less about his college degree.

No, said his old boss. You're a snob. You didn't go to grad school so you're dropping out. You think it's beneath you to work your way up in the office, too dull. Let me tell you something, you're wrong about that.

Carson went back to the company, not because he thought the old man was right, but because he didn't care what work he did anyway, how boring it was. And he didn't like being called a snob.

He trained as a claims adjuster and that was still what he did, though he was on his third company now.

"Last week I went out to a family whose house burned down in the middle of the night." Lydia was sitting on the swing seat on the deck and Carson was lying on his side, just out of kicking distance, he

92

said. "Situation like that—I'm there the morning after they just lost everything—you have to understand how they're feeling. You have to deal with them right. Their world got torn apart, and there you are with a set of forms."

"What happened?" said Lydia. "The whole house burned?"

"Electrical fault. That's what it looks like. You always have to consider arson, but you can tell a lot from how people act. You learn how to read them, figure out who's faking, who's got something to hide. The investigation has to happen, but I usually know if it's going to turn up anything."

"He was right, then, your old boss. It's not a dull business."

"There's the paperwork," said Carson. "But there's a lot more to it. Last year I had a claim made by the university. They'd insured an exhibition of artworks that was moving around the country. It was being displayed on campus for three months—big sculptures made out of scrap metal, road signs, fenders, railway sleepers. There were twenty-three pieces out on the lawns, and one goes missing. I drive into the city and go to the campus to see the dean of arts. I interview her and her colleagues and I'm getting nowhere. The best theory we have is someone's come with a truck and stolen this sculpture in the night."

"What would they do with it?" said Lydia. "Who'd put it out on their drive if it's stolen?"

"Right. So I ask the dean to show me where this sculpture had been and we walk across to the other side of the campus. There's nothing to see but I ask what's in the nearest building and she says it's the workshop, where the maintenance guys hang out. I say I'd like to talk to them. The head of the workshop doesn't know anything, so I say my good-byes and get in the car to go home and make my report.

"But as soon as I turn the engine on it strikes me that the workshop guy was holding back. As we were talking he never looked away, not even once. People who lie overcompensate because they've heard that liars can't meet a gaze. That's the popular opinion out there."

"What did you do?" Lydia slipped off the seat and sat cross-legged on the deck. A papery moon had insinuated itself into the pink and gold sky. A flycatcher took a bath in Madeleine's water bowl.

"I go back to the workshop and say, I think there's something you'd like to tell me. This time the guy looks away to the back of the room. There's a long workbench that's been put together out of different metals. I say, where's the rest of it? Alessandro, one of the workers, took the aluminum siding to repair his trailer. Pablo thought the railway sleeper would make a good mantel for his fireplace. Nothing had been wasted. They were recycling a heap of dumped garbage as far as they were concerned."

Lydia laughed. "Good for them. I hope they didn't get in trouble."

"We worked it out," said Carson. "Sometimes you catch a bad guy in this business. This wasn't one of those times. Sometimes," he rolled onto his back and rested his head on clasped hands, "the bad guy is the insurance company. There are companies that aim not to pay out anything, even when the claim is fair."

"That's terrible. Imagine if your house burned down and you couldn't get the insurance money."

"Yup," said Carson, staring straight up at the sky, at the few shy stars overhead. "I do. Imagination is part of the job. Thinking yourself into someone else's shoes. Now I'm imagining you might be getting hungry and I'm imagining driving over to Dino's and getting us a pizza. How does that sound?"

While he was out Lydia worked through the magazines and found what she was looking for in four of them. Her sons were organizing a concert in Hyde Park in September to commemorate the tenth anniversary of her death. She didn't experience the agitation she had expected. She knelt with the magazines open on the couch in front of her, looking at the photographs. "Thank you," she said out loud. The concert was a lovely thought but she was grateful most of all for the way they had got on with their lives.

Rufus scrambled onto her knee and she put her hand on his back and felt the rapid rise and fall of his rib cage. She picked him up and buried her face in his fur.

When she heard the door she closed the magazines and tossed them into a pile. She followed Carson into his kitchen and watched as he cut the pizza into slices and got out the plates.

"I know what you're thinking," he said.

"Tell me."

"You're thinking how lucky you are to have such a handsome dude at your beck and call. Am I right?"

"Something like that," said Lydia. She'd been thinking Lawrence wouldn't disapprove of this. She wasn't letting him down. "I was thinking about how I'm doing okay. How I'd do just about anything not to rock the boat. I'd like things to stay as they are."

He turned around to her. "Done enough of the boat rocking, huh? Next up for you, the rocking chair."

"You're not out of kicking distance anymore, so watch it."

"Not out of kissing distance either."

"The pizza will go cold," said Lydia.

"I'll heat it up. Right now I've got something more interesting in mind."

Later they watched cable, a slick heist movie that slid down like a pint of ice cream. When it was over Carson went into his study and came out with an envelope.

"Here," he said, "the last photo I've got of Ava. Her handprint's in there as well."

Lydia opened the envelope. "She was three? Four?"

"Three and a half."

"She's gorgeous. Those pretty little teeth."

He sighed. "For a long time it made me so upset that her mother couldn't send me a letter or a photo. Once a year would have been fine. But I gave up my rights. And she never responded to anything."

"That must be tough."

"Maybe she was right, though. Maybe it was better that way. Clean break. It might have been harder to see her growing up from a distance."

"I don't know," said Lydia. "I don't know about that. At least you'd know that she's okay."

"She could find me now, if she wanted. Ava, I mean. She's twenty-five, an adult. If that's what she wanted, she could track me down."

"Oh, Carson, she might not even know about you. Or she might think you wouldn't want that. And it would be so difficult. It wouldn't be easy, unless you're still in touch with her mother."

He sat down next to her and put an arm around her shoulders. She slid a couple of fingers between the buttons of his shirt. "Sarah moved," he said. "My letters came back. The phone number I had didn't work. I think about getting on the Internet, but then I think it should be Ava's decision, her choice."

"I'll bet Ava grew up fine."

With his free hand he cupped her chin and drew her face very close. He didn't speak. Then he let her go. He took the photograph and the handprint and put them back in the envelope.

He said, "Would you trust me if you needed to? I'm not going to ask you anything else."

A swell that started inside her chest spread through her body. The tips of her fingers prickled. "Yes," she said finally. "I would."

The next morning she swung out of Carson's front door dressed in yesterday's jeans and T-shirt and paused a moment on the stoop. Rufus ran back up the steps to see what was going on. She breathed in the air that was soft with the scent of pine trees. Most of the time it didn't occur to her to appreciate the small things. Like going out in the same clothes as the previous day. Being free to do that.

She wondered if it was the same if you'd been in prison. Years later maybe you'd be boiling a kettle or shopping for drain cleaner and start marveling at how you were allowed to do these things whenever you chose.

"How daft is that?" she said, as she got in the Sport Trac. She had to start the engine three times before it caught. Then she clarified her question to Rufus. "Comparing myself to an ex-convict."

Rufus thumped his tail on the seat as if he couldn't agree more. He lay down and started chewing surreptitiously on the seam.

It wasn't prison, but getting out was just as hard. Princesses were always locked in towers in fairy tales. In reality there wasn't a tower and there were no locks. You stood at the top of a crystal staircase a mile high in glass slippers, and there was no way down without breaking your neck.

Lydia chatted with Hank and Julia who were today's volunteers at the shelter and made sure they knew which dogs they were going to exercise.

Hank wrote everything down with his stubby pencil. He read back the list. "Thank you, Lydia," he said. "You've got us all organized."

He was a regular volunteer, a retired embalmer who had worked at J. C. Dryden and Sons for nearly thirty years. Such extensive proximity to death had equipped him with a calmly accepting attitude to life. It was a quality that was useful when working with the trickier dogs. Sometimes he seemed to move in slow motion, but he never flapped and never fussed.

Lydia went into the yard to find Esther.

Esther was squatting by the kennel at the far end, the one where they put the snarliest dogs to try to keep them calm. She looked glum as she straightened up.

"They should be shot," she said.

"Morning," said Lydia. "Who?"

"These damn breeders who do this to the dogs." She looked down at the young pit bull who was pressed up to the wire, saliva hanging down from his jaw. "We can't home him. There's no way. They're breeding these dogs to be killers. I've seen puppies attack each other at eight weeks old. It's not natural."

"What are we going to do with him?"

"I don't know," said Esther. "Look at this." She kicked at the remains of something on the floor. "I was doing the adoptability test with him. I took his food away, no problem, passed that with flying colors. Then I put the cat in the kennel and he locked on immediately. You can see what he did to it. His prey drive is in overdrive."

"Couldn't risk letting that happen to a real one," said Lydia.

"Nor to a child," said Esther. She scraped the mechanical cat together with the toe of her boot. "I don't know what we're going to do."

"I could work with him," said Lydia. "But even then . . ."

"I don't know what we're going to do, period," said Esther. "We're going to be out of money soon. The bank's not willing to extend the overdraft."

"Oh, I see. There's got to be something we can do."

"We've had cake sales," said Esther. "I've made three million jars of blueberry jelly, that's what it felt like. We've been around with the collecting tins. I'd sell my body, but I don't think we'd get any takers, do you?"

"I'm going to think about it," said Lydia, "while I exercise Topper and Zeus."

At lunchtime Hank and Julia went to the coffee shop and Lydia sat outside with Esther on the bench.

"Chicken pasta salad," said Esther, passing the Tupperware. "I've been adventurous today. Actually, I ran out of rice."

"I was never one for dogs when I was younger," said Lydia.

"A dog's happy when you're happy," said Esther. "You come to appreciate that in time."

"When I was a kid I had a nanny who brought her dog with her. She lived in the house. The nanny, I mean, and the dog as well. I remember being horrible to that dog. It was a poodle, a nervy little white poodle. I held it out of the window once and threatened to throw it. It was a long way down."

"Was it the dog you hated, or the nanny?"

"I wasn't going to do it," said Lydia. "I would never have actually done it. But of course I got in such trouble. Which was what I wanted, instead of Daddy just drifting through the nursery and looking vague. I was horrible to all the nannies. After Mummy left. I thought they were trying to be her, and I couldn't let them. I was six when she went off with another man. I used to think that if I really loved her then I'd have the courage to behave so badly that she'd just have to come back. So it was all my own fault that she didn't, because I was cowardly. That's six-year-old logic for you."

"Did you still see her? After she'd gone?"

One of the dogs started barking. The others whipped up too, and Lydia waited as if for a train that hurtled through without stopping at the station, until she could speak again. "Yes, at weekends. It was miserable. She cried when we arrived, my brother and I, and she cried when we left and I felt guilty the whole time. Sometimes I wished that she'd died instead of gone away."

"And then you felt even guiltier."

"And how," said Lydia.

"You see," said Esther, pointing at Rufus, who was tripping along with his tail low to the ground, "when it comes to dogs, only one of you is ever going to feel guilty, and you know it's going to be your four-legged friend."

"Hey," called Lydia, "Rufus, what have you done?"

She didn't find out until the drive home, when she discovered that he'd been in the car and chewed the seam off the upholstery on the passenger seat. The stuffing was coming out. "You bad puppy," she told him, but he was playing the innocent by then.

After swimming her lengths in the pool she soaked in the bath and tried to read the book she'd picked up at the drugstore. Before she got to the end of the first chapter she gave up on it. She dried off and put on her robe. There were a few books on the shelf in the bedroom, none of which she wanted to read again. She thought about the books she had read on Islamic art when she had dated an art dealer whose specialist area that was. When she was dating a doctor she read books about anatomy. Lawrence had given her some novels the last time she saw him, big fat books most of them, written long ago. He had so much faith in her; he thought she could tackle them. She'd wanted to prove him right but she'd been nervous about getting started, and then she'd moved from that first house in North Carolina and one of the boxes had got lost in the move. Reading for someone else's sake wasn't part of her life now, anyway. She wasn't about to go to the library and take out some hefty volume about the insurance industry.

She cut out the pages she'd found in the magazines and stowed them in the box she kept locked in the closet, with all her letters, her documents, her alternative documents, and everything else she needed to keep secure. Then she pottered around in the kitchen, listening to the radio, and thinking about her conversation with Esther. There had to be a way to keep Kensington Canine open. There wasn't another rescue place in the area. If it closed down, what would happen to the dogs? What would happen to them without Esther, and what would happen to Esther without them?

In the night she woke to find Rufus standing close to her pillow and quivering. "What is it?" she said. "What's the matter? Did you hear something?" As she spoke she heard the shattering of glass downstairs. Her heart thumped so hard that she put a hand to her chest as though to quiet it. She looked on the bedside table for her cell phone and remembered she'd left it downstairs. She slipped out of bed, trying not to make the floorboards creak. Standing still she listened again. Nothing. Perhaps she should stamp about to try to scare off whoever was downstairs. But if they'd been bold enough to break a window, surely they wouldn't take fright that easily.

She tiptoed over to the closet and unlocked it. It opened with an agonizing creak. Rooting to the bottom of the box, she found the gun. She'd bought it years ago when she'd thought she needed it because she lived alone. She'd never taken it out of the box before, except when she went to the shooting range to learn how to shoot it. She checked that it was loaded, as if the bullets might have mysteriously fled of their own accord.

There was another noise from downstairs, too muffled to make out what it was. She was at the door of the bedroom before she remembered she was naked and had to creep back to the foot of the bed to pick up her robe. Rufus tried to go out of the door ahead of her but she shut him in and went to the top of the stairs.

"Get out of my house," she called, and could have kicked herself for that shake in her voice. "Get out. I've got a gun." Should she have said that? What if the burglar had one too? "There's nothing valuable in here," she added as an afterthought.

What was she waiting for? Should she go back to the bedroom and barricade herself in? Lock herself in the bathroom? Give him time to go away? It seemed like the best idea. That's what she should have done straightaway. Let him take the television and the toaster. They could be replaced.

She tiptoed back to the bedroom, although tiptoeing was pointless now, scooped up Rufus, and went to the bathroom and locked the door. Rufus licked her hand with great care and attention while she listened with every fiber and sinew for footsteps on the stairs.

After she could bear it no longer, when the strain of waiting and listening seemed like it would kill her anyway, she unlocked the door and went gingerly down the stairs. She held the gun out in front of her but expected at every moment that the attack would come from behind.

She could see across the open-plan sitting room through to the kitchen and the moonlight shone in on the culprit, sitting on the counter, bold as you please. Rufus raced ahead of her yapping glee-fully and tried to jump up at the squirrel that flicked its tail in contempt and swished through the open window. The glass that it had knocked off the counter lay in silver streaks across the floor.

Oh my God. Lydia heard Amber's voice, what she would say when she told her the whole story.

She went around the house and checked all the windows and then got back into bed, although now she was wide awake and reviewing the situation. If it had been an intruder would she have shot him? If there was no other way to defend herself? Was there any point having a gun that you weren't prepared to use?

There wasn't anything of value in the house, the usual electronic goods, none of them fancy. But an intruder wouldn't know that. He might just keep searching and searching, getting more and more angry that he wasn't finding anything, except a wallet with a few dollar bills and only one credit card.

There was the bracelet. She'd forgotten about that. The one she'd been wearing when she slid down off the back of the yacht. In her old life it wasn't an object of great value, more of a trinket, bought on a whim. She'd forgotten how much she'd paid for it but it was probably worth more than anything else she owned, apart from the house and the car.

The bracelet. That was it. That's what she could do. She could go into the city and find a jewelry store and sell it. She couldn't wait to see Esther's face when she brought in the cash.

Chapter Thirteen

11 February 1998

I entertained a hope. I have never admitted it, not even to myself. But it is true. It was a long time ago. Perhaps the residue lingered longer than I wish to own even now.

There have been women in my life I have cared for deeply. Maybe I should have married Gail. We discussed it. I said I was willing. Don't do me any favors, she said. The whole thing fizzled out, but that doesn't mean it had to be that way. I could have tried harder with her.

I entertained a hope. How ridiculous. What could possibly have happened? An elopement, perhaps, of princess with palace aide?

Now here was the crux of her problem. Leaving aside any of my personal inadequacies, a relationship with the likes of me would have been hardly less preposterous than any of those she actually pursued.

One of her bodyguards, for instance. He was a likable enough fellow. Married, but hard to blame him for not resisting her charms. How would that have worked out if he hadn't been swiftly excised from his post? A cavalry officer. He fitted the bill of dashing love interest, but impossible to imagine (although she did) a future in which their lives could align. It was no better after she divorced. Who could take her on? Not a humble and decent doctor, determined to live a quiet and serious life. Was there another royal house into which she could have married? The answer to that is no. She'd had her fill of royalty. A billionaire financier, in the footsteps of Jackie Onassis? She thought of that. Of course she was a glittering prize. But she was a shed-load of trouble and billionaires, it seems, fall into two camps: those who like expensive baubles and wish not to have their lives excessively disturbed by them, and those who prefer to partner with their intellectual equal, and also wish not to have their lives excessively disturbed. To find a man who was worthy of her affections meant finding someone who had a purpose in life, and anyone with a purpose in life was not prepared to be subsumed—or eaten alive—by her all-encompassing fame.

She filled in time with her doe-eyed playboy. But she wanted something real.

12 February 1998

Gloria was here again this morning. After she took my blood pressure she circled my arm with her meaty fingers. "Now," she said, "you look like you could do with a bit of feeding up." I do like her cheerful brutality. I said I was merely fashionably slim. (In truth I know I am on the downhill slide.) "Tell you what I'm going to do for you," she said. But she didn't tell. She put her coat on and went out. I thought perhaps she was shopping for ingredients and would spend an hour or so in the kitchen making hearty, nourishing soups. She returned with a plastic bag full of tinned shakes, the kind that bodybuilders drink. "Two a day," she said, "on top of your meals. Do *not* let me down."

The funny thing is, I don't want to let her down. The last thing I want to see in her eyes is disappointment.

While she was sorting the meds and making her notes I sat by the window watching a dog chase the waves off the beach. "Penny for them," said Gloria. I said I wasn't thinking about anything. "I'll keep my nose out," she said. I told her I'd let her into a secret. When a woman asks a man what he is thinking and he says, "Nothing," the woman is frustrated, and the man is rather pleased to be thought so deep. In truth he was probably blank, a condition quite alien to women, unless in the pits of despair.

What I was thinking about was an evening about ten years ago at the Royal Opera House in Covent Garden. It was a VIP evening with celebrity guests, singers, and dancers. There was going to be one top-secret special surprise performance. I knew she'd been rehearsing the dance—balletic but set to a pop tune—for weeks. When she slipped out of the royal box to get changed I couldn't look at the stage any longer. I kept watching the prince and as she received a standing ovation, a curtain call, another curtain call, and then another, his face turned to stone. She was twenty-eight years old and in love with her husband and the more the audience loved her, the more he cut her out of his heart.

The next day I accompanied her on a visit to an old people's home. Earlier, she had been in tears. "Everyone loved it, didn't they? Everyone apart from my bloody husband." No doubt I said something horribly unctuous, because then she tore me apart. I had missed the point. The point had not escaped me, I was evading it. The dance had been for him.

The retirement home was just outside London, the oldies gathered in a semicircle in the sitting room. They broke out in a smattering of applause and "oohs" and "aahs" as she entered, and I remember thinking how terribly destabilizing it must be to win the adoration of strangers, and earn a cold shoulder at home. She chatted away and showed no sign of her earlier distress. Truly, I don't believe she was hiding it. She became absorbed in their stories and ailments. When one woman spoke of losing her husband of nearly fifty years and started to cry, she reached out and stroked her face. Another inmate, wheelchair-bound but chafing against confinement, began to sing aggressively, stymieing the conversation. The ladies clucked with embarrassment but their glamorous visitor was unperturbed. She took up the tune. The room filled with crackly voices belting out "The White Cliffs of Dover," followed up with a rendition of "Some Enchanted Evening." There wasn't a dry eye, including my own.

She is a star in more ways than one. Her intuition rarely lets her down. Except, of course, when it comes to the men in her life.

13 February 1998
Three weeks and two days to go until I board the plane and see her again. What is she doing with her days? What am I doing with my days? I haven't touched the book.

Three weeks and two days to go. I'm like a six-year-old counting down to my next birthday.

14 February 1998

Today I asked Dr. Patel if she believes in an afterlife. "I'm a Hindu," she said. "I believe in reincarnation." I admired the way she challenged me with those molasses eyes. Strange how I failed to notice her beauty before. She waited for me to take up my intellectual cudgels. We are quite the debating club at times.

Me too, I said, I believe in reincarnation. I didn't elaborate. I think I may have offended her; she thought I was poking fun. Maybe what I should have said is, I believe in another chance.

15 February 1998

I spend my time by the window. Or I go out for a walk. The phrase I always have in mind is "to clear my head." Some hope.

I have been trying to weigh the reasons. Which one tops the list? I shift them around and around. She needed to go. What is the point of sifting and ordering the reasons? What difference does it make?

Will I reach a point of clarity if I write it all down? That's what I used to suggest to my students when they were floundering. Writing sharpens the argument. Any weaknesses in your thesis will emerge.

The trouble is that not all of her reasons were sound.

She believed "they" were "out to get her." In her mind, the evidence had mounted steadily since the death of that unfortunate chap, the protection officer who was removed from his duties after their relationship was discovered. He died in a motorcycle accident. Or "accident." She could never speak of it without making the sign for inverted commas in the air. That's how far "they" would go. How ruthless "they" could be. Who, exactly, "they" were wasn't always clear to me. Nor to her, I suspect. Though sometimes she did point the finger directly at her father-in-law. Never at her mother-in-law, I noted, who either by her role or her bearing remained uniquely above suspicion.

Was it pure paranoia when she had KP swept for bugs (I had to recommend a firm), or felt along the wheel arches of her car to check for a tracking device? I'm minded to think not entirely. I too felt that the release of that taped phone conversation with a lover was a setup, aimed at balancing, so to speak, the books, when her husband was similarly embarrassed. Her thoughts went first to the children on that occasion, as they always did. But they were too young then (ten and eight, I think) to be aware, still shielded then by youth.

I advised her emphatically against giving up royal protection, though I knew how headstrong she is and that her mind was already made up. She couldn't stand the feeling that they were "keeping tabs" on her. She wanted to be free. And she had convinced herself that the powers that be wanted her dead. It was an assertion she came to make in my presence with alarming frequency. She spoke of it to other confidants too and it was reported—as confidants do not always live up to their name. It has been grist to the conspiracy theorists' mill.

"Lawrence, don't you see?" she said to me calmly one day, when we had been walking in the KP garden and had taken a seat in a clematis-laden arbor. "I've always been an inconvenience to them. I won't go quietly, and it drives them crazy. They think I should lie down and die."

I averred that they had certainly underestimated her. (It was always difficult not to get caught up in her worldview while in conversation—I too spoke of "they" and "them.")

"It's worse than that." She picked a purple-starred blossom and pulled its petals off. "I won't oblige them so they are going to have it arranged. I'll be driving somewhere and my brakes will fail. Something that looks totally innocent. When it happens, you won't believe it, will you?"

I was rather at a loss that first time. I think I opened and closed my mouth while failing to emit a single word. She thought that terribly amusing. "What's the matter?" she said. "Can't you say something? Let's hear some of your dictionary talk."

16 February 1998

I wonder if she believes it still? At the extraordinary distance she has traveled, can she see how absurd it was?

It was not the best of reasons for plotting her escape. Even as I write that, it throws up an issue instantly. She may have been delusional, but to feel that one's life is in constant danger is a horrible way to live. Not that she is a physical coward, quite the opposite, but the desire to remove oneself from a deadly threat, real or imagined, is totally understandable. Moreover, and more importantly, she was convinced that the boys were going to lose her, one way or another. If she didn't go through with our plan, "they" would have her assassinated.

There were reasons that were real enough.

Press exposure and public scrutiny—I hardly know where to begin. She had lived with it for such a long time, why not carry on indefinitely? Perhaps that question is built on the premise that one eventually becomes immune to these things. I wonder if anyone does. We rather assume it when we see the magazines and newspapers full of personal comments on the starlets of the day. It's the price of fame, we say to ourselves, and loose change at that.

This is my only "insider" knowledge: she never took it in her stride. After the announcement of the end of her marriage (the formal separation, I mean) the hounds of hell were unleashed. "Put your fucking head up and act like a princess," a photographer screamed at her. He couldn't get the shot he wanted because she had her face turned to the ground. She cried on the telephone. The paparazzi started saying vile things to her in order to get her to cry. The shot would be more valuable if she had tears in her eyes. Or if she flew at them in a rage. Just rise above it, I used to advise her. As if she could act like a robot, as if she were not entitled to the ordinary human emotions.

I was with Gail one Saturday morning (shortly before we split up) and we stopped off at the newsagent's to buy a newspaper to read in the café over breakfast. When I turned around from the counter after paying for the *Times,* Gail was reading the front page of a tabloid. "So mean," she said, shaking her head. She opened the paper to have a look at the inside photo spread. "I don't know." More head shaking while she perused the text. She closed up the paper and handed it to me, thinking perhaps that I would want to purchase it. I put it back on the stand. I couldn't help reading the headline over once again: PRINCESS LUMPY LEGS.

They'd got a shot of her running from her gym to her car in a pair of Lycra shorts. It was her daily routine: a short drive from KP to the public gym, an early morning workout sandwiched between two quick games of cat and mouse with photographers, going in and coming out. Cellulite was alleged. I knew the call would be coming, and come it did. I took it outside on the pavement and watched Gail through the plate-glass window, sipping her cappuccino.

Did it hurt? Of course it did. The pettiness didn't make it any easier. "Even for that," she said, "they come after me."

When I was working for her, I used to think that if only she had a proper public relations staff, these things would never happen. We'd be able to protect her. Turn her into Marlene Dietrich, a royal version of an old-fashioned movie star. Envelop her in mystique and ice-cool iconography. Control the agenda and set the tone.

But we don't live in that kind of world any longer. And she isn't that kind of woman. Dietrich's bisexuality remained secret for the greater part of her life. Lydia, as I must get used to calling her, when she wasn't having her secrets exposed, got busy exposing them herself.

That impulse grew and grew. Not all of it was bad. She spoke about her bulimia in a way that was truly courageous. My admiration scaled new heights. Every time, however, she revealed herself emotionally, she upped the ante. She turned herself into "fair game."

Nothing was out-of-bounds. And Lydia fed the monster that came close to destroying her. At first she thought that she could tame it, train it, make it roll over and beg. It was apparent that was not so. Yet she was compelled to feed it more and more. Certainly, she liked to see photographs of herself in the newspapers. She looked at them all, more or less every day, and it was to her chagrin when she did not appear. Certainly, she played tactically when she could, using or creating a photo opportunity to curry favor with the public, or to steal the limelight from her ex-husband. A junkie might shoot up an extra dose to get through a difficult occasion but that does not, I'm afraid, make him any less of an addict.

It frightened her. "There's only one way for it to stop," she said. "As long as I'm here, it will just go on and on."

17 February 1998

Lydia, Lydia, Lydia.

There—like a lovesick teenager.

I am merely acclimating myself to her new name. It will trip more easily off the tongue when I see her for what I have no doubt will be the final time.

I am a little too tired to write today.

18 February 1998

My headache was blinding earlier today, but I seem to have recovered this afternoon. I use the term *recovered* somewhat loosely, of course.

She won't stay in North Carolina. I don't know where she'll go next, but I gave her some suggestions and, more importantly, emphasized the places from which she should stay away. Old haunts, basically. The Hamptons, Martha's Vineyard, New York. I am quite convinced that no one would recognize her, but if she saw one of her friends that would be unfortunate for her.

I developed a cover story for her to use with her neighbors. It had the beauty of simplicity. She had divorced recently from an American man (I forget where I suggested she say they had lived, but somewhere far enough away not to invite questioning), and wished to enjoy some solitude and countryside before moving back to England. As a couple they had driven through this part of the state once and she'd been struck by how pretty it was.

Lydia said, "Oh God, you do make me sound dull."

I replied that she was free to embellish as she saw fit.

"I'm going to do exactly what you tell me to do," she said.

I said that would be a first, and she smiled.

19 February 1998

Dr. Patel asked me about her this morning. "Tell me something about your former employer," she said.

I wasn't sure to whom she was referring, so I gave her a quizzical look. At least I attempted it. I have noticed in the mirror recently whilst brushing my teeth that I am unable to raise my eyebrows. I don't know why that should upset me but it does.

"Her Royal Highness, the Princess of Wales." Dr. Patel is a great one for formalities. She insists on addressing me as Dr. Standing and I have given up encouraging her to use my Christian name.

I said that the HRH title had been stripped away after the divorce. Dr. Patel received the news as a personal blow.

As far as I'm aware, I have never mentioned this part of my curriculum vitae to my tumor doctor. I asked her how she knew.

"I see your brain scans," she said. "It's all up there. All your history."

I laughed and laughed. Quite disproportionately, but she seemed pleased. Why, Dr. Patel, I said, I do believe you have made a joke.

"Was she a good mother? Or was it all posed for the cameras?"

It wasn't faked, I said.

Dr. Patel nodded. She accepted me as an authority on the subject. Then she reverted to business and suggested I start thinking about either a live-in carer or a hospice for the final days.

Do I have to start thinking now? I asked.

"Not now," she said, "but soon."

Chapter Fourteen

Grabowski knocked on the car window, and the kid, who was reading a newspaper spread over the steering wheel, startled before rolling it down.

"On a stakeout?" said Grabowski. He gestured to the back of the station wagon, the camera bags on the backseat, the ladder poking out of the trunk.

"John Grabowski?" said the kid. He wore a white T-shirt with a cartoon bunny and a slogan—HIP-HOP IS DEAD. It was tight enough for Grabber to see the outline of his nipple ring.

The car was parked outside the bed-and-breakfast when Grabowski walked back after lunch at the bakery. He wondered if the kid had gone inside and scared Mrs. Jackson with his piercing, and what he had said to her.

"I take it Tinny sent you."

"No," said the kid, getting out of the car. "Told me where you were. But he didn't send me. I wanted to meet you—the legendary Grabber Grabowski." He held out his hand.

Grabowski ignored it and looked up the street. He didn't like the idea of being seen with this kid who had paparazzi written all over him, although around here they wouldn't know a pap if he bit their noses off. Still, it made him uncomfortable.

"Let's go," said Grabber. "We'll take your car." Best get the car shifted, because there was one person (maybe) who'd know just what she was looking at if she walked by.

"There's a bar over in Gains that you'll like," said Grabber, going around to the passenger side.

He didn't know any bar in Gains but they'd find something. Then he'd find out what was going on. He had an idea already, put it together pretty much the instant he saw the car.

Tinny had called him again. "What's up, Grabber? What's holding you? I'm telling you, man, I've got more work than I can handle. You know what's going on around here?"

He reeled off a list. An actress back in rehab, a pop princess shaving her hair, the heiress to a hotel chain booked for driving while under the influence and about to be sent to jail.

"This year, listen to me, man, 2007 is going down in history. It's the year of girls going wild. You coming down to get a piece of the action, or what?"

Grabber said he was on his way.

"That's what you said last time." Tinny paused. "What are you doing? What's got you by the balls in—where'd you say?—Kensington?"

Grabber had spun him a line, but Tinny smelled something. That's why Grabber had found this rat boy staking out the B and B.

The kid was wasting his time. Grabber, most likely, was wasting his time. Over the last few days he'd thought about nothing but Lydia. He'd followed her home from work. He'd followed her when she went into town on Wednesday at lunchtime, and down the street where she bought sandwiches, and then to the clothing store. What did he have so far? Same height, same build, same swing in her step. When she was leaving the kennels, she called out to the old gray-haired lady, and her voice was not the way he remembered it. Not so different, but not the exact same way. Her laugh, though, sent a shiver down his spine. Sometimes you had to think with your spine in this job.

They were in Gains now and he had to look out for a bar. "Take a right," he said. "I think it's down here."

There was that guy who was obsessed with Jackie Onassis. She had an injunction taken out against him, and he wasn't allowed within fifty feet of her. He kept on taking her photo. Every day he'd turn up at her apartment building. He ended up back in court. He still couldn't stop. The guy was nuts. But Grabber knew how he felt.

"There it is," he said. "You park. I'll line up the beers."

The kid jangled into the bar and pulled up a stool. The way he walked, loose-limbed, like his bones didn't join together, got on Grabber's nerves.

"What d'you want to know?" said Grabber.

The kid grinned. "Like, I don't know. Wanted to meet you. Hear the stories—how you got some of those, like, really famous pictures."

It was bullshit. No wonder Tinny wanted him in LA. This kid couldn't grease his own arse with an entire pack of butter.

"Yeah," said Grabowski. "Which ones?"

"You got the ones of her pregnant in a bikini, right?"

"Listen, Bozo," said Grabber.

"It's Hud, actually."

"Listen, Hud, I didn't take those shots. That wasn't me." It riled him, but this kid didn't have a clue. He'd grown up in an age when actresses posed naked with swollen bellies on the covers of magazines. He couldn't imagine the stink those pictures had caused. Grabber had been on the island. He could have taken the shots but he hadn't. He did have some principles.

"Right," said the kid. He scratched uneasily at his nipple ring.

"Let's cut the crap. Tinny sent you, didn't he?"

Rat boy chewed it over. "Yeah," he said. "Tinny says you wouldn't be here unless there was something going down. You got a scoop on something, is what he says."

Grabowski took a pull on his bottle. "And he told you about those pictures. Did you even know who she was?"

Hud shrugged. "Just about."

"Well, Tinny's memory is obviously cracked. But stick around. LA's got nothing on Kensington."

"Really?" said the kid, leaning forward. He had long dark eyelashes like a cow's. His tongue showed when he talked. Grabber resisted the urge to tweak that nipple ring right off.

"Yeah, really. Might look like Hicksville but I'll tell you what's going on."

"We can work as a team," said the kid.

"As long as it goes no further," said Grabber. "Don't even tell Tinny. We don't want word getting out."

"I swear."

"Know the place I'm staying?"

"The bed-and-breakfast?"

"You're smart. Madonna is in the next room."

The kid twitched. But it wasn't enough to get him going. Madonna, he'd have snapped her plenty of times.

Grabowski looked down the bar as if to check he wasn't being overheard. "She's there, and guess who she's banging."

"Who?"

"Swear on your mother's life."

"I swear. You're not going to regret this, I promise you."

"We're a team now," said Grabowski. "You're not going to let me down."

"Damn it, we're a goddamn team."

"I'm trusting you," said Grabowski, putting his lips up close to the kid's ear. "She's banging Hugh Hefner." He let that sink in. "Hugh Hefner, Santa Claus, and the seven fucking dwarves, in the Kensington bed-and-breakfast. Don't tell anyone."

There was a long pause while rat boy decided how to take being treated like the jerk that he was. Then he laughed. "Shit," he said. "I told Tinny. I told Tinny this was dumb. I drove all this fucking way. I got straight in the car and fucking drove. Only stopped when I had to piss."

Grabowski decided he was being too hard on the lad. He was only Tinny's foot soldier, after all.

They had another beer and then another one, and Grabowski, in spite of himself, found that he was glad of the company. He'd spent too long on his own. Maybe that was why he was chasing ghosts all over town.

115

They talked cameras and lenses. The kid wanted to know what he used. Canon, always, for everything from 35 to 500 millimeters, Canon power drives, Quantum Turbo battery, Nikon flashgun. The kid said he used a PalmPilot sometimes. The targets never even knew they'd been snapped. He thought he'd invented photographic subterfuge.

Well, if he wanted to hear about legends, Grabowski could tell him a few.

"You heard of Jacques Lange? No, never mind. He wanted to get a shot of Princess Caroline of Monaco taking her exams when she was a schoolgirl. He got into the classroom somehow. And he had a Minox hidden in his packet of cigarettes. Creativity," said Grabowski. "There were no PalmPilots in those days."

"That's awesome," said the kid. "I never even heard of a Minox."

"You ever hear the story about how I got friendly with your boss?" said Grabber. He sounded like an old-timer, and he knew it, but he guessed that's what he was. "I'll tell you. It was Necker Island. You know where that is? British Virgin Islands. Right. It's privately owned so all the press were staying on other islands nearby and going out on boats to try and get shots. Yes, it was her. Bang on, you're smarter than you look. She did a ten-minute photo call and then we were all supposed to leave her alone. There was an American television and photo crew. They were the flashiest guys in town and they hired a submarine for sixteen thousand dollars a day. Thought they'd got us all beat. When they got down by Necker they told the captain to put up the periscope. The captain just looks at them. There's no periscope. It's a submarine for watching fish, not an effing U-boat. Me and Tinny, we laughed ourselves stupid in the bar over that."

"Tinny wants you in LA, man. Said if it turned out you just had your head up your ass, try and bring you back with me."

"I'll tell Tinny you tried your best."

"So what you really doing here?" said the kid.

He told the same story he'd given Mrs. Jackson. He was working on a Robert Frank–type project—exhibition and book, small towns in the United States and England. Photographs and text by John

Grabowski. She was going to clock all the camera equipment at some point, so he'd found a way to work it into his résumé.

The kid had never heard of Robert Frank. Probably he had never heard of Brassaï or Cartier-Bresson. There was no room for art in this business anymore. Grabber had sold plenty of out-of-focus shots in his time and was glad of the money, but he'd come up the old way. He could compose a frame.

Grabowski sighed and ordered another round. "If you take people's photos without their permission, what does that make you?" he asked.

"I don't know. Paparazzi."

"Maybe," said Grabowski, "but remember, the people in those Robert Frank pictures didn't agree to be in them either. They didn't sign model release forms."

The kid dabbled in the bowl of peanuts and rained a few into his mouth. "People are snotty sometimes," he said, chewing, "when I tell them what I do. Then I say, hey, I got a photo of that actress making out on a beach, and they say, oh, let's have a look."

"Of course they do," said Grabowski. "By the way, what did you say to my landlady? Did you say you were looking for me?"

The kid narrowed his eyes, offended, apparently. "Wasn't born yesterday. I didn't go in. I don't go in unless I know what I'm going to find and I'm ready for it."

"Good lad," said Grabowski. It was after five o'clock and the bar was starting to fill up with construction workers. You could see where the hard hats had left a red band across their foreheads.

He had to work out what to do about this Lydia. Was there a move he could make without scaring her off? That's if he wasn't entirely deluded. At least the photographer who'd stalked Jackie Onassis hadn't been obsessed with a ghost. But there was no way Grabowski could leave. If he didn't pursue it, he would always be haunted by the opportunity he might have missed. A pair of blue eyes, a ring of green around the right pupil, a familiar walk, a laugh that set him tingling. It wasn't much, but it was enough to stop him walking away.

"I'm not intrusive," said Hud. His cow tongue explored his bottom lip. "I'm not one of those guys. I never rammed anyone with my car.

I never broke into anyone's house. I'm just doing my job. Live and let live, you know."

It was evening and Grabowski didn't know what to do with himself. He ran his fingers around the rosary, sitting on the edge of the bed. He paced the room. What he needed was a way of deciding. Was it worth pursuing or was it too ridiculous to contemplate?

It was possible. Anything was possible. But how could he prove it? What could he do to find out? If he was right and he started asking too many questions around town she'd take off as soon as she heard.

Patience, he told himself. Think of it as a stakeout. It may be the longest of your life, but if it pays off . . . He almost felt sick with excitement. Maybe Cathy would have him back.

He was running ahead of himself now.

He couldn't ask questions around town just yet, but he could start asking questions back home. He made a call.

"Nick," he said, "I know it's late but I've got something I need you to do."

Nick worked in police records and, unofficially, for Grabowski. He was good at turning things up, knew where to look and how. Of all the people that Grabowski had on his "payroll"—doormen, waiters, nannies, PRs, drivers—Nick was the most useful.

"It'll cost you," said Nick, his standard response. He sounded wide awake. Although Grabowski had, over the years, called him at all hours of day and night he had never once caught him asleep.

"Lydia Snaresbrook," he said. "Mid-to-late forties. Find out anything you can."

"That's it?" said Nick. "Just a name, no DOB, nothing else? What are you looking for?"

"I don't know. It's a pretty unusual name. Find out how many people we could be talking about first."

"So I check out the General Registry Office, all the Lydia Snaresbrooks born between, say, 1955 and 1965. What do I do then?"

"I don't know," said Grabowski. "Just call me as soon as it's done."

Chapter Fifteen

20 February 1998

A good mother, yes, she was. She is. (More and more I find myself tempted to write of her in the past tense.) As strange as it sounds, it was one of her reasons for leaving. It bears its peculiarities and complications.

She believed she would be "bumped off," as she quaintly put it, thus depriving her sons of a mother in any case. That wouldn't have been sufficient. She'd have been willing to live with that risk if that had been best for them.

But she had a growing conviction that her presence was destabilizing to her boys, had convinced herself that the circus that surrounded her would be increasingly detrimental to them. And, of course, she was determined that once the dust had settled, she would be able to see them again.

21 February 1998

I lay down for a few minutes yesterday thinking I would come back to the diary, but I fell asleep and when I woke up I remained in something of a daze until it was time for bed.

I was still there when Gloria came this morning and she rang on the bell three times (she'd forgotten her key) because I didn't want to answer until I had my dressing gown, which proved a little difficult to locate, and a struggle to get on.

"Right, we've got my visits planned for next week," she said, after we'd completed our rituals. "Let's get the schedule organized for the week after."

I mumbled something about possibly not being here.

"Course you will," she said.

She thought I was predicting my own demise.

I told her that I was planning to go to Washington to complete my researches in the Library of Congress.

"Well, that's lovely," she said, as if I had announced a trip to Disneyland. Then she put down her pen and placed her hands on the planner that was still open on her lap. Her hands were almost as large and square as the pages. "What does Dr. Patel have to say about that?"

My vagueness on the point made her purse her lips. Finally she said, "You've got someone traveling with you, I take it."

I said it wouldn't be wise to go on my own, thus avoiding the direct lie.

"Your sister . . . Patricia, is it?"

She's on the phone to me every day, I said. And call she does. I've been putting her off coming down again but I may have to give way before I fly off to the States.

22 February 1998

Have I examined my own motivations? Perhaps not sufficiently. Compared to living out my final days entombed in libraries, was it not thrilling to execute a covert operation, my first since I was seconded from the FCO to the secret intelligence services back in my youth?

I adopted a modest disguise (the old standby of beard and glasses) of my own in Recife, when I was waiting for the assignation. There were paparazzi in town and it was just about possible that one of them would recognize me as her old private secretary.

When I hired the rowing boat, I came face-to-face with one at the jetty. If I hadn't already been covered in sweat (the weather was baking) I would have perspired profusely at that point. I knew him and therefore he knew me, that was my first instinct, like the inverse of the small child who is convinced that he has disappeared from view simply by covering his face.

My training, thank goodness, kicked in. I knew not to walk away without ascertaining whether there was any possibility he had seen through the disguise.

I walked up to him and gestured at his camera equipment. "There's a pelican feeding frenzy the next cove round. Thought you might be interested—you a wildlife photographer?"

He looked me up and down briefly, my Hawaiian shirt and bald knees, a bearded and bespectacled ornithologist, of no interest to mankind. "No, mate," he said. "Stick around. You'll see a different kind of feeding frenzy soon."

I told Lydia about this little adventure. She's quick on the uptake. The way she held that magazine up to her plastic surgeon in Rio was quite brilliant. I think she will be okay.

23 February 1998

The book recedes. I read through the first three chapters yesterday and winced at all those dusty phrases.

I do not care. My legacy is not one that resides between the covers of a book. She resides in this world. I can be satisfied with that. I did right. I think I did.

What will she do? We discussed possible lines of employment. She said, "I'm not qualified for anything."

I disagreed strenuously, and asked her to think of all the experience she's had, all the skills that she's gained, all of her natural talents. It is a conversation we will continue. Financially speaking (I worked out budgets and she actually paid attention as I talked them through) she won't need to work for a long time, but I think work will be helpful in many other ways. Without it she may fall into festering, develop new obsessions, or simply die of boredom.

The boys, I was going to write about them, and found myself waylaid. They were the reason in the end.

Two weeks until I see her. I already have my bag packed.

24 February 1998

The day has passed while I looked out of the window in reverie. I was turning over in my mind times long gone. Scenes from my childhood, from the classroom, walking on the broads, Christmas gatherings, the blue-tiled walls of the Ankara consulate, a meal of pâté and bread in Provence with Gail on our first holiday. Funny what stays with you. It doesn't add up to anything, it doesn't have any shape, and yet it is a life.

The boys. How could any mother leave her children? And she is as devoted as they come. No, it wasn't for the cameras, although at times she played off "the other side" (her husband) by public displays of fun-loving, affectionate mothering. In comparison he looked so stiff.

She was terrified of losing them. She said to me, "Don't you understand what's happening, Lawrence, they're trying to cut me out." The first Christmas after the formal separation she had to leave the boys at Sandringham. She spent Christmas Day alone at KP. "They let me know when I can have the boys and when I can't. It's as if they're not my children, they're properties of the crown." And, in a way, she was right. She went on. "First they took my title, now they're trying to take the boys."

25 February 1998
The problem was certain to grow. The boys' loyalties were divided. I believe they felt guilty about how much they loved being with their father and grandmother at Balmoral (a place that their mother hated), away from the glamour and glitz and clicking cameras. They adored her, but they had already begun to grow uncomfortable about her behavior, especially the eldest.

When she drove up to his school to warn him that the television interview that she'd secretly recorded (what a sensation that caused!) was about to be aired, he gave her the cold shoulder. She called me and said, "He looked absolute daggers. I thought, my own son hates me. I can't cope with this." An hour later she called back and they'd been talking on the phone, everything was sunny again. But the episodes piled up like a multiple-car crash. There'd been "The Book of Revelations," as she referred to it, that infernal biography with which she had covertly cooperated. There'd been scandal after scandal, affairs with married men, phone pest allegations, screaming at photographers, wacky therapies, more unsuitable men, briefings to tabloid reporters—denied and then exposed, rumors and photographs and allegations plastered all over the world. He was old enough (and his brother was getting that way) that it embarrassed him to the roots of his molars.

She wanted to stop but she couldn't. The cycle was speeding up. And she feared that it was harming him in a way she couldn't prevent. Ashamed, as well, that she was slipping into an unhealthy dependency on her sons, her eldest in particular, whom she had started to call five or six times a day.

It was an echo of the desperation to possess them completely with which she drove her lovers away. They would receive, at her own conservative estimation, around twenty calls from her in any twenty-four-hour period. There was no proof of love that was proof enough in her mind.

The time when I came closest to falling out with her was when I suggested that she stop visiting her son at Eton so frequently. It was stifling to have your mother turn up three or four times in one week, and the other boys would delight in teasing him. She was furious.

She threw me out of KP by getting up and ringing for the butler. "Dr. Standing would like to be shown out," she said. That was vicious. Calling me Dr. Standing, and suggesting I didn't come and go by myself all the time at the palace, or would no longer be doing so.

Two hours later she was on the phone and sobbing. She said, "You're right. But I can't help myself. Poor child. What a dud mother he's got." She was desperate not to suffocate him, not to burden him with divided loyalties or her woes. But her patterns of behavior—she knew it—were so compulsive that it seemed like an impossibility.

My heart bled. Dr. Patel is most welcome to cut up my brain after I am gone and examine the cells beneath a microscope. But if she is looking for this particular part of my personal history, she will have the wrong organ under examination.

A dud mother. I don't think so. For them she would have done anything that lay within her capabilities, and to leave them, I firmly believe, was her greatest act of selflessness.

Was it misguided? That has yet to be seen, and I won't be around to find out. For my part, I cannot pretend that is what compelled me to help her. Her reasons were not my own. I feared for her sanity. I postulated that her increasingly spectacular recklessness would lead to her early and spectacular demise. And I wanted to be close to her. Even the most loyal of courtiers fails to leave his own interests entirely aside.

I have never agreed with her that there might be a time, in the future, when she might make contact with them. She has all sorts of unworkable schemes for doing so. It certainly cannot be done without risking her secrecy, and it would inflict terrible psychological damage on them, her resurrection much more so than her death. I have always tried to make that clear to her. I do have faith that it is a conclusion she will reach in time. Deep down, I suspect, she already knows it, but in order to leave them it was necessary for her to convince herself otherwise.

26 February 1998

Not long now. Ten days. I think I will need a driver. I will take one part of the way and then a taxi or two. I am a careful man.

27 February 1998

The excitement has made my left eye blind. That's the way I like to think of it. Quite suddenly overnight. The vision has been blurry from time to time, but this morning I tested it, as has become my habit, and it doesn't see anything. No choice but to use a driver from Washington now.

28 February 1998

Patricia arrives later today. She's bringing a casserole down with her on the train. Lamb and flageolet beans. The thought of it rouses my appetite.

Lydia, oh, Lydia. I hope my appearance will not distress her. I am not an appealing sight. My left, blind, eye wanders around in its socket—it makes me look a little mad.

She has frequently been viewed as such. "The firm" was strictly of that opinion, except when they had her down as a manipulative little schemer who knew exactly what she was doing. The public had other ideas. What seemed like madness to her in-laws was viewed as courage by the public, more often than not.

It was far from a simple relationship, though. Photographs of her in distress sold newspapers. As did salacious gossip and columns. Then—"Why does everyone hate me?" she would say.

Her decision to leave has been her most selfless act. But she is a complex woman. Perhaps it was also her greatest act of narcissism. No more swings in the barometer of public approval. She has ascended the firmament now, her worth beyond measuring; beyond dispute she is loved.

1 March 1998

Patricia has gone to bed. The casserole has taken up residence in the freezer—my appetite lagging somewhat behind expectation. I have forced down a shake, but my stomach is not keen to hold on to it and I think it may come up again.

I must finish this diary and put it through the shredder. It has kept me going through these days that truly I have only been counting down. Its purpose has been served.

2 March 1998

I said good-bye to my sister, she returned to London this morning, and she could hardly keep back the tears. Nor could I. She is a good sort. We discussed arrangements for the funeral. She was kind enough not to ask about the book.

Six days to go.

I have to stop writing this. More and more memories. It is enough to keep them in my mind. What will become of Lydia? I wish I could answer that with confidence, work it out and write the answer down. The past is difficult enough to see clearly. An historian should know that. At the future we can only guess.

One thing I do know: if she is undone, it will be by a man. Is it inevitable? Given her uncontrollable passions, her headstrong, head-long tumbles into doomed relationships.

I cannot answer with certainty, but I know that I know her well, perhaps better than any of her relations, her lovers, her friends. (Others have fallen off the wagon of her favor while I remained, by virtue of my dogged devotion.) All those obsessions, those disordered and manic searches for comfort (in food, in therapies, in love) do not bear the indelible stamp of a flawed personality or a psychiatric basket case. I have observed them as the response to a life lived in a permanent state of crisis, conducted at an unbearable level of scrutiny, in the toxic and highly flammable stratosphere of fame.

Others have coped. That doesn't convince me. Nobody else lived it at her level, with her constraints, in the nonstop multimedia age. There is no fair comparison that I can find.

I believe that she will make a life, because her desire is so strong. That's what I want to believe.

3 March 1998

Today my headache is bad and my good eye is blurring on and off. I'm not too worried. It took a long time for my left eye to go completely. Still, I must rest. And tomorrow, the final installment.

Chapter Sixteen

3 July 1998

Dear Lawrence,

I hope you're going to approve. Mr. Walker was willing to extend the lease for another six months (just as you said) but I had to get away. I was suffocating in Gravelton. Honestly, I couldn't take another minute.

Does that sound ungrateful? It's the last thing I mean to be. You said I'd need somewhere quiet so I could catch my breath. I'm sure you were right. You're always right. Anyway, I'm still in North Carolina and I've rented an apartment in Charlotte, in a big building right in the city center. And I have a feeling that I've turned a corner. I thought you'd want to know. This entire last week (I've been here for three and a half) I haven't cried once. Not a single time. There's no one I can tell that to, apart from you. Lillian, I could say (she's my neighbor across the hall), guess what, no tears from Monday to Sunday. She's seventy-six years old and keeps three tortoises and plays mahjongg with her cronies. The day I moved in, two suitcases, three boxes, she came round with a potted orchid and a bottle of disgusting sparkling wine, so sweet it made my teeth ache. We polished it off anyway, sitting on the balcony, while she told me about the Italian language course she's doing. In November she's going to Rome and Florence and she's aiming to be reasonably fluent by then. I sat there thinking about what my aims are. Not crying for a whole day, that's what I decided. And now I've gone a whole week. I wish you were here to tell me well done.

There's such a lot I need to talk to you about. I tried to call you three times in March, but of course I knew there was only one possible reason. You'd never let me down. I've been alone all my life and I keep telling myself that this is nothing new. Alone when Mummy left, and Daddy had his head in the clouds. Alone at the palace, alone in my marriage, always and always alone.

No, don't worry about me. I have my head above water. I'm not a lost cause. You didn't waste your time. That's all I wanted to say.

With my deepest affection,
Your Lydia

7 July 1998

Dear Lawrence,

I have a confession to make. I called the boys too. There was only the automated answer service. Then I tried to imagine what you would say about it. That's how I've been stopping myself from doing it again. So, you see, you're still here for me, I can still hear you when I concentrate.

Lydia

10 July 1998

Dear Lawrence,

That wasn't all I wanted to say. I wanted to say thank you, but I still don't know how. I do know that no other person on earth would have done for me what you did. No one else ever understood. I remember trying to say thank you, and I remember how silly it sounded. We laughed about that, didn't we?

I've cursed you sometimes for not saying no to me. You could have said it would be impossible. Why didn't you? You helped me lose everything. Is that the action of a true friend? Oh, Lawrence, what a dark heart I have. I've hated you for helping me. If only you'd turned your back and walked away.

No, I haven't had the best of weeks, maybe you can tell, even though I haven't said anything about it. Even so, this is a thank you letter. I don't just mean for carrying through "our little plan." I mean for standing beside me through the years. For seeing me at my very worst and never judging me.

Is it better late than never? Couldn't I have opened my mouth when you were still around? I wonder if we could have been happy together. Did you ever wonder that? I know you did.

With fond memories,
Lydia

5 August 1998

Dear Lawrence,

I've tried a few times to write a diary. You said it would be good for me. But I'd rather talk to you than talk to myself.

I'm in trouble with Lillian. I don't care. She can go to hell. Who does she think she is anyway? She's in trouble with me. She opened her door just as my new gentleman visitor was leaving this morning. Still sticking her nose in. She watched him walk down the hall and when he'd got in the lift she said, Lydia, I'm really concerned about you. Utterly brazen, like that. I told her where to stick it, the old witch. I said, you have no idea what you're talking about, and I've had enough interference for several lifetimes, thank you very much. I'd appreciate it if you'd leave me alone.

I absolutely will not stand for people telling me what I can and can't do. I never let myself be pushed around, did I? God knows they all tried hard enough. If they didn't break me, then some old lady in Sta-Prest slacks and penny loafers isn't going to succeed where they failed. When she comes knocking on my door she's going to find it closed.

She should have minded her own business. Sometimes I need a bit of company. You understand that, don't you? I can't make do with an old lady and three tortoises. I'm still a young woman and I haven't joined a nunnery. What was the point in moving to the city if I'm not allowed to have my bit of fun? I'd be letting us both down, Lawrence, if I didn't try to make the most of my life. I'm not putting up with lectures from anyone.

I'm going to get ready for my night out now.

Your ever-hopeful Lydia

25 August 1998

Dear Lawrence,

I've written you three letters now and you've replied, in your own way, to every one of them. Isn't that strange? I found you a bit disapproving last time, which surprised me. That's not like you. If you're going to carry on being like that I'm not going to tell you anything anymore.

I shall live as I please. If I don't, then what was the point of it all? Tell me that. I bet you don't have an answer, do you?

I've made a new friend, Alicia. She works at Skin Deep, beauty and tanning salon, and she's going to get me a job there. Don't laugh. You know I did my own makeup on many occasions. And you said it would be good for me to work. Alicia says I can get trained up to give facials and do eyebrow shaping and waxing and it only takes a few weeks. I'm going to get paid for pulling hair out of people's crotches. What's wrong with that?

I've been going out a lot with Alicia. I'm not drinking to excess, if that's what you're thinking. She drinks more than I do. Before, I could never go out and have a few drinks, because how would that have looked? Now I've got some catching up to do. It does help. Lawrence, I'm not turning into a drunk. I'm careful not to drink in the day. Alicia mixes her drinks and I stick to only wine and vodka. If it was getting out of hand I'd tell you. I've never hidden anything from you.

I feel you watching me, Lawrence. Why so stern? I want you to smile a bit more often, please. I'm making a go of this. It's not easy, you know.

Lydia

19 September 1998

Dear Lawrence,

Do you have the tiniest inkling what I'm going through? Did you think I could survive? Did you take that into consideration when you were making your ever-so-careful plans?

Did you just want me to yourself?

Lydia

20 September 1998

Dear Lawrence,

I'm sorry I spoke to you like that. I'm ashamed. Every day is such a struggle, but what did I expect? I wanted to write to you about my life and tell you how much it has improved since I saw you last November. I had a sense then that it would be the last time we would be together and I should have said a proper good-bye. Still, I waited for you in March. I kept hoping. All the beds I have sat beside, and I couldn't sit at yours. I'm sorry I wasn't there. You know that if there was any way . . .

With love and gratitude,
Lydia

21 September 1998

Dear Lawrence,

I wanted to be able to tell you that the depression has lifted. I wanted to tell you that it's all been worthwhile. At least that there is light at the end of the tunnel, or sometimes I think there is.

I have to acknowledge the progress that I've made and not beat myself up for the progress that is yet to come. That's what my therapist always said. You're my only therapist now. I listen to what you say, believe it or not. Perhaps more than I ever did when you were alive.

I'm cutting down on the drinking. And I'm starting my training at Skin Deep tomorrow. You'll be proud of me in the end.

Now for an early night.

Love,
Lydia

22 September 1998

Dear Lawrence,

I have done my first day's paid work since I was nineteen years old. Actually, that's not quite true. I don't get paid for the first month, while I learn how to sterilize tweezers and heat wax, but I do get free facials and manicures and two free massages. Alicia and I went to the diner for lunch and she told me all the gossip about the other girls. She has an ankle tattoo and a sense of humor and sassy five-inch heels. She grew up in a trailer park, but I've never had any difficulty mixing with ordinary folk. Also, her mother is an alcoholic, so we have that in common, don't we? Not that Mummy would ever admit it.

We don't have an actual uniform but we have to wear black trousers and black shirt and over the top of that a black tabard with Skin Deep *embroidered in white letters. Also a name badge, but I'll only get mine at the end of the month. What do you think? Can you believe I've found myself a job?*

Kisses,
Lydia

25 September 1998

Dear Lawrence,

I think I might have found my absolute forte. Who knows, in a couple of years I might be doing makeup for celebrities. Maybe for some of my old friends! Wouldn't that be a riot? Today, Alicia was doing makeup for a wedding and she was making a perfect dog's dinner of it, so I stepped in. All my usual tact and diplomacy, of course. The bride was really very grateful. I also did my first facial, under supervision, but it was supremely easy. The reality is, having had more than my share in the past, I knew more about it than my so-called supervisor, Alicia.

Good night, my sweet savior.

Your Lydia

28 September 1998

Dear Lawrence,

You said it would get easier and, little by little, it has.

At first I was so scared of everything and everyone, I practically jumped out of my skin when anyone spoke to me. And you, you wise old owl, told me it wouldn't be half as difficult as I thought. I mean the part about talking to people. No one gives me the third degree. I started telling Alicia how my husband always made me feel like a dunce, and I started thinking maybe now she's going to ask all sorts of tricky questions. I was getting the answers ready in my head. She just said, yeah, my ex used to call me Dumbo. Then she used some ripe language. We were having a drink at our favorite bar and she had her eye on someone. It was a bit annoying, really, because I was quite in the mood for a heart-to-heart, and she was hardly listening. I wouldn't say she's a slut, but sometimes she comes close. It would be nice to find someone who's a bit more on my own wavelength.

Just imagine, Lawrence, if she knew. She'd be singing to a different tune, wouldn't she?

Kisses from your semiqualified beautician,
Lydia

2 October 1998

Dear Lawrence,

We'd talked a lot about all the "stages" I would go through. I tried to keep that in my mind but I didn't always manage it. Despair is like a trump card. It wipes out everything else. I'm doing so much more now. In Brazil I lived the life of a slug. Two and a half months of lying on the sofa, and for the first couple of weeks, until you came back after the funeral, I didn't even have a television! Somehow it was beyond me to go out and buy one. I was used to having everything done for me. I remember you'd left the fridge and the cupboards stocked and I stayed inside and ate tinned soup and lumps of cheese.

You'd told me that when people are tortured (how do you always know everything?) they get through it by dividing time into slices. So they breathe through the next thirty seconds. If they've made it through that, they can make it through the next thirty. You meant I should slice up the first year into months and weeks and days. Get through one "stage" at a time. But there were days when thirty seconds seemed about right.

I thought you were just trying to put me off. I should have known you never talk out of your hat.

Respectfully yours,
Lydia

3 October 1998

Dear Lawrence,

The mind plays tricks on us. Last night I was remembering those first weeks in Brazil as totally desolate. Mostly they were. But there were moments when I'd soar. I'd put the radio on and dance around the house, because I'd done something so huge. We'd done something so huge. I felt totally invincible. If I could do that, I'd be able to do anything. I was free. For the first time in my entire life I was free.

Then you came, with your bag of newspaper cuttings, and that was the most terrible and wonderful thing. A heart can't actually burst, can it? I thought mine would. But there's no limit to how much a person can feel.

When you'd gone, I think I went downhill. I hardly got out of bed and I don't remember eating anything.

Eventually, I started setting myself little goals, like getting out of bed at a certain time, or showering and getting dressed before breakfast. Eating breakfast was another goal. Going to the shops before lunchtime. Rationing myself to a certain amount of television. I think the first ration was five hours. Doing some sort of cleaning task. Half an hour of practice with my voice tapes. Spending an hour in the garden topping up my tan. I know it doesn't sound like a lot, but believe me, it was as much as I could do back then. If you thought you found me in a bad way in November when you came back again (I know, I saw the look on your face) you should have seen me before when I was hardly functioning.

And now I'm working. I'm actually going out to work! Another couple of weeks and I will even get paid for it.

Love from
Lydia

4 October 1998

Dear Lawrence,

I've just read the last couple of letters through, and I can really see how far I've come. Sometimes it has been one step forward, two steps back. I think you told me to expect that. You do think of everything, don't you?

When you left me in Gravelton that was another shock to the system. Once I was in the States, I was supposed to begin my life. You prodded me, gently as always, in the right direction. Go and talk to the neighbors. Look for jobs in the local newspaper. Get back to some sort of exercise. I'm afraid I didn't do any of those things.

What did I do? I bought a load of novels (you know, my usual kind) and I read and read. I walked past the school gates, morning and afternoon, just to hear the chatter of children. In the evenings I watched television or stared in the mirror, trying to see if I was recognizable from any angle, in any light, with my hair a particular way.

One or two people came over and introduced themselves. When I heard the click of the garden gate I'd panic. As if I was about to be flushed out. We'd have a little chat and then they'd go and I wouldn't be relieved, I'd be . . . flat.

I was invited to a Christmas party and everyone was very polite and friendly but they weren't exactly queuing up to speak to me. My first party in my new life and I'm not even belle of the ball!

I did get quite friendly with a couple of women. Sometimes they invited me over for dinner with their husbands and children. I think they felt sorry for me.

In the local grocery store they were advertising for a sales assistant. I thought maybe I could do that. It can't be hard to learn how to work a cash register. I decided I'd go in the next day and ask about the job, but when I got there I couldn't summon the courage. I turned around and went home.

I had a hunch, though, that if I moved to the city things would just turn up—opportunities. I was right, wasn't I? Alicia came along. Skin Deep came along. You should see me at the salon. Alicia's clients have started asking for me!

Better get my beauty sleep.

Your Lydia

5 October 1998

Dear Lawrence,

I am making strides, aren't I? You taught me a lot of things about how to cope. Lots of practical stuff. Sometimes I found it irritating, because I liked to think I knew it all.

All the household finances—I'm managing very well now. Honestly, I am. I write it all down like you told me to. But I still had more to learn. You told me to budget for the monthly bills. I thought you meant the grocery shopping and the telephone. I suppose you did, but it was quite a surprise when the first bill came for the electricity. I don't know what I imagined before—that the electricity came with the house? That it was free? You walk into a room and switch on the light in KP and nobody ever tells you how much it costs. When I walk out of a room now I switch off the light. You see, a whole new me!

Your semiqualified citizen,
Lydia

15 October 1998

Dear Lawrence,

I need your disapproval like I need a rash on my face. Take your stupid raised eyebrows and shove them. Go on, back off, go away. I'm not listening.

And do not tell me to calm down.

Lydia

16 November 1998

Dear Lawrence,

No, I haven't been sulking. I just haven't felt like writing to you. Either way, it's silly. When I write to you, I'm writing to a dead person. When I don't write to you, you still don't go away.

I've moved. I lost two months' rent that way, but I don't care. I didn't want to be in Charlotte any longer. Yes, I did fall out with Alicia, since you ask. Not that it's any of your business. I'm making a fresh start. I'm committing myself to it. You'll see. This time it will be different. I'm not letting myself get sucked down ever again.

Polite and friendly but a little bit aloof. That's the way I'm going to be from now on. I'm glad I have your approval. Thank you.

My love, as always,
Lydia

18 November 1998

Dear Lawrence,

Guess what I did today. I went to Mark Twain's boyhood house. It's about an hour's drive from where I'm living now, and it's been turned into a museum. I haven't read any of his books. I'll bet you read them all, because you've read everything. Those books that you gave me got lost in a move. The removal company lost a box. I gave them hell, of course, but it didn't bring the box back.

I went on a riverboat cruise on the Mississippi in the afternoon. So beautiful. I think I'm going to like it here. It was time for a complete change, and I didn't much care where I went really, but I have a good feeling about my new home. I made a good decision, didn't I?

Your Lydia

20 November 1998

Dear Lawrence,

The house I'm renting is one-story, brick, two bedrooms, in what they call a "ranch style." It's not the prettiest house ever but it's clean and tidy and fine.

The neighbors are quiet and respectful, and you can set your watch by the yellow school bus and the postman's van. Does it sound dull? I think I could definitely be friends with Maggie, and Liza Beth (not Elizabeth, thank you). Next door there is a Mormon family, the Petersons, who called on me after I'd been here for a week or so, all dressed in their Sunday best. If Mr. Peterson has a second or third wife (how many are they allowed?) he didn't bring her around. Only one wife and five children. He said if I had any fixing up that needed doing he'd be glad to help. That's sweet, isn't it?

I've done some impossible things in my time, haven't I, Lawrence? I know

I've said this to you already—after the first date we went on, I told my friends I was going to marry the Prince of Wales. Well, it turned out to be no idle boast. Then I did the impossible again and divorced him. And now—living an ordinary life. Without being totally miserable. That's what I want. Can it be beyond me to achieve such a thing? Sometimes it still seems like a distant dream.

In all my dark hours, when I could scream and howl, I find myself turning to you. When I swam out that night, one year, two months, and ten days ago, maybe I wasn't in my right mind. It wasn't only a folly but a kind of atrocity I committed. How can I live with that? By reassuring myself that you, sane, sensible, careful, rational Lawrence, didn't tell me that it couldn't be done. That it shouldn't be done. I have more faith in your judgment than I have in mine.

Maybe it's time for me to stop writing these letters. I should really be standing on my own two feet by now, shouldn't I?

Affectionately yours,
Lydia

25 November 1998

Dear Lawrence,

You thought I'd never be able to see the boys again. Does it feel good to be right? Does it? How smug are you feeling now?

I'll never be able to bring them to me. The idea is monstrous. You knew that. You should have made me see. I relied on you and you let me down. Why didn't you make me see?

Lydia

27 November 1998

Dear Lawrence,

Less than a month until Christmas. The shops (the stores, as I call them now) are full of decorations and fairy lights. My second Christmas. I wonder if I will be on my own again this year. I should be used to it by now. They weren't letting me have the boys anyway, were they?

I was a bit sharp with you in my last letter. That's only the tip of the iceberg. There's not a day, not an hour, when I'm not battling to keep it down. Yes, it's always about my boys but I can't write about them.

Maybe there will be a time, when they have children of their own (that's what I keep thinking) when they would be able to understand. I have to believe that. They will come to me and I will explain. They'll forgive me, won't they?

I know it can't be soon. I damaged them once and I can't risk damaging them again. I have to be very, very sure. I have to wait.

I'm glad I can still talk to you. You're the one person who never abandoned me. Sometimes I felt the boys had abandoned me. I know they didn't. But those feelings came up. Have I shocked you? No, you already knew.

Yours in admiration,
Lydia

3 December 1998

Dear Lawrence,

I have spent the entire last week in a lather. Somehow I convinced myself that Maggie knew. I was having coffee one morning with her and Liza Beth and Elsa Peterson, and Elsa said, "How long did you say you've lived in the US, Lydia?" and Maggie said, "Lydia's quite mysterious when it comes to her past." She winked at me. I totally froze. I mean, that's the first time someone's said something like that. And the wink! Why wink like that unless you know something?

I glossed it over. But I kept thinking about other little comments she's made. Like, one time, she said I was very maternal, a natural with her kids, and she kept asking about how much time I'd spent around children. I practically had my bags packed. For five nights straight I didn't sleep at all. Joe Peterson came over to mend the kitchen tap that was dripping (he's been a good neighbor and friend) and he said, "Lydia, you look all tuckered out." I cried and cried. He sat me down at the kitchen table and we had a sort of heart-to-heart. I've been in desperate need of that. You can't imagine how hard it is, not having a single friend in the world.

You're thinking it can't have been much of a heart-to-heart because there's so much I have to hide. Well, for once, Lawrence, you are plain wrong. There was plenty I could talk about. Like how it's difficult to be a woman living alone, how I hardly know anyone in the neighborhood, how my marriage never stood a chance, how I don't know what to do with my life now that it is entirely mine, to do with whatever I like. Joe is a very easy person to talk to, very patient, very kind. By the time we'd finished talking I had calmed down. Maggie came around the next morning to ask if I'd like to help with the costumes for the school Christmas play. Of course she hasn't a clue. I'm going to do some sewing. I haven't done any for such a long time.

Isn't it astonishing that even though I'm nobody now, people still think I'm worth knowing?

I think that eventually my boys could be proud of me. What do you think? Maybe all three of you will be proud of me.

With my love,
Lydia

6 December 1998

Dear Lawrence,

I got cracking with the costumes straightaway. Three outfits for three wise men out of three old sheets. Not exactly haute couture but I made a tidy job of them. Maggie's coming round later with the next batch to be sewn, the shepherds. I know this is a big leap to make, but perhaps I will end up doing something professionally after all. Designing dresses, working in fashion. You did say I have all sorts of experience that I'll be able to put to good use. You're the fourth wise man.

Joe popped over last night and we had a lovely chat again. He's offered to tidy up the yard for me, it's running a bit wild. I said I'd pay him, but he wouldn't hear of it. People can be so kind when you least expect it.

I always felt my grandmother's presence, even after she left this earth. People scoffed when I used a medium to contact her. You never did, but now I do think that was a bit silly. I can talk to you without help from anyone.

Your Lydia

12 December 1998

Dear Lawrence,

Looks like I'll be on my own again for Christmas. No one's speaking to me. Not Maggie, not Liza Beth, obviously not Elsa Peterson. I felt like going round there and saying, look Elsa, I don't want your husband, you can have him. Why did he have to tell her? He said, "Lydia, it would have been on my conscience." So now he's told her it's all okay for everyone except me.

I have to get away from this place. Don't expect me to stay here after all this.

139

Have I done something so very bad? Is it always me in the wrong? Why are you blaming me, and not him? Am I the one person in the entire world who never deserves to be happy?

Lydia

30 January 1999

Dear Lawrence,

I'm not even sure that you care where I am or what I'm doing so I haven't bothered to write to you. For your information, I've moved again, but it's not so very different here. Was my life really worse than this before I dived off the boat? Tell me that. In what way is this an improvement?

I don't know. Maybe it's better because I've stopped caring. If you can stop caring then you can't be hurt. In the morning I wait for the day to end. After that I wait for the night to end. They always do. The next day and night always come around. You can rely on that.

I can hardly hear you, Lawrence. Speak, if you have anything to say.

I am still your Lydia

25 February 1999

Dear Lawrence,

I can't write down a scream, can I? I can't write down endless blank hours. Write it down. Write it down, you tell me. But what? Here I am. I exist. I'm making these marks on the page. I must exist. I am no more alive than you.

Talk to me.

Lydia

14 March 1999

Dear Lawrence,

If I could keep the vomiting down to once or twice a day that wouldn't be too awful. You know, at my worst it was six or seven times in one day. I'm nowhere near as bad as that. It's not as though I'm harming anyone.

You are really very faint. You haven't left me, have you?

Love as always,
Lydia

27 March 1999

Dear Lawrence,

Every day for the past month I have wanted to write you a proper, long letter and tell you everything. I have all these thoughts swirling around. Then when I sit down there's nothing. I'm all empty again. I go and eat. You know what I do after that. It's getting worse. What shall I do, Lawrence? I want it to stop.

With love,
Lydia

11 April 1999

Dear Lawrence,

I left my life. I left my children. I left everything. And I left you. I let you die without me there. How could I have done that? I could only think of one person. So I left everything but I took that one person with me. I thought I was leaving her behind too.

With my useless but eternal love,
Lydia

14 June 1999

Dear Lawrence,

You know I've moved on once more. Another fresh start, a new beginning. I thought you would be skeptical but you seemed to approve. That makes a difference, you know. I feel you watching over me again. Always when I am walking I feel you near. So I walk and walk.

You were with me when I made an appointment with the craniosacral thera-pist a few days after I moved in. "Ma'am," you said, "if I may be so bold as to venture an observation—you have tried all of these therapies before." I told you to be quiet, of course. And to stop calling me ma'am. But I didn't go. I canceled the appointment, and instead I went for a walk. I have to say you were right. It is surprisingly difficult to be angry with anyone, even with yourself, when you are surrounded by trees, trees, and more trees. I always hated the country. My husband's mistress was mistress of our country house. "Their" country house, I should say. Balmoral was bloody awful, as you know. Endless jigsaws and shooting at animals. I couldn't stand it.

Now it's just me and the trees, and I can walk without wondering where the photographers are and where the pictures will appear. My legs are stiff at the end of the day. I am getting muscles in my calves. Swimming helps stretch it all out. I toyed with joining a health club but it was very expensive, and I'm not touching the money you said to keep aside for when I'm ready to buy a house of my own. The municipal pool is only crowded at weekends.

I have to think about getting a job. The money for bills and food and rent won't last forever. Thank you for reminding me.

Your devoted,
Lydia

23 June 1999

Dear Lawrence,

I don't know how long this calm will last. I don't trust it yet. But I'll carry on doing what I'm doing. If nothing else I'm going to be very fit. I find myself looking forward to the day: walk, swim, walk, that's all. I don't have to drag myself out of bed.

In hope,
Lydia

2 July 1999

Dear Lawrence,

I have been thinking it all through, over and over, on my walks. I changed everything, so I thought everything would be different. And nothing was. Not really. Not different enough, anyway. I always had someone to blame before. I've run out of culprits now.

Sometimes I don't think at all when I'm walking. I look at the colors of the leaves. I look at the way the moss shines on a stone. Or I find myself squatting down, studying creatures on the forest floor. Today I watched two huge stag beetles locking antlers. Then I went for a swim in the afternoon. I was starving this evening. It's good to eat when you're hungry. I'd forgotten that. In the last month I've only had four episodes. Not perfect, but a lot better.

Thank you for bearing with me.

Your Lydia

6 August 1999

Dear Lawrence,

You can't escape from yourself, but you can learn how to live with yourself. You can try, anyway. If it's possible for someone else to teach you how, I never found that person. And goodness knows I looked hard enough.

I just read through all my letters. Still demanding, aren't I? No more, I promise. I've kept them all in a box and I'm going to hang on to them. Maybe at some point in the future I'll look at them again.

Truly yours,
Lydia

30 August 1999

Dear Lawrence,

I'm going to stop writing these letters now. I can choose what to put in a letter and what to leave out. As though you can only see what I want you to see. A letter just gives you a tiny bit of a person. I'd like to give you more than that, my whole life as a letter to you.

There will be days when I don't make you proud. I hope they will be few and far between.

I always knew when I fell short of your standards, Lawrence, even when you pretended to approve. You did that too often. You were too kind.

There's that little lift in your eyebrows. I know what you're thinking. Tomorrow, she'll be writing again to tell me off for something. That's okay, Lawrence. Maybe I won't be able to change. I might manage it, though, if I put my heart into it. I nearly said, if I put my mind to it. I'd rather count on my heart, wayward though it has been sometimes.

I see you, Lawrence. I know you see me.

Your ever-loving
Lydia

Chapter Seventeen

When Wednesday came around again Lydia helped Amber change the window display. They lifted down the four mannequins and stripped them and dismembered their arms. The mannequins bore their indignities with Mona Lisa smiles.

"I was thinking I should put the evening gowns in," said Amber. "But maybe all four would be too much."

"No, go for it," said Lydia. "Let's make a splash. How many have you sold?"

Amber smiled ruefully. "One. Plus the one you insisted on paying for."

"Let's get to work. We'll have them lining up and down the block."

They tried the peach chiffon first but the tone didn't work with the mannequin's coloring.

"No," said Lydia. "Not unless we give her an instant tan."

They took it off and replaced it with the blue taffeta. Lydia stepped onto the platform and Amber handed up the mannequin. The dress needed pinning in at the back of the waist, and when she had done that Lydia whisked around to the front to check the alignment across the collarbone.

Mrs. Deaver from the drugstore waved as she passed by at a pigeon-chested strut. Across the road, Sonia from the florist added pails of yellow and white chrysanthemums to the display outside her store. She wiped her hands on her apron and stretched her back and then leaned against the doorpost, her movements as languid as a cat's. Kindergarten had let out for the day and mothers and children paddled casually, stopping and starting, between the lakes of sun that fell between the buildings and the cool pools of shadow in front of the stores. They eddied generally in the direction of the bakery, from which the children emerged with a swoosh of sugar-fueled high hopes.

Albert Street was wide and generous. A grass verge extended the sidewalk on the east and the road itself was wide enough to turn full circle with a horse and cart. The town hall crowned the north end with erect Georgian symmetry, and the stores that mingled with the houses bore fascias and awnings in tasteful cottage-garden hues. The buildings, all clapboard or half-timbered, had air around them. It was the town's main street but it wasn't squeezed. It was a street with room to breathe.

Lydia looked to see if Mr. Mancuso would emerge from his bungalow. He liked to sit out on his little steel tube stool at this time. There he was, beaming as always, as if he couldn't believe his luck in living through another day. He was getting so frail now that perhaps there wouldn't be too many more. He set up the stool at the bottom of his stoop, and when a child stopped to have his cheek pinched Mr. Mancuso nearly fell off his stool in delight.

Six weeks to go, thought Lydia, until Albert Street put on its finery for the annual fête. She was looking forward to it. She smiled to herself. There had been a time when she could scarcely stay in one city, one country, one continent, for more than a day or two without being burned by the apparent certainty that she was in the wrong place. She'd step off the jet and be wondering if she had better cut short the trip.

Now she lived here round the seasons, three full cycles so far, through the calendar of annual events, and the daily parade, and she let herself (though she smiled at it) be cradled by the quiet rhythms of this place.

"What shall we do next?" said Amber. "The green silk?"

"Yes. Now give me the progress report."

"Phil?" Amber checked herself in the mirror and smoothed down her skirt. "We had dinner, it was nice. I thought he'd call yesterday but he didn't. Do you think he'll call today?"

"Oh, so you like him? You didn't sound too sure before."

Amber groaned. "You're right. I wasn't."

"And now you are?"

Amber arranged herself on the fainting couch. "A week or so ago I'd have said I wasn't really interested. He's nice, good manners, bit short, bit of a potbelly, not particularly handsome but nice eyes. The kids have met him—only in passing, because he lives so close, but I think they'd get along okay. He's a dentist. He talks about teeth a lot."

"Wow," said Lydia. "That's a big subject."

"I know!"

"If you like him, you like him."

"A week ago I could take it or leave it. I was thinking it might be . . . a little fling, maybe." Amber got off the couch to help with the next mannequin. "Honestly? Last week I'd have said he was nice but kinda boring. This week? If he doesn't call me, I'll die."

Lydia laughed. "And if he does you'll run away to Acapulco with him."

"Oh, why am I always like this?" said Amber. "I *know* he's not exactly thrilling but when he calls I'll pee my pants."

"I think Mrs. Deaver sells incontinence pads," said Lydia.

"Oh my God," said Amber. "Seriously, I've got to start doing my pelvic-floor exercises more regularly."

"You know I'll babysit for you," said Lydia.

"How's it going with Carson? Are you two good?"

"Hang it," said Lydia. "This shoulder won't sit right. Think we need to get the steamer out."

"I'll find it," said Amber, but she stayed where she was. "Are you in love?"

Lydia shrugged. "We're doing fine," she said. "I do tend to clam up on him though."

"Guess you haven't known him that long. I mean, it took you a while to tell me everything."

She hadn't told Amber everything. But she had let her suppose, and those suppositions had turned into facts as far as Amber was concerned.

Amber said, "Do you think that . . ." She stopped and composed her hair, and then spoke in a rush. "Do you think that your ex would actually try to find you? I know you don't like to talk about him. And what would happen if he did? What would happen if he showed up right now?"

"It wouldn't be him," said Lydia. "It would be someone else."

"Like a private detective?" said Amber.

"You know," said Lydia, slowly, "I don't think anyone's looking. That's what I think. I wanted to disappear. I couldn't stand it anymore. And when you do that you always feel like you've got to keep looking behind you. The rest of the world moves on. I've got to move on too. I've got to stop being such a numskull."

"You're not a numskull," said Amber.

"I am. I failed all my exams. Twice. I left school at sixteen without a single qualification."

"That doesn't mean anything. Means you had your head in the clouds, maybe."

"Right," said Lydia. In her old life she could never shake the feeling that she was an absolute dunce. Her husband saw to that early on. He was the intellectual, and she was the brainless clotheshorse. She could read a briefing for a charity meeting and remember all the facts and figures she needed, but she put the confidence on like a suit. Underneath she was butt naked.

She'd still say she was thick as a plank but she didn't mean it anymore. If she'd put her mind to it she could have tackled Lawrence's books. She wasn't educated. Nobody had cared how she did at school, least of all her. Maybe she was just a late starter, but she felt ready for something more than the drugstore novels now.

"Oh," said Amber, "on your birthday, I'm getting the girls together, throwing a little tea party for you after work."

"Thank you," said Lydia. "Can we fill one teapot up with wine? And I've got to tell Tevis, the weekend straight afterwards, I can't make it to the cabin. Carson's taking me to the ballet in New York."

"New York? Ballet? Shut up! We'll do the cabin another weekend. Two birthday weekends instead of one. Will you wear the gown?"

"Absolutely," said Lydia. She wouldn't. It would be over the top.

It wasn't her real birthday. But that's what it said on her driver's license and passport. There was her real birthday and her official birthday. She had known long ago that she would never be Queen, but she had never thought she might end up with two birthdays just like her mother-in-law.

Queen of Hearts. That's what she'd said she wanted to be. How grandiose that sounded now.

A couple of customers came in and Amber sold a gray shift dress and a pale blue cashmere vest. The window display was much admired, and Sonia and several of the neighboring storekeepers came in to say as much. Mrs. Jackson rapped on the window and when Amber walked over from the counter to see what was up, Mrs. Jackson pointed at the mannequins and mouthed "Look," through the glass.

"As if we might not have seen them," said Amber.

"I think she likes it," said Lydia.

Mrs. Jackson bowled through the door. "Oh," she said, "look at those! They are beautiful! If I were five years younger . . ."

Lydia knew not to look at Amber or they'd set each other giggling right away.

"How's Otis getting on, Mrs. Jackson?"

Mrs. Jackson fluttered her hands. "I've said it before and I'll say it again: I'm a martyr to that dog. Couldn't live without him of course."

She set down her shopping and slipped off her shoes and sat down on the couch. She wore heels even for a trip to the grocery store. Her bare legs were mottled with an excellent array of colors, like the inside of a mussel shell.

"Lydia, I've got a guest staying with me whom I'd like you to meet."

"Forget about matchmaking, Mrs. Jackson," said Amber. "Lydia's spoken for."

"That wasn't my intention, I do assure you." Mrs. Jackson had been a leading lady in Kensington's amateur dramatics society. It was a source of great regret to her, as she had previously informed Lydia, that the society had died—of natural causes, if you can call everyone spending their evenings sitting in front of the television natural. She had to make do now with the impromptu stage and scripts of life. "Lydia is dating Carson Connors. I do keep up with the news," she said, as if she had gleaned the information from CNN.

"Who's the guest?" said Lydia.

"A gentleman from England," said Mrs. Jackson. "And I've told him all about you. Oh, yes, I said, we're quite multicultural around here. Lydia's as British as they come, but we've taken her as one of our own."

"Thank you, Mrs. Jackson," said Lydia. Amber disappeared into the stockroom, apparently choking on a cough. "When would you like me to come?"

"I'm ever so busy this week, it's spring cleaning. I turn all my mattresses once a year, pull the armoires out, all the pelmets come down, everything. I've told him I've made an exception and he can stay, and I won't even ask him to change rooms. He's creative, you see."

"Yes, I see," said Lydia.

"So come next week, one afternoon."

"I don't work Wednesday afternoons. I could come then. Will he still be with you?" Mrs. Jackson's guests tended to stay only a day or two.

"He likes the quiet," said Mrs. Jackson. "I don't disturb him, so of course he will. Stay, I mean. Anyway, I thought, I must invite Lydia. It's not often we get a Brit, is it? You'll want to talk about . . ." She waved a bejeweled hand.

"Yes," said Lydia. She'd lived here three years without hearing another British accent. She wondered what had brought him here.

"You'll make him feel at home," declared Mrs. Jackson. "It's a lonely calling, isn't it?"

"I'm sure you make all your guests feel at home, Mrs. Jackson."

Mrs. Jackson received the compliment with a regal incline of the head. "So it's all arranged," she said as she inveigled her feet back into her unwelcoming shoes. "I'll make my famous scones."

Amber came out of the stockroom after she'd heard the door open and close. "I couldn't keep it in," she said. "I had to go and laugh into the leftover winter coats. I hope she didn't hear me."

"I don't think so. Have you had her famous scones?"

"Naturally," said Amber. "And they're pretty good. Who's the mystery guest, anyway? Did she say? Is he from London?"

"No, she just said he's an artist or something. I didn't want to ask too much."

"In case you set her off?"

"Something like that."

"When she said, we're so multicultural, that's when I had to go in the back room."

"She's a sweetheart, though, isn't she? We shouldn't make fun," said Lydia. An English boarder at the Kensington bed-and-breakfast. The first, as far as she knew, in three years. There could be any number of reasons . . . Mrs. Jackson had had a Japanese guest last year.

Amber shrugged, and started tidying up for the end of the day. "I know it seems like a silly idea of hers, like, why would either of you want to meet just because you're from over there. But it might turn out you have something in common. You never know."

When she began her lengths Rufus kept pace with her for the first dozen or so, urging her on like a cox from the tiled shore. Then he wandered away to look for raccoons in the undergrowth. He loved frightening himself with them.

Lydia swam a hundred lengths, trod water for a few minutes, and then went back to a steady crawl. She lost herself in the movement, or rather the movement became lost to her. As if she had ceased to push against the water and she were still as it flowed around her.

She had forgotten to bring a towel out and she shivered as she dripped through the kitchen. Her cell phone had a new text message from Carson. He'd had to go out of town on a claim for a couple of days. She texted him back and went upstairs to shower.

If he brought up the idea again, maybe she would move in with him, or he could move in with her. Would she ever tell him everything? If she was even thinking about it then it wasn't impossible. Lawrence would be urging caution. Actual urging was never his style. A significant pause, a quick twiddle of the thumbs, maybe the telltale eyebrows a little raised. He'd seen her lovers come and go, seen the end of each affair in its beginning. But Lawrence stayed the distance. Lawrence was always there.

Chapter Eighteen

No one, Grabowski decided, would voluntarily incarcerate themselves in such tedium. If it was really her then she must bitterly regret
the position in which she'd put herself. Lydia went from home to
work, to the grocery, and either home again or to her boyfriend's
house. Grabowski followed her in the car. She made regular stops at
the bakery, the boutique, the drugstore, and sometimes ate out at the
Italian restaurant. The boredom would be intense. To live life at dazzling breakneck speed and then end up in this endless drag of to and
fro would be unbearable.

Just as she had the previous Wednesday, Lydia left work at lunchtime
and strode over to her car. Grabowski, on his knees behind the trash
cans, had his longest lens trained through the gap. For a moment when
she turned her head straight toward him he thought the game was up.
She got into the car, and when she pulled out onto the road, Grabber
hoofed it back to the Pontiac and followed at a relaxed distance. There
was no danger of losing her. In the old days he had come to predict her
patterns, erratic though they were, had developed an instinct for her
moods, her swings, and where they would lead her, to the therapist, the
astrologer, or the airport. Now the choices were minimal. When she
parked and went to the bakery he stayed in his car and waited to make
sure he was right. She headed straight for the clothing store.

He already had shots of her in this location and there was nothing
more to be gained so he went back to the bed-and-breakfast.

Mrs. Jackson caught him on the way in. "John," she said, "how are
the juices? I won't keep you a moment, just come into the parlor."

The sitting room was a graveyard of teak and rosewood furniture, scattered with faded tributes of floral cushions. In the back corner, Mrs. Jackson's husband dozed in his planter's chair with his feet up on a carved giant turtle. Otis raced over the ottomans and couches, snaking back and forth like a balloon that had been blown up and let go. Grabowski nearly sat on the damn animal.

"It's coming, Mrs. Jackson, the work is coming along," he said. Mr. Jackson was pretty much deaf, so there was no need to keep their voices down.

"Splendid. I won't ask to look at even a page or a single photo," said Mrs. Jackson, which meant that she would pretty soon. "Even though," she added, "it would be a delight to see which vistas you've captured in our little town."

"I appreciate that," said Grabber. "You're a very sensitive lady."

Mrs. Jackson primped her lips self-deprecatingly. "Do you remember I was telling you about Lydia?"

Grabowski's cock twitched. Was it possible he had fallen into some kind of sexual obsession without even realizing it? That the rest was bullshit, that it was all about how much he had fancied her in that first second when she looked up from stroking the dachshund on the sidewalk?

"Lydia?" he said.

"The English lady," said Mrs. Jackson. "Works with the dogs."

"It's coming back to me," said Grabowski. Mr. Jackson snorted in his sleep.

Mrs. Jackson tutted at her husband. Grabowski wondered if he ever moved from that chair. He seemed to be there every day. Maybe Mrs. Jackson dusted around him. She dusted every day because of her allergies. Perhaps she dusted her husband as well.

"I've invited her over," said Mrs. Jackson, "next Wednesday, for my famous scones. She'd love to meet you, that's what she said. Chat about England and all that. It's not often she gets the chance."

"That'd be lovely, Mrs. Jackson. Have you fixed a time?"

In his room he uploaded more photos and sorted through what he'd got. Yesterday she'd had sunglasses on but today he'd got some clear shots of her face. He checked and rechecked the eyes. Since he'd noticed how uncannily similar they were, he'd spent hours overlaying photos, checking the exact size and shape and spacing. Most of all he had scrutinized the slender broken band of green, tiny flecks lacing around the right pupil. In a single shot it might have been a trick of the light. The next day he couldn't get the angle—it had to be fully frontal—and the day after that her face was in shadow and he knew from experience that the color wouldn't show up then. After that his bad luck broke and he got the shots he wanted. It was there all right.

What did that prove, though? What had he got? And what would happen when Lydia came around for the famous scones? He had to know what he was doing by then. Either that or avoid the situation. Be called away suddenly on urgent business.

If his theory was correct, then how could he prove it? You could identify a person by their iris scans, but that was no use without an initial record with which to compare them, and it wasn't as though he had an iris scanner in his briefcase. What about fingerprints? Fabulous work, Grabowski. Get her prints off the teacup next week and then all you need is her criminal record, you idiot. DNA, dental records, whatever. The whole thing was pie in the sky.

She couldn't have vanished without an accomplice. Maybe Mrs. Jackson's appearance belied her history and she was actually a secret service operative, trained in espionage and subterfuge, and she had arranged the escape. Perhaps she was planning to lace the scones with arsenic and dispose of his body in the river. It was about as credible as anything he'd thought of so far.

He closed his laptop and headed for the door before deciding it would be safer to take it with him. His room bolted only from the inside. Daft really, not as though they couldn't be stolen out of a car. But cars had, for so many years, served as his office that he felt more secure with his work stowed in them.

He found the bar in Gains and ordered a beer with a bourbon chaser. At this time in the evening the construction workers had already moved on or gone home. There were a few couples at the tables, some youngsters at the pool table with jeans belted under their butts, and in the booth that ran along the back wall there was a party of women, soccer moms on a night out. If they were anything like Cathy they'd be wearing their spandex underpants and best bras for each other, and when they got home to their husbands they'd let it all hang out and wear an old T-shirt to bed.

Grabowski tried to see himself in the mirror behind the bar but it was so densely shelved and stacked with liquor bottles that he could only see one eye and one side of his hair, streaked with gray. He was going to drink his way through the three different bourbons and then as many as possible of the eight different single malts. He ordered another round. The barman sliced lemons and stacked up the slices in a glass. He made up dishes of chips and olives and stowed them under the bar. Busy-work, thought Grabber. The way to get through a shift without dying of boredom. He had to get out of this place before he went insane.

A warm wind blew a woman through the door. She pulled up a stool two down from Grabowski.

"Scotch on the rocks," she said. "Don't gimme the list," she said when the barman opened his mouth. "I don't care."

She wore a fake fur jacket despite the season, and it probably never got that cold. Her legs were longer than a marathon. Her ankles looked too thin in those platforms.

"I been drinking here two years," she said to no one in particular. "Do I still have to explain myself?" She raised her glass. There were lines of dirt beneath her fingernails.

"Seen enough?" she said to Grabowski. "Want me to strip?"

"Didn't mean to stare," he said, looking away and then back.

The woman laughed.

"Well," she said, "not a whole lot to look at around here. A man can be forgiven."

"If I buy you a drink, how about that?"

She shrugged off the jacket in what seemed to be a gesture of acceptance. Grabowski moved to the stool next to her.

"So, what is it that you do, Mr. . . ."

"John. I'm a photographer."

"Is that a fact? And what do you photograph?"

"People. I photograph people."

"So you do portraits. And weddings? Studio shots of families to use on their holiday cards?"

"You don't sound impressed." She was attractive, in a been-around-the-block kind of way. She wore her dress short and her blond hair long, tied up high off the back of her swan neck. Her hands were grubby, like a child's, but he could see now that it was paint beneath her fingernails.

"You do what you gotta do," she said. "Where you from?"

"From out of town," said Grabowski.

She laughed again. "No way."

"What about you?"

"I move around," she said. "Been here two years, but I'll be moving on."

"I meant, what do you do?"

"I paint, John. That's what I do." She tapped her glass and the barman filled it up.

"And what do you paint?"

"People," she said.

"Portraits?" said Grabowski. "Family portraits to hang over the mantelpiece?"

"Ouch," she said. "Guess I deserved that."

She lived on the second floor of a two-family house in a huddled street where the garages spilled out their storeroom innards onto the driveways and the cars were all parked in the road. It took her a couple of minutes to stalk around the living room, turning on all the lamps. None of them gave out more light than a candle, and many had been draped with scarves, which struck Grabowski as a fire hazard.

Grabowski asked to use the bathroom. He splashed his face with water and thought about washing his cock but decided that would be tempting fate. He avoided looking in the mirror in case he didn't like what he saw. The light in the bathroom was the inverse of the sitting room and it would be unforgiving.

He still didn't know her name.

"Hey," she said, when he returned. "Would you like to see some of my work? My studio's in the back."

He didn't want to see her work. If it was terrible that would make him feel bad.

"Yes," he said, "maybe afterwards."

She laughed. "Afterwards. Okay, I see. You wanna get down to business."

"Not if you don't want to," he said, and suddenly he didn't want to anymore. He thought she was nice, he liked that she was lippy, liked the way she squared up to him. But the whole thing was sad and weary. It wasn't her fault, though, and if he left now that would be rude.

"Relax," she said. "We're just chilling here."

In bed she closed her eyes while he worked steadily. He couldn't tell if she was enjoying it or not. He felt the sweat gather at the small of his back and roll down his flanks. He studied her face, she could have been sleeping, with the smallest smile on her lips. Open your eyes, he told her. She opened them. Look at me. She held his gaze for a short while, then closed her eyes again and wrapped her legs around him.

"Was it okay?" he asked afterward.

She was cross-legged on the bed, rolling a joint on a magazine. She said, "I came, didn't I?"

"But was it, you know, good?"

She laughed and lit the joint and took a deep inhale. "So what do you want, a medal?"

"Sorry. It's been a while."

"My art sucks," she said. She was smiling and looking away, and rubbing at her thigh.

"No," he said, "it doesn't. Why don't we go and look at it? I'd like to see."

"Fuck off," she said. "Don't patronize me."

Grabowski sighed internally. It was a method he'd developed with

Cathy, where he let his breath seep back into his bones. Women were liable to go berserk if you sighed when they were working themselves up.

"Don't put yourself down," he said.

"I'm not," she said, and her face crumpled. "It just sucks, that's all."

She switched on the television and they watched it sitting up in bed, like an old couple. He was weary to the bone. He didn't even know if she wanted him to stay. If he asked then she'd take that as a sign of his insensitivity, because he should be able to tell what she wanted, although they had only just met.

"You can go if you want," she said, as if she had read his mind. Her eyes were red from the weed. She was older than he'd thought at first.

"Perhaps it's best," he said.

When he was dressed he said, "I'll call you."

"Right," she said. "You don't even know my name."

"I'm sorry," he said, and he meant it. He wasn't sure what it was that he'd done wrong but he felt almost overwhelmed with sadness.

"Get out," she said, and turned the volume up.

He had only just fallen asleep when he was woken by his cell phone. He groped for it in the dark.

"Christ, it's the middle of the night, Nick."

"I don't know what gave me the idea, but I thought this was something urgent."

"Yeah, okay," said Grabowski, turning on the light. "What have you got?"

Nick cleared his throat, the way he always did before giving his report. "Lydia Snaresbrook is not a common name. I only found three potentials. One was born in Stirling in 1954, bit outside your age range; the second was 1967, which was over the other side of the bracket, age-wise. The third was born around the right time, in 1962 in Wiltshire. Her parents are recorded as Mary Joanna Snaresbrook, housewife, and Joseph Renfrew Snaresbrook, banker and US citizen. So she's the one I worked on first. I haven't done the others yet. Thought you might want to hear this right away."

"I'm sure you've got your meter running," said Grabowski. Nick's information never came cheap. "So better get on with it."

"I couldn't turn anything up on her."

Grabowski waited. Nick wouldn't call in the middle of the night with nothing to tell.

"I couldn't find anything. Not a marriage certificate, driving license, parking ticket, credit record, not one damn thing."

"The lady vanishes," said Grabowski.

"So I checked the deaths register."

Grabowski held his breath.

"Lydia Snaresbrook was born on the twenty-fifth of April 1962. She died on the thirtieth April of the same year. A cot death at five days old."

Grabowski couldn't speak. He offered up a silent prayer of thanks.

"Grabber," said Nick. "Are you there?"

"I'm here."

"So what do you want me to do now? Want me to trace the other Lydias?"

"No. That's fine. That's good work. Figure out what I owe you and let me know."

"Was it helpful?"

"Yeah, it was helpful," said Grabber, trying to keep the excitement out of his voice. "I mean, it wraps it up."

"Okay, boss," said Nick. "Wraps what up?"

"It was nothing," said Grabowski. "Dead end. Listen, I'm going to get some sleep, but thanks for the call."

There was no way he could sleep, so he didn't even try. He went over the pictures that he had one more time. He paced the room. It was happening. This was really happening. The biggest scoop of his life. The biggest fucking scoop of anyone's life. And it was his.

It was his to fuck up. He had to get everything right. At four o'clock in the morning, when by rights he should have had a hangover, his head was clearer than it had been in years.

He didn't have to *prove* anything. Of course he didn't. All he had to know was that he wasn't being a total prick. He should have asked Nick to e-mail him copies of the birth and death certificates. He'd do that in the morning. American father on the birth certificate. Maybe whoever had planned all this for her had been able to procure a dual passport on the back of that.

There were other shots he needed to get. He didn't have any good ones of her with her boyfriend. Never the right angle from wherever he'd been hiding, on their tail. He knew how the piece would run: front page, six inside double-page spreads at least. As long as he knew what he knew, as long as he made the story stack up, the papers would print it. Actual proof wasn't necessary. The papers didn't need that when it was a story they wanted to run. They'd insinuate an affair between two celebrities out of no more than a kiss on the cheek. He knew how they'd do this. COULD THIS WOMAN BE . . . That's how the headlines would read. Ten years after her disappearance in mysterious circumstances, after crank sightings and bizarre assassination claims, could this small American town hold the secret to what really happened that fateful September day? In the spirit of inquiry and the public interest . . . They'd send the reporters and they'd turn up on her doorstep and by the time the news broke she'd have fled in the night, unless she could explain herself.

Grabowski went into the bathroom for a glass of water. He looked in the mirror. He rubbed his hand over his stubble. He checked his profile. A little heavy in the jowls but not bad. His hair was still thick, and if anything the gray suited him better than brown. Cathy used to tell him he had kind eyes, before she decided she hated him. He stared at them and wondered what was kind about them. He'd always thought they looked a little mournful himself.

What if he was wrong about Lydia?

Grabowski went and sat down on the bed and worked the rosary beads through his fingers.

He didn't have to prove anything. Only to himself, beyond all reasonable doubt. And there was only one way to do that.

Chapter Nineteen

Lydia found her rubber boots in the staff room and went to hose down the kennels. The volunteers had set up two grooming tables in the fenced grass run behind the yard and were working on the Kerry blue and a white-socked mongrel who had come in yesterday thatched with mud and twigs. The other dogs sprinted the length of the run or indulged in darting skirmishes or pottered amiably between the fence posts sniffing each one. The hose water hit the ground and sparkled where it sprayed up again. Lydia looked over at the far kennel where the pit bull was housed. He sat glumly at the wire door. After he'd bitten Topper on the foreleg he'd been condemned to solitary exercise.

Esther came out of the office. She wore her army fatigues and her work boots, with her gray hair tied up beneath a cap, and Lydia thought she looked distinguished, like an off-duty general.

The pit bull turned circles of delight as Esther approached. "Wouldn't it be great," Esther called back to Lydia, "if people were this pleased to see you every time you walked in the room? I only put him back in the kennel ten minutes ago." She opened the kennel door and received the dog's ministrations and slipped him a piece of basted bone from her pocket. She locked him back in.

Lydia turned off the hose and began sweeping down with a broom. "Well, it might get a little wearying in the end."

"You're right," said Esther. "Thing is, you'd know it was an act. But the dog's always genuine."

Lydia laughed. She wondered if she should tell Esther about her plan with the bracelet because now there was going to be a delay in getting the money. This morning she'd driven into the city and the first three jewelry stores she visited didn't deal in secondhand. The next two did usually but they weren't buying at the moment because the market, they said, was poor. They told her places she could send the bracelet that would pay her for the weight of the gold. Lydia knew that the inlaid garnets would be worth more than that. The last place she tried was interested but the guy who did their valuations was away on vacation. They told her to come back in around ten days.

"How long can we keep going," said Lydia, "if we don't get some more cash in?"

"We're not going down without a fight," said Esther. "I've arranged a personal overdraft. Something will turn up." She shrugged and dragged the hose to the next kennel.

Lydia decided not to say anything. She didn't know how much she would get for the bracelet, and how much it would solve.

"You ever get the sense that Rufus knows how you're feeling?" said Esther.

"Yes," said Lydia. "Guess that's me projecting onto him."

Esther scratched the back of her arm where she'd just caught it on the wire netting. She was forever covered in bruises and scrapes, as if she completed an assault course every day. "Maybe," she said, "but not necessarily. Dogs are more sensitive to humans than any other animal. If you hide a dog's toy and then look over to where you've hidden it, a dog will follow your gaze. No other animal can do that. Even a chimp can't do that, and they're supposed to be a whole lot smarter, whole lot closer to us."

"I'll start giving Rufus more credit, then," said Lydia. "By the way, I'm going out for a drink with the girls this evening if you'd like to come."

"Thanks," said Esther, "but I won't. I've got some bookkeeping to do tonight. See if I can squeeze some blood out of a stone."

They met at Dino's, the Italian restaurant, and got a table by the river, which was overhung with weeping willows. The water shone green and gold in the sun. The restaurant walls were covered in rustic hand-painted plates, and in the open kitchen the Mexican chefs threw and caught and stretched pizza dough in a kind of cabaret.

"Let's get prosecco," said Amber.

"Okay," said Tevis, "are we celebrating something?"

"Only life in general," said Amber.

"Wait a minute," said Tevis. "Here, take this crystal. No, just let it lie flat in your palm."

They all looked at the hexagonal stone on Amber's hand until Tevis obscured it by placing her palm a few inches above it.

"I'm getting a reading," said Tevis. "Yes . . . yes . . . got it. Amber's in love."

"I am not," said Amber, blushing.

"Amber," said Lydia, laughing, "you're not holding out on us?"

Amber pushed her bangs out of her eyes. "Well, I had another date."

Tevis set the crystal spinning on the table. "Did he come back to yours or did you go back to his?"

"Neither. We kissed on my front steps."

Tevis took off her jacket, rolled her shirt cuffs, and let down her hair, as if her Realtor's business-wear was too constricting for this conversation. "That's always the best part," she said. "Downhill all the way from here."

"Oh my God, I hope not," said Amber.

"I'm just kidding," said Tevis, giving Amber's hand a squeeze.

"It was great, though," said Amber.

"A dentist should know his way around a mouth," said Lydia.

"He does," said Amber. "You know, I think I could really fall for him."

"If you haven't already, you mean," said Lydia. She looked at Suzie, but Suzie seemed hardly to be listening. She was slowly shredding pieces off a paper napkin and rolling them between her fingers.

Amber groaned. "I wouldn't admit this to anyone but you guys. So today I found myself daydreaming, about Phil, of course. And I was imagining maybe I get trained as a dental hygienist and we go to work together every day, and maybe we don't get to talk that much because we'll be busy, but there's the lunchtimes . . . and, well, you know, I wrote the whole romance in my head."

Lydia, Tevis, and Suzie looked at each other. "Amber," said Tevis, "you are nuts. Do you know how dull that would actually be?"

"I know!" said Amber, squirming her shoulders.

"What about Closet?" said Lydia. "Where would that fit in?"

Tevis grew serious. "One step at a time, Amber. Treat it like a fling for now, don't run ahead of yourself, and certainly do not start thinking of your life in terms of his. Maybe he'll turn out to be the best thing that ever happened to you. Maybe he'll turn out to be a jerk. Don't go all dizzy over a kiss."

"Oh, I won't," said Amber, "not really. I've got my feet on the ground." She raised her glass to toast the fact, and give it some much-needed bolstering.

When Suzie came back from the restroom she sat down heavily in her chair, as if exhausted by the excursion.

"What is it?" said Lydia. "Are you okay?"

Suzie chewed on her bottom lip. Lydia saw that she had used concealer under her eyes. Perhaps she wasn't sleeping properly.

"I'm fine," said Suzie. "No, I'm not. I'm worried about Maya. The principal called me into school the other day."

"Mrs. Thesiger?" said Amber. "What did she want? I had to see her last year—remember Tyler and the graffiti in the bathroom business? She was very good about it, very calm. Is Maya in trouble now?"

"I wish she was," said Suzie. She forced a smile, a flash of teeth, their bold irregularity.

"Is it her grades?" said Tevis. "I wouldn't worry about that. She's a smart kid. She'll tune in when she's good and ready. Or when the teacher actually has something interesting to say."

"It's not that," said Suzie. "You remember how it was when you were in school, how all the kids banded together, kind of into categories? So at lunchtime you'd get the druggies sitting together, the jocks, the nerds?"

"The hippie types," said Tevis, shaking her auburn hair in front of her eyes. "The Deadheads."

"It's still like that," said Suzie, "only now you get these new groups. The anorexics, the cutters, girls who just want to . . ."

"Dissolve," said Lydia.

"It's a self-esteem issue," said Tevis.

"Maya's started hanging out with them," said Suzie. "Mrs. Thesiger said she wanted to bring it to my attention."

"With the anorexics or with the cutters?" said Amber.

"There's an overlap, apparently." Suzie chewed her lip again. "Anyway, she said maybe it would be a good idea for Maya to see the school counselor. When I got home I was shaking. Maya's not even fourteen for another five months. She still plays on the swing in the yard. Then I got to thinking, she's been saying all these things about her lunch box, about throwing food away, and I've just been ignoring them. What a shitty mother I am."

"All mothers feel like bad mothers at least some of the time," said Amber. "That's what being a good mother means. You're not a bad mother at all."

"I don't know," said Suzie. "So when the school bus drops her off I practically pounce on her at the door. I try to talk to her about it but she gives me the most withering look. I mean, you should see this look. It could strip a tree of its leaves. And really, I want to slap her. Really, I do."

"But you didn't," said Lydia.

"No, I didn't. But you know she's always wearing those long-sleeve T-shirts. I never get to see her arms. I'm not allowed in the bathroom when she's taking a bath. So I grab her, I actually grab her, and I pull up her sleeves, and she's got these little cuts up her left forearm."

"What did you do?" said Tevis.

"What could I do? She won't talk to me. I call Mike, he's out on patrol, but he comes over, and she won't talk to him either. She shuts herself in her room." Suzie massaged her temples with her fingertips. Her short black hair tufted out and when she lowered her hands again, Amber stroked it gently down.

Amber said, "Have you arranged the school counselor yet?"

"Got an appointment right away. But Maya just sat there, apparently. Gave him the napalm stare."

"I could try," said Lydia. "If you want."

Suzie looked at her gratefully. "Maya loves you. And Mike says I've got to lay off her and stop being so anxious. Says he's going to take me down to the station and lock me in the cooler if I don't calm down."

"I'll take her out somewhere," said Lydia. "At the least we'll have a nice evening." She hoped Suzie's gratitude would be justified.

"Let's get another bottle," said Tevis. "And I know we're all going home to eat, but would anyone share a plate of antipasti and maybe a little garlic bread?"

They got more prosecco and a platter of antipasti, fava beans, artichoke hearts, red peppers, pecorino, and green and black olives, fat and garlicky.

Suzie said, "Mike won't want me breathing on him tonight." She smiled and the heaviness seemed to have lifted from her.

"Garlic is actually supposed to be good for your sex drive," said Tevis.

"Where do you come up with this stuff?" said Suzie.

Lydia was reassured by this return to form, Suzie throwing out quick jabs like affectionate little punches on the arm.

"I'll bet you can't keep your hands off him this evening," said Tevis. "Then you'll see who's right."

Suzie picked a whole clove of garlic out of the olive oil. She put it in her mouth. "Fat chance," she said. "I can barely remember the last time we did it. Maybe a couple of months ago, maybe even three."

"It can come and go in phases," said Amber. "Is it you? Or is it him?"

"Me," said Suzie. "I still find him attractive. We're still affectionate with each other. It's just . . . I find myself making excuses, you know, more and more these days."

"That's okay," said Amber. "When I was married, and I didn't feel like it, I'd go through with it anyway. Then he'd be kind of mad at me, because I wasn't really into it. One time he just rolled off and snatched up his pillow and went to the spare bedroom. Said he'd had more fun picking his nose. Guess what I mean is, if you don't feel like it then it's good that you can say."

"Your husband was an asshole," said Tevis. "But we already knew that. Did you tell him where to get off?"

Amber made a neat little grimace, wrinkling her nose. "No. I started faking, that's what I did. You know, ooh, aah, oh yeah, *there,* shudder, gasp, collapse."

"Ha," said Tevis. "Every girl knows how."

"It'll come back," Amber said to Suzie. "With you and Mike."

"Sometimes," said Suzie, "I fake that I'm asleep so he won't try to start fooling around. Sometimes I fake a headache . . . I'm always so tired at the end of the day, it just seems like it'd be another chore, you know, like another load of laundry when you thought you were already done. And I can't be bothered, honestly. I think maybe I'll feel like it tomorrow, and then I never do."

"Does he mind?" said Lydia. "Do you talk about it?"

"I mind!" said Suzie, sitting up and declaiming. "I mind. God, when I think back to how I used to be. Me not wanting sex? Please! I was the girl with the feather cut, the pink bomber jacket, the snuggest shorts, the hottest ass."

The restaurant was starting to fill up with diners now and Lydia had to tuck in her chair to make more room for the table behind them to be seated. She glanced back at the elderly couple who was waiting courteously for Suzie to notice also and let them pass.

"Me and Mike, we got together in high school and we went at it. I mean we *went at it.* I could do it standing up. I could do it in a broom closet. I could do it in roller skates."

"Roller skates?" said Amber.

"Roller skates, up against the wall. It was tricky," said Suzie. "Now it feels like too much effort to even open my legs."

"Suzie," said Lydia. "You need to let these people through."

"Oh, excuse me," said Suzie, shuffling her chair. "I do apologize."

"That's okay, dear. Thank you," said the lady. She held herself like a dancer, shoulders back, chin parallel to the floor, one foot pointing out at an elegant angle. She reached back for her husband's hand. "About the sex, dear," she said to Suzie. "You think your libido's died. But it hasn't, it's just gone into hibernation. When it wakes up again—" She pulled her husband's arm around her trim waist and leaned her head back so that they came cheek to cheek. "Well, it wakes up again and it is, simply and beautifully, the most marvelous surprise."

There were times when it would be upon her suddenly, a surge inside her, like an electric current with no place to discharge. The enormity of what she'd done, the pain of losing her children, the pain that she had caused them.

She sat in the Sport Trac outside Carson's house and leaned her forehead against the steering wheel. If she could break open her rib cage with her bare hands, she would rip out her heart. If she could drive a knitting needle through her skull, she would mash up her brain. If that would stop the memories from coming unbidden, then she could be peaceful now.

A single image had floated into her mind. Her youngest in his high chair, with his fat cheeks and downy hair and his vague little yet-to-be defined eyebrows. His brother's eyes shining with pride as he turned for her approval because he had just fed the baby with puréed carrot from a plastic spoon.

She thought about Lawrence, how he'd worried that she would be upset when she saw her boys growing up happy without her. Even Lawrence, who understood everything, didn't understand about that.

Carson's house smelled of cedarwood. He'd made a new handrail for the staircase a few months ago. When he'd bought the house several years back, it had been a wreck. It was an old house, older than the town, cross-gabled and wood-shingled, with a grand Palladian window on the upper floor that let in the wind. The shingles regularly fell off the walls and roof and Carson kept patching them up.

"When are you going to sort out the curtain?" said Lydia.

"I'll get around to it," said Carson.

"Says the man who doesn't like to leave a job half done."

He raised an eyebrow at her. "It's functional, isn't it?"

"Carson," said Lydia. "It's a sheet."

He looked at the sheet in question as if the observation had taken him by surprise. "When I found this house and fell in love with it I knew none of my old stuff would look right here. I didn't have that much. It was a modern apartment and it was pretty minimalist."

"So's this," said Lydia, looking around at the sparse furnishings.

"Mostly I worked on the house. I redid the guttering, repaired the eaves where they were crumbling, worked on the antebellum plumbing, needed some help with that in the end. It was satisfying, anyway. And I wanted to get some furniture that looked right. First thing I started with was the couch."

"It's very nice."

"Maybe, but it took me so long to find it, it was so much effort, and then once you've got it, you sit on it and you never think about it again. What's the point?"

She laughed and walked over to the Ping-Pong table that was folded against the wall. "Least you've still got room for this. I'll give you a game."

"I'll go easy on you," he said.

"You better not. I'll know if you're letting me win."

They played three games and he didn't let her win. He tried to teach her how to spin the ball by slicing it. She was watching his eyes more than his hands. She was examining the hollow of his throat, the way it always looked a little sunburned. She was looking at the freckles on his forearms.

"I've got to have a rest," she said.

"Yeah," he said, "you wore me out."

She hit him on the leg with her paddle. "What was the job you had?" she said. "Where did you go?"

He sprawled on the couch with his thumbs through his belt loops. "It was a burn job. A house in Alabama."

"Didn't they have someone more local?"

"It wasn't even my company. I was just helping out."

"Why? What happened? I mean, is that normal?"

"That sheet's not so bad, is it? If I start looking for curtains I know it will drive me nuts. I won't know what to get." He actually looked worried.

"Leave the sheet up," she said. "It's fine. You were saying about the job?"

"This guy's house burns down in the middle of the night and he puts in a claim. His insurer checks through his history. You do that as a matter of course. Anyway, the adjuster sees he's got two previous, both with my company."

"You make it sound like a criminal record."

"Some people have a run of bad luck. They say lightning never strikes twice. You work in this job long enough you know that's not true."

"But three times?" said Lydia.

"I turned down his second claim. The first one was before I joined the company and on the forms he said he was intending to rebuild but he didn't. That always gets my interest."

"I like your neck," said Lydia. "I've been meaning to tell you that. But carry on. I am listening."

"Thank you," said Carson. "It's nice to have my neck appreciated. So, Stevenson, this guy, the next house he has burns down too. It's all around the town that he's torched it for the insurance. This is Roxborough, it's a hardscrabble town, and all the bars that Stevenson goes drinking in, I hear the same story, how he's been boasting about the money he'll get."

"That doesn't mean he was guilty, necessarily. Maybe he just liked bragging. Maybe a lot of people didn't like him. You had to prove it another way."

"I couldn't," said Carson. "I couldn't actually prove it. Couldn't locate the cause of the fire, no actual witnesses. I couldn't prove it, but I could turn him down, and I did. In my view he was lucky he wasn't in court for arson. He didn't see it that way."

"Was he angry?"

"Just a bit. Gave me some flack."

"What sort?"

"Abuse, you know, calling my house in the middle of the night, that sort of thing. The difficult part was, even though I knew I was right, there was room for the tiniest bit of doubt. What if he was really the hapless victim, and I was making his life hell? This third house two years later laid that to rest."

"How stupid must he be?" said Lydia. "Wasn't it going to be obvious?"

"He moved state, he switched insurers. Lot of people don't realize we access each other's records."

"Aren't you concerned," said Lydia, choosing her words carefully, "that he might find out you've rumbled him a third time? The guy sounds a bit . . . unstable."

"He probably won't know that. And even if he does, I'm not going to lose any sleep over it."

"What if he's, you know . . ."

"Crazy? Comes after me with a shotgun?" He took her hand. "Look at it from his point of view. The first time everything is plain sailing. No one dies, no one gets hurt, he gets his money, no one loses a thing. As far as he's concerned the insurance company can afford it. Then I come along next time and mess things up. He was responding. He was pissed, but I never thought he was a nut job."

While he was talking she leaned in and rested her head against him. She could feel the vibrations of his voice from his chest to her temple. At night when the light was off and he spoke to her as they lay in the dark she felt as if that was all she needed, as if it would be possible to live suspended in a space where the only things that reached her were the touch of his breath on her shoulder and the sound of his voice in her ear.

She looked at Rufus, lying on his back on the rug, exposing and offering his soft belly to the world. He was always at home here. Esther would say that he was acting how she was feeling. Esther, just possibly, was right.

Carson took Madeleine and Rufus out for a stroll before bed. When he came back he lifted the sheet at the living room window and peered out at the front lawn.

"What's out there?" said Lydia.

"Nothing," he said.

"Admiring the view?"

"Did you hear Madeleine barking?"

"I did. I thought maybe she saw a squirrel, a raccoon."

"She went for something in the oleander. I had to pull her away. I don't know what it was."

"Not a claimant?" said Lydia.

"Sadly," said Carson, "I don't think I'm important enough to have acquired a stalker of any kind."

Chapter Twenty

Did the boyfriend know? Grabber was in the sitting room of the bed-and-breakfast, the parlor, as Mrs. Jackson called it. In less than an hour Lydia would be arriving. Mrs. Jackson was out getting a Brazilian wax or hiring an orchestra or something. It was difficult to imagine what more preparations she could be making. The entire day so far she had been scurrying around the bed-and-breakfast preparing. Five times, no less, she had apologized for disturbing him in his room. If only she knew who she was actually receiving she would self-combust on the spot.

Did the boyfriend know? Grabowski kept asking himself that question. Last night he'd had the notion that maybe he'd glean something by staking out the house. Somebody had to have helped her. Maybe it was him. He didn't remember seeing the guy in the days before she "died," but she had a lot of people swirling around her and that didn't mean anything. A bodyguard who'd been on the yacht, maybe. It wouldn't be her first time for that.

He didn't even manage to get a shot of them together. He got a shot of her resting her head on the steering wheel as she sat outside. Clearly a lot on her mind. He remembered the day she had driven alone to Eton and sat just like that in her car before getting out. A private moment of reflection. Well, private if he hadn't followed her there. At lunchtime the radio news announced the divorce. She'd been gathering herself before seeing her son, so he would be fore-warned.

Last night the front door was unlocked and she went straight in. Later, the boyfriend went out for a walk and Grabowski was still in the bushes, watching the house. He wasn't exactly sure what he was hoping to learn. He wasn't going to use his flash even if they came out together. Then the hound went for his foot and he'd thought that the game was up.

But the boyfriend pulled his dog away and left it at that. He'd raised the curtain at the window after he'd gone inside and taken a cursory look. Grabber decided he'd learned something after all. If the guy knew anything, he'd be protecting her. He'd be on the lookout. No way he'd be leaving his door unlocked, even after all this time he'd be on his guard.

Now he had to concentrate on the task at hand, before Mrs. Jackson came bustling back. How could he set it up?

There was one thing he needed to achieve at this meeting, but he had to work out how.

He looked around the sitting room again. There were two mirrors, one over the fireplace and the other on the wall to the right of Mr. Jackson. If he stood just here . . . But there was bound to be a preliminary fanfare at the door when Lydia arrived, so having his back still turned when she came in would seem unnatural.

Mr. Jackson stirred in his sleep. His hands twitched on the armrests. This man could sleep for king and country. Perhaps he was nocturnal. Grabowski doubted it. He probably simply transferred from chair to bed. He looked older than his wife, his old man's trousers high above his waist. His forehead melted over his eyebrows, and his eyebrows over his eyes, his nose drooped over his top lip, and his chin cascaded down his neck, a fleshy cascade of features trickling ever down.

He needed some kind of prop. If he could sit right here—he placed a chair at an angle in front of Mr. Jackson—then he could see in the mirror that reflected the doorway. He needed to look as though he was absorbed in something. What could he use? He hunted around the sitting room. If he printed out some of his small town photos he could lay them on this card table. He shifted the card table too. But it was too late to get anything printed. He could be playing cards, solitaire. No, a card game with Mr. Jackson. That was it; otherwise why would he be sitting in such close proximity to him anyway? Now he had to find a pack of cards. And wake up Mr. Jackson. Both tasks appeared challenging.

"Mr. Jackson?" he said. He tried again and louder this time. "Mr. Jackson?"

No sign of life. If he died in that chair how long would it be before anyone noticed?

Grabowski shook the old man's shoulder. "Mr. Jackson?" he shouted.

"Exactly," said Mr. Jackson, sitting bolt upright.

A lifetime of pacifying your wife, thought Grabowski. That's how you end up, agreeing in your sleep.

"Mr. Jackson," he said, deciding it was better to collude in the fantasy that the old man had been awake all along, "I was wondering if you would like a game of cards."

"Don't play cards," said Mr. Jackson, placing his feet back on the carved turtle that served as his stool. "Never have, never will."

"That's a pity," said Grabowski.

"I'd play you a game of chess." Mr. Jackson made an attempt to smooth his straggly white eyebrows. "These need a trim. Hardly see a damn thing. Take my advice, never get old."

Mr. Jackson told him where to find the chess box and Grabowski set it up. He practiced keeping one eye on the mirror without lifting his neck so it appeared he was concentrating on the board. He had a clear view, and all he needed was a few seconds. It would prove it to him either way.

Twenty minutes to go.

Grabowski made his opening move.

"Son," said Mr. Jackson, "what do you say to a little whiskey? See that cabinet over there? Use the teacups. What she don't know won't hurt her, if you get what I mean."

Grabber decided he could use a drink, just one, he was getting a little jangly.

* * *

"You boys playing nicely?" said Mrs. Jackson. "You wouldn't believe how far I had to go to get the clotted cream!" She was wearing her knotted strand of pearls. She'd had her hair freshly set. Her voice was perpetually addressed to the back of the auditorium but it lifted with extra verve and vibrato today.

"You carry on," she said, and gestured as if waving away all offers of help. "I'll get the tray ready."

Grabowski moved his bishop from king four to queen five. He practiced again with the mirror. He turned his head to the door and back again, making a mental map of how clearly she would see him. She would see him all right. And she wouldn't realize that he could see her.

"Oh, Mr. Grabowski!" Mrs. Jackson was calling him from the kitchen. Grabowski checked his watch. One minute past five. She could arrive anytime.

"Oh, Mr. Grabowski!"

"Hello there."

Mrs. Jackson's voice was so animated she was practically singing. "Would you mind awfully giving me a hand?"

Yes, he would mind awfully. He would mind awfully if she cocked this whole thing up for him. He had to stay in his seat in case Lydia arrived.

Mr. Jackson attempted a wink. His eyebrow didn't exactly spring back in place. He helped it along with a finger. "Play it safe," he said.

"I'm coming," Grabowski called out, and nearly tipped the chessboard over. He had to get back to his seat as soon as possible.

At twenty past five she had still not arrived. Grabowski was losing the game. Mr. Jackson had all but cornered his king with a castle and two pawns. Mrs. Jackson was on sentry duty at the window. Grabowski's shoulders were beginning to ache from hunching over the board.

Mr. Jackson was due to make the next move. It was like waiting for a tectonic plate shift. But the last thing Grabber wanted was for the game to be over before Lydia arrived. He wouldn't be hurrying his opponent along.

"Here she is," trilled Mrs. Jackson. Grabowski tracked the sound of her heels across the floor. The muscle of his right shoulder went into spasm. He needed to stretch it out but he didn't dare move.

He was in the exact right position, his view as clear as it was covert.

"Now, boys," said Mrs. Jackson as she and Lydia entered the room. "Sorry to interrupt the tournament but there are introductions to be made."

Grabowski waited a few beats as if lost in thought, before turning toward them, rolling his shoulder. "Beginning to seize up there, Mrs. Jackson. And your husband seems to have me on the run."

"Lydia Snaresbrook, John Grabowski," said Mrs. Jackson, flourishing her arm at each in turn.

"Pleased to meet you," said Grabber. He stood up to shake hands.

She returned the line with perfect equanimity and he looked directly into her eyes. "I'd say please do finish," she continued, "but I think you may have lost your opponent rather than the game."

Grabowski looked at Mr. Jackson, who had indeed fallen asleep. Lydia laughed her crystalline laugh, and Mrs. Jackson trumpeted hers, before ushering them to sit down.

"Would you care for another scone?" said Mrs. Jackson. "They don't keep long. Lydia, will you take a few home? Oh, Otis, please get down from there." She went to rescue Otis, who had jumped from tapestry stool to rosewood side table, and from there to the top of a vacant black-lacquered plinth that rocked on its base as he tried to maneuver himself into position to scramble down.

"So what do you write about?" said Lydia.

"He's a photographer too," called Mrs. Jackson. "I'm going to take these dogs in the backyard. Come along, Rufus. Yes, and you, Otis."

He had rehearsed this over and over all morning, how this conversation would go. He'd practiced some of his answers out loud. Before she had swum into view in the mirror he had been rigid with nerves. Now that the distance between his feet and hers was no greater than the length of a telescopic lens, he was supremely calm. In his mind he composed a frame of the two of them together, as if snapped from the other side of the room. Him with his arm resting carelessly across the back of the sofa; her on the Queen Anne chair with ankles neatly crossed.

"Oh, and a photographer," said Lydia. "What kind of pictures do you take?"

She betrayed not a single sign of discomposure. They had been chatting for some time and she had answered all his questions with self-deprecating humor and charm. Of course she would be good at this. He had been practicing a single morning. She for ten years by now.

"I'm working on a project about small towns over here and back at home. Street life, local color, local characters. But basically I'm a photojournalist. I've taken photographs of a lot of famous people over the years."

"Celebrities?" said Lydia. "That must be fascinating."

Even before this new life, lying was part of her daily routine. He guessed it had to be. All the things she'd get up to, the way she'd try to cover her tracks. Spinning stories to favored columnists, smuggling men into her apartment, denying their existence. She had a reputation for slyness. You couldn't blame her, but it was well deserved.

"You name them," he said, "actors, musicians, royalty, television presenters, the lot."

Lydia poured out the tea that was left in the pot. "Gosh, that does sound glamorous. What made you decide to switch from that?"

He was careful not to look at her too hard as she played out her moves.

"I'll switch back," he said. "This project won't pay many bills." Maybe he would actually do this mythical project. If he got rich enough (and he might) that's what he would do. "But I kind of slid into this, to be honest, started taking the photographs, then the whole thing kind of grew."

"Peace and quiet," said Mrs. Jackson, bustling back, "now that the children are playing outside." She blew her nose. "Oh dear, these allergies. I need to take an antihistamine. I thought you two would get along. Not just the British connection. I do have a knack for predicting how well people will mix. We used to do a lot of entertaining, and though I say it myself, my soirees were quite famous, because I knew exactly who to put with whom. Excuse me another moment. I'll be right back."

Lydia smiled at Grabowski. He smiled at her and for a moment they were genuine conspirators, allies in their amusement.

"The whole thing just grew," said Lydia. She was, perhaps, more handsome than beautiful in her jeans and gray T-shirt. Although her blue eyes were luminous.

She had a reputation for slyness. He wouldn't dispute it. She had a reputation for being dim. Grabowski wouldn't go along with that. Not as clever as she thought herself, but far from stupid. She'd work her little tricks. When he first started photographing her, before the engagement was announced, he'd been hanging around outside her apartment block when she'd come down carrying a suitcase and two bags.

"If you give me a hand to the car," she'd said, "I'll let you take my picture."

She offered to carry his camera in return. She kept him talking while they walked to her mini and he stuffed the bags in the back. Before he knew it she'd jumped into the driver's seat and wound the window down. "You're a poppet," she said, and drove off with his camera. He got it delivered to the office a week later.

"I must be getting old," he said. "You know you're getting old when you start wondering if you've done enough with your life. Guess the attraction had gone a bit, you know, out of the celebrity thing. All that's pretty ephemeral."

"And you're writing about the towns too?" She kept the conversation flowing easily. Perhaps, thought Grabber, a shade too easily. A few conversational bumps in the road between strangers would be more realistic.

"I'm working on a text to go with the photographs. Writing's not my strong point, but I'm getting along."

His cell phone rang. "Sorry," he said, and pulled it out of his pocket. "Gareth, mate, I'll call you back."

"Don't hang up," said Gareth. "You're sitting on a fucking time bomb and you don't know it. I need to talk to you right now."

"I've got to take this," said Grabowski, "if you don't mind."

He walked upstairs to his room, passing Mrs. Jackson on her way down. "Bring your camera with you, Mr. Grabowski, when you're through. If you'd like to take a picture of Lydia and me for your art project, I'm sure we'd both oblige. Don't be shy."

"This better be important," said Grabowski. His agent had a sixth sense. He knew all the wrong times to call.

"It's not a matter of life and death," said Gareth.

"Great."

"It's more important than that. It's a matter of money. I talked to your publisher today and they are not going to extend your deadline. It's already pushed to the wire. You've got to shit or get off the pot."

"You have such a way with words."

"I sweat blood for you," said Gareth. "Don't let me down."

"Gareth," said Grabowski, "fuck off."

"Are you sure you can't stay a little longer, Lydia?" said Mrs. Jackson, when Grabowski walked back into the sitting room.

Lydia stood up. "I'm taking Maya out to the movies," she said. "I'll just collect Rufus and then I'm afraid I do have to go. I'd love to take a couple of those scones with me, they're so delicious."

"Isn't she splendid?" said Mrs. Jackson, as Lydia went out to get her dog. "Didn't you bring your camera down?"

Grabowski ran the permutations. If the old lady was still going on about it when Lydia said good-bye, how would it look if he refused? How would it look if he said yes? What about if he agreed reluctantly? He could think of ways in which any of those options could seem suspicious. He'd like to strangle his landlady with her pearls. When he thought what care he had taken, how well it was going, and then she comes along with her innocent, preening sabotage.

"Do you know what?" he said, lowering his voice. He looked earnestly into her eyes. "Do you know what, I'd love you to be in my book, Mrs. Jackson, but let's do it tomorrow when the light's better. Just you and me."

"Oh, the light," she said, fluttering her sparse lashes, "that is *so* important. When I was directing stage plays, it was only the local amateur dramatics society, but we were quite the professional outfit and I always . . . Ah, Lydia, are you off?"

"Thank you so much," said Lydia. "I do have to go, yes. It was a pleasure meeting you, Mr. Grabowski. Good luck with everything."

"I had a dog when I was a boy," he said, looking at Rufus. "Highland terrier. He ran into the road, got hit by a car. I was completely devastated."

"You poor thing." She touched his arm.

They accompanied her to the front door. "One thing I wanted to ask you," she said, turning, "what was it that brought you to Kensington in particular? There are a lot of small towns to choose from, aren't there?"

He didn't miss a beat. "I worked a lot in Kensington, the one in London, covering the royals. When I saw it on the map, I thought, well, I've got to check that out. What about you?"

"I was actually looking in some of the other towns in the county. But I couldn't find the right house, then I found it, in Kensington. I do love it here." She waved back at them as she ran down the steps, carefree and girlish, her long dark hair lifting off her shoulders, and for an instant it was hard to believe that she wasn't just what she seemed to be.

Grabowski took his laptop and his camera bag and got in the Pontiac and drove. He couldn't stand to be shut in his room right now, he needed to drive and think. If he decided to review what he'd got in his laptop, well, he was used to working in a car. He didn't want Mrs. Jackson coming in to ask questions about what she no doubt thought of as tomorrow's "photo shoot." Bless her, though. Bless Mrs. Jackson. She'd been very useful. It had been easy to avoid Lydia. (Why had the name stuck? Was that a sign that he wanted to let her go, didn't have the guts to see this through?) Even in a town this size it had been easy to avoid Lydia seeing him, because if you're the one doing the following you know where the target is. The problem doesn't arise. But meeting her without blowing it, that would have been difficult, without dear old Mrs. Jackson on his side.

Lydia had hardly put a foot wrong. It almost seemed a shame that wasn't enough. But that was just life. She'd played a good game. He'd give her that.

One slipup she'd made—she wouldn't realize it—when he'd said that he photographed celebrities she didn't ask for names. Who? she should have said. Everyone wanted names, except her because she already knew.

He couldn't fault her really, though. That would only have given him more material with which to speculate and what he had needed was to prove it to himself before he took the next irreversible steps.

He should go and celebrate. But he wouldn't go back to that bar. He didn't feel like being around anyone right now, not that failed artist for sure. He pulled over at a liquor store and bought a bottle of Woodstone Creek, and swigged it from the brown paper bag.

"Here's to you too, Mr. Jackson, partner," he said, raising the bag aloft. "I'll remember you in my prayers."

He'd had a clear view of Lydia in the mirror and she hadn't seen him looking. By the time he'd shaken himself out of his chess-induced reverie she'd composed her face. But there was no mistaking the shock of recognition that had initially flooded it. He was the last person she'd expected to see there. Hats off to her for recovering so well. He lifted the brown paper bag again.

Chapter Twenty-one

The movie theater outside Havering was a multiplex in an arid shopping mall with air-conditioning that left you so dry that afterward you could shed your skin like a snake. Lydia reached into her purse and applied her lip balm. The movie playing to a house that was three-quarters empty was a teen comedy drama but she hadn't the faintest idea what was happening. Maya slurped her Coke and laughed. Lydia gave a cursory laugh because she didn't want Maya to think she wasn't sharing the experience. When she glanced at her though, Maya was too wrapped up in the screen to notice anyway.

How could it have happened? How could that man have ended up in Kensington? The dread she felt when she saw him hunched over that chessboard was like her lungs filling with water. It was lucky that he was the kind of arrogant man who doesn't leap to attention when there's an introduction to be made. He just sat there looking at the board. Bad manners, she thought, had their uses. It gave her a moment to catch her breath.

She ate popcorn and stared at the screen. It was hopeless to try to follow the story now.

She had to get a grip. What would it have mattered if he'd seen her that first instant, looking a little flustered? She had to stop being so paranoid.

He hadn't recognized her. Of course he hadn't. In the hour they had spent talking there was nothing—she'd been running over and over it—that he'd said, no glance that he'd given, that made her think otherwise.

She had known him the second she walked in and saw him. He'd been around from the start, before she had even got engaged. From then on, until the final days, he had been a constant presence. He wasn't one of the worst. He always called her ma'am. Even after the divorce.

And ten years later he turned up on her doorstep? How was it possible? What had led him to her?

It was all getting twisted again. Nothing had led him to her. He hadn't found her. He hadn't a clue.

What would Lawrence say about it? She didn't know. She couldn't think. Where was Lawrence when she needed him?

"Lydia?" said Maya. "Lydia, what did that bag of popcorn ever do to you?"

Lydia looked down at the bag of toffee popcorn. She was twisting the half-empty packet hard, as if she were trying to wring its neck.

Afterward, in the ice cream parlor, Maya opined about the movie while eating a triple scoop of chocolate chip with hot fudge sauce.

"It was kinda dumb. Like, you know what's gonna happen in the end. It was all so obvious."

"I know," said Lydia.

"It was good, though. It wasn't boring, even though I guessed everything ahead of time."

Maya had black hair and dark eyes like Suzie, and Mike's pale complexion, which made for a striking combination. She wore a zip-up red hoodie and flapped her sneakered feet as she talked. They were sitting on stools at the narrow ledge that ran down the side of the parlor. If Maya was troubled, she wasn't showing any sign of it right now.

"I think we should go for a walk down by the river," said Lydia.

Maya licked the edge of the sundae dish where the sauce had trickled over the side. "In the dark?"

"It's safe," said Lydia. "We won't go too far."

Maya shrugged. "No, I meant, what's there to see? In the dark. Also, Leon Kramer? His brother fell in the river, this stretch of it? He got typhoid or malaria or something? He was in the hospital for, like, a month."

"Maybe Leon was pulling your leg," said Lydia. "Anyway, we're not going to be falling in."

The path by the river was built like a seaside boardwalk with little wooden jetties set into the water at intervals. They passed a couple of walkers heading in the opposite direction and then they were alone on the path. Maya flipped her hood up and zipped the top right under her chin. She had her hands in her pockets. She slapped her feet against the boards as she walked.

"Are you okay?" said Lydia. She could see why John Grabowski might decide to check out Kensington on his travels. Hadn't the name intrigued her too?

"Yes," said Maya. "I was getting bit. On the back of my neck."

"It helps to talk to someone," said Lydia. "If there's anything you're worried about."

"Oh God," said Maya, grabbing her arm.

"What?" Lydia's heart began to race. Had he come for her already?

"No, don't look," said Maya, practically dragging her along. "That was so gross."

They passed a pair of teenagers convoluting on a bench.

"Did you see them making out?" said Maya. "That was so gross."

Lydia laughed. "You just watched people making out in that movie."

"That's different," said Maya. "My mom told you, didn't she?"

"She's worried about you." Maybe the best thing to do would be to leave town until Grabowski had gone.

"My mom is so dumb," said Maya. She stepped off the boardwalk to the riverbank and walked down to where it started to slope away into the water.

Lydia followed. What did she think she was going to say to this girl that would help her? She wasn't sprinkling princess fairy dust anymore. The afflicted did not glow in her presence.

"It was my idea," said Lydia. "Us going out to the movies together. Don't blame it on your mom."

Maya picked up a stone and threw it into the river. "I hang out with whoever I want. She can't stop me. At school, I mean."

But why should she leave town? Lydia picked up a handful of stones. Why should she do that? Why should that man have any power over her life? Why didn't he just go away?

"I guess she can't."

"My mom is so dumb," said Maya. "She thinks I'm dumb, but I'm not."

"No one's saying that." One time he'd followed her to her therapist's home. That was before the world knew she was in analysis. He'd wanted to get a picture of her coming out of the house. She'd stayed inside for hours and someone had kept a lookout for her. When he'd left his car to go and relieve himself or buy something to eat or whatever it was that he was doing, she'd slipped out. She wrote him a note and put it under his windshield wiper. *You lose. You didn't get anything.* In the therapy session they'd been talking about techniques she could use to calm herself. By the time she'd got into her car again she was brimming with rage and spite. She was beyond that now, out of its reach, and out of his.

She hurled the stones into the river.

Maya was regarding her carefully. She pulled down her hood as if that would help her to see better. "My mom says if you're angry you should go and thump a pillow."

"Now that *is* dumb," said Lydia. "Smash some crockery. It's more fun."

"You're not mad at me, are you?"

"Of course I'm not."

Maya unzipped her hoodie and took it off. She held out her arm. "See that. That's what made Mom go ballistic. Those scratches there."

"They look quite nasty," said Lydia. "What happened?" There were three long red marks down Maya's arm.

"Next door's cat got stuck down the storm drain. I pulled him out, ungrateful critter."

"Why didn't you tell your mom?"

"Why should I? She started yelling before I opened my mouth. And I'm not anorexic either, if that's what she's been telling you. I thought Zoe Romanov was really cool? People say she's a white witch and everything and she keeps a rabbit's foot on her key ring even though she's a vegetarian? I sat with her for, like, a week. And all she talks about is calories. She's so boring. I get enough of that at home."

"I'm sure your mom didn't mean to fly off the handle," said Lydia. "She was probably just a bit stressed."

Maya hugged herself. It was starting to get chilly. "Like duh," she said. "I know. She's always stressing. It bugs me. What does she have to be stressed out about?"

When Maya had gone up to bed, Lydia told Suzie what she had gleaned.

"I am a prize ass," said Suzie.

"You were worried about your daughter. That doesn't make you any kind of ass."

"I'm a world championship ass," said Suzie. "I should know my own daughter. I should give her more credit. Mike said I was over-reacting. I didn't listen to him either. Let's go and open some wine."

"I need an early night," said Lydia.

"One glass," said Suzie. "Then an early night."

"I'm beat," said Lydia. "I've got to go home."

"Okay. I'll let you go. Think about what you want for your birth-day. I'm going shopping this weekend."

"A surprise," said Lydia. "I've invited Esther to the party next Tues-day. I hope Amber won't mind."

"She'll be delighted," said Suzie. "You do look tired. Get a good long sleep. And Lydia, thank you."

Lydia did not get a good sleep, and the next evening as soon as she arrived at Amber's house she regretted coming out. She should have stayed at home.

"Tyler and Serena are both on sleepovers," said Amber, "so we are free as birds. Where shall we go? Why don't we hit the freeway, see where we end up?"

Lydia pulled a face. "I'd rather stay here."

"Go to Dino's, you mean?" Amber took a compact out of her purse, adjusted the line of her lipstick with her finger, and then added some more where she'd just dabbed it off. "What do you think of this shade?"

"Let's watch some television," said Lydia. "I can't be bothered to go out. I'm not in the mood."

"Oh," said Amber. "Sure. We can stay in. We can talk just as well here."

Lydia switched on the television. "I am so exhausted."

"How about a cup of tea?" said Amber.

When Amber came back with the tea she sat on the sofa next to Lydia and they took little sips of conversation between the lines of voice-over of a wildlife documentary about whales.

"How was your evening with Maya?" said Amber.

"Maya's fine," said Lydia.

Amber waited. She didn't press. It was irritating.

"I'll tell you another time," said Lydia. She wished Amber would tell her to snap out of it.

After a while, Amber said, "If there's anything in particular you'd like for your birthday . . ."

"No, there really isn't," said Lydia. "Sorry, I'm a bit tetchy today."

She could feel Amber dying to ask her why. What could she tell her? It wasn't something she could tell anyone.

They watched together for a while.

Amber picked up a magazine and started flicking through. She was still reading it when the documentary finished.

"I think I should go home," Lydia said. "You don't want me sitting around here all grumpy."

"I do," said Amber. "What are friends for if you can't be grumpy with them?"

"What's in the magazine?"

Amber showed her. "Everyone thought they had the perfect Hollywood marriage. Turns out he'd been cheating on her for years. I feel sorry for her. It's so awful."

"Do you really?" said Lydia.

"How could anyone not?" said Amber. "The latest one was a pole dancer. She's not even pretty."

"And now everyone knows. Don't you think that makes it worse?" She should just go home. This conversation was pointless. Was she going to take out her frustration on Amber?

"When my ex was cheating it ate me up," said Amber. "The thought of everyone knowing, and feeling sorry for me because I was such a sap. You only turn into a sap when everyone knows."

"Why don't you leave her alone then?" said Lydia. It came out stronger than she'd intended, and Amber looked startled.

"Who?"

"Wherever she goes now she'll have someone ramming a camera up her nose."

Amber closed the magazine and tossed it on the floor. "I think it's terrible."

"You think it's terrible," said Lydia. "Why do you think they want the pictures? Why . . . oh, never mind, I should go home." Lydia stood up. "I'll see you soon."

Amber didn't answer, she smoothed down her skirt and folded her hands on her lap.

"Amber, I'm just snappy this evening. Okay?"

"Sit down a minute," said Amber. "I know what you're saying."

"It doesn't matter," said Lydia.

"It's like crocodile tears, that's what you're saying, isn't it? I don't really feel sorry for her. No, Lydia, let me speak, please." She said it more gently than Lydia deserved. "These magazines can be so mean. I know that. And maybe it's mean of me. I look at these rich and famous people and see that they have problems too. Maybe that shouldn't make me feel better about my life but sometimes it does."

"We'll talk tomorrow," said Lydia.

"I've read about her for years," said Amber. "I see her on television, I've seen most of her movies. And I do feel sorry for her, whatever you say."

"Amber," said Lydia, "I'm too tired. Let's just leave it, okay?"

She parked by the house and strode toward the swimming pool, Rufus on her heels like a ball of fluff that had stuck to the back of her shoe. By the time she reached the lawn she'd taken off her sweater, and by the time she reached the tiles she'd pulled off her T-shirt. She kicked off her shoes and peeled off her jeans. Rufus barked. "Rufus," she said, "shut up."

She took off her underwear and when she dived in she swam along the bottom in the dark until she hit her head against the steps at the shallow end. She came up for air and then flipped onto her back. Between the black of the sky and the black of the water she floated, thoughts leaking out of her, jellyfish and phosphorous, she could see them spreading across the pool. She flipped over and hung facedown, eyes open, in the water. Now she could see nothing. Her legs started sinking and she kicked them up, keeping her face under the surface. She was freezing and her lungs were burning. She stayed as still as possible. When she thought she couldn't last any longer, she blew out hard through her mouth and kicked to force herself down. She reached the bottom and placed both palms flat on the tiles and let herself go. She inhaled too soon as she came up. Rufus barked and she coughed and retched, and flailed to reach the side.

She clambered out and doubled up and coughed until she vomited a long thin stream of milky water. Her legs were shaking with cold. A huge bug flew right at her, buzzing like a stun gun. It crashed against her shoulder and she screamed. Rufus kept up his din. As she ran for the house she hit her toe against something sharp but she didn't stop until she got to the back door which was locked, she'd have to go back to find her jeans and the key. She beat on the wood until her fists were sore, then she slid down and sat on the ground and sobbed.

She sat with her foot up. The cut bled down the valley between the tendons of her big and second toes and laced around her ankle. In a minute she would get up and clean it off. How horrible she'd been to Amber. That was unnecessary and she would apologize. She'd forgotten what a bitch she could be.

She had to stop being so angry. The fact that she'd recognized him didn't mean there was any chance of him recognizing her. He hadn't turned up at the kennels today. He wasn't camped outside her house.

All she had to do was stay calm. She watched the blood drip onto the cushion.

If he did recognize her . . .

He didn't.

But if he did . . .

She flexed her foot and raised her leg and the blood flowed down her shin.

Did she want him to? That rush she felt the instant she saw him, was it pure dread, or was it mixed with something else?

Her cell rang. "Just wondering how you're doing," said Carson.

"I'm wounded."

"In body or soul?"

"Big toe."

"That sounds bad. Want me to come over?"

How careless she had started to become recently. How willing to let down her guard. As if nothing could ever go wrong for her now. "Thanks, but I think I can handle it."

"I could come anyway. If you like."

"I'm ready to curl up and go to sleep. Another night."

"Okay," said Carson. "You handle your toe, I'll handle the rejection. I'll see you tomorrow, right?"

Maybe John Grabowski had done her a favor showing up here. It served as a reminder. Not to get too comfortable. Perhaps he was an angel in disguise. "I'm not sure," said Lydia. "I'll call you. I've got a busy week."

Chapter Twenty-two

On Saturday morning Grabowski rose early, took his laptop and camera bag, and got in the car. He wanted to be out of Kensington today. Thursday, the day after Lydia had come around, he'd lain low. Mrs. Jackson had draped herself in various positions around the bed-and-breakfast and the yard and he'd obliged her by snapping away. He still didn't have a shot of Lydia with her boyfriend but he couldn't risk anything. She would be edgy now, she'd be checking over her shoulder and in her rearview mirror. He had to proceed cautiously.

Yesterday he had ventured out to take more photographs that might be used as background, the wooden sign that read, "Welcome to Kensington," the view over the river, the town hall, the quaint stores on Albert and Victoria streets, the street signs themselves. He'd driven all over town, looking for the best vantage point, for the frame that would be accompanied by the caption that read, "Could this sleepy little town hold the secret to a royal mystery?" They'd make out there'd been a mystery all along, ignore the fact that only the UFO spotters had ever seriously considered it as that.

He'd written the captions to each picture over and over. Not that he'd get any say. When he laid his head down on his pillow and closed his eyes he'd see the headlines in gigantic block capitals. SHOCK WAVES FELT AROUND THE WORLD . . . PRINCESS "DISCOVERED" IN U.S. BACKWATER . . . RISEN FROM THE DEAD . . .

Yesterday, while he was still trying to stay out of her way, he could have sworn she was following him. Three times he'd seen the Sport Trac a couple of cars behind. She should have been at work, not cruising around town.

He pulled into the forecourt of the diner where he'd first spotted Kensington on the map. He needed a shot of this place, where the story began. They'd want him to go through it, exactly how it had all unfolded. There was a fluttering in his stomach. He was hungry. He was also nervous as hell. This was going to be so huge, it was almost unimaginable. The media would descend like a plague of biblical proportions. They'd all want to interview him. His life would change. This was the lull before the tsunami. He was going to need some serious backup.

Patience, he told himself. Put it together. There were a few more things he needed to get in place. He wasn't going to open his mouth too soon. He wasn't going to turn paranoid and rush in before he was ready.

Out of nowhere he felt a pang that hit him like a blow to the solar plexus. Was he going to do this to her? The world at her feet, and she moved heaven and earth to get away from it.

Since Wednesday he'd been in such a high state of tension that he'd hardly eaten. After breakfast he'd feel better. A waitress, the same one who'd served him before, came out of the diner and lit a cigarette. She squatted on her heels with her back against the wall.

He should get out of the car and eat. In a minute that's what he would do. He took his rosary from his pocket and examined the crucifix that hung off it, the silver-capped borealis blue beads. When his mother had given him the rosary, on the day that he left home at eighteen, he'd hugged her. To her he was still what he'd always been, a little altar boy.

He worked the beads through his fingers and thought about Lydia. If he could let her be then he would. But it wasn't possible. She was here. She was alive. She had lied to the entire world. To her own children who'd followed her coffin. And it wouldn't be right, it would be wrong of him, to look the other way.

"How are the waffles?" he asked the waitress. She had a safety pin in place of a top button on her blouse, but it didn't look too safe, the fabric pulled apart and showed her bra.

"To die for," she said.

"Really?"

"For five bucks and coffee thrown in?" she said. "What do you think?"

He ordered them anyway, with a side of bacon, and when he finished eating he opened his laptop and reviewed the shots he had of Lydia. There was a good one of her coming out of the clothing store, her hair was tied up and she was smiling and waving at someone across the street. She was wearing a camisole-style top, showing her swimmer's shoulders. There was a series of shots of her getting into her car at the kennel. A brilliant clear shot of her face, straight on. He'd crop in on her eyes for the cover picture. The same blue as his rosary beads. Pictures of her house, from all angles. He didn't have one of her coming out of the front door because there wasn't a position from which he could take it unobserved. He had one of her at her bedroom window though, which he'd taken from the bushes. She still had the same habit, on waking, of looking out at the new day. When she'd taken her boys to Disneyland he'd got a shot of her in her dressing gown at six o'clock, drinking coffee standing at the window of her hotel suite. That single picture had paid for his entire trip.

The waitress refilled his coffee cup. "That your girlfriend?"

She'd flirted for England in the early days. That image she had, of being shy, was never real. She'd look down at the ground so it was difficult to get a straight-on head shot but that didn't stop the banter.

"Just a woman I know," he said.

The waitress bent down to get a closer look. Her shirt strained dangerously. She straightened up and noticed the camera bag on the seat next to him. "You a photographer?"

"Tell me something," he said, zooming in on Lydia's face. "Does she remind you of anyone?" The waitress was probably in her mid-thirties, old enough to remember.

"No. I used to do some modeling," she said. "When I was younger."

They'd all been a bit in love with her. Then she'd turned on them. *Why don't you leave me alone?* It was disconcerting when she'd scream like that. And the answer was so obvious it left you with nothing to say. To be honest, after all those years, it felt like a betrayal. How could she expect them just to go away? She'd given up her police protection too. What did she expect?

"Nothing raunchy," said the waitress. Her face was sweaty. She had open pores on her nose. The flesh that ran down from her armpit to her elbow swung slightly when she lifted the coffeepot. The way she lacked self-consciousness made her quite sexy. "I did some nudes. But nothing raunchy," she repeated. "She's pretty, your girlfriend."

"She's not . . . not what you think."

The waitress picked up his plate. "Yeah?" she said. "In my experience, people rarely are."

What else did he need? He'd take it to the *News of the World*. No, *The Sunday Times*. Tell Gareth to negotiate an "exclusive" that would last a day. It was going to explode. The photos were the core. Then birth and death certificates. They didn't exactly prove anything, other than that there was something suspicious about her identity. What he needed now were a few bits of titillating circumstantial evidence. A quote or two from her friends. Any snippet that could be tied to her past, any background information she'd slipped up on. He had to be cautious, but he also had to be quick.

Was she actually following him yesterday? If so, she wouldn't have seen anything suspicious. He was out taking shots of Kensington yesterday, which tied in neatly with his cover story.

If she thought he was on to her, wouldn't she simply skip town, vanish? If she did that, he'd still have the pictures, could still press ahead, and it would only add to the intrigue.

Yes, she'd just go.

Unless she wanted to get caught.

Perhaps she'd had enough of living this dreary life.

Grabowski sipped his coffee. He looked over at the waitress, filing her nails at the counter while a man in a baseball cap tried to chat her up. Something in her studiedly casual stance told Grabowski that the man's luck might be in.

If she wanted to go back to her old life, how could she go about it? Turn up at KP and pound on the gates? This way she'd create the fireworks, the circus, the mayhem she'd always kicked off. She was a perpetual manipulator. She was a puller of strings, and an expert in denial.

It was more likely she had been running errands than following him. It was only his nerves playing up.

How much surgery had she had done? Definitely the nose. Maybe the lips as well. What else had she gone through? Her voice sounded different, had she trained it? In ten years she hadn't picked up an American accent but she'd lost her own, the accent of the upper classes.

He had to stop this daydreaming and sharpen up his plan. This afternoon he'd go into the clothing store, pretend to be buying something for his wife, and see if he could strike up a conversation. She seemed to be close friends with the woman who ran it. There might be a way to turn the talk around to Lydia. Saturday today. On Monday, when she was safely out of the way at work, he'd break into her house. There'd be something in there to spice up the proceedings. Something she'd taken with her, a recognizable piece of jewelry perhaps, a family photograph. Something that nailed the story to the front pages. The second he got out of there he'd have everything uploaded and ready to e-mail from the bed-and-breakfast. A call in to Gareth first. Shit or get off the pot. It was Gareth who'd be soiling his trousers.

He watched the boutique for a while from across the road, pretending to browse at the florist. Best to go in when there were no other customers. He scanned the street again to make sure Lydia's car wasn't there.

Cathy wouldn't have him back. She'd never got along with his mother. Never made the effort. This was going to change his life anyway. And who knew what he'd want himself when it was over?

First time he'd met Cathy he'd been in a pub brawl the night before. How it had got started he couldn't even remember by the next day. His fighting days, thank God, were over a long time ago.

The clothing store was empty now, except for the owner who was rehanging clothes from the changing room. He wasn't sure how to run the conversation. He'd have to play it by ear. Of course he'd tried Mrs. Jackson, but she hadn't given him anything useful. The same vague details that Lydia had supplied herself, about having moved to America with her husband, living in several different states, getting divorced, settling down in Kensington. Mrs. Jackson wasn't intimate with Lydia and even if she had been, she was too firmly enthroned at center stage to be capable of reflecting the bit players.

"Are you looking for something special?"

"Something to take back to my wife."

"My name's Amber. I'll let you browse. Just let me know if you need help with anything."

Grabowski picked up a beaded cardigan. "This is nice."

"Oh, that's pretty," said Amber. "It's a safe bet. What size is your wife?"

He considered. "She's tall and slim. Size ten, maybe."

"That a UK ten? That'd be a size six here. Are you staying over with Mrs. Jackson?"

"I am." She was going to be talkative. He might get something. But maybe his timing was off. Wouldn't it be better to wait another day or so, then tie it up immediately with a swift visit to Lydia's house?

"Lovely," said Amber. "Did you meet my friend Lydia? Mrs. Jackson invited her over for scones."

"I did. We had the famous scones." He walked over to a rack of long gowns and picked one out.

"That's my favorite," said Amber. She was a pocket-size blonde, a little bland, a little babbly. "Lydia has that very one. She looks absolutely stunning in it. What kind of coloring does your wife have? Does she have dark hair?"

He lifted the gown and examined it front and back. This Amber was definitely a talker. And she'd repeat this conversation to Lydia the second she saw her. "My wife's a blonde," he said, "very pale."

"Ah," said Amber, "well, what about this blue taffeta, here, take a look. What do you think?"

It would be better, as well, to get something on tape. He'd have to buy a digital recorder and have it switched on in his pocket. He should have thought of that already. *For a ha'penny worth of tar,* his mother would say. Well, he wasn't going to spoil this ship. He was going to make sure it set sail.

"That's very nice," he said. "Could I have a look at some others?"

Amber showed him all the gowns, pointing out details, naming fabrics, explaining how they sat at the neckline. "Lydia's one is stunning, though. Did you have a good chat about London?"

He evaluated two dresses distractedly, holding them up for comparison. He wasn't going to show any interest in her friend. When she relayed the conversation there would be nothing to make Lydia twitch.

"What do you think?" she said. "Do you have an instinct about what would be right?"

He had an instinct that what would be right would be to wait until Wednesday afternoon. If Lydia had an initial suspicion he'd have done nothing by then to strengthen it, quite the opposite, stayed right out of her way. She took every Wednesday afternoon off work and spent it here, in the boutique. That gave him a clear run at the old woman at the dog place. If he played it right he'd get something useful out of her, a quote from the employer. Then he'd go to the house. Four more days and he'd have what he needed. And not long after that this town would be on the map for all time. This was Chappaquiddick, Roswell, and Dealey Plaza rolled into one. This was twenty-four hours a day, worldwide saturation coverage.

"I can't decide," he said to Amber. "I'd better think about it."

"Oh, please do," said Amber, smiling sweetly. "It's never good to rush into things."

Chapter Twenty-three

After brunch at Tevis's house on Sunday, her boyfriend and Suzie's husband began dragooning the kids for a hike in the woods. Lydia wondered if she should go with them. She was restless. She didn't want to sit still. But she couldn't make up her mind to get out of her chair.

"Maya," said Mike. "Get your ass in gear. We're hitting the trail."

"Why can't I stay here?" said Maya. "I hate walking."

Mike grinned at her. He was tall with sandy hair and freckles and he always had the bit between his teeth. Just looking at him right now made Lydia even more exhausted. "Don't make me cuff you," he said.

Maya turned to Lydia. "Always the same lame old jokes."

"Old ones are the best ones," said Mike, slapping his thigh. "Why did the chicken cross the road?"

"Oh God, Dad," said Maya. "You really do live in the Stone Age."

"LAPD answer—we don't know, but give us five minutes with the chicken and we'll find out."

"I'm staying here," said Maya, tucking her legs up on the chair.

Suzie came out of the kitchen onto the deck and stacked more dishes. "Has Steve gone ahead?"

"He's loading the troopers into the wagon." Mike put his hands on Maya's shoulders. "Whaddya say we take Rufus with us too, if it's okay by Lydia?"

"It's okay with me," said Lydia. Mike, she could see, was trying to steer Maya away from a confrontation with her mother.

"You, young lady," said Suzie. "Scram."

Maya opened her mouth but Mike bent down and whispered

something in her ear that made her laugh. "Come on, Rufus," he said, "we're going for a walk."

Rufus was glued to the top of Lydia's feet. She pulled them out from under him. "Go," she said. He picked himself up and moved five inches to curl up over her toes. "Okay, stay."

When they'd seen the men and children off, Suzie, Amber, and Tevis rejoined Lydia at the table.

"Wasn't Carson supposed to come too?" said Tevis.

"We sort of had an argument last night," said Lydia.

"Oh dear, is everything okay?" Amber looked at her anxiously.

"It's fine," said Lydia. She smiled to cut the questions. "We both needed a bit of air today."

"The guy from the bed-and-breakfast came in yesterday," said Amber. "Looking for something for his wife. He seemed nice."

Everyone, thought Lydia, seemed nice to Amber. She was indiscriminate in her liking. And if Grabowski was poking around in Amber's store, maybe Lydia wasn't being paranoid. Maybe he was going all over town, asking questions. "What did you chat about?"

"Nothing, really," said Amber. "He was interested in the evening gowns."

All day yesterday, she had been trying to put it out of her mind, telling herself she was being stupid. On Friday she'd taken the day off work and followed him from morning until late afternoon. It was more difficult than she thought it would be to do that without him noticing. Many times she'd lost him because she'd held back too far, when there wasn't much traffic around, and knowing her car was distinctive. Years ago, time after time, she'd had him on her tail and lost him with her reckless driving. This time she'd crept behind and all she'd seen was him driving around taking photographs of town signs and the river. She'd tried to make up her mind to stop torturing herself. By evening, of course, the doubt had crept back in. And now Amber was telling her that Grabowski had been sniffing around. Her first instincts had been correct.

"Which one did he buy?" said Lydia.

"He couldn't choose," said Amber. "He's coming back next week. I told him best not to rush the decision."

"Did he mention that we'd had tea together, with Mrs. Jackson?"

"He did. Or I asked him," said Amber.

"What else did he say?" What she wanted to know was what Amber said. All the things that she had told Amber, she'd been getting so sloppy.

"Nothing really. Told me his wife's a blonde. He was interested in the same dress you've got but I thought maybe it wouldn't suit her coloring. I told him how fantastic you look in yours."

"What else did you tell him?" said Lydia.

"You interested in this guy, Lydia?" said Tevis.

"What else did you tell him?" said Lydia. "I'm just curious, that's all, because to tell you the truth, he didn't seem like a nice man to me. He seemed a bit seedy."

"Oh," said Amber. "Was he? Well, he wasn't there for long, and we talked—I talked—about the dresses."

I failed all my exams, twice. Why had she told Amber that? Why did she give away information like that? How many other things had she told Amber and Esther and the others that Grabowski could piece together? My mother left when I was six. Only the other day she'd been telling Esther. Careless, stupid, witless. Carson's dossier might be pretty thin but Grabowski's would burst at the seams if he managed to gull all her friends. Her so-called friends.

"Lydia," Tevis was saying. "Lydia, are you all right?"

They'd give her away. Why had she ever thought that wouldn't happen?

"Lydia?"

Endless betrayal. Her life had been one endless betrayal. She could never, ever, trust anyone, and she should have learned that so long ago. On her honeymoon, which her husband spent making calls to his mistress. No, long before that. When her mother left her sitting on the stairs and walked out to the car, carrying her suitcase.

"Lydia," said Suzie.

This was crazy thinking. She had to pull herself out of it. She should have gone for a walk with the kids. A long walk and then a swim.

"Do you want a glass of water?" said Amber.

Lydia shook her head.

"Do you have a headache?"

She looked at the three of them, the concern on all their faces. "I'm sorry," she said, "I've got a few things on my mind."

"Thought we'd lost you," said Suzie.

Lydia gave her a smile. She felt a blush of shame for the way she had just written off her friends.

There was a pause in the conversation. The breeze started to pick up, and the sun ducked behind a cloud. Tevis's yard was small with a gravel and herb garden that smelled strongly of thyme when the wind blew. Beyond the herb garden was a little pond filled with rushes and water lilies.

"I'm going to stretch my legs," said Lydia. She wandered down to the pond.

Last night Carson had come over. It was terrible. She'd made a terrible scene. Why had she done that? It had been so unnecessary. Rufus was fussing at her feet. He really could be trying sometimes. She picked him up. The whole of yesterday she'd been staving off thoughts that there was anything sinister in Grabowski's presence. Running through the doubts, like a never-ending load of laundry, around and around in her head, faster and faster on a spin cycle, tangled, mashed up, blurred. By the time Carson had arrived she had been so on edge she flinched when he kissed her hello.

She had hardly been able to speak. "You know you can talk to me if you want to," said Carson. "About anything. I'm here."

She had wanted to scream at him then. No, she couldn't talk to him about anything. She couldn't tell him anything at all.

"Thank you," she said through gritted teeth.

"Really," he said. The sincerity in his eyes was scalding, unbearable. "If you don't want to let me know you, that's fine. We'll carry on as we are. But there's not much I wouldn't do for you. I hope you know that, Lydia."

"What would you do for me?" she spat. It was a stupid thing that he'd said. "What would you really do?"

He took her hand. "Try me," he said gently.

"Would you leave everything?" she said. She was practically shouting. "Would you leave your home, your job, your friends?" He didn't realize, she had to make him realize, that when he said something like that he had to mean it. "Would you sacrifice everything if you had to, to be with me? I don't think so." She snatched her hand away. If Grabowski was going to expose her, then that would change the rest of his life. That's if he stayed the course, which he wouldn't, when it came down to it. If she had to take off suddenly, would he come with her, without any explanation, at a moment's notice? She wasn't foolish enough to think that. What if she did explain? But no, it was hopeless.

He tried to answer but she wouldn't let him. "It's all cheap talk. We have a nice time together. We sleep together. It's company for both of us. But that's it. Don't go talking about how there's nothing you wouldn't do for me, because you don't know. You've got no idea."

She was trembling. She wanted him to wrap her up in his arms and tell her everything would be okay. She wanted to fill the hollow of his neck with her tears. If he said to her now, you have to tell me everything, she would let it all come tumbling out. Everything. She couldn't hold it in anymore. Whatever happened would happen. She was sick of it, sick of trying to control every last little thing.

He didn't say a word. He rubbed the back of his neck and looked up at the ceiling.

After a while, when she already knew it was too late and the moment had gone, he said, "I'm a serious person, Lydia. When are you going to start treating me like one? I don't want to play any games."

She cried then, and he held her but the distance between them was vast, too great to fill with her tears. How could she ever explain herself? If she tried, how could he possibly understand? It wasn't his failing. Perhaps one person could never understand another. And in her case it was too much to ask of any human being.

* * *

She went back to the deck, where Amber was talking about Phil, recounting where they'd been on their date.

"So," said Suzie, "you think this is going to be a regular thing?"

"Last night at dinner," said Amber, "he was talking and I was listening to him, and making comments, you know, back and forth."

"That's called a conversation," said Tevis.

"But I wasn't really in the conversation," said Amber. "I was just looking in on it and thinking, wow, that conversation sounds dull. I hope that woman knows what she's doing. I hope she doesn't get landed with that guy who's sitting there talking about his IBS."

"IBS? Was he talking about his finances?" said Suzie.

"Irritable bowel syndrome," said Tevis. "You haven't even slept with him yet and he's talking about his irritable bowel syndrome?"

"He has to be careful what he orders," said Amber. She giggled.

Lydia took her place back at the table. "You sounded quite excited about him last time."

"I know," said Amber. "Do I seem fickle? I do think he's really nice."

Lydia patted Amber's hand. "You're the most generous person I've ever met. You think everyone's really nice."

"Oh," said Amber, "well, mostly they are."

"That's something you've taught me," said Lydia. "Or something I'm still trying to learn."

"So is it all off?" said Suzie.

"I think I'll let it wind down," said Amber.

"Sounds like it reached a great climax, though," said Suzie. "Talking about his irritating bowels. Man, you should've made a home movie out of that."

"Dang," said Tevis. "I forgot about dessert. I got two huge tiramisus in the refrigerator. Anyone want some?"

Lydia tidied the kitchen while Tevis washed and cut strawberries and spooned the tiramisu into bowls. She stacked plates in the dishwasher and scrubbed out a pan. There was no way Grabowski could have been following her. Every day she'd been looking over her shoulder, checking the rearview, watching out for him. The only one who'd been doing any following was her.

The danger of destroying her world came from only one person. Herself. She was her own worst enemy. A year after she'd swum into her new life she'd imagined that a neighbor had worked out who she was. What a frenzy of paranoia that turned out to be.

There was a pressure, a storm cloud, building inside her. How long was she going to live like this anyway?

She picked up a dirty chopping board and knife. When she'd washed it, she carried on turning the knife over in her hands. She thought about the blood running down from her toe, over her foot and onto her ankle, the crimson flower unfolding, blossoming. She looked at the knife. Let it out, she thought. If she could just let it out. The smallest puncture, a tiny valve, a lancing, a leeching, a bloodletting.

"Leave the dishes," said Tevis. "Let's take these desserts outside."

Lydia dried her hands. She had to calm down.

"Ready?" said Tevis.

She didn't want to calm down. Why should she? Was this her life forever? Always holding her breath. Forever tiptoeing. She surged with rebellion, an adrenaline rush that nearly lifted her off her feet. How long since she'd soared like that? In the old days, when she was knocked down, didn't she always spring up again?

"Tevis," she said, tossing the towel aside, "I want a tarot reading. Can we do that first?"

The sitting room was a cave of eastern treasures: Indian wall hangings, Indonesian furniture, a large onyx Buddha presiding on a Japanese tea chest. Tevis retrieved her tarot pack and sat on the floor by the coffee table in lotus position. It had a mermaid done in mosaic. Lydia sat at the opposite end.

"Is there anything in particular you want to find out from the reading?" said Tevis. "Don't tell me what it is. Just have it in your mind." She wore a crinkly cotton top and the string tie with which it laced at the chest ended with small gold bells. "I'm going to deal a Celtic cross," she said. "Have you ever had this done before?"

"Yes, but ages ago," said Lydia. She'd done it all. Tevis looked so easy in her skin. She never cared what anyone thought. Right now she looked positively serene.

Tevis laid out seven cards in a cross. "Now this part is called the staff," she said, putting down another four cards.

The cards couldn't tell her what she wanted to know. Tevis couldn't tell her. No one could tell her. She had to get out of here. She had to go somewhere. Anywhere. She had to go right now.

Rufus ran in to investigate what was going on. His tail knocked some of the cards to the floor.

"Let's not do this," said Lydia. She picked up the rest of the cards and shuffled them back into the deck.

"It won't matter," said Tevis. "I can just deal again."

"I know, but I've changed my mind. Rufus changed it for me. He's very wise, you know." Lydia forced a laugh. She should at least have a swim. Try to clear her head.

Tevis gathered the cards and put them back in the pack. "You're not into this stupid hippie stuff."

"Do you believe it?" said Lydia. "Tarot, runes, horoscope, chakras, channeling?"

"This week, at work," said Tevis. She piled her hair on top of her head while she thought, and stuck a pencil through it. "This week, at work, I showed five houses, I made about fifty calls, I read or sent maybe a hundred e-mails. I drank fifteen cups of coffee, had six meetings with colleagues, I went to the bathroom twelve times. I read about the new regulations for escrow accounts. I did three new valuations and prepared half a dozen contracts. I got two runs in two pairs of hose. The highlight of everyone's week was when the new watercooler arrived." She paused. She stuck out her bottom lip and shrugged. "I don't know which is more nutty. All this stuff I do outside of work, or the stuff that I do all week."

Lydia parked and walked up Albert Street to the pharmacy to buy some aspirin. Her headache had become intense. She'd take some pills and have a swim and after that she'd be able to think more clearly, work out exactly what to do and when.

Albert Street was dead, nothing moving. How long could she bury herself here? It was about time she reminded herself that she didn't actually die.

She should move. What she should do was move to New York or Washington and begin living again. It was time. Lawrence had given her a contingency plan, another passport and identity, in case she ever needed it. Most likely she didn't, and she didn't want to learn again to answer to another name. But she should reinvent herself elsewhere in any case. She was a kennel worker in Kensington when she could (she was still attractive enough) be a socialite in Washington.

She would come across old friends there. If she managed to infiltrate some of her old circles . . . she smiled.

In the pharmacy, Mrs. Deaver was getting ready to close. "I'll be quick," said Lydia. "I just need some aspirin and a mascara."

"You take all the time you need," said Mrs. Deaver. "If you want any help, let me know."

Lydia picked up a bottle of aspirin. The cosmetics rack was at the back of the store. She examined a couple of mascaras, slipped one in her pocket and put the other back on the shelf.

Mrs. Deaver rang up the Bayer. "Couldn't find what you wanted in the back there?"

"No, Mrs. Deaver. Actually, I decided I didn't need it after all."

She said good-bye and stepped out on the street and scanned it in both directions. In her old life she couldn't set foot outside without checking first where the cameras were. She walked back up Albert Street, imagining the photographers walking backward in front of her, others to the side calling her name. Was she going back to that? Is that what she wanted? There were goose bumps down her arms. Hold tight, she told herself. Hold tight. It was going to be one hell of a ride.

Chapter Twenty-four

He had two days to kill before Wednesday and they'd be the longest two days of his life. Was there anything he could do to speed this up? A thousand times over he'd checked his work. There was nothing he could do now but wait. He wanted the "interview" with the woman who ran the kennel. And if he waited until Lydia's regular afternoon off there was no chance of bumping into her there. He'd be careful how he asked the questions. With a bit of luck, the old woman would be oblivious, wouldn't report anything back to Lydia. Lydia wouldn't run before the story broke.

Last night he'd lain awake worrying about whether he should e-mail some photographs to Gareth as backup. What if the bed-and-breakfast burned down? He knew it was stupid. He was taking his gear everywhere. If he lost it, which he wouldn't, he had a copy on a memory stick in the desk drawer. E-mailing would be dangerous. If someone in Gareth's office saw it, it would be all over the Internet, no way it could be controlled. He'd fly back with everything safely and securely loaded on his laptop alone. Gareth would arrange a meeting with *The Sunday Times* and he'd show them. He wouldn't be handing anything over until the money was agreed.

Patience. Ten years without a single story that he really gave a toss about. Another two days was nothing.

The bar in Gains opened at noon and Grabber arrived as the barman was pulling the shutters up. He played some pool with a mechanic who had one leg shorter than the other, and a rolling, pirate gait. He drank diet sodas and kept one eye on his bags and another on the door. If that woman showed up he'd get out of here.

Not that he had anything to feel guilty about. But he could do without any scenes.

How much would he get for the exclusive? A million wouldn't be too much. A million would be too little, in fact.

He took a stool at the bar and ordered a beer. He tried to think of something to say to the barman, but the guy had a face like a wasp sting and to concentrate on drying glasses he probably needed both his brain cells.

When he saw the lads in the pub back home, they'd give him a hard time. That's how it was when someone did well. They had to take a ribbing, stop them getting too big for their boots. Jealous as fuck, they'd all be. But pleased for him. Most of them. He'd be buying the rounds all night.

The old woman at the dog place. He had to think how to play it with her. He had to invent a reason for talking to her, a reason that would open her up. Once he had her confidence it would be easy to lead her in the right direction, to turn the talk to Lydia. All he needed was a handful of details, which he'd get on the tape recorder in his pocket. He'd buy one tomorrow. Almost anything would add heft to the story. "So, Mrs. Jackson said Lydia grew up in Southampton." "Oh no, dear, Lydia grew up in . . ." It didn't matter what she said. It would be useful either way. If Lydia had told the old lady anything true about her childhood, of course the paper would run that as a consolidating fact. If she'd made up stuff, the paper would run it anyway, as confirmation that she'd woven a nest of lies around her false identity.

And it wasn't difficult to get people to talk. You only had to flatter them a little. He'd had years of practice. One afternoon he got a tip-off that she'd taken the boys to a movie in Leicester Square. He didn't find her car parked anywhere nearby, and he didn't know if he was wasting his time. There were no other photographers in sight. If she was inside, she'd given everyone the slip.

He'd gone into the foyer and ambled around, left his camera back in the car, of course. He pretended to read some of the movie reviews that were posted on various pillars. Then he bought a ticket for a later show and struck up a casual conversation with a ticket attendant. Said he hadn't been to this cinema since he'd come just after it was opened. Wasn't it opened by the Duke of Edinburgh in 1985? Yes, it was, said the attendant, there's a plaque right over there. Grabowski turned around to take a look, although he'd already seen it. And did the Duke ever come to see any films here? Not to my knowledge, said the attendant. You'd be too discreet to tell, said Grabowski. The attendant was fairly bursting. Well, I'm not supposed to say, but the Princess of Wales is in right now, with both her sons. Really, said Grabowski, is she as beautiful in real life as she is in the photos? She's amazing, said the attendant. You know how amazing she looks in the photos, well, she's even more amazing than that.

He knew what he'd say to the dog lady. And it hardly mattered what she said to him. It would all be great context. Lydia's wonderful with both people and animals. Lydia hasn't said much about her past. Lydia takes sugar in her coffee. It didn't matter. It would all help feed a story, and the appetite would be insatiable. Everyone would lap up every detail of what her employer said, they wouldn't be able to get enough of it, and they'd make of it whatever they liked.

"I'll have another beer," said Grabowski. "Hey, what do people do for fun around here?"

The barman looked at him suspiciously, as if he'd asked a trick question. "Fun?" he said, mauling the word. "Well, on the weekends some folks go hunting. That's quite popular. You a hunting man?"

"No," said Grabowski. He'd lain on his belly in the gorse at Balmoral, but it wasn't deer he'd had in his sights. "Not into blood sports."

The barman nodded. "It's exciting. Can't explain it to someone who's never done it. But you have to have a license, they got strict laws about that."

He spent the day in the bar, nursing one slow beer after another. By evening he was half-hoping that the woman would come in because he was going out of his skull with boredom. She didn't show.

Around ten o'clock he drove back to Kensington, parked, stowed his gear, and then decided to walk up to the liquor store, though he didn't know if it would still be open; this town was a graveyard after nine.

It was so quiet on Fairfax that his footsteps sounded rudely loud. On Albert an old man shuffled out of his bungalow, coughed, and shuffled back inside. The streets were deserted, barely a car passing through.

When he wanted to cross there was a single vehicle, approaching from the left. The driver wasn't speeding, he'd have plenty of time. He stepped off the curb and instinctively turned to check for any traffic from the right. An engine roared and he swung to face it, startled. The car from the left was hurtling at him, its headlights gunning him down. For a moment he was paralyzed, not knowing whether to turn back or run straight ahead. There was a voice shouting *No!* It was his voice. He was running for the other side of the road, the car was nearly on him. He was running for his life, the engine ripping at his ears.

It wasn't going to hit him, it was terrifying the way it had revved up, but it had been far enough away that . . . Before he finished the thought, the car swerved sharply toward him. He screamed. This was it, he was going to die.

He braced himself for the impact, as if by steeling his chest and arms, he would be ready for a ton of metal smashing into him at eighty miles an hour.

The speed the car was going, it got up so much wind it nearly whipped him around when it swerved right and passed.

"Fucker," he yelled after it. "You fuck . . ." He stopped. That was Lydia's Sport Trac.

She'd tried to kill him.

She was on to him.

He closed his eyes and crossed himself.

What did this mean? He tried to think, with his heart still jumping out of his shirt. What did it mean? It meant one thing, clearly. He was going to have to speed this whole thing up.

Chapter Twenty-five

On Monday evening Lydia went to Esther's for dinner and on the drive back across town to home she tried to focus on how great tomorrow was going to be. She'd asked for another day off but she'd go into work in the afternoon and present Esther with the money she'd raised from selling the bracelet. The valuer was supposed to be back tomorrow, and she assumed she'd be getting a check on the spot.

Over dinner, Esther had told her that she'd secured more funding from the ASPCA. It wouldn't be available for another few weeks, but all they had to do was make it through.

"I know we're having tea at Amber's tomorrow," Esther had said, "but I wanted to do something for your birthday too. I'm not sure that you know how much I appreciate all that you do."

Esther wasn't one for hugging, so Lydia didn't inflict that on her.

Yesterday evening she'd been so whacked out, she'd been thinking all sorts of things. Why would she leave this place? Why would she put herself on the rack again? What she'd found in this place was some peace. And she had found some friends.

"John Grabowski," she said aloud, "you've got a lot to answer for."

There was something she hadn't worked out yet about his presence here. Was it a total coincidence? Was she supposed to believe that? She had tried.

She stopped at a red light and drummed her fingers on the steering wheel.

She had to believe it, or else she would drive herself mad. Raise all of the demons that she thought she had slain.

Once again she ran over it. He'd shown no sign of recognizing her.

He hadn't been following her, she'd checked so carefully. She had followed him.

The light turned green. She sat there. Something still wasn't right. There had to be something she'd missed. She put the car in drive and moved off. They'd met on Wednesday and he hadn't tried to come near her since.

Not since. But what about before? That was the first time she'd seen him, but what if it wasn't the first time he'd seen her?

How long had he been in town? Mrs. Jackson had come into Amber's store and invited her to meet him. That was a whole week earlier. If he'd seen her before, he'd already have all the pictures he'd need.

What was he waiting for? Why was he toying with her?

She gripped the steering wheel as her stomach lurched. This could not be allowed to happen. She would not let him, he had no right. *No-right-no-right-no-right.* The words jammed in her brain.

It wasn't a raccoon in the oleander outside Carson's house.

Damn him. Damn John Grabowski. What gave him the right?

The town peeled past her on either side. There was nothing and no one on the road as it spooled out ahead and all she could think of was John Grabowski and how much she hated him.

Out of nowhere he stepped onto the road. Lydia didn't hesitate. She put her foot down on the gas. He would take her life if he could. He would take it and he wouldn't have a single regret. She slammed her foot to the floor. He was running, but she'd get him, he wouldn't get away. At the last moment she swerved to avoid him and by the time she reached home the sweat that had drenched her ran ice-cold down her back.

She stood in the shower and soaped her face, neck, arms, hands, chest, thighs, shins, feet. Her sanity had slipped through her fingers more easily than this bar of soap. It wasn't Grabowski who was torturing her. She was torturing herself. This roller coaster of doubts and emotions—she'd chosen to get on it, and if she didn't like it, then she should choose to step right off again. Hadn't she learned that by now? That was the hardest lesson. It was no good blaming others. It was no good lashing out. She'd had to leave everything and everyone just to discover that you were the only person responsible for your own peace of mind.

When she got out of the shower there was someone ringing the doorbell. It was after ten thirty. Nobody came around at this time.

She could make up a dozen stories to blame Grabowski for this—what?—this relapse. They were just stories in her head. Was she getting some sick kick out of them? All she'd seen, with her own eyes, was him going about his own business. And then she'd nearly run him down.

He had come over to confront her about it. The doorbell rang again. She didn't know what she could say. And it would serve her right to have to deal with him now.

She opened the door in her dressing gown.

"I know it's late," said Carson. "But can I come in? We need to talk."

She opened a bottle of red wine and got the glasses and sat down on the sofa, expecting him to sit next to her. He sat down opposite.

"I've been thinking about what happened the other day. We seemed to tie ourselves up in knots."

He smiled at her. It was a smile that was full of regret, as if this was all over, as if he'd come to say good-bye.

"Couldn't we forget about it?" said Lydia. "Just carry on?"

He leaned forward in his chair, and for a confused and aching moment she thought he was going to get up and come to her, but he just bowed his head and let it hang. When he lifted it again he said, "I know I said I wouldn't ask you anything, but I have to. I want you to talk to me."

She studied his face, as if she had to memorize it. The lines on his forehead, the mole on the right side of his jaw, the chapping on his lips. His eyes sought hers.

"We always talk," she said.

"You know what I mean." He held her gaze and there was a sad light in his dark eyes, and she knew exactly what it meant.

Still, she would try to hold on. "Don't do this," she said. "We were fine as we were."

"Stop pushing me away, Lydia. I don't know the first thing about you and every time I try to talk to you, you act like it's all over."

"Isn't it?" she said.

He shook his head. "There you go again. What is it that you're hiding? What dark secret do you have that you can't share with me?"

"I'm sorry," she said. She bit her lip. She thought about the blood coursing down her foot. She imagined it running down her arm, down her body, let it flow.

"That's it?" he said. "You're sorry? What kind of answer is that? Are you a bigamist? Are you working for the FBI? Did you kill someone? What? Aren't you making this so much more difficult than it needs to be? What can you have done that means that I'm not allowed to know anything about you at all?"

"You know quite a lot about me," she said. "You know that I . . ."

He cut her off. "Lydia, stop it. Stop fucking with my head." He stood up, and she knew that was it, that he was going to leave. He came and sat down next to her.

"I say I'd do anything for you, and you tear into me. How am I supposed to take that? More or less, you call me a lying son of a bitch. Is that how you really feel?"

"No," she said. The word came out enveloped in misery.

He put his arm around her shoulder and pulled her into him and kissed her softly on the cheek. "I'm not expecting you to spill your guts to me now. I know you better than that. What I'm asking is, do you think we're going somewhere with this, and if we are, will you believe me that I might just be able to understand whatever it is that you find so difficult to say?"

All she had to say was, *yes*. All she had to say was, *I'll try*. But she cared too much about him to tell him something that could never be. "Please don't do this," she said.

He pulled away from her. He slumped his head back against the sofa, as if she had finally defeated him. For a long minute he didn't move and she watched him and listened to the blood pounding in her ears.

"Okay," he said at last. "Okay. There's a couple of things I need you to know. One is that I love you. You may not want to hear that. The other is that I'll be there if you ever change your mind."

As soon as she woke the next morning, Lydia went to the bedroom window to look out on the new day. It was early. The pale yellow sun was skeined in a light haze, the dew lay milky on the grass, the surface of the pool ruffled and flattened, the maple leaves danced in the breeze. On the lawn, a rabbit stood on his hind legs and quivered, ears pricked, head swiveling, checking for dangers from every direction. Lydia leaned her forehead against the windowpane and her breath steamed up the glass.

Today was her birthday. In real life, it wouldn't be her birthday for another couple of months. In real life she'd be turning forty-six, instead of forty-five.

What real life? This was her real life.

She put on her black one-piece, picked up a towel from the bathroom, and went down to the pool.

She swam for almost an hour and all the time that she was immersed she felt no pain, as if it was rinsed from her body and soul, as though it had dissolved in the water, drained away.

Afterward, she fed Rufus and then made scrambled eggs and toast. She poured the juice and the coffee and sat down at the breakfast bar. She sat and looked at the plate. She pushed it away and covered her face with her hands, as if someone might see her cry.

It was inevitable, what had happened with Carson. It was only ever make-believe that she could share her life with him, with anyone. What she wished was that there had been a way of going back and doing it over without hurting him. That was impossible too.

She had to pick up the pieces now and carry on. The life that she'd made was a life worth living and it was up to her to do that. She had a place to live, her work, her friends, who accepted her for who she was. For who she wasn't. For who she was now.

These last few days she had seesawed. It was the old, old pattern returning. But it was up to her. No one was pushing her into it. She alone was responsible. It made her shudder, the fantasy that she'd briefly entertained, of going to live in Washington and insinuating herself back into her old social circles, staging a comeback, slowly revealing herself like some tawdry striptease act.

An image inserted itself into her brain: Grabowski's face in the headlights, one arm thrown up in terror, his mouth opened in a soundless scream. She had been out of her head, as if it wasn't her who was driving, pure paranoia taking over the wheel. He hadn't hunted her down. That was impossible. It was a coincidence that he was here and there was no way, under these circumstances, that he had recognized her. Even so, it was natural that his being here made her uncomfortable. She could have dealt with that maturely, accepted that it was unfortunate but that she'd have to leave town for a short while to stop herself worrying. Instead, she'd turned the whole thing into a drama.

Should she go away somewhere today, come back when Grabowski had gone? There were things she had to do today, and it would be awful to miss the party Amber had organized for her. Perhaps she should go tomorrow.

What would Lawrence advise? He was always full of wise words. Wise words and kindness. What would he say?

He had told her a story about when he was waiting to meet her in that bay in Brazil, walking on a jetty and coming across a paparazzo he recognized from days of old. When a small child holds a cushion over his face, he said, they believe themselves invisible. They have not yet developed what is known as a theory of mind. They are not able to project themselves into the mind of the other person, and look out, as it were, from their point of view. We adults, he said, sometimes do the opposite. I believed, for a few moments at least, that because I had recognized him, he must have recognized me. In other words, what I was doing was projecting a great deal too much.

Lydia removed her hands from her face. In her previous life she had felt conspiracy all around her. Constant spying and constant betrayals. She had even believed she would be killed.

She was a danger to herself. That was closer to the truth.

If she had ever been the victim, the target of conspiracy, she was no longer. The world did not revolve around her. She wasn't the center of the universe.

She got up and cleared the plate of food that she had not touched.

This morning was not going to be spent wallowing. She would go into the city and sell her bracelet and take the check to Esther. The biggest birthday present she could give herself would be to stop thinking about nothing but herself. She wondered what Carson was doing. This afternoon she would take Zeus and Topper and go for a long walk in the woods. She scraped the plate into the garbage and ran water over it. Out the window she watched the rabbit nibbling at the grass.

She picked up her car keys from the kitchen counter. She checked her cell to see if Carson had sent a text. Then she pulled open the knife drawer. Ten knives all in a row. She ran her finger along from one blade to the next. She counted them up the line and then she counted them down. As she turned, she used her hip to bang the drawer closed.

The jewelry store was inlaid with polished wood and bloused silk, like the inside of a casket. The air was stiff with the ticking of clocks. While Lydia waited for the valuer to come out from his office, she perused the lines of silver and gold necklaces, all laid to rest on yards of pale purple silk.

"A beautiful day, a beautiful woman. What more can a man ask for?"

"Hello," said Lydia. "I've got a beautiful bracelet for you."

"I'm Gunther. I don't want your bracelet. I want to take you out for dinner."

Lydia laughed and slipped the bracelet off her wrist. Gunther appeared to be wearing his pajama top. His hand shook with some kind of palsy as he took the piece from her. The liver spots that spread across his face ran up over his bald head. There was a skittish gleam in his eyes.

"What?" said Gunther expansively. "You don't like my outfit? Hannah," he said to the woman behind the watch counter, "she don't like my outfit. Tell her she should see how I scrub up."

"Don't mind him," said Hannah. "He's only fooling. Gunther, quit fooling around."

Gunther pulled an eyeglass from his pocket. He winked at Lydia. "Feminist," he said. "Can't get no sense outta her."

He laid the bracelet on a piece of green felt, turned a lamp to shine on it, and leaned over with the eyeglass.

"You sure you want to sell?"

Lydia nodded. "Yes, please. I'd like you to buy it, if you can."

"Sure you wouldn't rather run away with me?" He plucked at his pajama top. "Don't let this pull the wool over your eyes. Rich ones are the eccentric ones. Regular Howard Hughes you're lookin' at, right here." He wheezed an old man's laugh.

"Gunther," said Hannah. "Cut it out."

"All right, all right," he grumbled. He turned the bracelet over and examined how the garnets had been set. "Know what's wrong with the world these days? Everyone's so darn serious."

It was, as Gunther had said, a beautiful day. Lydia put the car windows down and Rufus stood on the passenger seat with his front paws up and his coat glossed back in the wind. The check was in her purse, and the sun on her face was fine. If she kept her mind on what was good in her life, if she put one foot in front of the other instead of whirling around so much she didn't know which direction she was heading, there'd be peace at the end of this solitary winding road that she had taken. She had to try to stop thinking about Carson. The car made an ominous noise, a rattling in the engine. She listened intently but it had gone, as suddenly as it had come, and perhaps it had only been another figment of her imagination.

"Hey, Hank," said Lydia. "Esther around somewhere?"

"Hello there, Lydia," he said. "How are you?"

"I'm great," said Lydia. "How are you?" She should know better than to try to rush the preliminaries with Hank. There were certain rituals, certain dignities, to be scrupulously observed.

"I'm doing great too," said Hank. "Thank you for asking." He wore his shorts down to his knees, socks with his sandals, and Lydia had never seen his shirt untucked no matter how hot the weather.

"I can't seem to find Esther." She didn't want to hurry him, but she was excited about handing over the check, nearly nine thousand dollars, made out directly to Kensington Canine Sanctuary.

"Oh, Esther went out for lunch," said Hank. "Say, I hear it's your birthday, Lydia. I didn't get you a present, only heard about it today. But happy birthday, anyway. And may this day bring you whatever your heart desires." He bowed at the waist.

"Thank you, Hank. That's lovely. Do you know where she went?" Esther never went out for lunch. She brought chicken rice salad in a plastic box every day.

"Afraid I don't," he said. "Heard you were taking the day off."

"I've got a . . . surprise for Esther," she said. "Something I'd like to give her. What time did she leave?"

Hank consulted his watch. "About an hour ago, should be back soon. Went with the English fella she was showing around this morning."

"What did he look like?"

"Oh," said Hank, raising a hand in slow motion, "about this high, gray hair . . . Hey, Lydia, you off now?" He called after her, "Good news, he's interested in making a big donation."

This was real. This was happening. Sniffing around Amber and then her workplace. Grabowski was going to let the world know that he had found her. She had to be out of this town forever within the next hour. Her hand was shaking so much she could hardly get the key in the ignition. When she finally managed it, the engine turned over once and died. Damn it. Goddamn it. She thumped her hand on the horn. She tried again and then again. "For fuck's sake," she shouted. "This is not happening."

Hank was at the window. "Car trouble, Lydia?"

"Hank," she said, trying to steady herself, "you have to give me a ride home. Please."

"I never heard you swear before, Lydia," he said, rocking back and forth on his sandaled feet.

"I'm sorry," she said, scrambling out of the car. "I just really need to get home now."

Hank drove his Volvo like a hearse. It was all she could do not to scream. "Could we go a little faster, please, Hank?"

He notched it up by three miles an hour. "Someone's in a hurry," he said.

Her first instincts had been right. Why hadn't she listened to them? It would still have been too late to stop him, whatever he'd got he'd use it anyway. But all this time she could have been running, and she was still here, telling herself she was crazy. Telling herself there was nothing to fear.

"That English fella," said Hank, "had a border collie when he was a boy. Got run over by a truck. Its name was Zorba, same name as my first dog. Now, what are the chances of that?"

"Not high," said Lydia.

He dropped her off in the driveway and Lydia thanked him and ran for the door. She ran back toward the car, shouting and waving. "Hank! Hank! Stop!"

"Need some help with something?" he said, poking his head out of the window.

"Can you give this to Esther for me?" She pulled the check out of her purse.

He whistled as he looked at it. "Ain't that so kind of you. Giving out presents on your birthday." She sprinted off and she heard him hollering behind her, "You take it easy now, Lydia."

Chapter Twenty-six

All night long as he staked out the house, Grabowski tried to imagine what it was that she could be thinking. After he'd watched her tail-lights disappear down Albert Street, he'd run back to the bed-and-breakfast knowing he had to act fast. His initial decision had been to get the first available flight back to London. By the time his foot hit the front steps he'd realized that would be a mistake. He knew what he had to do. He grabbed his computer and his camera bag.

Now he couldn't make sense of her inaction. He was shivering behind a thick stand of viburnum at the perimeter of the yard, wish-ing he'd thought to pick up his jacket. He couldn't work it out. Either he was missing something or else she was barking mad. She'd tried to kill him, or at least tried to scare him off. That meant she knew he was on to her and since she didn't have the bottle to run him over, she would have to take her passport and leave. If he pursued her to the airport and through security he'd be able to get a shot of her waiting at the gate. Even if she spotted him, it would make the story more sensa-tional. It didn't matter that as soon as she landed she'd be on another plane to somewhere else. There'd be a paper trail behind her that the authorities would follow.

The boyfriend had arrived and then left. She'd summoned him to say good-bye for the last time. After that, the light had come on in her bedroom and she was surely packing a case. He was paranoid that somehow she'd slipped out without him hearing or seeing a thing. He crept back and forth, keeping watch on the house front and back, then repositioned himself at the side. The car stayed where it was on the drive. It was nearly morning now and she still hadn't gone anywhere. Maybe she wanted to get caught, after all. In that case, why try to crush him beneath her wheels?

He snapped a twig off the viburnum and broke it into pieces. It didn't make any difference what her motivations were. He was a photographer, not a psychiatrist. But to be truly excellent at this job, you did have to know your subject. There were times when he'd felt like he knew her better than he knew his wife. He could predict her mood swings more accurately and knew more about the structure of her day, her shopping habits. To be fair, he'd devoted more time and thought to her than he ever had to Cathy.

What the hell was going on? Why wasn't Lydia leaving? An insect crawled over the back of his hand. He brushed it off and there was another crawling underneath his sleeve. He tried to shake it off, undoing his cuff to let it fall out. It was still there. He rolled up his sleeve and slapped his hand along his arm, but he could still feel it crawling, tickling, nesting among the hairs. He rubbed and scratched.

He checked his watch. Even if she was going to get a morning flight it would still have made more sense for her to drive off in the night and go to a more distant airport. He'd had enough of this waiting around, he wanted the final chase, the final photos, the adrenaline pumping. He wanted to be on the flight home. Within the next forty-eight hours he'd be meeting with *The Sunday Times*. He'd be meeting with Rupert Murdoch.

Just before seven o'clock she appeared at her bedroom window, and shortly afterward the back door opened. He sprang to attention. This was it. Time to roll. She came out in her bathing suit. God, she looked great, but what on earth was she doing? He reeled off some pictures.

For close to an hour she swam lengths and he didn't know what to do. Somehow he had the feeling that she was jerking him around, as if she had developed some elaborate plan, and he was only a pawn in her game. The stakes were so high it was making him paranoid.

After the swim she went back inside and out of view, presumably upstairs. When she finally appeared in the kitchen, which he was watching through his long lens, she had got dressed and she pottered around, apparently making breakfast. Surely after that she was going to leave.

She didn't eat a single mouthful, just sat at the counter with her head in her hands. It was nearly ten o'clock. What was she doing? If she was going to carry on as normal and pretend nothing was happening, she should have been at work about an hour ago. He pulled out his cell phone, rang the dogs' home, and asked to speak to her. Lydia, he was told, would not be coming in today.

Finally, she lifted her head. Now she was going to move. But she didn't. She sat there staring into space, her lips parted slightly, her eyes red, her entire demeanor catatonic. He gave it a while longer but then he decided he had to revise his plans in light of the strange way she was acting. If she was going to try to sit this out then fair enough, but he had to get moving. He'd go and get his "interview" with the old woman at the dog sanctuary. Then he'd check back at the house. If she'd gone, good luck to her, he'd have plenty already, and as he crept along behind the bushes toward the road he felt a little dizzy from lack of sleep and from knowing that at long last he was counting down the final hours.

Lydia flew upstairs as soon as Hank dropped her off. Her mind was racing so fast she could barely make out a single thought. Her arms and legs seemed to know what to do, as though they were receiving clear instructions from elsewhere. She was pulling out clothes from her closet. She was pulling out a suitcase. She was in the bathroom, picking up her toothbrush and random items from the shelf and running back to the bedroom and throwing it all in the case.

Now she was kneeling at the window and opening the wooden seat and digging around for she didn't know what. Whatever else that she needed was in the box in her closet. She sat on the floor and checked through the items. Her passport, and the other passport that she had never used, the papers for the savings account in that name which had so far lain fallow, thank you, Lawrence, for thinking of everything. The photographs of her boys that she'd cut out and collected over the years, she would take them of course. All her letters. The gun she would leave here, she couldn't take it on an airplane. It couldn't protect her anyway. Where was she going? It didn't matter. She'd take the first flight available, and then there'd be time to work it out. Her driver's license was already in her purse. Oh God, she was stupid. She sat on her heels and closed her eyes. She was back at the bed-and-breakfast, walking into the sitting room and seeing him for the first time. Now she was opposite him, sitting in the Queen Anne chair, making polite conversation. They were standing together on the stoop and he was telling her about the highland terrier that he'd loved, and she was touching his arm. Hadn't he told Hank it was a border collie? Oh God, she was stupid, wasting time. She didn't have the car. She should have called a taxi first, and the minutes were slipping away.

As she began to dial the number she heard a noise, the shattering of glass downstairs.

Esther, the old woman, hadn't been as talkative as he'd hoped. Lydia was a good worker, that's about all that he'd got, a few comments about her dog-handling skills. The fact that most days she ate Esther's chicken rice salad for lunch. As he drove back to the house he turned it over. Every word about her spoken by her employer would still be printed, each worth its weight in gold. Esther hadn't exactly been cagey but she had steered the conversation ever inward to the workings and finances of the shelter, to how his proposed substantial donation would be used so carefully. She'd posed for a photograph.

It crossed his mind that Esther was deliberately going out of her way to protect her employee's privacy. But what did she imagine there was to hide? It was impossible that anyone knew Lydia's true identity. Over the years she must have woven the most incredible web of lies.

He parked a distance down the street and approached the driveway on foot. The car had gone. She had finally come to her senses and left. Taken the sporting chance that he'd given her.

About three hours had passed and she could be stepping onto an airplane soon. The passenger manifests would turn her up, unless she'd chosen simply to drive off and hole up. Maybe she had other aliases. It would all come out in the end. He approached the front door. It was locked. He tried the back door and it was locked as well. Then he tested each ground floor window to see if she'd left any open. A few interior shots would cap it all off brilliantly. It was worth searching the rooms as well for any clues she'd left behind in her haste. It wasn't as though she'd spent the morning preparing.

There was a stack of firewood by the shed. He jogged over and selected the largest, heaviest piece. Standing at the kitchen window he hesitated for barely a second. In the maelstrom that was about to explode, the detail of a little breaking and entering was not going to be high on the agenda. He smashed the window and heaved himself up and inside, straight onto the counter.

The ground floor was open plan and he'd already shot it through the window. He wasted little time, quickly reeling off a few more angles. The best place to start searching would be the bedroom. The best shot to get would be of the bed that she had slept in. As he walked upstairs he was working out which way to turn on the landing. He'd seen her several times at her bedroom window so he already had a mental map of the interior geography. This humble home, he thought, captioning the photograph of the simple beech wood kitchen cabinets, this humble home . . . he reached the bedroom door, began to turn the handle. This humble home has witnessed . . . no that wasn't right. He walked into the bedroom. For a moment he thought he must be hallucinating. He let the camera fall from his hand and it swung on the strap around his neck and hit his chest with a thud.

"Hello," she said, leveling the gun at his head. "Were you looking for me?"

There was no hurry now, that was the thing. It was a relief. She waited patiently for a reply, and while she waited she looked him closely up and down. His pants were torn across the right thigh, his shirt was crumpled, one of his cuffs hung loose and the other was buttoned. He was unshaven and although his hair was gray, his stubble was black as an old bruise across his jowls. There was a leaf sticking out from the sole of his loafer. Grabowski had never been what she'd call a sharp dresser but today he looked as if he'd spent the night in the bushes. That wasn't unlikely.

"Were you looking for me?" she repeated.

He raised his arms slowly, responding to the gun she supposed. It hadn't occurred to her to say, put your hands up.

It looked as though he was trying to speak and she encouraged him by nodding.

He managed a single word. "No."

"I see. Not looking for me." She lowered the gun to her lap. His arms floated down in slow motion.

She raised the gun again, her finger on the trigger.

"No," he cried, this time in alarm.

"Why are you here?"

Beads of sweat were beginning to pop up on his forehead. "I'm . . . I'm . . ." he stammered.

"Sit down on the floor with your legs crossed," she said. "And put your hands behind your head," she added. Since she was seated on the bed, it would be better if he was down lower and in no position to spring at her.

When he was down, she continued, "You were saying?"

"I wasn't looking for you," he said. He never took his eyes off the gun.

"Then what are you doing in my house?" she said. "If you don't mind my asking."

"I mean, I wasn't looking for you before . . . before I found you. You were dead. It was an accident."

He was quite handsome, she'd always thought. He was getting a bit of a belly. A drop of sweat had run down into his eyebrow. She had to concentrate. "You're not explaining very well."

"I was here by accident. I've been traveling around and I saw Kensington on the map, and then . . . and then I saw you."

His right eye was stinging with sweat but he didn't dare move his hand to rub it. As he'd walked up the stairs to her bedroom he'd thought he was high on adrenaline. That was nothing. Right now he was so pumped he could feel his pulse in every limb, every finger, every toe.

"But I'm dead," she said. "You can't have seen me."

She was sitting on the edge of the bed, in her faded jeans and a pale pink shirt. Her hair was clipped back off her face and she was side-lit from the window and she looked calm and beautiful.

"I'm dead," she repeated.

She was crazy. She was still pointing the gun at him.

"Okay," he said, "that's right."

She started to laugh, a small giggle, then another and another, until she was holding her free hand to her stomach, shaking and laughing and bobbing the gun up and down. If it went off she could kill him. She couldn't mean to kill him. He twisted away and ducked his head as her hand wavered around.

"I'm sorry," she said, drawing her feet up onto the bed and steadying the gun on her knee. "It's not funny." She wiped away a tear. "I don't know why I was laughing. The tension. All the tension. Me saying I'm dead, you thinking I'm crazy and you have to agree so I don't shoot you." She paused. "I'm not, you know."

He didn't know whether she meant not dead or not crazy. "I know," he said. "I know."

She gazed at him intently. The tiny flecks glinted in that deep blue iris. At this instant they shone not green but gold. "That's our whole problem, isn't it?" she said. "Until a few minutes ago it was only my problem. The fact that you know. But now it's your problem as well."

How the fuck had he walked into this? Is this what she was setting up? How had she lured him in here? Always the manipulator, always pulling strings. His mouth was dry and his heart was still racing. It was difficult to think with that gun pointing at him. Why the fuck hadn't he gone straight back to London?

"You know what they say," he said. "'A problem shared is a problem halved.'"

"Does it feel like that to you?"

"I feel like there's a lot to talk about," he said. Out of the corner of his eye he saw a little white and gold heap on the bed vibrate. Her dog had stood up and was giving himself a good shake. He'd been so focused on her and the gun that he hadn't even noticed the dog was there.

"Like old friends?" she said. "Like old friends catching up?"

* * *

As soon as he'd said it, she realized that of course that was what he would want. There was no end to her stupidity. When she'd watched him walk into her bedroom and seen his face convulse with disbelief, she'd thought that at least she could slow down and think, that he wasn't in charge of her anymore.

Of course he'd want to keep her talking. He'd sent all his pictures of her to the newspapers and they'd all be on their way here.

"When did you send them?" she said.

"What? No, I haven't. I swear I haven't. I haven't sent anyone anything."

"Get up. I want you to stand up."

"I have to use my hands to help me," he said. "Is it okay to put my hands down?"

He didn't look in the best of shape. He'd probably hurt his knees if he tried to get up from cross-legged without giving himself a push. "Yes, but move slowly. Don't make my finger twitch."

When he was up she said, "Okay, hands behind your head again. Now two slow paces towards me. I don't want your body blocking the door when you fall."

"I swear to God," he said. "If you let me go I'll give you my camera. You can wipe the memory. No one else has got anything."

How would it feel to kill him? If she pulled the trigger now it would be done. "The problem is," she said, "you have no way of proving that. It's difficult to prove a negative."

He looked a little unsteady on his feet, and there was a vein crawling down his temple like a fat green caterpillar. "My camera and my laptop," he said in a creaky voice. "It's all on there. I didn't e-mail. I was going to fly home today. I didn't e-mail because . . ."

"Why not? Why didn't you do that?" If he believed she was going to kill him would that force him to tell the truth? Would it force him to lie with all his might?

"Because I don't trust anybody," he said. "It'd be all round the Internet before I'd even touched down at Heathrow."

She remembered something from one of their little chats in the early days. "You're Catholic, aren't you, John? Would you like to say your prayers?"

"I've got a rosary in my pocket," he said. "Is it okay if I get it out?" It would give him time to think as he pushed the beads through his fingers.

"Which pocket? Okay, very slowly, and keep the other hand behind your head."

He should have gone back last night. But he always went the extra mile, it's what made him so good at his job, it's what earned him his reputation. Right now it was what might have earned him a bullet. He let his eyes stray from the gun and work carefully over the room as he moved his lips as if in silent prayer. The dog was standing at her hip. The bed was neatly made, with embroidered cushions and bolsters along the headboard. There was a dressing table with some perfume bottles and a few necklaces strung over the mirror. The lid on the window seat was up, partially obscuring the glass. He couldn't dive out the window anyway, he'd kill himself. If there was something he could pick up and throw, he might be able to overpower her.

He said a Hail Mary out loud. He looked straight in her eyes as he said it. His heart rate had slowed, just having the beads in his fingers. She wasn't going to kill him. If she killed him she'd have the police chasing her, how would that be better than photographers?

"Why don't you put the gun down?" he said. "Put the gun down and then we can talk properly. There's nothing to be afraid of. I'll let you have my camera."

"Do you think I'm not going to kill you?" she said. She sounded disappointed.

"I think . . . I think you wouldn't be so stupid."

"You broke into my house," she said. "I'm a woman living alone. You broke in through—which window?—the kitchen, let's say, and crept up to my bedroom. You saw me for the first time a couple of weeks ago and since then you've become obsessed. It's all there—all the evidence on the camera, taking pictures of me in the street, at my work, even through my bedroom window. Am I right? Am I hitting the spot? I think your face is saying so."

"Mother of God," he said. She had it all planned. She'd set him up.

"Who else will see what you saw? Was it the eyes? Is that what struck you? Did you spend hours comparing them? Yes, well, I don't think anyone else is going to be doing that, do you? To finish the story—you come in here and attack me, try to rape me. I manage to get the gun out of my drawer and I warn you, but you just keep coming at me, you leave me no choice."

His tongue seemed swollen, perhaps he had bitten it, and it got in his way when he spoke, so that every word was labored. "It's not too late," he said. "You don't have to do this. Just let me go and I'll give you everything. I leave the country—I leave and I never come back."

She sighed and stroked her dog's ears absently. "For that to work, I'd have to trust you."

"You take all my equipment," he said. "You go anywhere you like. I'll have nothing and no way of tracing you."

"That just raises another problem, John. You see, I like it here. I don't see why I should leave, I'd like to stay."

Chapter Twenty-seven

He looked as though he might pass out so she told him to sit down again. Shooting him had sounded like a remarkably practical solution.

"We can both walk away from this," he said, looking up at her. "It can be over and done. I didn't send anything to anyone, there's no one I trust, not even my agent."

She wondered if he'd cut his leg when he'd climbed through the window. She said, "That's a sad state of affairs."

"Gareth's all right," he said, "but you never know, someone in his office . . ." He trailed off. His breath sounded heavy, uneven.

"You forced me to act in self-defense," she said. In a way it was true.

"I worked with a partner once," he said. His shoulders were rounded, his back was hunched, as if he was slowly collapsing into the fetal position. "Tony Metcalf, he was sort of a mate. Trip to Mauritius. We got some shots of you at the pool looking fabulous. This was before digital and we developed them in the bathroom."

"You did this to yourself," she said. It would still be murder.

He talked faster, and he was looking up at her, always seeking her eyes, hunting for any sign of weakness, of compassion. "Stunning photos," he said, "front-page stuff, really glamorous. We persuaded a tourist to take the photos back to London, because we were staying on with you, used to do that a lot in the old days. I let Tony do all the negotiating, we'd have a joint byline."

"How many cameras do you have with you?" The way he was wittering on now was making it hard to think.

"And there they were," he said, "front page next day. Cathy, my wife, she called and told me. Tony had taken my name off, the bastard. I never worked with a partner again."

"How many cameras?" she said. "And where are they? Is your computer at Mrs. Jackson's?" The gun was starting to feel heavy in her hand.

"Two," he said, unfurling a little. "This one around my neck and the other in the car. I'm parked on the street. My laptop's in there as well."

His back was aching and his knees felt like they'd been placed in a vise, the screws tightening every few seconds. He'd been standing up all night and now he had to sit on the floor like this with his hands behind his head. And she wouldn't let him talk.

He tried again. "You can come down with me. We'll go and throw the whole lot in a wood chipper."

"Don't be ridiculous," she said. "And please be quiet."

The door to the right of the closet opened on to her bathroom. If she allowed him to go and relieve himself there might be something in there he could use. He'd got himself beaten up before, there was that time in Spain, the hotel gorillas, but he'd never faced a gun. He looked at her again. At first she had looked at ease, as if it were perfectly natural to receive him in her bedroom with a gun pointed at him. Now she was rubbing at her wrist and her cheeks were red, he didn't want to risk making her more agitated. She wouldn't let him go to the bathroom anyway.

"I can't march you down the street with a gun pointing at your back," she said. "If you tried something, I couldn't shoot you down there. I have to shoot you in my bedroom."

He tried to tell himself she'd never do it. If he got up now and walked over to her, she'd scream and shout but she wouldn't pull the trigger. He shifted his weight from one buttock to the other, and she lifted the gun and cocked her head and met his gaze straight on. She was crazy enough, she was always unstable, a ticking time bomb, a human hand grenade lobbed right into the heart of the royal family.

"You'd have me on your conscience all your life," he said.

"Who says I would?" She smiled sweetly at him.

It had been a mistake to tell her that nobody else knew about this. When she'd asked him straight-out, when he was still sweating in terror, it had been his first instinct, as if that would put him in the clear. What he should have done was lie. If he'd told her that it was too late, that the cavalry was already riding into town, then she wouldn't be able to murder him and innocently justify it.

She might, on the other hand, have shot him then and there, out of pure fury.

He had to keep her talking.

"Can I ask you a question?" he said.

He didn't look so terrified now, but she could hear the fear in his voice. Women who stand up for themselves, who don't take it lying down, are always thought to be crazy. Esther had told her that. In the old days, right from the beginning, when she wasn't pliant, they wanted to put her on medication. She wouldn't have it and that proved how mad she was. Well, it was useful now, him thinking she was mad enough that she might do anything at all.

"Why did you do it?" he said. "Why did you . . . do what you did?"

"I had my reasons."

"But, surely," he said.

She waited, but he didn't continue. "Surely what?" she said.

"I don't know. Is it okay if I lower my hands for a while? My shoulders are killing me."

She didn't see why not. There was nothing he could do, sitting there cross-legged on the floor.

"Thank you," he said. "You must have been very unhappy."

"Thank you for your concern," she said. "I'm touched."

He worked his knees up and down and she could hear his joints click. "There were good times as well, weren't there?"

Her eyes pricked.

"I remember some good times," he said.

She felt the tears forming and fought to hold them. "Why did you have to come here?"

234

* * *

If she really wanted to kill him she could have run him over on Sunday night. She hadn't had it in her to do it then, and she wouldn't do it now. While she blinked back the tears he looked around the room again to see if there was anything he could grab and throw at her, just to push her off balance for a second or two while he leapt up and knocked the gun out of her hand. A book was lying on the floor, but it was too far to reach.

"I'm sorry," he said. "I told you. It was an accident."

Her cheeks were really burning. The more emotional she grew, he saw this now, the more disabled she would be.

"You didn't have to do anything," she said. "You could have left. You could have left me alone."

"I'm sorry," he said again. And he did feel sorry for her, in a way. "But you know, there's not a single person, if they'd been in my position, who would have done differently. Can you understand that? I'm really sorry, but it's true."

She sniffed and didn't say anything, as if she didn't trust herself to speak, but she nodded her head slightly.

"Remember that fashion awards evening in New York?" he said. "I think it was ninety-four. You were staying at the Carlyle, and when you arrived at the event there were about two hundred policemen holding back the crowd. They were all there for you." He paused to see how she was taking it. She showed no sign of wanting to cut him off. "The photographers were going wild, pushing and shoving each other, all trying to find the best angle. I remember a couple of supermodels trying to get a bit of the limelight. We yelled and screamed at them to shift their scrawny arses."

He was talking on and on and she was trying to focus on what had to happen now. They'd been sitting here for too long. With her free hand she stroked Rufus's head and he pushed his nose against her palm.

She would have to leave this place, that much she knew. Beyond that, she couldn't think. On her dressing table there was a silver powder compact that Amber had given her. She should take that. And the shell necklace that Maya had given her at Christmas.

"When you were staying at the Brazilian embassy in Washington . . ."

It didn't matter what he was saying, as long as he didn't move. She heard her cell phone bleep and reached back for her purse without taking her eyes off him. "I'm still watching you," she said, as she glanced down at the message. *Happy Birthday. I miss you. Carson.*

"And there was that night at the White House . . ."

The tears ran down her face. She was so tired of fighting everything and everyone. It would be better to give up now. She turned off her cell phone.

"And when you were on the dance floor . . ."

She wished he'd shut up and go away so that she could sleep. He'd been talking for what felt like hours, and the tears wouldn't stop coming.

"You see," he said, "there were a lot of good times." He was speaking softly, as if to an infant in the crib. "A lot of good times. And there can be again. We can work this out together, you and me. Work out how best to play it. Imagine how amazing it's going to be, how totally breathtaking."

"What?" she said, wiping the tears away. "What are you saying? What is it that we're working out?"

He was walking on eggshells here—no, worse, he was tiptoeing around a battered ego, not knowing exactly where the fractures lay. The dog jumped off the bed and lay down on the floor in a pool of early evening sun. It was a pretty bedroom, he thought, simple and uncluttered, a white bedspread, dove gray walls, a few splashes of color in the cushions. This humble home . . . the words ran through his head again. Keep it together, he told himself, keep it together.

"Is it okay if I shuffle over? Lean against the leg of the dressing table. There, that's okay, isn't it, I'm just shuffling really slowly, like this."

He wasn't going to push it hard. It had to seem like her idea as much as his. Let it sink in a bit. She wasn't condemned to live like this forever. There was a way back and he could help her make it happen. So far, so good, all the old stories of her glory days had her in tears.

"What?" she said again.

"If you wanted," he said. He paused. "If you wanted, you could go back."

She smiled at him, but it was a smile he couldn't read. "Could I?" she said.

The spaniel got up and wandered around the room, and then puttered over to him. He moved his hand slowly up to the dog's head. "There," he said, "that feels good, doesn't it? How long have you had him?"

"Nearly three years."

He stroked along the dog's spine and then withdrew his hand to his knee. The dog came forward, looking for more petting.

"It wouldn't just be for you," he said, as the dog climbed onto his lap. "Think of your boys. What it would mean to them, to have their mother back."

The gun was limp on her leg, her shoulders were slumped, she'd lost her poise, lost her bearings. He fussed with the dog, reaching one hand under its belly. Another minute or two and she'd be sobbing like a baby.

The sound of her voice startled him, he cracked his head up against the table leg. "I do think of them. I think of them every day."

"Exactly," he said in a soothing voice. "They must miss you as much as you miss them."

"And is it your considered opinion," she said, "that it would be best for them? Have you given it a great deal of thought? Have you thought about it every day for ten years? Every day. Well, have you?"

She was bolt upright on the edge of the bed. Her free hand was clenched in a fist and her other was greatly animated. There was no knowing what she would do. He had to make his move. If he lifted the dog to his chest, pretending to cuddle him, he could lean right back and get some traction, enough to hurl him straight at her.

"Rufus," she called. Rufus sprang off Grabowski's lap and jumped back on the bed. "Good boy," she said.

"Well, have you?" she repeated.

He pressed his eyes closed and sighed. "No," he said. "I haven't."

They sat for a while in silence. She knew what she had to do, now she had to summon the energy to do it.

"Who helped you?" he said. He'd stretched his legs out in front of him. His head was crooked against the table. "How did you do it?"

"The camera around your neck, the one in the car, the laptop. What else?" she said.

"That's the lot." He was sliding farther and farther toward the floor. "You can't have done it on your own."

"I don't believe you," she said. "What else?"

He rubbed his hand over his face, over the dark bristles on his jowls. "Does anyone here know? What about your boyfriend, kept him in the dark as well?"

"No one knows," she said. "Except you."

She stood up and he lifted his head. She pointed the gun straight at it. "Now, I'm giving you one more chance. What else?"

"All right," he said. "The bed-and-breakfast, left desk drawer, a memory stick. Little plastic and metal thing, about this big." He showed her with his fingers. "That's the backup."

"Give me your car keys," she said. "Slide them over on the floor. And your cell phone. Now the camera. Thank you."

When he'd done it, she told him to get up and open the closet. "Get inside and pull the door closed."

"Be reasonable. You're not going to leave me in there."

She didn't answer and he got in among her clothes. "Haven't you had enough?" he said. "Whatever you wanted to escape from, it can't have been your dream to live like this."

"Close the door," she said. She walked over and locked the door. It wouldn't hold him for long, but maybe long enough for her to be away from here. She picked up her bag and his stuff from the floor, scooped the compact and the shell necklace off the dressing table into her purse, then knocked on the closet door.

"Tell me something," she said. "What kind of dog was it you had that got run over when you were a boy?"

She heard a muffled snort. "I never had a dog."

"No, I thought not," she said.

She ran down the road and found the Pontiac and headed into town, to the bed-and-breakfast. For a moment she thought her vision was dimming, that perhaps she was going to pass out, but it was the sky turning, in what seemed like an instant, from dusky pink to purple and black. She fumbled for the headlights. How long before he dared bash his way out of her closet?

The hail drummed down on the hood, annihilating any possibility of thought. It was as much as she could manage to peer through the windshield and keep the car steady on the road.

She rang the bell and when Mrs. Jackson failed to answer she rang again and tried to see through the front bay window. The light was on and through a gap in the curtains she could see Mr. Jackson installed, as ever, in his chair, and for once he seemed to be awake, he appeared to be reading.

"Mr. Jackson," she yelled. She banged on the pane. "Mr. Jackson, it's Lydia."

She tried the bell again. Mr. Jackson didn't hear very much at the best of times, and with the thunder and the crackle of hail he wasn't going to hear anything.

"Mr. Jackson!" But her voice rose thinly against the storm and drifted away on the wind.

She drove east, to the river, left Rufus in the car, and scrambled down the bank carrying the laptop, the tape recorder she'd found with it, both cameras, and his phone, sliding on the carpet of hailstones. It was coming down so hard it stung the back of her neck. When she was nearly at the bottom she fell on her side. She gathered the phone and the recorder and, still sitting on the slope, hurled them as hard as she could, out into the water. She got to her feet, picked up the cameras and the laptop, slid the last couple of yards, and stood at the water's edge. Then she laid them in a row on the ground.

She picked up the first camera, held it by the strap, and started to spin it around, higher and higher, and she could see it even as she looked out in front of her, a dark shape, darting, flitting, like a bat circling overhead. She let it go. It flew to the center of the river. She hoisted the other camera. The laptop she flung so it went spinning, skimming, a flat white stone across the surface, and when it hit it floated for a few long seconds before succumbing to the suck of the current.

She was drenched by the time she got back in the car and shivering, although she felt hot, not cold. If she called and left a message for Mrs. Jackson . . . what could she say? Don't let your lodger in tonight? Get the locks changed, please? She turned on her cell phone. Three messages from Amber. Oh God, she was supposed to have been at her birthday party. Nearly quarter to nine, thirty-five minutes since she'd left him. She'd taken all her things downstairs then gone back up and told him she was going to sit there for half an hour and compose her thoughts, and that if she heard him move an inch she'd shoot him through the door. Then she'd taken her shoes off and tiptoed down the stairs. Without his car it would take him half an hour to walk to the bed-and-breakfast.

And then what? She had to think rationally. Of course she had to get out of this place, but was an hour going to make any difference? Grabowski would go to the newspapers with his backup copy of the photos, but he'd have to make his story stick. It would be coming out of nowhere. She looked different enough, had been dead long enough, that even the tabloids wouldn't touch it without asking him a few questions.

She just wanted to get to the airport. Why risk anything more than she had already? Wasn't she in this situation now because she had delayed and delayed?

All she had to do was call Amber and tell her sorry. Then she could go. She pressed the button to return the last call, but before it connected she hung up.

Chapter Twenty-eight

It was too dark in the closet for him to see his watch. He squatted on his haunches, pushing her shirts aside with his shoulder. How the fuck? How the fuck had he allowed this to happen? Was she really sitting in the bedroom or had she gone? He wouldn't put anything past her. She was totally insane.

"Hello," he said cautiously. She didn't answer. That didn't mean anything.

He stifled a groan. She'd taken his car and she'd be going straight to Mrs. Jackson's. Then she'd excuse herself to the bathroom and go up to his room. It was all over. Unless, by some miracle, he got to the bed-and-breakfast before her.

His back was excruciating, his thighs were hurting, his jaw was so tense it had locked and he could hardly swallow. Anger and frustration wetted his eyes. For fuck's sake. How long had he been squatting in the dark? He leaned over to his left and pressed his ear against the inside of the closet door to see if he could hear anything. "Hello?" he said again. As if from far away he heard a bang, the shirts swung over his face and he swatted blindly, panic flashing through his body, whacking himself on the nose as he flailed. Something clattered and he scrambled to the back of the closet, curling his arms around his head.

His heart was pounding so loudly it seemed to echo around the sides of the closet. He took deep, slow breaths. Nothing was happening. He was getting claustrophobic. No shots had been fired, she hadn't called out to him. A hanger had fallen and he'd practically wet himself.

He stood up and pushed through her clothes and shoved hard

on the closet door with both hands. Then he turned sideways and rammed it with his shoulder. He stood back and kicked it twice. Mrs. Jackson was going out this evening, she'd been talking about it for ages, a supper out with her old amateur dramatics associates. Mr. Jackson would be asleep in his chair.

There was still a chance. He felt his strength returning, he wasn't spent yet. He clenched his fists and pumped his arms, getting the blood flowing, summoning the rage. With a howl he turned on his left foot, banged his head on the rail as he leaned back, and let fly a karate kick that splintered the wood and broke the lock.

He started at a run but he was soon out of breath and had a stitch in his side. Unless he'd slept on his feet at any point, he'd been up all night. There was a crunching noise in his head, but he ignored it, he wasn't going to pass out now. He jogged to the end of the road and stood there under a streetlight, wondering if there was a shortcut he could take. The sidewalk shimmered white. He crouched briefly to the ground and picked up a few grains and watched as they dissolved on his hand.

A car was approaching and he tried to flag it down. It didn't stop and he swore beneath his breath. He set off at a jog again.

Thank God he'd kept his key for the bed-and-breakfast separately from his car key, and she hadn't thought to ask for it. Not as clever as she thought she was. A dog barked from behind a fence, a television glowed in a window, a woman passing in the other direction gave him a wide berth. He probably looked a bit of a state. The stitch was agony and he held his side and willed himself to run faster.

He saw the flashing light reflected blue off the scattered hail before he heard the siren. The police car pulled ahead of him and stopped. Two officers got out and stood in front of him with their hands on their hips.

"Can I see some ID please, sir?"

He had to play it cool. He ran a hand through his hair, as if that would make him appear any less disheveled, as if it would help. "Of course," he said, pulling out his wallet. "Is there some problem?"

The cop, the short one, barely glanced at the driver's license. "Mind if I ask you a couple of questions, sir?"

Grabowski felt the wind on his thigh where his trousers were ripped. It blew on his face, and he hoped it was enough to cool the anger that was rising. "I'm in a bit of a hurry, Officer, is there any way we could do this later?"

The silence with which his question was greeted was maddening. He looked from one to the other. The short guy was tapping Grabowski's driver's license against his leg. His partner, a pencil in a uniform, a gingersnap, still had his hands on his hips.

"Afraid not, sir," said the short one. "Can you tell us where you've been this evening, sir?"

There was no way he could explain. And he had to get to the bed-and-breakfast before Mrs. Jackson got home and gave away the crown jewels. "I've been for a walk," he said. "I've been for a walk and now I'm going back to Fairfax, to the bed-and-breakfast where I'm staying."

"We'd like you to come down to the sheriff's office, sir."

"Why? Can't a man walk down the street anymore?" For a wild moment he considered making a run for it. He imagined sprinting, outrunning the squad car, dodging bullets, leaping fences, scrambling, bloodied but not beaten, to victory.

The tall cop spoke for the first time. "There's been a break-in reported. You fit the description." He picked between his front teeth with his thumbnail. "Be a good boy, let's go."

"I can explain," said Grabowski, panic rising, gabbling, "but later. Or you could come with me now and I'll show you something that explains everything."

"That's funny," said the tall one. He slapped his partner on the back. "We want him to come with us, and he wants us to go with him. Which way should it be?"

"Let's get you in the car now, sir."

The way the little squirt kept calling him sir was calculatedly infuriating. But he wasn't going to lose his temper.

"Time," he said, "is very, very precious." He groaned inwardly. Why the hell did he say that?

"I'll arrest you here if I have to, sir."

This was too fucking much. He'd had it. These two fucking jokers. "If you don't stop saying sir at the end of every sentence . . ."

"Yes? If I don't stop, what happens then, sir?"

"Look," he said, choking on his ire. "Look, I'm sorry, this is very, very complicated. If I could just collect something from the bed-and-breakfast on the way to the sheriff's office . . ."

"Cuff him," said the tall one. "He's not cooperating."

"I haven't done anything," yelled Grabowski. "You can't arrest me for walking down the street."

The lanky bastard was in his face faster than a ferret. "How about I arrest you for resisting arrest," he said. *"Sir."*

"Fuck you," shouted Grabowski. The cop was practically standing on his toes. He was asking for it. Even as he was telling himself not to do it, Grabowski could feel his hand form into a fist, and as it connected with that snub and satisfied nose he experienced, for a fraction of a second, a sense of pure unadulterated bliss.

The interview room at the county sheriff's office in Roehampton was so hot that as Grabowski looked across at his lawyer he imagined the plastic chair beneath him melt and fuse to his backside.

"I'm not sure I've got this clear," said the lawyer.

"Christ, I've been over it three times already." Last night, on the metal rack that supposedly passed as a bed, he'd scarcely got any sleep at all. His clothes, which he was now wearing for the third day in a row, were stinking. "And you've hardly made a single note."

The lawyer had pimples on his neck, he was fresh out of school, and his mouth, for the last hour, had twitched and twitched. "Let me see," he said, pretending to consult his pad. "You're a British photojournalist, on vacation in Kensington, and yesterday afternoon you broke into a private residence at forty-five Cedar Road, where you were taken hostage by . . . a woman whom you believe . . ." His mouth twitched again. "A woman whom you believe to be living under an assumed identity. Her true identity you are not, at this moment, prepared to divulge. But you also believe that when you are able to prove this true identity at some undefined point in the future, the charges against you will be dropped." He flipped his pen between his fingers. "Mr. Grabowski, the charges against you are assaulting a police officer and resisting arrest. And I'm not *entirely* clear what you propose the mitigating circumstances to be." His lips finally gave way to a smirk.

Grabber wanted to reach over and squeeze that spotty neck until his head oozed and burst. "Listen," he said. "Listen, I told you—I haven't been here on some fucking holiday."

"I'm sorry, yes, you did. You've been in the States for . . . two months, working. Do you have a work visa?"

Grabowski laced his hands together and squeezed until his knuckles turned white. It was so hot in here he could barely breathe. "No, I do not have a work visa."

"Well," said the lawyer, "that's the least of your problems now."

The arrogant little fuck was in a suit and tie, hadn't even taken off his jacket, but he didn't seem to be perspiring at all.

"Why do they keep it so hot in here?" said Grabowski. "Is there something wrong with the heating? Somebody ought to complain."

"It's a little warm. Mr. Grabowski, I'm not sure you appreciate exactly how much trouble you're in."

He didn't know why he'd even bothered trying to tell this jerk what had happened. It was worth one more try. If he couldn't persuade his own defense attorney, he'd never convince anyone of the truth. "I know this is hard to follow," he said, in what he hoped was a mollifying tone. "The reason they were trying to arrest me was because I'd broken into her house, that's how it began, and we got in a scuffle because I was trying to get back to my room to pick up a vital piece of evidence."

The lawyer scratched his scrawny neck with his pen. "So here's where you start to lose me. There's nothing on the charge sheet about any break-in. No one's said anything about that. Officer . . . let's see . . . Johnson and Officer Nugent say they were on routine patrol on Montrachet Street at approximately nine fifteen last night when they saw a man, possibly a vagrant, staggering and possibly intoxicated."

"That's a lie," said Grabowski.

"The sidewalk was in a treacherous condition due to the hailstorm that had just passed, and they decided to see if they could be of any assistance. That's when you attacked . . . Officer Johnson. Were you, at that time, under the influence of either drink or drugs?"

"It's all lies," shouted Grabowski. "Are you ever going to listen to me?"

The lawyer—Grabowski couldn't remember his name, but he probably answered to Asshole—left a prim little pause before he spoke. "I understand that you're upset," he said. "But you have to understand that I'm doing my job here, the best I can. What I'm doing is trying to help you. Now, are you intending to bring a complaint against this . . . the lady in question? Or have you done so already? I didn't see anything in the file."

Grabber shook his head. "She's already gone."

"Gone where?"

"I don't know."

The guy nodded, as if this were the first sensible thing Grabowski had said. "And what about this . . . er . . . vital evidence? Has it been—secured?"

"She took it," said Grabber. "It's gone too." Last night, by the time they'd taken him in, processed and fingerprinted him and filled in the forms, chewing on their pieces of straw, it was well after midnight and all hope had disappeared. If they'd let him have his one phone call first he might have been able to sweet-talk Mrs. Jackson into barring the door.

"And could you share with me, Mr. Grabowski, who this woman really is? As you believe it's of great importance to your case."

Grabber pressed his fingers to his temples. He gave them a little massage. If he came out and said it . . . could he make the guy listen seriously? He knew the answer to that. All it would earn him, if he tried to explain, was the possibility of a psych report. "Forget about her. She's not relevant, nothing happened, forget what I said before."

The suit kept on nodding, as though to say that they were finally getting somewhere, as if the entire matter had been cleared up at last.

"Certainly, if those are your instructions, Mr. Grabowski," he said. "And how do you intend to plead?"

"Not guilty," he said. "Now, how fast can you get me out of here?"

"You'll be able to post bail after the arraignment."

"And when will that be?"

"Court's a little backed up. I'd say you're looking at Monday or Tuesday, possibly next Wednesday."

"I'm not staying in here for a week," said Grabowski.

The lawyer scratched under his chin with his pen. "You can pay bail with a credit card or I can arrange a bail bond, let me know and I'll do what's necessary. Let's hope it's not a whole week, look on the bright side, could be a day or two sooner than that."

For the next hour he paced his cell, frying with indignation. What had happened to the breaking and entering allegation? Now he looked like a crazy person, someone who attacked the police at random in the street. She must have called it in hoping he'd get picked up, and then called back and said it was all a mistake. It wasn't as though she would ever want to face him in court.

This wasn't justice, this was a travesty. It was an outrage. His human rights were being abused and there was nothing he could do about it, there was nobody who would listen. And she'd toyed with him, trapped him, cornered him like an animal. A person had a right to go about his business without interference from anyone, a person had a right to walk the street free from . . .

The door swung open. The desk sergeant who had taken his fingerprints filled the frame. "Someone up there likes you," he said.

"What?" said Grabowski. "Are you transferring me now?" He knew he'd be going to the county jail until the day of the first court hearing.

"Said someone up there likes you," the sergeant repeated. "Or you are just one lucky motherfucker."

The Pontiac was parked outside the bed-and-breakfast and the taxi pulled up behind it. Grabowski paid and stepped onto the sidewalk.

He used his front door key. Mr. Jackson was in his chair but didn't stir as Grabowski crept up the stairs. He wanted to get out of there without having to chat to his landlady about where he'd been for the last two nights.

He went straight to the desk and opened the left drawer. Of course it wasn't there. He'd known it wouldn't be. Even so, it didn't prevent the crash of disappointment. She'd beaten him hands down. He changed his clothes and packed up. The car key was on the desk. Perhaps he should think himself lucky, like the sergeant had said. Officers Johnson and Nugent had withdrawn the charges and he was free to go. They'd filled in the paperwork incorrectly, that pair of knuckle-draggers, and when the trial came up it would have got thrown out on a technicality. "I was you," said the sergeant, "I'd try to avoid running into those two. They ain't gonna be happy, they ever see your face again."

"Yeah?" Grabowski had said. "How happy they going to be when I sue?"

He wasn't going to do that, there were better things he could do with his life than spend it with lawyers. In any case, he had actually hit the cop, and if you hit a cop you got arrested, it was inevitable.

He put some cash in an envelope for the nights that he owed, left it on the bottom stair, and snuck out.

There were two cars in the drive, no sign of the Sport Trac. He couldn't leave without checking that she'd actually gone. He walked up to the house. A woman was coming out of the front door that stood open. She was writing something down on a clipboard as she walked and it took a moment for her to look up and notice him.

"Hi, can I help you?" she said.

"I'm looking for Lydia."

"I'm Lydia's Realtor, Tevis Trower. I'm afraid she's not here."

"Oh, right," said Grabowski casually. "She putting this place on the market, then?"

"Yes, I've just been measuring for the brochure."

"Will she . . . be back later, do you think?"

"She had to go overseas at short notice, dropped off the keys this morning."

"Ah," he said, "where'd she go?"

The Realtor shrugged.

"Do you think the crockery and glassware should be packed before or after the open house?" The voice called from inside the front hall.

"I'm just coming, Amber," said the Realtor.

But Amber, the little rabbity blonde from the boutique, came out on the porch. "Oh, *hello,*" she said. She tucked her hair behind her ears. "How are you?"

"I'm great. I was going to drop by your store later on."

"Oh, do," said Amber. "My assistant will be there, she's got a good eye, she'll be able to help you. I'd come and help you myself, only I've got to get Lydia's house sorted out. I'm not actually doing it today, I'm just making lists of what needs doing and then if I get some time on Sunday, I'll come in and make a start. The clothes to Goodwill, whatever she's left behind, the lamps and so on to the antiques store on Fairfax, the crockery we haven't decided what to do with . . ."

She burbled on and he listened, and waited for a chance to steer the conversation.

The Realtor checked her watch, anxious to get moving, but Amber, in full patter, didn't notice. " . . . The furniture we decided we'd leave and see if we could include it in the sale. If not, there's an auction house I know and can go there. Of course the cost of shipping it all the way to South Africa is prohibitive. Anyway, we'll all miss her." She fidgeted with the tie of her wraparound dress. "Did you not know that she'd gone? Were you hoping to see her?"

"There was something," said Grabowski, "that I was wanting to talk to her about. Did she leave a forwarding address by any chance?"

Amber shook her head. "No, she's going to be in touch just as soon as she's settled."

He looked at the Realtor, who was dangling the clipboard, swinging it slightly, growing more and more impatient. "Guess she'll be keeping in touch with you because of the house sale," he said.

"You'll have to excuse me," she said. "I need to get back to the office."

"Didn't mean to keep you. If you've got a phone number, an e-mail address, anything?"

The Realtor had her car keys out, she was striding down the drive. Grabowski pursued her. "Sorry," he said, "but she can't be selling the house without keeping in touch."

She had her car door open. "Not that it's any of your business," she said. She got in the seat. "Not that it's any of your business, but she signed over power of attorney for the sale. I believe there's been some kind of family crisis, but I don't know, I didn't pry." She closed the door.

He knocked on the window and she opened it. "What happens to the money then? How does she get that?"

"What's it to you?" She started the engine.

"All I'm saying is, you must have a way of getting hold of her if necessary, and if you could just . . ."

"The money will go into a client account and then when she's ready she'll claim it. Anyway, in this market that's many months off. Maybe a year." She raised the window and backed the car down the drive.

Amber was at his shoulder. "If you like," she said, "I'll tell Lydia you're wanting to speak to her. When I hear from her, that is."

He felt sorry for Amber, the way she'd been duped by the woman she thought of as a friend. "You won't," he said.

"Won't what?"

"Doesn't matter," he said. "Listen, I've got to get going. Don't think I can make it to your store after all. I'll have to pick up something for my wife at the airport."

"Oh, are you leaving us?" said Amber. "I hope you've enjoyed your stay in little old Kensington. Perhaps you'll come back one day. I know there's not a great deal that goes on here, but it's a very friendly place," she said, smiling up at him. "I hope you've found it that way."

He managed to get a window seat in coach on a direct flight. There was some turbulence on the ascent and he looked out at the scudding black clouds. The plane jolted and shuddered as if it were scraping along a hard surface. And then they were clear and the clouds were below, draping a tattered veil over the earth.

She had a brother in Cape Town. He knew that the chances were slim but he had to try. If she was there and he watched the house day and night, it was possible that he'd find her again. There was no guarantee that she was in South Africa, just because that's what she'd told her friend. The reality was she didn't have any friends, they didn't know her, but he knew her and if he gave it long enough, thought hard enough, never gave up, he'd find her in the end. She'd beaten him once but it wasn't over yet, he would find a way to track her down.

He had to get some sleep on the flight. Grabowski closed his eyes and tried to float on the sound of the engines, allow the deep vibration to fill his consciousness so that he could drift away. He saw her, she came to him, sitting on her bed. The sun slanted in through the window, lighting her up beautifully, and she was radiant and calm and he stood there transfixed, drinking her in. *Were you looking for me?* He could see the longing, the yearning, in her eyes. *It was an accident,* he said. She nodded in encouragement and he took a step forward, lifted his camera, and she lifted the gun and held it to her head.

Chapter Twenty-nine

The cabin stood a spit away from the lake, tucked in among the pines. It had been around two thirty in the morning when she arrived and she hadn't made it as far as either of the bedrooms, lying down on the dusty couch in the moonlight with her hands between her knees, and waking with a crick in her neck and the sun lapping around her ankles. She was hungry. Yesterday she hadn't eaten. Amber had packed provisions, and she walked outside to retrieve them from the car.

On the seventh attempt she got the stove lit and set the kettle to boil. While the water was heating she ate a bread roll, scattering crumbs everywhere. Rufus sat at her feet, waiting with exaggerated patience. She didn't have dog food but she had half a meat loaf from Amber's refrigerator. She found a saucer in the cupboard and chopped up a slice for him.

After breakfast she put on her boots and they walked through the pine trees on a bed of needles that was springy damp, a few mushrooms sprouting here and there, the occasional fern glowing emerald green against earthy brown. From time to time they came to a clearing painted with wildflowers, dabs of pinks and whites and yellows across the grass canvas. She kept the lake just in view in the distance to her right so that eventually they would come full circle, back to where they'd started.

When she'd hung up the phone yesterday before it had connected to Amber's number, she'd driven around to say good-bye in person. They'd all been there, waiting for her. She'd intended to stay for a short while but hadn't left until after midnight, while all the plans were being worked out.

She walked out of the pines toward the lake, Rufus scampering ahead to the slate shore. They'd been out three hours and had come two-thirds of the way around, another hour and a half to get back to Tevis's cabin, she could see the long sloping roof, like a letter A written in the trees. They'd passed a few other houses and crossed a couple of tire-made dirt tracks that suggested more cabins deeper in the woods, but they had seen no one. She looked out across the shimmering water, the dense green of the forest, to the blue hills smudged across the horizon. A shadow passed overhead and swooped to the lake and rose up in slow and silent commotion, the fat silver fish wagging in the eagle's claws.

She'd told them something had happened that meant she had to leave and wouldn't be coming back.

"Why don't you let us help you?" said Esther. "Maybe we can fix it."

"There are things I can't tell you," Lydia had said. "And I don't want to lie to you."

"What you can't tell us we don't need to know," said Esther. "Tell us what needs to happen now."

She walked to the edge of the water, sat down on a rock, and pulled off her socks and boots, her jeans and T-shirt. The slate was sharp on her soles and then gave way to shingle that massaged her feet as she waded into the water, bright insects skimming the surface, chasing trails at her fingertips. She tried to keep her feet on the bottom as she went deeper, the water at her waist, sternum, clavicle, she wanted to walk until it was over her head but her feet were rising, her hips lifting weightless in the water and she started to swim.

When she grew tired she turned on her back, stirring her wrists and ankles to keep herself afloat, staring at the flat blank blue overhead. She flipped over and swam back to shore and sat on the rock to dry.

Last night, Suzie had called her husband and he had called back as soon as he'd picked up Grabowski and taken him in. "You feel bad about what you did?" said Suzie. "Man breaks into your house, comes into your bedroom, he needs to get what's coming to him."

"Take my car," said Tevis. "I can borrow one from work. Go to the cabin. I haven't got it cleared out and set up, but no one will know you're there except us."

"What else do we need to do," said Esther, "to make it possible for you to come back?"

She put on her clothes and called to Rufus, who had ambled into the woods. They set off, this time hugging the shoreline, and she marched with the sun on her back, and in the red, brown, and black slate, flecks of gold sparkled out.

By the time they reached the cabin her legs were aching and she kicked off her boots and sat down on the couch. There were cobwebs in each corner of the ceiling and rivulets of dust everywhere. The curtains, which were half-drawn, were pale yellow, almost translucent, at the top and solid mustard below the ledge, as if over the years the color had trickled ever downward to form a thick crust at the hem. The air smelled of old carpets and damp cardboard and very faintly of the thickets of dried lavender that were bundled up on the table.

Her cell phone rang and she pulled it out of her pocket.

"He's gone," said Tevis. "I followed him to the airport."

"It's beautiful up here," said Lydia. "I'd like to stay a few days."

"Take all the time you want. Amber went to Mrs. Jackson's this morning and got that thing you needed out of his desk. The stick with all the photos. She threw it away."

"I still don't know," said Lydia, "if I'll be able to come back. Will you call me if . . . if anything else happens?"

"I will, but Lydia—this is the last place he's going to look for you now."

"If I could tell you . . ." said Lydia. "You know, if I could tell you, I would."

"It's like Esther said. You don't have to tell us anything."

She stretched out on the couch with her hands behind her head. If Grabowski had lied to her, if he'd already sent the pictures, then by this weekend at the latest Kensington would be under siege. That's why she'd come out here, in case it all went up in flames.

All the cobwebs were abandoned, dilapidated, spiderless. There were boxes half-filled with books and magazines on the floor below the empty shelves. Perhaps the previous owner ran out of space in the car and didn't think it worth another trip back. Would Grabowski have lied? If he'd lied to her, he wouldn't have been so desperate to reach the bed-and-breakfast to get that stick. He'd hit Mike on the nose. Poor Mike. She'd caused a lot of trouble for her friends. Perhaps it would be best for everyone if she moved on, started again.

She thought about calling Carson. She hadn't replied to his text. But what could she say? She'd allowed herself to start spinning a fantasy about telling him everything. The fantasy had been that he would understand. That one person in this life would understand. What she had to understand was that she would always be on her own.

Was she on her own? Her friends had done more for her than she had any right to expect, but what kind of burden, what kind of strain, would be placed on those friendships now?

Always spinning fantasies. They were as empty as those cobwebs up on the ceiling. She'd thought she would be able to see her boys again, that she would find a way. If, ten years ago, she had been the person she was now, then she would still be with them, they wouldn't be motherless children. They weren't children any longer. It was hard to imagine now the person she had been. If she met that younger self, how much would they have in common, and what would they say to each other?

The next morning she walked and swam and then she started to straighten up the house. There was no vacuum cleaner but there was a broom and she rolled up the rugs and started with the ceilings. She found a duster and a can of polish under the sink and cleaned the shelves and the table, unfolded the chairs and wiped them down. Then she swept the floors, and Rufus got in the way and sneezed and sneezed. In the kitchen she mopped the linoleum, scrubbed the tiles with a nailbrush, and scraped the mold off the grouting. She polished the taps until they shone.

Whenever she paused for breath, John Grabowski floated into her mind. There was a moment when she had considered squeezing the trigger. What if she'd done it? Could she have done it? Was she capable of killing a fellow human being? She couldn't have done it. She told herself she couldn't have done it. There was a moment when she might have. And for what? For doing, as he'd said, what anyone else in his position would do.

She took down the curtains in the sitting room and bedrooms, washed them in the sink, and hung them over the fence that ran around the front deck. She cleared out the cupboards in the kitchen and washed the plates and dishes, wiped the shelves with a damp rag, and put the crockery away. Then she started on the bathroom, scrubbing the stains on the toilet, scouring the inside of the bathtub, washing and drying the mirrors, buffing them up with a twist of old newspaper.

Amber had given her some sheets that she now stripped off the bed. She dragged the mattress outside to air. Took the other one out as well. Then she dusted and swept the bedrooms and cleaned all the windows. By now it was getting dark, and she ate some bread and cheese and gave Rufus a pâté sandwich.

She looked through the boxes for something to read. There were fishing and gardening magazines, more old newspapers, a bird-spotting handbook, an old car manual, an encyclopedia, cookbooks, travel guides, a series of hardback atlases, and a few battered paperbacks. All but two of the paperbacks were novels in French and her French wasn't good enough. She set them aside. Of the remaining two, one had lost its cover and the first few pages. The other was *Crime and Punishment,* one of the books Lawrence had given her.

She switched on a lamp and sat down on the couch with the book in her hands. She read the back cover, turned the book over, and set it on her lap. She hoped Lawrence hadn't been alone when he died, she would have been with him if she could. "If I'm not there on that date," he'd said, "it can mean only one thing." She'd stayed up all that night, waiting, knowing in her heart that he wouldn't come, knowing what it meant. At dawn she had gone into the yard with a lighted candle, picked some flowers to lay at the foot of an oak, and said a prayer, a funeral without a body.

Lawrence had thought she could read this book. She opened it to the first page but she couldn't see the words for the tears. And he was always so kind to her, thought so much of her, that it was probably another way of showing his love. It didn't mean that she was actually up to it. She closed it and put it down.

She went outside and looked at the star-strung sky and at the silver moon that had fallen onto the velvet lake.

On Friday she swam first and then walked for the rest of the morning. In the afternoon she polished the wardrobes and tried to get the brass handles to shine. The oven looked as though it had seen a few cremations and there was no oven cleaner, but she did her best to scrape out the worst of the charred remains with a knife. When she was nearly through, her hand slipped and she cut her thumb. She ran it under the water until the skin turned puckered white and the bleeding had stopped. Then she cleaned the stove top and the kettle, scalded the pans with boiling water, and scrubbed them with a wire brush.

She swept the deck and pulled the weeds out of the gaps in the wooden steps. What else was left to do? She wiped her hands on the seat of her jeans and her forehead with the back of her arm.

The rugs were still rolled up at the back of the sitting room and she fetched them outside and beat them with an old baseball bat until the dust no longer exploded with each swipe. She took them inside and laid them down.

After supper she sat outside with Rufus on her lap and thought again about calling Carson. Would he want her to call? If she told him who she had been would he still see her for who she was now? There was no way to tell him anything without telling him about her monstrous crime. He had given up his daughter, but she had already been taken from him. And a mother who leaves her children can never be forgiven by anyone.

Every day, for the rest of her life, she would ask herself the same question: could she have stayed?

To begin to know the answer she had to meet herself again, the way she was then, to remember how things had been. It was like meeting a stranger. Could she introduce that troubled stranger to Carson? Expect him to understand?

She stroked Rufus's ears and he whimpered in his sleep.

On Saturday her cell phone bleeped a text message alert and her spirits soared. If he'd texted again she would call him and they would find a way through. It was Amber, *Just checking you're okay.* She sent a message back to say she was fine, not to worry, and thank you for everything.

She walked and swam, wired up the tears in the window screens, and rubbed linseed oil into the deck furniture.

She thought about Carson cutting up the tree in her backyard, the specks of sawdust across his collarbone. She tasted his sweat. She heard his voice. She felt it in her chest. "Putting yourself in someone else's shoes, that's part of the job. I never thought he was crazy."

The next day she followed her morning routine of walking and swimming. Every step and stroke took her farther away from John Grabowski, made her believe that he had really gone, that he was no longer on her heels. She shook him off. She found her balance. He would still be looking for her, and he would never understand that the person he was looking for was no longer to be found.

She couldn't think of any more tasks to do around the house. She mopped the kitchen floor again. Then she went to the boxes and flipped through the gardening magazines. She looked at an atlas. She picked up the coverless novel and started reading, still sitting on the floor.

She moved up to the couch and read on. It was about a character called Ivan Denisovich Shukhov, an inmate in some kind of prison camp. She turned the book over and flicked through, trying to find the author's name. All the characters' names were Russian so the author was probably Russian too. It was an easy book to read, short sentences and nobody spoke like Lawrence, straight from the dictionary. The prisoners had to work at a construction site and they were so cold and hungry that all they could think about was how to survive another day. It was forty degrees below zero and the prisoners were badly clothed. If they added extra layers beneath the prison uniform they were punished. Shukhov thought about the piece of bread he'd saved from breakfast and sewn in his mattress.

She thought he would die by the end of the book, that would be the story. The conditions were so extreme, that would be what would happen. She read on. *Can a man who's warm understand one who's freezing?*

For the next four hours she read without lifting her head; when Rufus jumped up and wanted to play, she petted him but carried on reading. She moved around the couch, changed positions, stretched her legs, switched the book from one hand to the other, all without interrupting her flow. It was starting to get dark and she fumbled for the lamp. The guards were searching Shukhov and he had a piece of metal hidden in his glove. They didn't find it and she breathed easier. She wasn't so sure he was going to die, he was a survivor.

At the end of the book Shukhov was grateful to have lived another day. He'd decided it was a good day, he'd managed to get some extra rations. She closed the book and sat there filled with a longing, a yearning, so strong that it made her tremble.

She walked outside to look up at the stars. When she came back inside there was a new text on her phone, and this time it was from Carson. *Where are you? I miss you. Can we try again?*

For a while she sat and stared at the screen. She hadn't decided what was possible. Was she going to leap again into the unknown?

She got undressed and went into the bathroom and picked up a towel. Then she ran out of the cabin, across the deck and down the stairs, and without pausing ran thigh-deep into the water. She plunged in and swam in the dark and she was swimming away and toward and she saw Lawrence in the rowboat, the gleam of his bald head, bobbing up and down, and she raised an arm and waved at him, and he disappeared but she swam on.

Acknowledgments

My research for *Untold Story* relied on many books, articles, and websites about the institution of royalty, how it has evolved in recent years, and the role that the paparazzi have played in that change. In particular, I drew inspiration from the facts and insightful analysis contained in *The Diana Chronicles* by Tina Brown. I would also like to acknowledge my debt to four other books: *Diana: Her True Story* by Andrew Morton, *Diana: The Life of a Troubled Princess* by Sally Bedell Smith, *Diana and the Paparazzi* by Glenn Harvey and Mark Saunders, and *Paparazzi* by Peter Howe. I am grateful to all these authors.

A Scribner
Reading Group Guide

Discussion Questions

1. Monica Ali begins the novel with an intriguing pair of lines: "Some stories are never meant to be told. Some can only be told as fairy tales." What do you think these lines mean? Why did Ali choose to open her novel in this way?

2. Though the description on the book cover—not to mention certain details of the plot—make it clear that *Untold Story* is inspired by Princess Diana, why do you think Ali chose never to use Diana's name, or the names of her family or friends, anywhere in the book?

3. In Chapter Four, Ali introduces the diaries of Lawrence Standing, whom the reader comes to understand served as Lydia's secretary when she was princess and helps her orchestrate her escape into a new life. Now he reveals in his diary that he is dying of a brain tumor. What is the function of Lawrence in this plot? How does his perspective add to your understanding of Lydia?

4. In Lawrence's diary, he writes of Lydia as princess: "Time after time, over the years, she had come out of darkness (of her husband's betrayal, of her bulimia, of numerous scandals)

and dazzled the world. The deeper the darkness, the brighter she shone. Impossible to sustain indefinitely . . ." (p. 26). How do you take this explanation for Lydia's decision to escape her royal life? Do you think the real-life Diana would ever have contemplated such a radical choice? Why or why not?

5. Ali presents Carson as a seemingly perfect guy—game for chopping down trees, a "darn good listener," and more than willing to buy ballet tickets to please his girlfriend. Lydia, however, remains cautious. Why?

6. "What do they imagine I'm going to do all alone in these empty rooms?" Lydia (as the princess) asks Lawrence (p. 26). What portrait of royal life emerges in the book? Does Lydia's "suffering" as princess seem justified to you?

7. Of all the places in the world to where Lydia could have escaped, she chose middle America. Why? What qualities of small-town America benefit Lydia's ability to make a life for herself there? In what way does Lydia realize "she'd been wrong about this country" (p. 69)?

8. Rather than disregard entirely the true events of Diana's fatal accident in the Paris tunnel in 1997, Ali includes mention of a "Near-Fatal Car Crash" in Paris (p. 90). Why do you think Ali chose to transform that incident for the novel?

9. How would you describe the way Ali portrays Lydia's feelings toward her sons? How do her feelings compare to those of Carson toward Ava?

10. Lydia tells Esther that she was "never one for dogs" when she was younger (p. 98). Why do you think Ali makes dogs so central to Lydia's life now—with Rufus and her job at the dog shelter?

11. In Chapter Sixteen, Lydia's letters reveal the course of her first year in America. What mistakes does she make in her new life? Why is it difficult for Lydia to settle in one place? How is she different once she reaches Kensington?

12. Grabowski wonders why anyone "would voluntarily incarcerate themselves in such tedium" by living in Kensington (p. 152). But does Lydia find Kensington dull? What do her friends—Amber, Suzie, Esther, and Tevis—offer to Lydia that was, perhaps, absent in her previous life?

13. Ali presents Grabowski as a morally conflicted character. "Was he going to do this to her?" he asks himself, as he considers whether to expose Lydia (p. 193). How do you feel about the role paparazzi play in covering the behavior of celebrities? Do you think Grabowski's moral uncertainty is realistic? Compare Grabowski's willingness to expose Lydia with the reaction of Lydia's friends when she asks them for help.

14. What do you think happens to Lydia at the end of the novel?

15. In an essay in the British newspaper *The Daily Mail,* Ali writes that "Diana was not only the supreme icon, she was the supreme iconoclast. *Untold Story* is my salute to her." After finishing the novel, how do you view Ali's decision to write a "what if" story inspired by Diana?

Enhance Your Book Club

1. Using clues from the novel (e.g. North Carolina, Mark Twain's home, the Mississippi), try to trace Lydia's route through the United States on a map. Then allow each member of the group to reveal his or her own fantasy "escape." If you were forced to live incognito in a foreign country, where would you choose?

2. Turn your book club meeting into a tea party. Serve cucumber or cream cheese sandwiches, scones, and fruit. Look online for more menu ideas.

3. Read another novel inspired by a famous person, such as Curtis Sittenfeld's *American Wife* or Joyce Carol Oates's *Blonde*. Why do you think novelists find it so fascinating to take their fiction inside the mind of a character culled from real life?

A Conversation with Monica Ali

Why did you choose to write a novel inspired by Princess Diana?

Like all British women of my generation, I grew up with Diana in the background. I was thirteen when I watched her wedding to Prince Charles. I followed her evolution over the years into a global superstar. She was a lightning rod for so many different issues. Her appeal was extraordinarily wide, and you could see that in the crowds that gathered after her death—young and old, male and female, gay and straight, every color, every race, every creed. Some people didn't like her at all, and accused her of being manipulative, of bringing her troubles on herself. To those people she will always be the patron saint of the self-obsessed.

I didn't see her that way. The more I read about her, the more I admired her. When she got engaged she was nineteen years old, a virgin, uneducated, intellectually and emotionally insecure, with a troubled family background and eating disorders. She was supposed to be like a lamb to the slaughter. She was meant to put up with and shut up about everything. But she turned out to be tougher than anyone had imagined possible. She didn't just curl up and die; she took her own suffering and used it to reach out to others. People responded to that. She could be headstrong and reckless at times, and she certainly didn't follow the rules. I liked that about her.

Explain what you mean when you call *Untold Story* a "fairy tale."

It is a fairy tale, as it says at the beginning of the book! My initial idea had been for a short story—what if Diana hadn't died, what would she have been like in her forties? But when I started reading up about her in earnest, I homed in on one particular aspect—the fantasy Diana had of living an ordinary life. For her that could never have been anything more than an idle dream. But what I decided to do was to write about a fictional princess, Lydia, who does leave fame and fortune behind and go off to live this ordinary life. It stands the traditional fairy tale on its head. An Unhappy Princess who turns into a more contented Cinderella.

What drew you to set the novel in Midwestern America?

Partly I took my cue from Diana's fantasies. She talked of moving abroad as a possible way of escaping some of the circus that surrounded her. She always felt welcome in the States, and viewed the country (incorrectly) as somewhere there was no Establishment—having aroused the disapproval of the British Establishment. She also felt that America was a country that could somehow "absorb" celebrity the size of hers.

So that was the germ of the idea, to set the novel in the States. But of course my fictional princess, Lydia, goes there under an entirely different set of circumstances. She's living in America incognito. I chose the Midwest as Lydia needed to be away from the more cosmopolitan areas on either coast that she had known in her previous life. It also seemed in keeping with the central idea of the book—to give her a life that was ordinary, and to pose the question: What is actually important in life?

To some, *Untold Story* might seem like a major departure from your first two novels, *Brick Lane* and *In the Kitchen,* in which immigrant life in London figures heavily. Was writing *Untold Story* a different kind of project than your previous work?

Brick Lane was set in the Bangladeshi community in London; my second book, *Alentejo Blue,* was set in a Portuguese village; my third, *In the Kitchen,* is about an English chef from the north of England. They're all very different from each other, and *Untold Story* is different again. Although I think what they perhaps share in common is a preoccupation with identity. For example, in *In the Kitchen,* the chef, Gabriel, is metaphorically and then literally stripped of his identity as his world falls apart. In *Untold Story*, Lydia not only has to construct a new facade of her identity, she also has to construct a new sense of self beneath that facade.

What's important to me as a writer is to write about what interests me and to keep stretching myself as well. *Untold Story* has a thriller element that I hadn't written before, and I enjoyed the challenge of that.

Do you think real-life paparazzi are as morally conflicted as Grabowski? Why did you choose to make a photographer figure so central in the novel?

Grabowski draws a distinction between himself and the new breed of paparazzi. He came up in the old Fleet Street tradition and he thinks of himself as having some standards. He laments how those standards have now fallen away.

There's a cat-and-mouse game between Grabowski and Lydia that is central to the book's plot. But in a way, what was more important to me is the notion of complicity. Grabowski is a (lapsed) Catholic. I guess he carries our collective guilt, for the way that we (nearly all of us) suck up the details of celebrities' private lives.

Many girls grow up with the fantasy of becoming a princess. Lydia, as a princess, has the opposite dream—of becoming average, living a normal life. Was that an irony that appealed to you?

I think this comes back to fairy tales. Marrying a prince—we know, because Diana showed us—is no guarantee of happiness.

We have material comforts in abundance. We no longer need carriages and glass slippers. Neither do we really believe anymore in the benign transformative power of great wealth and fame (rather the reverse).

The modern Cinderella—with her fast, complex life—wants the simple things: independence, freedom, friends she can trust, and a good man to love. That's what I wanted to explore.